NO WIND

by

Judd Garrett

MAIN POINT PRESS
CHICAGO • LOS ANGELES

No Wind

Cover photo of the Jersey Shore is from the author's collection.

Designed and published by Main Point Press, an imprint of Bantry Bay Publishing, Chicago/Los Angeles.

Library of Congress Control Number: 2020941217

To contact the author or the publisher, email: MainPointPress@gmail.com, or call (312) 912-8639.

For information about special discounts available for bulk purchases, sales promotions, fund-raising and educational needs, contact the publisher.

Dedication

To my father, who loved the beach and taught me the game of baseball, and to my son Calvin, whose infectious spirit will always be in our hearts.

Frankie, Campbell, Kassity, Leigh and Charlie: There is no such thing as life with no wind. Your courage is inspiring. I love you.

To my wife, Erin, thank you for your love and support.

Prologue
(*Summer 1999, age 17*)

You can come back to your memorable places, but you can never go back to the time that made those places memorable.

My eyes scanned the sparkling sand and the crystal blue water, glittering in the sun as they descended the stone wall, silhouetted by God's golden rays. Their black dresses and dark suits were in stark contrast to everything I've ever known about this beach: the running, the playing, the laughing, the colors. They marched down the dunes in a slow, solemn procession. The girls held balloons, and the boys held the girls. Her mother trailed the pack with barely enough strength to take a step, head down, sobbing.

They stopped at the edge of the surf and bowed their heads as the white water flowed over their naked feet. They stood silent in rigid pairs performing the makeshift ritual. Dorian stepped into the oncoming waves and lifted the urn over his head, offering it up. He held it there, not wanting to let go, and then swept it across the horizon as the girls released balloons. The gray ash billowed into the blue sky, reaching as far as possible, and then vanished into the ocean, gone forever. They stood at the water's edge, their eyes fixed on the balloons until they disappeared into the heavens. They lingered, staring at the blank sky, uttering one more prayer, hanging on to one more memory. They hugged and wept as they staggered up the dunes. I should have cried, but I couldn't. I didn't have it in me. My heart was too damaged.

I thought more people would come, more people would care, but then how many would come to my funeral? How many would give it a second thought if I disappeared into nothing? It should have been me who was scattered into millions of pieces, my fate left to the will of the wind.

I continued to watch as they climbed over the thick boulders, and disappeared, returning to their lives. I remained, staring out over the ocean, searching for answers. Answers to the same questions that everyone will eventually ask. Questions that have been contemplated since the dawn of time. Questions that have never been satisfactorily answered. I believed there was something in that deep blueness that would make sense of all this, bring a remnant of peace.

My father used to say the ocean was forgiving, that the waves erased everything. The water flows, the wind blows, and the imperfections disappear. All is forgotten, and the beach is returned to its origin; unmarked, untainted, new.

My mother believed the ocean cured everything. There wasn't a childhood malady that couldn't be healed by bathing it in the ocean. "Go to the beach and let the saltwater get at it," she would tell us. So, I've always believed, always hoped, there was something magical, some healing power in that deep blue water.

And I always believed the ocean went on forever. It was eternal, melting into the endless horizon. Staring out over the ocean at that moment, I felt I was beholding the immeasurable hope and innocence of the new century stretching before me and with it, the days, the months, the years of the old would disappear, and I would emerge through this window in time as a new person.

In the distance, the faint gray outline of New York City rose up, a blemish on the flawless horizon. On this blinding clear day, I can make out the hazy green light of Lady Liberty reaching toward me, offering a promise that is as frail, as far-reaching, and as beautiful as she.

Fluffy white clouds drifted softly across the sky, and for a moment, I felt that the clouds were stationary, and I was floating by. The sun stared down at me, watching me, judging me, as it does every day, its golden rays raining through cracks in the mist, casting frothy dark shadows across the shore. Those touched by the light shone brightly, while others sat in darkness.

I wish it were that easy. I wish that God's bright, discerning eye fell on us discriminately, highlighting the best and veiling the worst. Then I could see what He sees, know what He knows, and understand what is right and what is wrong. But His eye shines down on all of us, the good and bad the same, offering light for everyone who needs it while the clouds arbitrarily decide who bathes in its warmth. And we are left to decipher beyond the dubious choices of the mist, my eyes forever blind to God's truth.

So, I searched for the truth by connecting the dots that led from my childhood to where I sat at that moment, hoping to see myself for who I was so I could live with myself for who I had become. How had all the promise shattered? Where had it gone so wrong? Will I get a second chance, not so much to start again, but to pick up the pieces of the broken promise, and figure out my rightful place in the world? Who I am, why I am here, and how I am to live?

NW

~ Part I ~

Chapter 1
(*Summer 1986, age five*)

"Let there be light!" God said, as he created the heavens and the earth from a formless void. He divided the white of day from the black of night, and then he separated the land from the sea. By doing so, he created the beach. The beach is just a fuzzy line scrawled on the edge of the world, the residue in the battle of life and death.

I was practically born on this beach. My father brought me here when I was six days old, and I spent my childhood playing on this thin slice of sand on the edge of the world. It was a magical time, a time of infinite promise and potential. My world was elastic and uncontained, safe and free. All I needed was a ball, and I held my dreams in my hands.

I met Dorian on this beach when I was five. I was making spectacular diving catches that saved the game for the Yankees when he first walked up to me, caked in sand and baked in the sun. Like the ball I was playing with, he appeared to have washed up on the beach. Without speaking a word, he walked over to a big, flat rock, and drew a pie-shaped grid in the sand with his heel.

"Here's a single," he pointed to the first box, "There's a double, that's a triple, and that's a homer." He turned and faced the rock ready to spring into action.

We played that simple game of bouncing the ball off a rock and trying to catch it for hours that day, diving and sliding for every ball. Derek Jeter never dove for line drives with more intensity than we did.

Dorian did not appear to be an extraordinary kid. He seemed like everyone else. He had the same wide-eyed innocence every kid has. He was my best friend from that first day on for no real reason. It was natural. We were the same height. We had the same hair color. It didn't matter that our houses sat on opposite sides of town, his along the river, and mine on the beach.

Dorian and I played all day, every day on the beach in the summer. It was the center of our world growing up. I don't know what my life would have been without it.

There was something reassuring about the beach that drew me in. The relentlessness of the waves. They keep coming and coming, again and again, drawing and redrawing the line, continually reshaping the face of the beach. In and out, in and out, ticking by like seconds on the eternal clock, the sand slowly slipping away, like an hourglass, counting down not the length of a minute or of an hour, but of the remainder of my life.

Every summer when I returned, the beach had grown a little smaller. As I grew, the beach shrank. It was slowly being consumed by the waves, as if the ocean resented what God had done, and the waves were methodically restoring the earth to its original nebulous state.

But now the beach, and my childhood, are gone, buried beneath these throbbing waves. All that remains is a hazy vision, etched in my brain, of running up and down the dunes chasing the ever-elusive ball.

◆

Galilee is one of the many small beach towns that speckle the Jersey Shore. It's not on most maps. It is a sleepy town with one main street adorned with large, two-story Century Homes on spacious lots, and lined with Victorian-style lampposts and hand-carved wooden street signs. The winding tributaries off the main street were cut by horseshoes, not horsepower. The disparity of wealth in the town runs the gamut, from Wall Street millionaires in mansion-like vacation homes, to poor crabbers and clam diggers squeezed into tiny bungalows.

During an ebb in the market, my father bought our three-story, Century Home, overlooking the beach with a backyard as big as a baseball field, for $40,000.

"You're a fool," Mother told him, "You could've gotten it for 35."

My dad fell in love with the house at first sight, and unwittingly made the shrewdest financial deal of his life. He didn't see the investment; he saw the uniqueness, the beauty that made the house so valuable. He was once offered $800,000 for the land alone, but he refused. "You can't put a price tag on 30 years of memories," he said.

On the day of the purchase, my mother snapped a quick Polaroid of him looking over his new home. He had that hopeful look of a life just beginning, still perfect, with so much ahead.

My parents were born before the start of the Great War, and my brother and sisters during our country's worst. It was as if our family skipped a generation and I, the youngest of the four by nine years, skipped everything. I felt like an only child and my father treated me like the son he had always wanted. I always believed that I was an accident, until I discovered there are no accidents, or everything is, so it didn't make any difference.

◆

As a child, my life overflowed with possibilities. I believed I could become anything I wanted. There were no roadblocks, no stop signs, no past. All there was, was future.

I believed in everything. I believed in magic, the Tooth Fairy, the Easter Bunny, Santa Claus, and God. I believed in honesty, right and wrong, good and evil. I loved without thinking, and I had no regrets, not because I hadn't made mistakes, but because I hadn't learned about the gray yet.

In my childhood world, the sun rose and fell by the hand of God, not by the Laws of Newton. I believed God heard all prayers and answered each one. I saw God everywhere and in everything.

"I think the moon's following me," I told my mother as we walked down the beach on an August night when I was five. It was like God's golden eye following my every step, watching me, judging me.

"We all think it does," she answered, "because we're so small and it's so big." I didn't understand because the moon wasn't any bigger than a nickel.

The following morning, minutes before the long yellow bus pulled in front of our house to take me to my first day of kindergarten, my mother squeezed me and whispered in my ear, "I wish I could freeze you and keep you like this forever." I turned my cheek to avoid her kiss because I didn't want to be seen for what I was, a child.

Dorian and I started at St. Francis Catholic Elementary School the fall after we met. The day before Dorian started kindergarten, he named himself. How he came to name himself is as bizarre as his life had been growing up.

His mother is the daughter of a local fisherman, but his father was a salesman from Paterson. The two met one day when he was in the area on business, and before long they were married and expecting their first child.

The day Dorian was born, his parents fought so fiercely over what to name their new baby that security guards had to physically remove his father from the hospital. The dispute was never resolved, and

Dorian left the hospital with no name on his birth certificate. For the first two years of his life, he was called Neal, his father's father's name, a man Dorian's father had never even met.

But on Dorian's second birthday, his father went out to the store to get ice cream and never returned. From that day forward, his mother called him Justin, the name she preferred, until the day before he was to start kindergarten, when she realized that no name was on his birth certificate, and he could not enroll in school without it. Out of curiosity, or maybe spite, she asked Dorian, "What name do you want to be called, Neal or Justin?"

He shook his head. "I want to be called Dorian." It was the only other name he could think of, a name he'd heard his grandfather say many times in a voice filled with love and affection. It meant "from the sea."

"That's a ridiculous name," she scoffed, "no son of mine is going to be named after a broken-down fishing boat."

"So? It's my name," he retorted.

"Fine." She scribbled the name in blue ballpoint pen on the line. "It's your life."

◆

School was not for me. All day long, I was told *sit up, shut your mouth, no smiling, no laughing, no playing.* I didn't understand. I was trapped, like I was in jail surrounded by cold cinder block walls, staring out of lead-lined windows at the sun-drenched playground. Fun and happiness were treated like sins in Catholic school.

I don't know if I always found trouble or if trouble always found me. Either way, we weren't strangers. That afternoon, as my first day of kindergarten wound down and the long yellow buses lined up on the blacktop, I saw a pink ball wedged behind a filing cabinet in the back of the room. I pried it out and gripped it in my hand.

"Betcha can't hit the blackboard," Jay, the smallest kid in the class, challenged me. It was an easy throw. My dad and I play catch from much farther away. The athlete inside me was bursting to come free.

"Oh yeah," I said, intent on proving I had the strongest arm in the class. "Watch this." And without thinking, I reared back and threw the ball as far as I could. It spun off my fingertips cleanly with a firm backspin and flew toward the front of the room in a beautifully symmetric arc. As it reached its apex, the door to the classroom swung open, and Sister Margaret Mary walked in with a big smile on her face. "How are my future Valedictor—." My perfect throw struck her left ear, knocking her habit half off. She staggered backwards.

"Who threw that!" she shrieked. Her eyes darted around the room. Her habit only covered the right side of her head. Quinton burst out laughing, and the 20 other five-year-olds crept away from me, creating a clear sight line from Sister to me.

"Jake!" our teacher, Mrs. McCallister, barked. I stood pressed against the back wall. I wanted to run. I wanted to hide. I wanted to slip in among the pack unnoticed. I looked at Jay, but he had stepped behind an American flag drooping off a wooden pole. Quinton was doubled over with his face buried in his hands.

I stood frozen, scared still. Sister straightened her habit, and walked directly at me, her face was burnt red and her eyes little black dots. I wanted to cry, but I knew I couldn't. It would be worse than anything she could do to me. So, I straightened up, prepared for whatever beating she delivered.

She leaned toward me. Her nose so close I could smell the coffee on her breath. She pointed her crooked finger in my face, and snarled, "You. I'm going to keep my eye on you, Jake Pearson. I'm always going to be watching you." I quivered at her words as if it were God himself speaking to me. Then she turned and walked out, leaving me alone in my embarrassment. It didn't matter that she'd always keep an eye on me, because I knew God was already watching.

NW

Chapter 2

"Remember, man, that thou art dust, and unto dust thou shall return." The priest's gravelly voice bellowed these mysterious words as his gnarled thumb pressed black ashes into my forehead. The church was unusually bleak that night, lit solely by the auxiliary lights surrounding the apse. The altar had been a dark, distant, foreboding place to me, a place I had never been, a place I had wanted to go, but was always too young. But this winter night, my mother told me to go up there with her. I didn't know why, but I followed anyway, falling in line behind a group of disjointed souls, shuffling along, searching for that unfulfilled promise of meaning.

We were Catholics. My parents were devout; church every Sunday, confession once a month, fasting during Lent, all seven sacraments. I did all the things I was supposed to, even though I didn't know why. God and religion were mysterious and confusing, but the Catholic Church intrigued me. There was something eerily appealing about its rigid solemnity. Comfort in its unbending structure, peace in its melancholy. Even though I didn't understand it, the Church made me feel I was a part of something infinitely important and eternally viable.

But that night, I didn't get anything except those black ashes, and that dark message. I turned at the altar and fell in line behind my father's thick back and saw the rest of the congregation staring back at me, marked with a black cross on their foreheads. Music simmered above the sparse congregation. I thought about the priest's words, how scary and yet pointless the whole thing seemed.

"What did he mean I was dust?" I asked my mother as we walked out of the church.

"It means we are all going to die," my brother whispered.

"Don't tell him that," she scolded him. "He's just a child."

"Why not?" he whined. "It's true."

I always knew that I was going to die. Everyone dies. But that was the first time someone told me that fact of life to my face.

"Don't pay any attention to him. He's just trying to scare you," I grabbed onto her arm and floated down the steps to the foot of the church.

I looked up at my mother's placid face. "When old people die, they become babies again, right?" I asked.

"No, Jake," she answered.

"Then where do we go when we die?"

"If you're good," she squeezed my hands, "to God."

I studied her quiet face. Even behind her wrinkling skin, her sagging eyes, and that black cross splashed across her forehead, her face was peaceful and beautiful.

What do I have to do? I thought. *How am I going to return to God?*

◆

My father swept my mother up in his arms and spun her into a tight embrace. "You can leave anytime you want, you don't have to stay," he said, staring deeply into her eyes.

My mother responded as she always had when he said that to her. "My yes is my yes, and my no is my no."

There was an innocence in my father's face when he looked at my mother, like a school kid on his first date. *How had he earned the right to that innocence?* I wondered. *And what did I have to do to deserve that look for myself?*

My parents loved each other, but they really liked each other, too.

There was a purity, an idealism, about my father. He didn't drink. He didn't smoke. He didn't stay out late with the boys. I never heard him swear. My mother once told me, "Your father's only vice is baseball, and that's because it almost destroyed him."

◆

Around age 10, I realized baseball was a religion to him, as important as being Catholic. Baseball stadiums were his cathedrals. The batter's box was his sacristy. He told sport stories as if they were parables and worshipped names like Ruth, Gehrig, Mantle, DiMaggio.

My father was the ultimate dreamer. He believed our wildest dreams were not only possible, they were probable, and it was our obligation to pursue those dreams out of respect for our Creator who placed those magical ideas in our souls. "A life without dreams is not worth living," he once said. "The dreams are the gift, not the realization of the dreams."

He was the supreme optimist. "You can be anything you want to be," he told me often, implying his unspoken belief, "as long as you're the *best*." If I wanted to be a baseball player, I was going to be a Hall of Famer. A writer meant the Pulitzer Prize. College was Princeton.

"Never settle for anything less than the best," he told me, "Never accept 'pretty good,' 'OK,' 'nice try.' Those are insults. Only the best."

My father was not simply a head-in-the-clouds dreamer. He had a rigid practicality to him, a consequence of growing up during the Great Depression.

"Everyone has a purpose," he told me when I was too young to understand. "A reason they were placed on this planet. We all must discover our purpose for being."

"I don't get it," I said, "What reason?"

"It's like," he explained, "you have to earn the air you breathe and the water you drink."

"I thought air and water are free," I said.

"Exactly," he exclaimed.

My father's idealism was so invigoratingly hopeful, it was hard not to embrace it. I believed if I found my purpose, my life would somehow become perfect, and my problems would disappear. So, I followed his dream. I reached out to baseball for meaning. It made sense at the time. My father played professionally. It was our nation's pastime. Babe Ruth and Mickey Mantle were as revered as Franklin Roosevelt and Jack Kennedy. I was not old enough to realize how improbable the dream of the big leagues was for someone like me. I was still too naïve to understand my limitations. "Why not me?" I thought innocently. "I could be the next Mickey Mantle."

The *Baseball Encyclopedia* became my bible. I studied it relentlessly. I consumed it. I memorized it. I wanted to understand baseball's meaning, so I studied its history, recorded by every statistic of every game ever played. Only those who played in the big leagues were allowed in that book, memorialized for eternity. You were either in or out. That book was the ultimate quantification of baseball significance.

Baseball is numbers. That's what I liked best about it. Numbers are honest. Numbers are true. Numbers don't lie. There are no gray areas. You always know where you stand. You either hit the ball or you didn't. Success and failure are clearly quantified. Numbers define the game. They give it meaning, structure, substance.

Many sticky summer nights, I sat on our couch, beside my father rocking in his chair, consuming the names and numbers in that green book, quizzing him under the blue glow of the Yankee game and the clipping voice of Phil Rizzuto.

Each new stat led to another and another, and yet another, hitting me from every direction, pouring over and through me like a multi-dimensional matrix. I searched through the maze of interconnected names and numbers, reaching out for the promise of some ultimate answer, but always leading me back to the beginning.

I knew if I was going to play for the Yankees, I would have to earn it. So I never objected to spending all that time in the backyard with my father. From the day my mother signed me up for Little League, my father took me out back and pitched me balls, hundreds of them, every day, in pursuit of a dream, a dream I inherited.

"Let's go hit," my father said to me that first day, so I ran to the back yard with my bat, my glove and my unblemished hope, and for that briefest of moments, I was a future big leaguer. I was a blank page.

That first time a father takes his son out to play ball is filled with so much potential. Every father looks at his boy flailing a bat, or chasing a ball, for any sign that he could blossom into a star. An accurate throw, a sharp hit, a one-handed catch, are evidence of what their fathers have suspected from birth, that their boy is special.

My father wanted that to be true. He needed it to be true. And if it weren't, he would make it true. Our time together was not the typical Norman Rockwell father and son baseball moments. He was not my father, and I was not his son. He was the coach, and I was the player. He saw all my flaws, and we worked tirelessly to fix them. For me, the Promised Land was not a gift at birth, but an earned destination, a path paved with hard work and perseverance.

"If you can hit, you can play," my dad told me that the first day, as I balanced an oversized bat on my shoulder. He stood on the mound, with two balls jammed into each of his pockets, staring in like a fiery relief pitcher brought in to save the game. Home plate was always 15 feet shorter than the actual distance, because, "that's the way Pete Rose did it when he was your age." He didn't pitch the ball underhand or toss it lightly overhand; he threw a quick, tight, straight ball down the center of the plate. I swung and missed.

"C'mon, let's go," he barked. "The pitch isn't slowing down, you got to speed up." And then he threw another, and another, and another, like a pitching machine, the balls flew at me in short regular intervals until there were none left.

My father believed the answers to all of life's problems could be found in the sixty-foot-six-inch stretch of grass between the pitching rubber and home plate.

"Let's go hit," was his answer to any of my problems. He believed the simple process of trying to strike the leather baseball with a wooden bat broke life down to its most fundamental and vital elements.

We hit for two hours the day his mother died. He pitched me nine buckets of balls that day. He never said a word. He just stood on the mound, stone-faced, and I swung the bat until every callous on my hands was ripped open raw.

Why couldn't my father be like the other fathers, a normal father? I asked myself often.

"He had major league talent," my uncle Roth often said about my dad. "He should have played in the big leagues."

But he never made the majors, though he never batted below .280 in 10 minor league seasons. After years of chasing, his dream died and his family was born. Unfulfilled dreams pass from fathers to sons as certainly as the cut of their chins, their unique gait, and their dream-killing flaws. He was determined not to allow his inadequacies to prevent me from realizing his dream. He never asked me what I wanted; it was simply assumed. He never cared about my hopes, my dreams.

It didn't matter. I would have done anything he asked, his idealistic dream-like outlook on the world was so irresistibly positive that anything he said, to my mind, was undeniably true. "You're going to be a major leaguer," he told me so often that I actually believed it.

"But you gotta earn it, be worthy of it." His message was as consistent as it was persistent. "What you're doing today in the cold, wet snow is why you'll be playing in Yankee Stadium someday."

I came to believe that being a Yankee was my purpose. I wanted it so badly, I could taste it. When I closed my eyes at night, I pictured myself in pinstripes, striding along the green grass under the lights of Yankee Stadium, looking up at the white facade, and the graffiti-laced train rumbling past. The image was so vivid, so real, so perfect, that waking left a harsh, cold emptiness.

Why not me? I naively thought. *I'm working harder than any other 10-year-old in the country. How many kids my age are taking 100 cuts of batting practice every day?* I was going to earn this. I could see his dream in each one of his batting practice pitches and its fulfillment in each one of my hits. Every time I struck the ball cleanly, I glimpsed my destiny.

"This is the most perfect place on earth," my father told me the first time I walked onto an actual baseball field. We had just climbed over the shiny new fence surrounding the Little League field, ignoring **NO TRESPASSING** painted in blood red letters, and I felt like we were scaling Saint Peter's gates and sneaking into heaven. I walked across the orange clay, scarring its sticky surface, saw the sharp white lines, the razor-cut green grass, and the bright white bases.

"Nothing can touch you here," he stated unequivocally. "All the problems, the worries, the cares of the world disappear. This is nirvana."

Every time I stepped onto a ball field, I stepped into a perfect world, a world that made sense, a fair and just world free from the deceit and depravity, a place to lose all sense of self, and I could only imagine the transcendence of playing in Yankee stadium.

◆

Unlike most kids who are force-fed their parent's regurgitated dreams, I never hated my father. I loved my father. I wanted his dream for him as much as I did for me. Baseball was my conduit to him. I believed if I hit the ball hard enough or far enough or enough times in a row, then he would see me as worthy, and if I made it to the major leagues, I would prove to him that my life was meaningful, and I was valuable, or that his life was meaningful, and he was valuable.

After every session, before walking off the field, I would put on my small mitt, crouch into my catcher's position, and my dad would rear back and fire the ball straight into the air. I'd jump up, throwing off my pretend mask, and watch as the ball would shoot up like a missile, race toward the heavens, climbing and climbing, and then it would stop, hesitate for a moment and fall back to earth. I would stand under it, drifting side to side like a drunken sailor, and there was always a moment when everything slowed down, when I actually believed I could catch that ball, but it always fell too fast, and struck my body hard,

Chapter 2

bouncing in the grass harmlessly, and I lay on the ground, embarrassed and bruised.

"One more!" I would beg him. "One more!"

He would simply say, "Big leaguers don't get two chances," and walk into the house.

NW

Chapter 3

"You're gonna be great!" my father told me when he dropped me off for the first day of Little League. I walked up to the field tentatively.

A tall man in royal blue tossed the ball lightly into the air and slapped it across the infield. The second baseman scooped it, flipped it to the shortstop, who snared it in mid-air, dragged his foot across the bag, and fired a perfect strike to the first baseman. I shuddered at the ease of their precision.

"Hey," the man in blue yelled at me. "The Knights are practicing here. Sharks stay in the lot till we're done."

We hated the Knights. They were the best team in the league, and one of the best on the Jersey Shore. The Sharks were the worst. We were the leftovers, the discards from the Knights. They were the rich kids, the kids with the best equipment, the sharpest uniforms, the most championships. We had nothing.

We shared the same field, but the Knights used the home dugout, while we were relegated to the visitors. Their dugout was adorned with rows of championships banners. Ours was barren.

Dorian, Quinton and Jay rode up on the same bike. "They're still here," Jay said. "They should've been done 10 minutes ago." Jay lived in the house across the yard from mine. His mother was a nurse and his father sold insurance. They were a small family, in size, but not in number. Both parents and all four kids were significantly smaller in height and weight than average.

"They always take extra," Quinton said. Quinton's family was one of the three black families that lived in Galilee. His father was the mailman, so Quinton knew everyone in town because everyone knew his father. He was tall and gangly, with a short, tight Afro, a big smile, and a bigger laugh. Everything was funny to him. He was like a young Satchel Paige, rail thin, lanky with a wiry whip-like left arm designed for throwing a baseball with great velocity.

◆

As we walked to the field, a green Oldsmobile skidded to a crooked stop next to the dugout, and Jerry staggered out onto the field, his bushy orange hair pointing in all directions, his black framed glasses tilted on his nose, and his red Chuck Taylors flopping plumes of dust with each step. Some mornings, as my yellow school bus rumbled through town, I would see him on the side of the road in an orange jumpsuit, dumping metal cans full of trash into the back of a garbage truck. He looked like a different guy from the vibrant coach I would see at practice later that afternoon. At 7 a.m., he was just another guy picking up trash.

Jerry gathered us all together. "This is what we're playing for, men." He held up a fading blue jacket with **NEW JERSEY STATE CHAMPIONS – GALILEE KNIGHTS - 1975** written on the back. "This was the best year of my life, and I'm going to do everything in my power to get each of you a jacket like this."

"What's he gonna do, steal them from the Knights?" Quinton whispered to me.

"Is there something funny?" He snapped his head at us. I shook my head. "You don't think we can win the championship?"

Quinton shrugged. "It seems a little unrealistic. The Sharks have only won one game in two years."

"It's only unrealistic if you don't believe it is."

Jerry lined up all of us 10-year-olds. "Now who's played ball before?" he asked.

"My dad played pro ball," I blurted out proudly.

"What's his name?" Jerry studied me.

"Jack Pearson."

"Never heard of 'im," Eddie Brickman snarled. "He never played pro."

"He did, too," I shouted "He played 10 years. Just 'cause you never heard of him doesn't mean he didn't play."

"It just means he sucked then," Eddie said.

"You suck," I said. "My dad played pro, and he was good."

"Yeah, who cares," he relented. "You'll never play pro."

After practice, my father didn't say a word as we drove home. He pulled the car sharply through every turn until it skidded to a stop in our driveway. "Never tell anyone I played." He cut his eyes at me. "You don't get credit for what I did. You gotta earn it yourself."

◆

I didn't get a chance to earn anything that season. I rarely played. Jay was the only 10-year-old who got in the games regularly.

"A walk is as good as a hit," Jerry would scream as Jay walked to the plate. Jay led off every game. He never hit the ball. He never swung the bat. He never had to. All he did was crouch so low that his strike zone became so small that it was virtually impossible for a young pitcher to hit. Jay had a one thousand on-base percentage that year.

"It's not fair that shorter batters get smaller strike zones!" I said to my dad. "Everyone should have the same strike zone."

"They have a shorter strike zone because they're shorter. If they didn't, taller batters would have an advantage."

"Taller players have an advantage in basketball, but short guys don't get to shoot on a nine-foot basket." I countered.

"Baseball's more equitable than basketball," my father replied.

It didn't seem so equitable. A guy with a 70-mile-an-hour fastball doesn't get to throw from 50 feet.

◆

We lost the first 10 games by an average of eight runs and were out of most games by the end of the second inning, but for some reason, I always remained optimistic. No matter what the score, what the inning, I always believed we had a chance to win. My mind was always deducing a mathematical path to victory.

"We can do this," I prodded my teammates as they trudged into the dugout for our last at-bat. "We only need eight runs. We got this. All we got to do is bat around the order once, just once. Everybody hits. Everybody hits. No one makes an out." I believed I could believe enough for all of us, but that glimmer of hope I sparked in their eyes always faded and died, usually in order.

And after each game, my dad and I waited in his car for everyone to leave the field, and for every car to pull out of the lot. We barely spoke, and when no one was around, we walked back onto the field, me carrying my bat, and he lugging the bucket of balls. He didn't even ask. It was just understood. We hit, and we hit, and we hit, for an hour after each game.

"I can do just as good as these guys," I complained after our eleventh loss. "I should be playing."

"Who's the coach of the Sharks?" my dad asked.

"Jerry."

"OK, let Jerry coach, and you play. Stop trying to be the manager, and start being a player, a good teammate," he told me.

And then one game, our best player, Billy Weaver, didn't show up.

"Billy's sick." I heard Jerry tell a parent.

"He's got ammonia," Eddie said.

"He drank ammonia?" Quinton asked.

"No, he's got ammonia."

"It's pneumonia," Jerry said, "Billy has pneumonia." He then pointed to me. "Jake, right field."

I sprinted to the outfield like I was playing in Yankee Stadium. Rarely did a 10-year-old start a Little League game, but I guess I was the best of the bench warmers. Through the first five innings, the ball never touched my glove. I stood out there like a lawn ornament, irrelevant. Still, I knew we had a chance.

My unfounded optimism was unnecessary. I stepped to the plate with the bases loaded, down by two with two outs. The last thing I remembered was the pitcher starting his wind-up. It was like I blacked out, but when I looked up, the ball was flying over the infield, and kicking up chalk as it hit the right field line for a base clearing double, and for the first time in a long time, the Sharks took a one-run lead that we gave away in the bottom of the inning.

After the game, as I walked to the car, I saw my dad and I could not contain a full-face smile.

"What are you smiling about?"

I didn't know what to say. I thought he knew, so I looked over my shoulder to where my hit landed.

"You lost," he said. "That hit doesn't count when you lose."

That hit did count. I started the next game because of it and never missed an inning the rest of the season. I slowly became one of the best players on the team. I was young, but advanced. No other kid had a former minor leaguer throwing him batting practice day in and day out.

◆

As I stood in right field the next game calculating a nine-run comeback, the temperature dropped, and a cold, haunting wind rolled over us like an invisible wave.

"Here it comes," a voice shrieked from the stands.

"It looks like the end of the world," someone called out as a big, black amorphous mass crept out of the horizon, spread across the field, and enveloped us in cold blackness, turning day into night.

We scrambled to our cars and raced to our homes. Streaks of lightning reached from the clouds to the ground like long yellow cracks in our glass sky. We plowed through the sheets of rain, thick drops pelting our windows, our wipers unable to keep up. My dad jerked the wheel back and forth, spraying rain puddles on other cars.

"Where do the birds go when it rains?" I asked him.

"All birds find shelter in the rain," he told me, "except the eagle. He soars above the clouds."

We sprinted into the house, and my mother met us at the door. "Lock the doors, and shut all the windows," she said very calmly. I ran from room to room shutting windows with the lightning cracking around me. We huddled in our living room, listening, feeling, sensing every sound.

I thought about the eagle, rising above the thunder and lightning, soaring above it all in peace and tranquility.

A sizzling flash lit up the house. Every muscle in my body tensed up, but my mother reached over and squeezed my hand. "It'll be OK," she said quietly.

"One Mississippi, two Mississippi," my dad counted like this were a game. "Three Mississippi, four Mississippi." Then, we heard the faint rumble in the distance. "Four miles," he announced. "Four miles away."

"I don't like these storms," my voice quaked.

"We've survived hundreds of 'em," my father stated calmly. "We'll survive this one."

The rain crackled against the house like sizzling bacon. The snapping and popping was so loud that I looked out the window to see if the house was on fire.

The house lit up again. "One Mississi—" and then the thunder roared again.

"It's right on top of us!" I said.

My mother rubbed my back. "Don't worry dear, nothing's gonna happen."

And when she said those words everything fell silent. No one moved or spoke for the longest moment. "It's all over," I thought, and my racing heart slowed. And then out of the quiet nothingness, the black sky blazed white, the thunder cracked, the house shook, and the rain fell in soft silence. We sat shaking in the stinging echo.

"Jesus, Mary and Joseph!" my mother shrieked, as the house shuddered to stillness.

"What the hell was that?" my father barked.

The lightning bolt struck so violently that we thought a bomb had exploded. And out of the ringing silence, sirens blared. And just as fast as we had run into our houses, we flowed out of them, flocking to the smoldering home, electrified with fear and awe, standing on sidewalks, peering over fences, trying to get a glimpse of the Thompson's house in the dying rain.

"Lightning doesn't strike in the same place twice," was the common refrain offered to the trembling souls watching the firemen rush in and out of the smoking house. The town's psyche was scarred like the 20-foot lash of burnt shingles across the side of the Thompson's home.

"It's a once-in-a-lifetime event, honey," my father assured my mother. "We should thank God the only damage was to some wooden shingles."

As we walked home that night, I turned to my mother. "What did the Thompsons do wrong for God to do that to them?" I asked.

"Nothing, dear."

"Then why would God do that to their house?"

"God has a plan for everything," she said, unconvincingly.

"I don't get it," I said. "The Thompsons are a good family."

"God works in ways we are not meant to understand."

I was confused. What plan could destroying a house be a part of? The older I became, the less I understood God, and the more I was told I wasn't supposed to understand Him. I just had to accept His ways.

I looked back at the Thompson's house, and told myself if I made the world, I would have made it fair and just, not one where good things happen to bad people, and bad things happen to good people, but I didn't have the power to make the world, so life would never be fair and just.

NW

Chapter 4

"Everyone is to write a one-page fiction story by Friday," Mrs. Armstrong told the class as she wrote **FICTION** across the blackboard.

"What's fiction?" I asked.

"It's all made up," Betsy Kelleher called out.

"Fiction is the lie through which we tell the truth," Mrs. Armstrong explained.

"You want us to lie?" Jay asked.

"Not exactly," she replied. "A fiction story is solely from your imagination. Most of the best books are fiction."

"What's so hard about that?" Quinton sneered. "If you can just write whatever you want, where's the trick? A true story. That would be tough."

"My dad says that even the true stories are fiction," Suzy Marx added.

The concept of fiction intrigued me. There were no right or wrong answers. I could make it all up. I could create the world that I wanted, a perfect world, a world that made sense from my own realities, a world I could get lost in.

I spent two hours that night writing my story in my Big Chief tablet. It took me an hour to write the first sentence, but once I found my voice, the rest of the words flowed easily. What was once a blank sheet of paper had become my living world.

I sprinted down the stairs and handed the story to my mother. "Read this, see if it's OK."

She looked at the paper, her eyes widened, and she broke into uncontrollable laughter. She picked up the phone and called my aunt but was laughing so hard she could barely read my story. I pleaded with her to stop, but she kept reading anyway. When my father came home, she was laughing so hard she could barely explain, so she just handed him the paper.

My father grabbed the paper, and his eyes scanned the words on the rippling page in his clenched fist. He didn't laugh. He walked straight to the utility drawer, pulled out a red pen, and with loud, aggressive strokes, carved up my story with the precision of a surgeon and the savagery of a butcher. He thrust the red-scarred paper back at me.

"Fix it."

Tears welled up. "It's good enough," I squeaked, "It doesn't have to be perfect."

"What..." he snapped his head at me. "What did you say?"

"It doesn't have to be perfect," I mumbled.

His sharp blue eyes cut into me. "Of course, it does. It always has to be perfect. Good enough isn't good enough."

I ran up to my room, ripped the paper into pieces, and threw it out the window. "I will never write another story, ever," I promised myself. And I didn't, I never rewrote that story, and I received an incomplete on my report card. I didn't care. I didn't know if I was smart or dumb, but I did know a letter on a card could never answer that question sufficiently. That question was answered in other ways.

◆

The following Monday, Mrs. Armstrong returned the works of fiction, and then announced, "Laticia Martin, Suzie Marx, Jeremy Keegan, Michael Bailey and Jay Griffin please stand, and go to Mrs. Powers' class for fifth and sixth period." She gazed at them proudly as they filed out of the room, while the remaining twenty sets of eyes stared at them enviously.

"These students are gifted," she stated so emphatically that I accepted it as the truth, and immediately concluded I was not. As I watched them walk out of the classroom, I thought that those kids must be so exceptionally smart they had to be intellectually quarantined from the "non-gifted" like me.

"Gifted?" Quinton roared after school. "The only thing Jeremy Keegan is gifted at is acting like a retard."

"Jeremy's pretty good at math," I said.

"He's a retard," Quinton exclaimed, "He can't even tie his own shoes. Ya know, Armstrong should've just told the rest of us, 'Y'all a bunch of dumbasses.'"

◆

"I used to be smart, but I'm really dumb," I told my mother that night.

"Of course not," she said, "You're very smart."

"I'm not in the gifted class," I confessed.

"That doesn't mean you're not smart," her voice melted. "Whoever didn't pick you as gifted isn't smart."

My father appeared in the doorway like an apparition. "You want to be gifted?" He asked so confidently that I believed if I said 'yes,' he would reach into his pocket and hand it to me.

I nodded at him, embarrassed, but hopeful, and he stared right into me with his steely eyes. "You want to be gifted?"

I nodded again.

"Turn off that damn TV and read a book for chrissake. You want it, you have to work for it. You have to do more than what you're doing, more than what those other kids are doing. It's not gonna be given to you. You have to earn it. They're not better than you, it's just more important to them."

"He's doing the best he can, Jack." My mom's consoling voice sounded weak and powerless.

"If he wants to be gifted, he has to do better than his best," he stormed out, leaving my self-pity in his wake.

"He's doing better than most kids," my mom shouted weakly.

Well, at least one kid, I thought.

◆

"Dorian," Mrs. Armstrong's voice rang out and a chill ran up my spine, "take the next page." Hushed laughter ran from desktop to desktop.

Dorian straightened up and stared down at his book. "T-Tr-Tr-Trust m-me..."

"My little sister reads better than that," Gregg Taggart laughed.

I sat behind him, struggling through every eternal pause and gut-wrenching stammer as if it were I who was battling from one word to the next.

"W-Wil-Wil..."

"Wilbur," I whispered to him.

"Shhh!" Mrs. Armstrong said.

"Wilbur, p-p-pe-people a-are v-ver-very g-g-g..." he pressed his nose tight in the page.

"*Hooked on Phonics* worked for me," Betsy Kelleher murmured loudly.

"Gullible," I said under my breath.

"Gullible," he repeated.

Dorian wasn't dumb. He was actually smart. For some reason, he just couldn't make out the words. He struggled turning groups of letters into sentences. Terms such as dyslexia and ADD were tossed around, but by the end of the year, everyone knew Dorian was being held back.

"Jake," Mrs. Armstrong called me over after class. "Let him do it himself. You're not helping."

"I'm helping him more than you. Why d'you call on him? Just so everyone will laugh him."

"Of course not."

"Then why don't you yell at the kids who make fun of him, instead of at me?"

"You worry about Jake, and I'll worry about the other kids."

◆

"Where's your b-b-b-boy fr-fr-fr-iend D-D-D-Dorian?" Mitchell Coakley and Gregg Taggart taunted me at recess.

"Shut up!" I yelled.

"Make me?"

"I don't make garbage, I burn it."

They walked right at me and pressed me into a tree.

I clenched my fist. I wanted to punch them both in the face but didn't know how to punch. I had never been in a fight before.

She came out of nowhere, and before I knew what happened, both boys were doubled over holding their shins. "Leave him alone!" she screamed.

"Oh, your girlfriend's got to protect you," Coakley laughed.

"Na-uh," I yelled back.

"Stop hiding behind your girlfriend's skirt," Taggart limped away. "Is your b-b-boyfriend D-D-D-Dorian j-j-j-jealous of your g-g-g-girlfriend?"

"Jake and Dawn sittin' in a tree..." Coakley chanted.

"She's not my girlfriend!" I screamed so loud that everyone on the playground stopped. I looked at Dawn's horrified face and waited. Then I yelled, "I don't even like her." She recoiled. "She's ugly!"

She sprinted across the yard with her plaid skirt flapping and disappeared into a side door of the school. I stood there stunned, motionless.

"Dude, that was totally messed up," Taggart laughed. "I can't believe you said that."

"Shut up," I told him as I walked away. "I don't care."

I did care. I knew I shouldn't have said that to her, but I wasn't strong enough not to. I was also more concerned about Dorian; how unfair life is to people like him. He couldn't read. It seemed like he couldn't do anything.

◆

"Swing!" the pack of fathers screamed as the ball approached the plate the opening game next season, and Dorian's bat waved and missed it by a foot.

"He's an embarrassment," his mom stated as he dragged his bat to the dugout. "I can't watch anymore of this." She marched to her car and never returned the rest of the season.

"You have a beautiful swing." Jerry patted his helmet. "If you ever make contact, you'll hit it right into the river."

But Dorian never made contact. He never hit the ball. He struck out every time. He swung at pitches over his head or in the dirt and let pitches right down the middle go for strikes. He was the worst player on the worst Little League team on the shore.

I was one of the best. I was always surprising myself. I played better than I ever imagined. I even felt sorry for those kids not as good as me, especially Dorian. It seemed unfair.

It started the first game of the next season, I stepped to the plate in the bottom of the sixth with two on, and two outs, down by one. The Sharks had not won a game in two years. I was scared. The pitcher was tall and intimidating with a rising fastball. I had not hit him all day, so when I stepped in the box, I told myself to swing at the first fast ball I saw no matter where it was. His first pitch flew off my bat on a line over the third baseman's head and fell safely onto the outfield grass. As I rounded first base, Quinton sprinted home for the winning run and everyone — the team, parents, friends — stormed the field, hugging and rolling around in the dirt like we had just won the World Series.

"Jake, game winning hit against the best pitcher in the league." Jerry reached into the pocket of his blue Championship jacket and tossed me the game ball. I proudly showed it to my father after the game.

He took the ball from my hand and tossed it into the gray bucket with the other batting practice balls.

"But Dad, I wanted to put that on the shelf in my room," I pleaded.

"It's more useful in the bucket," he winked. "Let's go hit." And I followed him out back. We never stopped working. I had to succeed. It was simply understood. I couldn't let my father down; I couldn't let him see me fail.

I rarely did that season. Five straight games, I collected at least three hits, and drove in the game winning run in the last inning. It was a stretch of success never before seen by a Shark team, and I was not only part of all those wins, but responsible for them. Each one of those hits made my dreams of the majors feel closer and closer.

"There's no better feeling than when you hit the ball like that," my father told me after my fifth game winning hit. "So clean, so pure, and as you watch that white ball fly through the blue sky and land safely on the green grass, all is right with the world."

Through the first 12 games, Jerry gave a game ball seven times. And whenever I brought a ball home still warm from a triple or home run I hit that day, my dad casually tossed it into that gray bucket with the other anonymous balls.

"You're gonna be a major leaguer," he told me after each one of my game winning hits, trying to imbed that delusion into my psyche, believing in the magic of self-fulfilling prophecies.

Jerry started calling me Chase Manhattan, proclaiming to everyone I was "money in the bank."

"What d'you got today, Chase?" Jerry asked me before each game. "A couple doubles? A homer?" I just shrugged, afraid to make a promise that I didn't know if I would keep.

I hated that name. I hated the pressure of that name.

"Get used to it, Money," Quinton told me, "It's all part of being the man."

In the last inning versus Highlands, we were down by two, and Jay walked to load the bases. *Why does it always come down to me?* I thought. I could feel the eyes of everyone locked onto me, expecting me to get a hit, to win the game. I picked up my bat, and slowly walked to the plate. Quinton grabbed me, and looked me in the eye, "One more time, E Pluribus Unum."

"Here we go again, C.M.B.," Jerry screamed. The first pitch bore down to the outside corner, and without thinking, I snapped my barrel into it and the ball flew to the right center alley clearing the bases for a game-winning double.

"He did it again! He did it again!" Jerry bounced out of the dugout and lifted me on his right shoulder. "Chase Manhattan did it again!" He paraded me around the infield. I was so relieved the pressure was gone that I pumped my arms with both index fingers extended in the air. "We're number one. We're number one," I pointed at the pitcher as he trudged off the field, head down.

I walked to the parking lot, picturing myself sprinting out of the dugout at Yankee Stadium, throwing out base runners, and hitting game winning doubles as I approached my dad's car.

"Get in!" He shoved me into the car and slammed the door. He wrenched the car out of the lot and drove down a long, dark road away from the field in edgy silence. He just stared straight ahead, driving in a big loop around the town without a word.

Then he turned to me. "You think you're better than that pitcher?"

"I hit him," I said.

"You work harder than him?" He sneered. "Play harder?"

"I don't know," I shrugged.

"That one hit makes you a better player, a better person?" I shook my head. "No."

"What gives you the right to taunt him like that?"

"I don't know," I said. "I didn't mean to embarrass him."

"You didn't embarrass him, you embarrassed yourself," he said as he pulled the car back into the empty baseball field lot. He flung open the door and popped the trunk. "Grab your stick," he told me, and we walked back onto the field to hit three buckets of balls.

◆

I knew I wasn't a better person than that pitcher, and I didn't know why I was succeeding. It was just happening like someone else was doing it. I began to believe that success and failure were somehow pre-destined, and my success was maybe God repaying my father for all his disappointments.

I also didn't know why Dorian was failing. I tried to help him. "Just watch the ball and swing," I told him because that's all I did. It seemed that everyone had advice for him, everyone knew how to fix him.

"On no occasion lift the bat off your shoulder," Jerry instructed Dorian before the Seaside game.

"Why?"

"You have a better chance getting on by the pitcher throwing four balls, then you hitting one pitch," Jerry explained.

"You want me to just stand there?"

"No, when you get in the box, dig in hard, take some big aggressive practice swings. Try to intimidate the pitcher, then don't swing."

The first three times up, Dorian took long swooping practice swings, but struck out looking each time without lifting his bat off his shoulder. He just watched three third strikes float past him, and walked back to the dugout, his face twisted in anger and embarrassment.

"He doesn't want to hit. He's scared to swing," the opposing coaches called to the pitcher whenever Dorian was up.

For five straight games, Dorian did not swing the bat and only reached base once. Finally, he turned to me in the sixth inning of a 10-1 loss, "I'm swinging," he said with a cool resolve.

"What about Jerry's orders?"

"I don't care. If I'm gonna strikeout, I'm not doing it just standing there like an idiot." He stepped to the plate with a gleam in his eyes and swung at the first three pitches. He missed them completely, but walked to the dugout with his head held high.

Jerry followed him to the bench. "I thought I told you never to swing, ever?"

"I didn't come here to not swing," Dorian said. "I'm gonna do it my way."

"Your way doesn't work."

"Yours didn't either," he replied.

Jerry smiled and walked away. Dorian turned to me. "I'm not listening to anybody anymore."

His first at-bat the next game, he swung at the first pitch, and the ball left his bat with such a resounding crack that everyone on the field stopped and looked. The ball flew so fast that when my eyes finally picked it up, it was bouncing beyond Sea Haven's wooden fence, and rolling across the street.

"I never seen a ball travel that fast," Jay's father observed.

"I told you if he ever connected," Jerry said as Dorian rounded the bases.

The rest of the season, he hit everything and never struck out again. With that one act of self-reliant defiance, Dorian turned from the worst player on the team to one of the best. Everything suddenly clicked. It all happened overnight. He became so good that Jerry moved him to fourth in the order and gave him five of the last six game balls.

I tried not to be jealous of him. It's wrong to be jealous of your best friend, but every so often a rogue thought squeezed into my mind uninvited and clawed at me. I didn't want him to fail. I just didn't want him to be better than me, but it seemed the better he became, the worse I did.

NW

Chapter 5

"Idle time is the devil's workshop," Mrs. Armstrong warned us as we filed out of her classroom on the last day of the school year. Dorian and I walked by her desk, and she grabbed his arm. "Stay with me after school today," she told him.

I stopped. "What are you doing with him?"

"This is not your concern, Jake," she told me.

"But..."

"This is for his own good. You can go get on the bus," she said.

When I stepped on the school bus, I knew what was happening. I knew they were holding him back. I sat down in my empty seat and felt alone for the first time.

Gregg Taggart walked on the bus and stopped next to me. "You know what the best thing about being you is?" His pointy teeth smiled at me.

"What?"

"You don't have to look at you," he burst into a maniacal laugh.

"Oh, yeah," I screamed, "but you do."

"Hey, Jakie where's your b-b-boyfriend?" Betsy Kelleher's grating voice taunted me.

"Where's yours?" I yelled back. "Oh, I forgot, you're too ugly to have a one." She popped up out of her seat.

"Mitch, Mitch, Mitch," ricocheted down the aisle, as he strolled onto the bus with his usual swagger.

Mitchell "Killer" Coakley was the most feared kid in school. He ran a newspaper delivery syndicate. He "owned" every paper route in Galilee and subcontracted them out to younger kids. He took in a hundred dollars a week without delivering one newspaper himself. His was a reign of terror. He chose you. You didn't choose him. Once, he dangled a third grader over the second-floor railing at school, until he agreed to deliver for him.

His tiny eyes darted back and forth, hunting for prey. He stopped next to my seat with a fiendish smile.

"What's wrong with you?" He leaned toward me, but I just looked out the window. "You're not going to cry, are you?" His warm breath licked my cheek. "Like a little faggot!"

He pressed his body up against mine, looking for a sign of fear or weakness. I didn't say a word. I sat there frozen.

"What, are you ignorant or something?" His lips grazed my ear. "You catatonic?"

The window was my only refuge. My eyes locked in on two water droplets as they raced down the glass.

"Let's see the baby cry," he grabbed my backpack. I lunged at him, but he stiff-armed me to the ground. He held my bag up, and everyone pounded the seats and stomped their feet. He unzipped the bag and lifted it over his head. He paused with a jagged smile.

"Dump it! Dump it! Dump it!" The mob chanted. Mitch grinned. "Dump it! Dump it! Dump it!" He thrust it higher, and then turned my bag upside down. Books, papers, and baseball cards fell to the floor and scattered everywhere. The seventh and eighth graders went wild, pounding, screaming, laughing. I scrambled to the floor, frantically grabbing everything I could reach. I sat there shaking as I pulled my life back together.

I'll never be that way. I promised myself. *Never.*

"Here." A gentle voice reached out and handed me a small stack of my baseball cards. Laticia stood there wearing the same ragged plaid jumper she wore every day.

She sat down next to me. "You don't have to worry about Dorian," she smiled softly.

"I'm not," I answered severely.

She waited to let my angry words dissolve amid the clamor. "He'll be OK." Her voice was as delicate as her face.

"How do you know that?"

She looked at me with her almond eyes. "He didn't do anything bad."

◆

I jumped off the bus and onto my five-speed and pedaled as fast as I could until my tires skidded against the gray stones of Dorian's driveway. I walked up the steps and through the front door. The windows were open, but nobody was inside. The old and tattered house was impeccably neat and organized; no clutter.

Johnny emerged from the basement, stopped, and looked at me. I never really knew who Johnny was or how he was related to Dorian's family. He never married Dorian's mother. He never adopted

Dorian or his sister Karen, but he took care of all of them like a father.

"Dorian's not back from school yet, huh?" I asked Johnny.

"Yeah, yeah, yeah," he stammered.

"Can I shoot some baskets?" I feigned a basketball shot.

"Right, right, right," he nodded, and walked back into the basement.

I shot baskets on their rusted hoop for about an hour, when Dorian appeared at the end of his driveway. Ms. Armstrong honked as she drove off. He walked slowly toward me. There was something different about him. "Hey, four eyes," I called out.

He walked over to me, took the ball from my hands, and quietly said, "I think these glasses are magic."

"Yeah," I agreed, "You couldn't see and now you can. Magic."

"No, something else. I'm seeing things I've never seen before," he peeled off his glasses. "Try 'em."

I carefully held them up to my eyes.

"What d'you see?"

"Nothing, the same. Everything's bigger and blurry but nothing different."

He held the ball up, "What does this look like?"

"A basketball."

"No, what color is it?"

"Orange?" I was unsure of what answer he was looking for.

He grabbed the glasses and kicked over a dusty mound of gravel exposing a spectrum of grays. He studied the various hues through his sparkling lenses, and carefully picked up a medium gray stone. "This... is orange."

"That's gray." I said skeptically.

"Well, this is the only orange I've ever seen." He eyed the stone. "I know a basketball is orange." He held up the ball. "But I've never seen this color before."

He grabbed a handful of grass. "I know that grass is green, but I've never seen this color before. When I was driving home, all these new colors kept coming at me, floating around me, like I could reach out and grab 'em."

"Where in the hell did you get those things?" Her shadow stood on the edge of the porch.

"Mrs. Armstrong took me to the doctor."

"The doctor?" Dorian's mother stomped down the wooden stairs and marched across the gravel driveway in her bare feet. "What doctor? Not our doctor."

"I don't know." Dorian looked away. "Just a doctor."

"You don't know. How much did they cost?" She stopped inches from his face.

He shrugged.

"You don't ever know a goddamn thing. I'll have to pay for those fancy glasses. Did you think of that? You didn't need those things. You were doing just fine without them."

"No, he wasn't," I said. "You should've taken..."

She cocked her right hand. "No!" she screamed, as her hand flew and her open palm struck Dorian on his left temple. His head snapped to the right, throwing his glasses across the driveway. They bounced off the gravel, and a sparkling lens shot out of the frame and slid across the rocks.

She walked into the house as Dorian groped along the gravel for the pieces of his glasses. I picked up the scratched lens and handed it to him. He pressed it back into the frame until I heard a subtle snap. He pushed himself to his feet and walked toward the porch.

"Get Johnny to put some Krazy Glue on that," I suggested as we sat down on the top step.

"It's funny," he smiled as he fiddled with the lens and slid his glasses back on. "On the way back from the doctor, I read a whole chapter of *Huckleberry Finn*, no problem."

"If you couldn't see," I asked, "how do you hit so good?"

"I stopped listening to everybody," he replied, "and I listened to the ball."

"How can you listen to a ball?"

"I don't know," he shrugged. "I just do. It's like, I can hear its echo."

NW

Chapter 6

"Great players play their best in big games," my father told me as our car snaked around packs of pedestrians on their way into Hendricks Field. American flags were everywhere, big and small, hanging and waving. Red, white and blue bunting fluttered in the wind along the fences, and the school band meted out "Stars and Stripes Forever."

That Fourth of July, Galilee shut down and everyone in town came to watch the Mayor's Trophy game. The Sharks had never beaten the Knights, ever, but this year, we finally had a chance. The bleachers were packed, standing room only.

Jerry stood before us prior to the game. "This is our year. We can beat these sonsabitches. Remember, this is for bragging rights the rest of the year, the rest of your lives. If you lose today, you'll never live it down."

He was right. We could beat these guys, and as we entered the last inning, we trailed by only one run. Quinton had struck out ten, I had three hits, and Dorian, with his new eyes and sonar-like ears, hit three triples.

I stepped to the plate with two outs, bases loaded in the last inning, in front of the entire town, everybody I knew. "Chase! Chase! Chase!" emanated from our dugout and the bleachers.

The pressure was always there. No matter what I did, each time I stepped into the batter's box, I felt like my life hung in the balance. If I didn't get a hit, I would never play in the major leagues, and my life would amount to nothing.

I worked the count to full. A walk tied the game, but a base hit meant victory; victory over the Knights, victory in the Mayor's Trophy game — unprecedented.

"One more time, Chase," Jerry shouted.

"A walk's a run," a parent called from the bleachers.

His last pitch streamed at me, high and outside. I was tempted. I wanted to swing. I wanted to drive it to right field. I wanted to beat the Knights, I wanted to be the hero, but I knew it was a ball, and I knew I couldn't put my bat on the ball, so I held my bat back and watched the ball all the way until it popped into the catcher's mitt.

"Striiike three!" The umpire pumped his right fist dramatically. The entire Knights team swarmed the field tackling each other. I stood at home plate just staring at the blue team rolling around in the dirt with the bat still firmly on my shoulder as if I were waiting for the next pitch, refusing to concede the victory.

"It'll never happen. The Knights are just too good," a random parent said casually. I walked slowly toward our dugout.

Mr. Brickman followed me along the outside of the fence. "Don't ever take strike three, ever!" He ripped off his cap and spiked it. I pulled off my helmet and fired it into the backstop. It ricocheted off a steel post and bounded down the third baseline.

"Son," the umpire grabbed my shoulder, "if you ever throw your equipment when I'm working a game again. I'll have you kicked out of the league for good."

I approached the dugout, and saw my teammates sprawled on the bench in a desolate heap. A big hollow ball began to grow inside me, filling up my chest. My face grew hot, my breath became short quick pants.

Jerry walked up to me, ran his fingers through his thick red hair and sighed, "I guess the bank was closed today, huh?" And walked away.

That ball continued to grow and grow, expanding into my heart, filling up my lungs, pressing against my Adam's apple, until it burst out of my eyes and streamed down my face. I pressed the heels of my hands against my eyelids, trying to stop the tears from bleeding out of me.

I walked to the parking lot, head down, eyes burning, face wet. I sat in the front seat of my father's car, staring out the window. I could still taste the dried salt pasted to my cheeks. I was afraid to look at him. He wasn't mad, just silent and serious. He finally turned to me.

"If I ever catch you bawling on an athletic field," he growled, "you'll never play again. Never."

"But, Dad." Fresh tears boiled up inside of me. "I let everyone down."

"I don't give a damn," he sneered. "Don't ever show you're defeated. Ever!"

I sat there in silence and waited. When the last car pulled out of the lot, he popped the trunk, grabbed the bucket of balls, and we went onto the field and hit for an hour.

NW

Chapter 7

"He's gifted," random voices commented from time to time the following spring. "He's special. He's got *it,*" filled the background of my life, but no matter how much I wanted it, those words were not meant for me. Dorian was gifted. Everyone knew it. He had that indescribable quality that set him apart. He had *it.* I could see it but could not put my finger on it. Excellence radiated from him like a sweet smell.

He played with an even confidence, as if he knew what was going to happen before it happened. His gift was baseball, and the price he paid must have been the house he was born into.

For some reason, I didn't continue to progress. With each passing day, I became more and more average, pulled back to the pack. I began to look up to Dorian like a little brother looks up to his big brother. He became everything that I wanted to be but wasn't.

Dorian playing in the big leagues was a reality even back in Little League. I knew the odds against one kid from a small town making it were minute, so the odds against two were infinitesimal. Only one man from Galilee had ever played in the major leagues, and that was 50 years ago.

As his legend grew, my dreams withered, starving in his shadows, scorched by his brilliance. My life slowly became a series of disappointments, continually falling short in front of my father's eyes. Some days, I was embarrassed to look at him. I was beginning to realize that I would never become what he so desperately wanted me to be.

I was average. I couldn't escape it. I was not the tallest or the shortest in my class, not the smartest or dumbest, never picked first or last on the playground. My family was not rich or poor. The more I looked around, the more I saw others just like me, and I slowly began to fear, through no fault of my own, I was sentenced to an uneventful middling life of banality; a nameless, faceless being, contributing little and easily forgotten. I was invisible. There was nothing wrong with being average, most people are. It becomes a problem, though, when the dreams of the extraordinary are misplaced into the mind and body of the ordinary, and they are forced to unwillingly accept their inadequate life with quiet despair.

Many nights, as I lay in my bed listening to the waves roll to the beach, and watching the lights from the cars on Ocean Avenue race around the walls of my room, I feared the only thing I would discover was there was no reason for me to be here, that I didn't deserve the air I breathed or the water I drank, and it might all be taken away. So, I worked harder and longer. I got a weekend job at the batting cages on the boardwalk so I could take as much batting practice as I wanted in the 90-mph cage. I was desperate to learn how to catch up to a major league fastball.

◆

We opened the next season playing in a tournament at the new baseball complex in Freeport. As we drove up the winding road outlined by apples hanging off of trees, 12 fully lit baseball fields rose up out of the orchards. Four of the fields were Little League-sized duplicates of Fenway Park, Tiger Stadium, Wrigley Field, and of course, Yankee Stadium.

"That pitcher has a foot on his hand," a voice observed as we walked up to Fenway. The pitcher did have a foot for a hand, or what looked like a foot. He had a stump at the end of his left wrist with four little stubs that amounted to round toes without nails. I stared at his misshapen hand as his fastball seared down the center of the plate and snapped frighteningly loud into the catcher's mitt.

"If we make the finals, we're probably gonna face him," Jerry pointed at him.

Stevonne Simpson played for Chelsey's YMCA. He had a grown man's body, tall and muscular, which gave him a physical advantage over everyone in the league, except for that third foot, or missing hand, but I never felt sorry for him. I knew it wasn't fair that God gave him a stump for a hand, but it also wasn't fair that God gave him a lightning bolt for an arm.

We rolled through the first three games, despite only two hits by me, but we won easily behind Dorian's four home runs and Quinton's 16 strikeouts.

◆

I walked through our front door, and my Uncle Roth was sitting at our dining room table. He showed up that morning out of nowhere, unannounced, as usual.

"Heeeeey, how was the big game?" he screeched.

"Jake's team made it to the finals today," my father announced proudly.

"That's unbelievable, kid, huh?" my uncle perked up.

I nodded.

"C'mon, how many times in your life do you get to do that, huh? And play in Wrigley Field, huh?"

"Thanks." I walked into the kitchen.

"Jake," my father followed me. "Go in there and greet your uncle the right way."

I walked back into the dining room to shake my uncle's hand, and I thought about what my father had stated unequivocally many times: "Roth should have played in the major leagues. He had Bill Mazeroski hands, Ozzie Smith hands."

I looked at him. "Let me see the hand." He stuck out his left hand with a grin.

"No, no, the other one."

He winked and held his right hand, almost proudly, turning it back and forth. He never made it to the big leagues because of that right hand or what's left of it. The top halves of his fingers were gone at mid-knuckle. The skin was scarred and melted. He held his hand up again for me wiggling his half fingers.

"Roth, make sure Sarah comes next time," my mom said, trying to change the subject.

"OK, Ginny," he nodded. "Sure."

I couldn't look away from Uncle Roth's deaf right ear. It looked like it was made of silly putty, while his thin, sharp beard covered up the warped and twisted skin on the right side of his face.

"Tell me how it happened," I asked.

"Jake, please," my mother admonished.

"It's OK, Ginny," he smiled at her. "This is our country's history. He should know about this." He stared right at me. "I'd been in country for a little more than a year. I was a short timer, only a few months left. The Cardinals had been sending me letters the whole time I was there. There'd been heavy fighting up in Lam Song, and we were sent in to clean things up, evacuate the wounded. There were some guys in pretty bad shape, shot up pretty good. We were pulling 'em onto the chopper when a grenade flew inside and skidded to a stop on the metal bed. It just laid there spinning in front of us. Everything slowed down. So, I just shuffled over and scooped it up. It was all instinct. I was in good fielding position, and I threw that sonovabitch out of the chopper. It exploded just as it left my hand. The next thing I knew, I was on a plane heading stateside, and I never fought in that war again. And I never played baseball again."

He looked down at his mangled dreams. "I guess I didn't have as quick hands as I thought."

"Jake, Jake!" my father barked from his rocking chair in front of the TV screen. "Best hitting catcher in baseball."

Number 31 dug into the box for the Dodgers, standing like a statue. The muscles on his forearms rippled as he gripped the bat. He took a deliberate stride and threw the head of the bat at the ball violently. The ball shot in a line over the second baseman's head.

"He attacks the ball. He's not afraid of nothing. He goes after every pitch. That's the way to hit!" my dad barked at the screen as if he were coaching him.

"Piazza," I whispered to Roth.

"I saw this kid in spring training when he was a rookie, Jack. Best young hitter I've ever seen."

"He reminds me of you." My dad pointed at me. "You attack the ball just like him. Beautiful. That's gonna be you someday."

◆

The next day, we played Chelsea's YMCA in the finals at little Yankee Stadium. Eddie sat down next to me on the bench before the game. "Where did you get that mitt?" he asked.

"My mom got it for me for my birthday," I said proudly.

He laughed. "See this word right here?" He pointed to four capital letters branded into the leather along the outside edge of the pinkie.

"What does it mean?"

"Blem?" He said the word as if he were offended. "Blem?" He repeated in disgust. "Your mom bought you a blem for your birthday. What is she, a dago, or something?"

"What's blem?" I asked.

He pulled the glove off my hand, inspected it, and sneered, "Instead of BLEM, you should have SUCKS stamped on it."

◆

Stevonne Simpson stood on the mound like a giant, pulsating black mountain, and I stood on the lip of the dugout, studying his motion like I knew what to look for. His first warm-up pitch struck the catcher's mitt with such a startling pop that everyone within earshot stopped to see what they just heard. It was such an intimidating sound that most kids were struck out the moment they heard it. But not me, I wasn't going to back down. I was going to attack like Piazza.

My first at-bat, I hit a hard grounder back at the pitcher. He bounced off the mound, and in one seamless motion transferred his glove perched on his stump into his right hand, fielded the ball, switched the glove back to the stump, and threw me out with his good hand.

We played them close the entire game, and entering the last inning, I was 0 for 3 with seven runners left on base and I also allowed one of Quinton's fastballs to bounce off my blem mitt for a passed ball that let in the go-ahead run. I walked to the plate with one out, runners on second and third, down by one. "Here we go, Chase," Jerry called from the dugout weakly trying to evoke some of last year's magic. I looked around. It really did feel like Yankee Stadium.

The first pitch was a fastball straight down the middle. I dropped my back shoulder and jerked my bat at the ball. It shot straight up. The catcher popped out of his stance and waved his arms, "I got it! I got it!" I stood idly next to him at home plate helplessly watching him settle under my hit. He took a subtle step to his left and the ball dropped easily into his mitt. He reached out and tagged me with the ball in my chest.

"He used to be good," a parent whispered as I walked back to the dugout. "Thank God, Dorian's up."

He walked to the plate with a cool confidence, like he knew what was going to happen. We all knew, and by the look on Stevonne's face, even he knew. He whipped his bat at the first strike he saw. The middle of his barrel caught the ball with a sweet *whap,* and it clung to the barrel for a perceivable moment, until he casually flipped it on a line over the second baseman's head. It skipped in the alley and rolled to the fence. Eddie wheeled around third and sprinted home. Dorian trotted down the line, touched first base and casually strolled back to the dugout, like none of this really mattered.

What's a Dago?" I asked my father on the way home. He looked at me with a sour expression and answered my question with two questions.

"Why? And where did you hear that?"

"Some kid at school said it," I told him.

"That," he said slowly, "is just another word for an Italian person."

"I don't think so," I said. I didn't understand why calling someone an Italian would be an insult?

"It's absolutely the truth," he affirmed, "but don't ever use that word yourself."

"Why not?" I asked, "if that's all it means."

"Don't ever say that word again. It's an ignorant word used by ignorant people. It's only an insult to you when you say it."

I had learned two new bad words, Dago and blem.

NW

Chapter 8

"You can't win if you don't play. Nothing ventured, nothing gained," echoed across the playground as the smell of popcorn and cotton candy floated over me. I strolled along the school yard, watching my classmates running from tent to booth, smiling and laughing, bobbing for apples, eating cotton candy, tossing rings.

A pang of jealousy bit into me. How I wished I was like the other kids, living without a care, without a concern, without a gnawing drive in the pit of my soul for something more meaningful. Why couldn't I just enjoy being a kid?

Then I saw it. On the top shelf of a red and white wooden booth in the middle of the schoolyard, a brand-new Wilson A-2000 catcher's mitt was displayed, the exact model that Piazza used. The one I'd been saving up for. The one my mom should have gotten me for my birthday. But there it sat, gleaming, within my grasp, inviting me. I was drawn to it. I had to get it. I walked up to the booth. In thick red paint, the words **PENNY PITCHING** were scrawled at the top; **QUARTER TO PLAY** was painted in tiny print below.

A fat man leaned into the booth tossing coins. The wooden ledge pressed so deep into his overgrown stomach, that I thought it would split him in two. A little brown-haired girl watched intently; fingers crossed. The man's thick sausage fingers rubbed the coin, and in one quick easy motion, let it fly. The coin floated in a soft arc over the game board, landed in the white, and slid to a stop just inside the big red circle. "Give it to me!" He snatched at the air.

A slippery looking man, with a long, curled mustache and a pointy face barked, "We have another choice winner!" as he pulled down a large bear and presented it to the young girl.

"You look like a good athlete," the slippery man smiled at me. "That Nintendo game has your name already written on it."

I nodded and pulled a quarter out of my pocket. I cautiously held it in my fingers and tossed it, hopeful. The glimmering silver arced over the board, landed heads up in the middle of the red, but slid to the white.

"Aw, that's a damn shame." His yellow teeth smiled at me. "Sooo close. Keep trying, you'll get 'em."

For the next hour, I tossed two pockets full of quarters toward those red circles, trying to somehow negotiate those silver disks inside the edges, but no matter where they landed, they always slid into the white.

"It's impossible to win," I yelled at myself.

"A nine-year-old girl won a pair of roller skates this morning," the man boasted with a wink.

I turned my last quarter over and over in my fingers as I contemplated my last chance, but the coin slipped out of my hand and fell inside the booth. I leaned over the ledge to grab it.

"That coin's been played," the slippery man yelled.

"I dropped it. I didn't throw it." I lunged at the quarter, but he scooped it up, and I flipped over the ledge, almost landing on my face. As I was pulling myself up, I saw it. "What's that for?" I pointed to a blue can sitting under the ledge with the yellow writing: WD-40.

"None of your business, sonny."

"That's not fair," I screamed. "You're cheatin'!" I pointed at him, but just as those words shot out of my mouth, the bright sunny day turned dark and cold.

The storm crept in quickly and silently, and thick, wet drops began pelting us. Everyone scrambled like ants after their hill had been stepped on, sprinting underneath the covered platform and staring out over the rain-soaked carnival.

The red and white booth stood idle in the middle of the driving rain and pounding thunder, tempting me. I eyed it, filled with false prizes and empty promises. Its emptiness, its ill-gotten gains called to me. *That was my money in there. Why does he get to cheat? Why does the school let him rip off kids?*

I stood under a big oak, waiting for a letdown, not of the storm, but of their eyes. Their eyes held me under that tree. I waited for my chance as the lightning cracked around me. Their eyes finally receded, and I broke out. My legs kicked high and my arms pumped hard. I ran across the field through the sweeping rain, leaped over the side of the booth and slid in the warm mud into a bucket. Quarters flew everywhere, mounds of them, glimmering like white gold.

I crouched inside the booth. Rainwater poured off my clothes. Thick drops slid off the red dots and pooled up in the white. I scooped handfuls of silver and jammed them into my pockets, my front pockets, my back pockets, my shirt pockets. I even managed to cram a few into that small fifth pocket in the front of my jeans.

I pulled myself over the rail, but a rusty nail snared my pant leg. As I yanked it free, I saw an eighth-grade girl on the platform pointing directly at the booth. I rolled over the side.

Three eighth graders and two men stepped into the rain and spread out over the field. The men sprinted right at me, one on each side. I was trapped, cornered like a wild dog. I darted left, then right, and then back left again, but they followed my every move. I had nowhere to run, nowhere to hide, nowhere to escape. I weaved in and out of the trees and around the booths as my captors slid and slipped in the thickening puddles. A roar rang out from the platform with each dart and dive, as the people rooted for my capture.

I ran to the back of the playground. The fence was too high to climb. I turned to face my captors. The five walked toward me, closing in, cutting off the yard, sealing any escape paths. The jingling in my pockets reminded me of my crime. I needed to give it all back and say I'm sorry, but it was too late, so I grabbed handfuls of coins from my pockets, and threw them into the rain, scattering them all over the playground until my pockets were empty.

I made a final desperate dash toward the parking lot, but a large wet hand grabbed my right shoulder, and slammed me to the ground. A cheer broke out as I laid covered in mud, staring into the blinding rain. I wiped the water from my eyes, and I saw the mustache, wet and drooping, no longer greasy and curled. His yellow pointed teeth smiled, "It's a damn shame."

He dragged me across the playground. "I didn't do it, I didn't do it," I punched at the air. "I don't have any coins," I screamed as he pulled me on the platform.

"Look." I reached into my pockets and pulled them all the way up to show they were empty, but four white quarters slid out of that fifth pocket of my jeans and bounced off my sneaker. He smiled that same smile right at me. "Sister will be very pleased to see you."

"He's the thief, not me," I pointed.

"Some jerk always ruins it for the rest of us," a woman sneered.

"That was the most fun all day," a man laughed. "They should have that every year."

They sat me down on a wooden bench facing the school. Drops of water fell from every edge of my body while the rain sizzled on the metal roof above.

I wanted to run away, but I had nowhere to run to, so I just stared straight at the wall, wet and ashamed, and out of the corner of my eye I could see him standing there, waiting. Then Dorian cautiously inched toward me, slapped a pile of coins on the bench, and ran away.

Sister Margaret Mary walked up with her beady black eyes. She was built more for playing middle linebacker for the Giants than teaching eighth grade math. She was short and squatty with forearms bigger than most of the boys' thighs. And she used those powerful arms to keep the boys in line; a push, a shove, an occasional swat. She wasn't abusive, just physical. I feared the power of her thick form, but I also pitied her miserable existence of being trapped in such a hideous form.

Sister handed me an envelope. "Bring this back on Monday with both your parents' signatures, and 40 dollars to pay for the lost coins." She reached down, scooped up Dorian's coins and walked away.

◆

"Why'd you take the money?" Jay asked, as we waited for his mom.

"It wouldn't have been right to just take the glove."

Neither Jay nor I said a word about the incident as his mother drove us home, and I completely forgot about it when I saw the flashing red and blue lights of the two fire trucks in front of the Panunzio's house. As we inched by, we saw the Panunzio's 20-foot chimney scattered on the ground, like a pile of children's blocks. "I swear," Mr. Panunzio was telling the fireman, "I thought the house was hit by a plane."

Half the town stood in the rain, frozen in collective fear, seized by the meaning of a second lightning strike in consecutive summers to consecutive houses along Ocean Avenue. Was this random chance, or part of a greater plan?

"There must be some magnetic field around here," Uncle Roth theorized, "drawing in the lightning."

"Are we gonna get hit by lightning someday?" I asked my mom.

"No, honey."

"Two lightning strikes on the same street is like winning the lottery or being killed by terrorists," my dad surmised. "Lightning won't strike anywhere near here again, mark my words."

"But why did the Panunzios get hit?" I asked. "Why does God keep punishing good people?"

"Lightning is not punishment. It's too unpredictable," Uncle Roth said.

◆

"You have to tell your old man," my uncle advised me when I told him about the coins that afternoon.

"I don't want to," I said. "I'm scared."

"Sure, you're scared," he nodded. "You did something dishonest, but the solution to dishonesty is not more dishonesty, it's honesty. Tell him the truth. You'll be fine. He's not gonna kill you."

"He might," I said.

He smiled and nodded. "He might."

◆

That night, my father's face remained stone-like as he stared at Sister's letter. I stood there with my head down. He looked at me, and without raising his voice, said, "Is this the way you want to live your life? Do you want to be known as the kid who stole the money? It's your choice. It's your life. Never trade your self-respect for a handful of quarters." He walked out of the room, and never spoke a word of the incident again.

I wished he would have whipped me or slapped me across the face. That would have stung less than the disappointment in his eyes.

I was forced to spend an hour a day after school for a month, clapping erasers and washing chalk boards with a dozen or so other kids who did those tasks so often it seemed like they were on the school's payroll. Sister always made an effort to remind me, "I must always keep my eye on you, Jake. Nothing in all creation is hidden from God's sight. Not even you."

She watched my every step, waiting for me to make a mistake, to reveal myself. In her eyes, I was guilty until proven innocent. Every so often, she would walk by and her eyes would screw tight onto me, saying *I'm watching you. I see everything. You don't fool me.*

"Nuns shouldn't act that way," I told my mom after a two-hour detention one Friday.

"Putting on that habit doesn't stop her from being human," she told me.

I was human, too. *Why should I forgive her humanity, when no one ever forgives me mine?* I began to realize, over time, my humanity was being revealed in all its wonder and weakness.

I was tempted by both the unattainable lofty visions of my father, and the nefarious expectations of others. Who was I? I was the only one who didn't seem to know.

I began to look at the world like God standing over Sodom and Gomorrah, but not searching specifically for one good man to save the rest; rather, for one good thing, one pure moment free from all the depravity, something that would tell me that there was a reason for the existence of us all.

NW

Chapter 9

"It's a life choice," Jerry told Jay through the rearview mirror of his green Oldsmobile as the warm salt air swished through the downed windows while we drove north on Ocean Avenue. "What do you want to be, a hitter or a walker?"

Jay just shrugged.

"God put you on this earth to swing the bat. I never want to see you crouching for a walk again."

"I just want to win," Jay said in his tiny voice.

"Then swing away. I believe in you," Jerry told him, and then turned to us. "You guys can be whatever you want in life. That's what makes America great."

"We can't be whatever we want," Quinton spoke up. "Only some can."

"In this country," Jerry snapped, "if you work hard enough, you can achieve anything. You can be president. You can even be a Yankee, if you want it badly enough."

"It don't work like that," Quinton said.

"Don't be afraid of your dreams, Q," Jerry told him.

"I ain't afraid of nothing, but I see it every day. No one works harder than my old man. You think that was his dream, lugging that bag around all day?"

◆

We pulled up to a field with IAMA hanging above the back-stop in red and green letters. For the first time since their inception, the Sharks had a winning record, and could finally compete with the best teams in the area. So, Jerry set up a challenge game with IAMA, the Italian American Men's Association, led by the infamous Vinnie Segreti, aka "The Hot Dog," the best player on one of the best Little League programs on the Jersey shore. The week before, Vinnie no-hit the Knights.

He was a legend, the most feared player in the area. He had the fastest fast ball in the league, as well as a knuckleball, a curve, a slider, a forkball, and a "slurve," a pitch he invented — a combination slider and curve; so dangerous that the Little League commissioner outlawed it because it was "potentially lethal."

Everyone in the stands looked like they were related, and the plate umpire looked like their coach's brother.

"That boy's at least 15," my mom said, sizing up the pitcher when she first saw him. Vinnie was tall, lanky, with a pencil mustache. He wore a gold cross against his hairy chest, a diamond stud earring in his left ear, an orange bandana around his neck and a tattoo on his left bicep. A pack of fully mature girls sat behind home plate cooing after every pitch.

When I stepped to the plate in the first inning, the Hot Dog walked off the mound, and held up three fingers. "Three, just three," he announced to the crowd, and the stands erupted. The fans pounded the chain link fence with such ferocity that the backstop began shaking.

He walked back and stood on top of the mound with his black, beady eyes staring in at the catcher. He reached his hands high over his head, arched his back nearly parallel to the ground, kicked his left leg high, and wheeled to the plate, whipping his rubbery arm right at me and a straight blur exploded in the catcher's mitt.

"Steeerike!" the umpire sizzled, and the backstop rattled.

The Hot Dog walked directly toward the squealing girls. He raised his index finger. "That's one! That's one." He strutted back to the mound with his solitary finger still raised above his head. He perched on the white slab like a bird resting on his pedestal.

"That's bullshit," Quinton yelled.

The Hot Dog looked over at our dugout, and pointed at Quinton, "You're next, buddy. You're next."

The next pitch was harder to see and popped louder in the catcher's mitt. "Steeerike two," the umpire screeched, the crowd erupted, and the cage shook.

The Hot Dog swaggered off the mound again, with two fingers high. "That's two. That's two."

"Protect the plate," Jerry called out. "Don't let anything by."

I crouched down, choked up two inches, opened my stance, and told myself, just make contact. Don't strikeout, put it in play.

I don't think I could have hit the next pitch if I swung a thousand times. I started to swing the moment the ball left his hand, but my bat came so late that I had a better chance of hitting the catcher's throw back to the mound.

As I meandered back to the dugout, the Hot Dog marched directly at me. "That's three," he shouted, his cold black eyes staring at me.

"That's three."

Dorian strolled to the plate next, and the Hot Dog glared at him. He climbed on the mound, and cautiously raised three fingers above his head. The steady din in the stands fell silent. The first pitch came in hard and low. And Dorian watched it sail into the catcher's mitt for strike one. The Hot Dog stepped toward his entourage again, "That's one," he said, in a more serious voice. "That's one."

The next pitch looked the same, low and straight. Dorian's looping swing missed the ball completely. The Hot Dog stood on the lip of the mound, raised two fingers, "That's two. That's two," he said more confidently.

He walked back up on the mound, looked over at the girls and winked. He reached his arms high over his head again and fired his next pitch. It left Dorian's bat in a high, far-reaching arc, and carried the length of the outfield like it was caught in a jet stream, until it clanged off the middle of the right center fence.

Dorian slid into third base a step ahead of the relay throw, bounced up and brushed the orange dirt off his uniform without a glimmer of satisfaction.

"That's three!" Jerry yelled from the dugout. "That's three!"

After five innings, the Hot Dog had 12 strikeouts, but Dorian had a triple, a double, stole home, and pitched five innings of one-run ball. We were tied one to one going into the sixth inning.

When Dorian walked to the plate for his third at-bat, the IAMA coach stepped out of the dugout and pointed to first base. The Hot Dog looked down and shook his head.

The catcher stood with his mitt out to the left. The Hot Dog wound and fired his famous fastball between the four and two on Dorian's back with a reverberating thud. Dorian fell to his knees, like he was shot. Jerry sprinted to him. Dorian rolled on his back, and his eyes closed slowly. He didn't move, except for short, involuntary gasps of breath.

Jerry peered up at the umpire, looking for an answer, expecting him to make the right call, so Dorian's eyes would open.

"Dorian! Dorian!" Jerry shook him, but he didn't respond. The raucous stands fell eerily silent.

"That's bullshit," Eddie's dad called out. No one else spoke. Everyone stared silently at Dorian's motionless body.

"I'm gonna kill that dude," Quinton seethed.

Jerry turned to the crowd, "Call an ambulance!"

Several women hurried to the parking lot. Jerry unbuttoned Dorian's jersey, and pressed his ear to his chest.

But then Dorian's eyes opened. He popped up as quickly as he fell and ran to first base.

The game became more intense, more physical; brush back pitches, hard tags, sliding spikes high, and the parents became louder with each pitch, mocking the opposing players, berating the umpires.

Quinton doubled down the left field line, and Eddie walked to load the bases. Jay stepped to the plate. He had already struck out three times. Jerry called him over. "Listen to me, Jay." He draped his arm around him. "If you lift that bat off your shoulder, I'm going to break it over your head. God made you short for a reason. Everyone has their role in life and your role is to walk. I want you to crouch like you've never crouched before."

We took the lead on a bases loaded walk in the sixth.

With two outs in the home half of the sixth, we led by one, but they had a runner on third. A sharp grounder between first and second bounced hard off Eddie's chest. He gathered it quickly and tossed a strike to Dorian covering first. The Sharks' parents erupted, but the base ump swept his arms "safe."

Eddie's dad staggered onto the field flailing his arms. "You goddamn dago," Mr. Brickman screamed. He stood nose-to-nose with the umpire, "What the hell you looking at, you guinea?"

Jerry sprinted out of the dugout, bear-hugged Mr. Brickman and tried to pull him off the field, but Eddie's dad torqued his body and threw Jerry to the ground. Parents from both teams swarmed the field, knocking Mr. Brickman to the ground, pushing and shoving, throwing wild punches at each other that only struck the air. Jerry herded us into the parking lot.

Dorian stood behind first base, still holding the ball as he stared at the melee, not understanding how a game of baseball could devolve into this, how it could bring out the worst in people. He turned and fired the ball high into the air. It streamed across the orange sky, fell beyond the fence, and disappeared into oblivion.

NW

Chapter 10

"The boundaries," Dorian stated very clearly as he inspected the beach, "are the rocks," he pointed to the row of boulders beneath the boardwalk, "and..." he looked to the blue horizon, "England."

Dorian could turn anything into a game. He created games out of nothing. They appeared in his imagination and all he needed was a ball and the beach. Sports games always brought out the best in him. They reveal what is truly inside of everyone, and maybe that's why he loved to play.

He used his right heel to cut two thick lines at the far ends of the beach. He drew the goal lines with his heels and the boundaries with his eyes. We played the game on the wet sand, on the edge of the world.

"When you cross the goal line," Dorian said, explaining the most important rule of Beach Rugby, "you must *touch* the ball *down* on the ground to complete the play. That's what *touchdown* means."

All kids were welcome. All types of kids; big, small, short, fat, boys, girls, would flock to the game, appearing on the field from nowhere, and step right into the flow of the action. We never slowed the game down. Dorian either threw the ball to the new kid, or he didn't, and that's how we knew which team the newcomer was on.

Dorian chose up sides quickly. He didn't divide us by size, speed, or athletic ability. He would study the pack of kids and state, "All blue bathing suits versus all non-blue bathing suits." Or, "Odd ages versus even ages." And the group always divided into two equal teams.

One day as we were choosing up sides, Tina walked up, wearing her rainbow-colored swimsuit and purple goggles. "Dorian Childs. Dorian Childs, can I play?"

"She can't play, man," Quinton objected. "Look at her. This is no joke, D.C."

"Why not?" Dorian asked naïvely.

Quinton pulled him to the side. "She's a retard. She's gonna get hurt."

"She's not retarded," I said. "She's got Down syndrome."

"Same thing," Quinton said.

"There is a difference…"

"She's going to get somebody hurt."

"She's no different than anyone else," I argued. "We're all different."

"Yeah, but she's not like everyone else."

"Neither are you. What if we said, no black kids?" I asked.

"That's different."

"It's only wrong if it's happening to you?" I asked.

Dorian turned to Tina. "Do you want to play?"

"Yes, I do, Dorian Childs," she nodded.

"You could get hurt," he warned.

She just nodded and smiled.

"If she doesn't play, then I don't play," Dorian said.

"I'm gonna run over her by accident," Quinton predicted.

"Be an athlete," Dorian said, and tossed the ball to Tina. She grabbed it, clutching it against her chest as she ran away from the pack with her legs flailing as they closed in on her. Just when Jay was close enough to touch her, she threw the ball straight up in the air and dove into the sand causing the pack to topple over her.

"See, she's gonna to ruin the game," Quinton said, flipping his hands in the air.

Tina played the entire game, running up and down the beach following the pack, waving for the ball, smiling at everyone, as if her infectious smile was the only joy she could bring to the world. She never caught a ball, because the only balls thrown to her were desperate, erratic throws that hit her randomly and sent her sprawling.

Dorian didn't wear his glasses when he played. He didn't need them. He had a sixth sense. He always knew where everyone was on the field. He always made the right cut, always found the open man. Maybe the healing powers of the ocean made his foggy eyes clear. Or maybe Dorian sprinting across that vague stretch of nebulous sand caused the hazy shades of gray floating in his eyes to become well-defined images.

The games lasted for hours, to the point of exhaustion, but we kept playing. We never kept score, or more accurately, Dorian never kept score. I did, every point, every game. And even though his team was always leading by insurmountable margins, he never used those points to determine who won or lost. The game always had to end memorably.

Deep into this game when we could barely take another step, Dorian grabbed the ball, and announced dramatically, "Next touchdown wins." All that had gone before, the running, diving, sweating, every touchdown, suddenly became meaningless. To Dorian, it would always come down to one final act.

He tossed the ball in the air. Quinton grabbed it and sprinted along the water's edge. He cut back across the beach, weaving in and out of blankets, spraying sand on sunbathers. He leaped over a beach chair, only to be trapped between an umbrella and a playpen, where he was tagged down by Jay.

He tossed the ball to the side, sand and frustration pasted all over his sweating skin. "There are too many damn people on this beach."

Dorian picked up the ball and burst toward the water. We chased after him, but stopped at the water's edge. He sprinted into the crashing waves and dove into the ocean.

He swam and swam, deeper and deeper, into the water. Quinton stood on the wet sand, not wanting to be lured into the web of the waves. Then, Dorian turned and swam north, toward the underwater goal line.

"He's trying to touch it down underwater," I screamed.

"No way." Quinton yelled. "You're cheatin'!" He leaped into the water after him.

Every member of my team followed. Once we were all in, Dorian ducked under the water for a long moment, popped up, and lofted the ball in a beautiful arc back toward the beach into the awaiting hands of the young girl in the rainbow bathing suit and purple goggles. She grabbed the ball clumsily with her palms, pressed it against her chest and sprinted toward the end zone. She leapt across the goal line, touched the ball on the ground and held it high in the air for the game-winning score. Dorian sprinted out of the water in a beeline to Tina, grabbed her and lifted her over his head, her big smile beaming over the Jersey shore.

It was the first time I was not angry or jealous that I had lost. Her smile erased all that. It's impossible to hold self-destructive emotions in your heart in the presence of such sheer joy. Dorian found beauty in places no one else would think of searching, and always seemed to find the thing missing most in his life.

◆

"This is illegal," I warned him that night, as he stood on top of the green dumpster. "It's wrong."

"It would be wrong if we didn't do this tonight." Dorian lived by his own rules which often make more sense than the ones everyone else lives by. He pressed his foot into the metal joint of a down spout clinging to the side of the big, white club and scaled the side of the building. I followed. We pulled ourselves over the high wall and stood on the top of the club, looking out over the coastline.

"This amazing," I said as I beheld the Jersey Shore; Atlantic Heights, Long Beach, Seaside.

Streams of red taillights and white headlights highlighted the roads and bridges, weaving the islands and the peninsulas into an elaborate tapestry.

"It makes you feel lucky," he said.

As dusk began to give way to the deep blue night, small white lights outlined boats on the ocean. And the distant skyline of New York City was vaguely defined by a thousand specks of light.

Just as the hazy dusk melted into night, glowing lights of gold raced across the sky like shooting stars, stopping momentarily at their climax to explode and spread their carnival of colors for the world to see. Red, white, blue, and gold flowered every beach, boardwalk, and marina across the Shore. Blooming balls of color sprung up all the way from lower Manhattan down to the faint glow of Atlantic City. On the water, solitary flares shot up from lonely boats, lighting up the dark water momentarily, adding their singular verse to our celebration.

After the last burst of color faded into the sky, Dorian stepped down off the highest part of the roof and looked out over the Olympic sized swimming pool. He leaned against the railing, studying the 20-foot drop to the deep end of the pool. He kicked off his shoes, peeled off his shirt and climbed up on the railing.

"What are you doing?"

Without a word, he sprung from the darkness into the soft, smoldering light above the pool. His half-naked body floated weightlessly above the glassy water with outstretched arms, arched back, and upward eyes. And when gravity took hold, he curled forward and plummeted like a cliff diver, melting into the water with only a slight ripple.

◆

I creaked open my front door and tiptoed inside.

"You can't hoot with the owls and soar with the eagles," a voice from the shadows said. My father stepped into the scant light. "The biggest game of your life tomorrow, and you're out all night."

"I'll be fine," I mumbled.

"You'll always be fine, but is fine good enough for you?" my dad asked. "Is it good enough for the Yankees?"

◆

Minutes before we took the field for the Mayor's Trophy game the next day, Jerry held a shiny new quarter in front of us.

"Watch it, Jer," Quinton warned. "Jake's here."

He smiled and flipped the quarter high into the air, anyway. It sparkled in the sun and dropped softly in the grass. "Heads," he called as he picked up the coin. "If I flipped this coin nine times and it came up heads nine times, what are the chances the next flip will be tails?"

"Ten percent." Eddie guessed.

"No, ninety," I corrected him.

Jerry shook his head.

"Fifty-fifty," Dorian said softly.

"Exactly. Fifty-fifty. It's always fifty-fifty. The last flip doesn't affect the next flip. What happened last week, yesterday, five minutes ago, doesn't matter anymore. The past does not dictate our future. Look at them," he pointed to the Knights warming up. "Are they better than us?"

"Yes," Quinton whispered under his breath.

"They're no different than us. They're not better than us. It don't matter how many times they beat us. If we win this one game, everything bad that's happened is forgotten."

A beat-up Monte Carlo pulled up next to the Knights' dugout. The passenger side door rumbled open and the cleats of a large black baseball shoe clicked on the pavement. Attached to the shoe was a thick, muscular leg, and when the rest of the body unfolded from the car, everyone stopped and stared. A shiny metal hook was where a hand should have been. A loud buzz swept through the stands as Stevonne Simpson walked onto Hendricks Field wearing a Royal's pin-striped uniform.

"We can forget about forgetting," Quinton said.

"I'll be goddamned," Jerry shook his head. "So they're gonna let him play."

"They can't do that," I protested, "he plays for Chelsea."

"I didn't think the league office would give in," Jerry muttered quietly to himself.

"He doesn't live in Galilee," I argued. "They're cheating..."

"His mom's in California for the summer," Jerry interrupted me. "He's living with his aunt in the Cove."

"The Cove?" Jay said. "That's not Galilee."

"Technically, it is," Jerry stated.

"My dad delivers mail out there," Quinton nodded. "It's the same ZIP code."

"But this late in the season," Jay said.

"I've been all through this," Jerry said, "I've made every possible argument."

Mr. Thorne, the Knights' manager walked up to Jerry and handed him three sheets of paper. "It's official."

"C'mon, Karl," Jerry scanned the paperwork, "you're not playing him, are ya?"

"He's on our roster," Thorne took the papers back from Jerry.

"Play him in the playoffs, if you want," Jerry offered. "But today? This is a Galilee thing."

"It's not fair," I said.

"Fair?" Thorne smirked at me. "It's legal."

"We should get him," I said. "They have two more players than us already. It's not right."

"We'll beat 'em anyway," Jerry predicted unconvincingly.

Stevonne Simpson struck me out three times on a total of nine pitches. He threw fourteen strikeouts for the game, but Dorian homered, Quinton tossed a two-hitter, and we were tied going into the last inning.

I stepped to the plate in the bottom of the sixth and two outs, with a chance at retribution for last year, and the rare opportunity to prove to the town that the Sharks weren't just a bunch of cast-offs. The first pitch I pulled long down the left field foul territory over the red shed. He threw two curves in the dirt for balls. Then I took a fastball down the middle for a strike. "Swing the damn bat," Mr. Brickman snapped.

I stepped back and looked out to left field. I didn't just eye the fence, I eyed the river. I dipped my back shoulder and yanked my bat at the next fastball, and missed it completely, but instead of the deadening pop of the leather mitt, I heard the hopeful rattle of the backstop. The catcher and I broke at the same time. I sprinted to first base as he scrambled for the loose ball.

As I closed in on the bag, the first baseman's eyes grew big and he lunged at me with his glove. The ball struck the side of my helmet, ricocheted and bounded down the right field line. I put my head down and raced in a tight arc around second toward third, and I slid in just ahead of the throw.

I stood 90 feet away from the potential winning run in the last inning with two outs and Dorian stepping to the plate. I didn't care how I had gotten there, I just knew I had given us a chance.

Thorne stepped out of the dugout and pointed to first base. Stevonne nodded. The catcher stood with his glove out to the left. Stevonne shortened his wind-up and threw the first pitch high and outside for ball one. He tossed the second pitch in the same place for ball two. Eddie Brickman was on deck.

Dorian stepped out of the box and stared at Jerry. Jerry walked up to me and whispered, "Be ready."

Stevonne threw the third pitch in the same spot as the first two. Dorian leaned across the plate, stretched out his thick bat, and plucked the ball out of the air. It dribbled down the third base line, zig-zagging inches inside the white chalk like it was trying to stop itself.

I sprinted straight for home, with one eye on the plate and the other eye on the dying ball. Home plate never looked so far. I slid hard and fast; my whole body crossed the plate before the third baseman even corralled the ball.

Jerry burst onto the field, arms held high, leading a band of flailing 12-year-olds. "We did it! We did it! We did it!" They swarmed Dorian, pulling him to the ground. I stood alone against the backstop and watched the Knights slowly trudge off the field into oblivion. They didn't seem so intimidating, I thought. They just looked like a bunch of kids like me.

"You won't see that again in my lifetime," a random voice declared from a pack of exiting parents.

NW

Chapter 11

"Jesus, Mary and Joseph," my mother paced in front of the TV, staring intently at the bright orange cone superimposed over the Atlantic Ocean.

We knew the hurricane was coming a week before it arrived. It was born off the tip of Africa, matured in the South Atlantic, and headed straight for Florida. It was first reported to have hit land somewhere in the Florida Keys, but a high-pressure system steered it out to sea and drove it north.

Every night that week we stared at the TV, hoping for some good news. The next landing site was to be a small town in Georgia, but the high-pressure system kept the worst of it off the coast.

A woman grasping a microphone on a deserted Georgia beach told the country in front of a rising sun, "This small hamlet is safe as the storm heads to North Carolina."

A gray-haired, leather-faced man proclaimed, "God showed us his love by turning that storm away from us. He saved our homes, our lives. He loves us."

My father stood, and angrily struck the TV knob, and the screen fizzled to black. "What about those poor bastards in Carolina who are gonna lose their homes tomorrow? Does God not love them? Are they not deserving of God's graces?" He looked straight at me. "People are ridiculous, Jake. Never forget that."

◆

The storm continued moving north up the Atlantic, again side-stepping the expert's predictions, and seemed to be heading right toward us. The wind came first, blowing for two days straight. The gusts blew so hard that they wiped clean the dirt and salt pasted on our cars. We could feel the house leaning with the force of each gust. Garbage cans rolled down the empty streets like tumbleweeds. And then came the rain. It came like the wind in swirling sheets that gathered up the drops of water and spun them around the yard like miniature waterspouts.

The house was dark from the wooden boards nailed over the windows. The streets were empty. White water poured over the seawall, turning the streets into streams. A fisherman rowed down Ocean Avenue past our house.

We sat around the kitchen table all morning listening to the winds grow stronger, and the banging of the shutters get louder. "Eleven fifty-eight, fifty-nine," my dad announced, tapping his watch. "Landfall in exactly 61 seconds."

My mother clutched a set of wooden rosaries, head down, her lips thinly mouthing her silent prayers.

"Sixty, fifty-nine, fifty-eight." He counted down dramatically. "Landfall... right... now."

Golf ball-sized raindrops flew across the yard and pounded the side of the house for an hour straight, unrelenting, a constant torrent of rain and wind and darkness.

"When will it stop?" I asked. "I can't take this."

My mom put her arm around me and squeezed tight. "It will be over soon," she whispered in my ear.

And then, like a light from heaven, the clouds opened, everything stopped; the wind, the rain, the debris all paused. The sun was bright, the sky was blue, white gulls soared overhead. It was a normal summer day.

And just when we felt safe with the clear sunlight overhead, a bright flash sizzled down from the heavens followed by a deafening crack. The house trembled.

"Jesus, Mary and Joseph!" my mom gasped.

Down Ocean Avenue, the front porch of a white Victorian home was split in two. Its roof sprawled out on the front yard.

"The Fitzpatricks," my dad finally said.

We all stared at the wreckage, processing that information silently. But we knew what it meant. The Fitzpatricks lived next to the Panunzios who lived next to the Thompsons. Three lightning strikes, three consecutive summers, three houses in a row. The lightning was moving south one house at a time directly toward us.

"Two strikes are a fluke," my dad said. "But the third is something else entirely." The third one made it real, like a force more powerful than luck was in control. The whole thing was eerily comical, and we used morbid jokes to quell our fears. We watched as the Connolly's garage was ripped open the next summer, and then the Mason's roof, followed by the Dodson's chimney. Each strike was closer and closer to my house. I felt that God was playing a sick game, hurling thunderbolts down at me, but missing on purpose as his strikes were picking off our neighbors, one by one.

"Why is this happening? What did we do to deserve this?" I asked my mother. "Why is God doing this to us?"

"God isn't doing this to us," she said. "God loves us."

"This is what happens when you live near the beach, on the edge of the world, where the two great forces of the world collide," my father told me.

I never believed we would get hit. Not really. But when our next-door neighbors' front porch was destroyed by a sizzling flash last summer, I believed. We were next in line, and there was no buffer zone, nothing, no one left to protect us.

NW

Chapter 12

"C'mon, Jake. C'mon, Jake. C'mon, Jake." My father's voice bounced off the cracking walls of my room. "Twenty-five minutes." I shut my eyes and fell back to sleep.

We lived four blocks east of the small white church with the big red door. My family never missed mass, never. It was not an option. We went, always, every Sunday, every Christmas, every Easter. Rain, snow, sleet, it didn't matter. Mass was never up for debate.

As high school grew nearer, I slowly began to question everything; all the things I had blindly accepted since birth. I no longer understood the necessity of church. I saw the rituals, the robotic repetitive responses, the voodoo-like superstitions that outsiders condemned and ridiculed, and I began to see the difference between belief in God and blind allegiance to a religion. But I was never allowed to question anything about the Church except in the dark, silent recesses of my soul. Mass had become a useless ritual. I could close my eyes and recite the entire mass verbatim. Why did I need a priest? Why did I need the Church?

"C'mon, Jake. C'mon, Jake. C'mon, Jake," rattled my brain. I opened my eyes and noticed the faint yellow light prying through my frost covered windows. I looked through the warped glass and saw millions of glistening specks spiraling to the ground and rolling hills of white everywhere. Everything was frosted over, shimmering in the glow of the new day. It was a beautiful sight, especially on Sunday morning.

"Jake. Jake. Jake. Jake," fired up the stairs. "Let's go! We gotta make nine o'clock."

The drifts were higher than the hedges, the stoplights were blocks of ice, and there was not a single tire track on the pristine snow-covered roads. I fell back into my bed, "We're snowed in," I yelled hopefully.

"Get downstairs right now," my father ordered.

I stumbled down the stairs. "The snow's three feet high."

"Your father was up at six digging us out," my mother said.

"You're lucky I didn't get you up," he squeezed my shoulder.

"We don't need to go. God knows we're snowed in."

"We're going," my father fumed.

"It's too hard to get there." I said.

"It was hard for Jesus to get to the top of Calvary, wasn't it?"

"Why do I have to go to church, anyway? I don't need church," I whined. Both my parents remained silent, pretending not to hear my blasphemy. "It's stupid. Stand up, kneel down, repeat what he says like a robot. Church is like a Hitler Youth Rally."

"Don't you ever use those words in the same sentence again," my mom snapped.

"Don't you want to thank God for all the good things he's done for you?" my father asked.

"Can't I be thankful in my bed?"

My father walked directly over to me, and very calmly said, "Get upstairs, get ready. We leave in five minutes."

I looked at my mom, pleading.

"Jake, you never know what God has in store for you," she offered.

The usually half-filled church was not even a quarter full as our snow-covered bodies trudged through the doors. "See? I told you," I whispered. "No one's here. We didn't need to come."

"Shhh," my mother said.

"Of course, we did," my father snapped.

We slipped into the last pew as the processional hymn abated. Father John greeted the small pack of half-frozen parishioners. "Thank you all for coming this morning. The effort getting here is as important as attending."

"Let's leave then," I whispered to my sister, and my mother shushed our laughter.

After the Gospel reading, Father John stepped in front of the altar. "He who is without sin may cast the first stone," his words reverberated through the nearly empty building. "Jesus said that to the men who accused a woman of adultery as he saved her from being stoned to death. People will claim that this line from today's Gospel is proof Jesus tolerated sin, but they always seem to omit the last thing he said. He looked at the woman and told her ..."

Father stopped and looked to the back of the frigid church. "Welcome," he spread his arms to two snow covered creatures stepping inside the door, almost blown in like the swirling snow. "God waits for all men."

Dorian and his sister emerged from the back of the church with snow plastered to their woolen clothes, and walked heads down up the aisle, and knelt in the first pew. Dorian placed his bowed head in his open palms against the rail.

The priest looked back up and said, "Jesus told her, go and sin no more. Simply because he did not condemn the sinner, does not mean he does not condemn the sin."

After the priest sat down, a girl stepped to the podium as organ music floated down from the balcony. She opened her tiny mouth, and a beautiful waif-like voice spread out over the scant congregation. Her soft, high-pitched melodious voice flowed up to the rafters and rolled back down, as if from heaven. She was as beautiful as her voice. When she released her final note, she stepped to the side and sat down gently. I couldn't take my eyes off her the rest of the mass.

◆

"We are all sinners, saved only by God's grace." My father stood uncomfortably close to the priest, sharing his interpretation of the Gospel story in the shadowy vestibule of the church.

"Dad," I prodded him to go.

The door burst open, and a puff of white, like frozen smoke, swept in and swirled around us. She stood just inside the door, like the statue of an angel with the fluffy white snow dancing around her dark hair. She walked straight to me. "Hi." She smiled.

"Hi." I leaned up against the wall.

She ran her hands through her hair, and the snowflakes floated around her.

"I thought your song was good," I said.

"You're just saying that to be nice."

"I'm never nice."

She smiled, and I reached out my hand. "I'm Jake."

"I know. We went to third grade together. Remember? I'm Dawn. We moved to Long Beach, but we just moved back."

I stared at her. I remembered the girl, Dawn, but she was different now, older. She had full flowing hair, and the blossoming curves and burgeoning chest of a woman. That was the first time I noticed those things about a girl.

"You've changed," was the only thing I could think to say.

"You haven't," she winked. "You're the same old Jake. I'll see ya in school tomorrow." And she walked away.

◆

That night, the church parking lot was overflowing with cars but empty of people. It was a bitter cold and clear night. I walked through the lot and into the pulsating gymnasium. There was not an inch of naked wood on the long benches of the bleachers.

"I guess it's easier to drive through the snow on your way to a gym than a church," Father John remarked to one of the parents.

She was sitting at a square card table in the main doorway, exchanging tickets for dollar bills.

"Hey, two times in one day," Dawn smiled at me.

"Five dollars?" I read the cardboard sign. "They never charged before."

"This is the championship," she said.

"I don't have any money." I patted my empty pockets.

"Go outside for a few minutes," she whispered. "I'll let you in after we shut down the table."

I stepped back out into the cold. It was peaceful, and frigidly still. A black silhouette crept in and out of the rows of cars. I peered down an aisle and saw the short squat form of Mitchell Coakley, slithering about, staring into car windows. I walked toward him.

He looked up at me with a hammer in one hand and a chisel in the other. "How's eighth grade treating you?" I asked as he approached. "Second time's a charm, huh?"

"Shut up, Pearson," he raised the hammer, "before I split your skull open."

He wore a black leather jacket, black leather fingerless gloves and a dark blue wool cap. Tiny particles of glass clung to his wool pants. I scanned the lot. Car windshields were destroyed in his path, cracked like the partial holes left after walking across thin ice.

"What are you doing?" My voice quivered, more from his presence than the cold.

He looked over at the rows of shattered windshields and then back at me. "Let me show you something."

He walked to the nearest car and brushed the fresh snow off

the frozen windshield. He placed the chisel firmly against the frosted glass and carefully tapped the butt of the metal with the precision of a sculptor. The glass slowly separated, and long screeching lines grew down toward the hood of the car.

"What are you doing?" I grabbed his arm but it didn't budge. He was one of those kids that was made solely of muscle.

"I'm doing 'em a favor." He pulled away.

"Favor? How's breaking their windshield a favor?"

"I only pick the windows that are already cracked," he pointed to a small hole on the top of this window. "See that? This way, the insurance will pay for a new one."

He held the chisel firmly against the glass, his naked pink fingers wrapped around the cold raw metal, and in one quick thrust, smashed the butt of the hammer into the blunt end of the chisel. A loud disturbing pop shattered the cold silent parking lot and the glass disintegrated into nothing. He went from windshield to windshield, exploding them into dust or cracking them like giant spider webs.

I was awed by the raw vitality of his unbridled depravity. Then, somehow the chisel ended up in my hands and the glass fragments on my pants. I ran from car to car. There was an exhilaration to the pop of the hammer and the explosion of the glass. It possessed a power, a control over others. The warm air trapped inside the car broke free with each pop and rose from the cracks as steam. I felt like the freed air, liberated yet chilled. After 20 minutes, half of the cars in the lot were smashed open, and I was dripping with sweat in the frigid night.

As I turned to leave, Coakley grabbed my shoulder. "You will never tell," he looked at me squarely. "Never. Take this to your grave." He didn't know I wasn't brave enough to confess.

I went inside and watched a quarter of the game, then waited by the back of the church in the biting cold until the game ended, comforted only by a warm waft of cigarette smoke floating by. I watched, hidden in the darkness, as people melted into tears beside their shattered cars.

◆

When I arrived home from basketball practice the next day, my parents were sitting at the kitchen table, serious. "How was the game last night?" my father asked.

"It was good." I was purposely ambiguous.

"Good?" His eyelids tightened in on me. "Mr. Gardner told me it was the most exciting game he's been to in a long time."

"Yeah," I quickly retreated. "It was an exciting game."

"I heard we went down by 18, came back, and won it on a three-pointer at the buzzer."

"Yeah," I nodded. "I didn't see that part."

"And why not?" my mom asked.

"I came late and left early."

"Then you didn't see what happened to those cars?" my mother asked.

"You mean in the lot?" I responded.

"No, parked on the roof," my father said sarcastically.

"I didn't see it, but I heard about it."

"What would possess kids to do something like that?" my mom asked.

"How do they know there were two kids?" I asked.

"Only kids would do something that stupid," my father said. "It's a shame, a lot of those poor people don't have coverage for that."

"Doesn't the insurance pay?"

"Some don't have comprehensive, just collision," he said. "I just don't know why anyone would do such a thing."

"They don't know right from wrong," my mom said.

"That's ridiculous," my father replied. "Jake knew right from wrong when he was five."

"It's not that they can't learn right and wrong," she said. "They've never been taught it."

"...Because no one believes in right and wrong anymore," my dad said and then turned to me. "I love you, and I'll do anything for you. But if you break the law."

"But Dad, I didn't..."

"You're the one who pays, not me. You're the one that goes to prison. They won't let me do that for you. I'll pray for you. I'll visit you, but you'll be the one behind bars. I get to go home." He walked out of the room.

◆

"Twenty-three car windows were destroyed Sunday night, and we know who did it," Sister Margaret Mary proclaimed to the whole school over the P.A. system. I froze at my impending doom. My life was over. I didn't know why I did it. I still don't.

"We're giving the perpetrators one chance to make it easy on yourself. If you come to us, the punishment will be much more lenient than if we come and get you."

"If they knew who did it," Quinton whispered to Jay, "they'd just come and get the jerks."

Later that day in the lunchroom, Mitch walked up behind me and whispered, "She don't know a damn thing. Take it to your grave."

Sister spent the rest of the school year investigating the crime, and throwing out idle threats, drawing lines in the sand. I was scared, but I didn't say a word to anyone, not even to Quinton or Jay. Nothing Sister could do to me would be worse than what Mitch would do if I turned us in. Out of nowhere, every so often, he would come up behind me and whisper, "To your grave."

A few weeks later at the end of sixth period, Sister Margaret Mary's sharp voice over the P.A. system cut in and silenced our class, "Mitchell Coakley, please report to the principal's office. Mitchell Coakley, please."

When I heard his name roll out of the brown speakers, my heart hesitated for a moment, and I tried to convince myself that he was always in trouble, always doing something wrong, and that announcement could be for anything. But then 20 minutes later, I heard, "Jake Pearson, please report to the principal's office. Jake Pearson, please."

She found out, I said to myself as I walked to the door. I should've confessed, or maybe Mitch cracked. My future was hanging on the honor of a criminal.

As I approached the office, Mitch was being escorted out by Sister Maureen. "He told," I thought. "I'm done. My dad's gonna kill me."

As he passed, he leaned toward me, and whispered, "To your grave," and continued down the hall and disappeared.

The sisters sat me down in a short chair and leaned over me. Sister Margaret Mary was the only one who spoke. Sister Maureen just sat there with a disgusted look on her face, listening to my every word, watching every one of my gestures, studying all of my facial expressions.

"You are what we call a usual suspect," Sister Margaret Mary said.

"Usual what?"

"From the first day you got here, I knew I had to always keep my eye you."

"I didn't do any..."

"We know what happened," she said. "Do the Christian thing and confess."

"Confess what?" I said in a trembling voice. "I didn't do anything."

"Don't play games with me," she said, her face reddened.

"I'm not playing games. I don't know what you're talking about."

"Make it easy on yourself, Jake. If you admit what you did, the punishment will be less severe. We may even let you graduate," she said.

They both looked down at me. "Well?" Sister said.

"I didn't do anything." I shrugged. "I'm not lying. I swear."

"Just remember, Jake, God's always watching. He knows what you did. What is forgiven on earth is forgiven in heaven, what is bound on earth will be bound in heaven."

My crime haunted me. The eyes of Sister, the leer of Mitch, the scrutinizing stare of unknown witnesses were everywhere. I could not escape my guilt. I wanted to confess, admit what I did, free myself, but I couldn't. I didn't fear the punishment as much as everyone knowing I was guilty. Eighth grade was almost over, I told myself. I would graduate soon, and move on to a new life, forgetting about this.

NW

Chapter 13

"You're a rare player," the tall man said as he reached out and grasped Dorian's hand. "We're from Bainbridge."

The Bainbridge School had never once entered my consciousness, not even as a remote consideration. Every student from St. Francis Elementary was destined to go to Cathedral High, the big Catholic high school fed by the five Catholic grade schools on the shore. That was our destiny the day we first stepped into Mrs. Gallagher's kindergarten class.

But that destiny changed the day two men in red golf shirts and white ball caps with a "B" stitched on the crown appeared at our games with notepads and stopwatches. I first thought they might be from the Red Sox.

The Bainbridge School was not meant for us. It was the rich school, for rich kids. Everything was given to them, and when it wasn't, they took it from someone else. And that's what they were doing with Dorian. They wanted him, so they came to take him from us, dangling an athletic scholarship in front of him.

Quinton, Jay and I were against it immediately. We voiced our disapproval, loudly. We dished out every type of "rich kid," "privileged life" stereotype, and topped it off with the inherent moral superiority of the working class.

I'm not sure if I was against him going because the rich school wanted him, or because the rich school didn't want me. Either way, this was a life-changing decision. The first significant one in my short life, and it wasn't even mine to make. A choice like this is rarely a singular decision but a trigger that sets off a series of unavoidable eventualities we must confront as we grow.

Growth then becomes a continual series of losses: loss of future, loss of possibilities, loss of dreams and imaginations, loss of innocence, loss of belief. The child loses all that is good for the sake of the adult, and we are left with experience and knowledge, and a bottomless pit where our beliefs used to live.

I didn't know who I was anymore because I didn't know what I believed in anymore. I looked out of my bedroom window that night, the rolling dunes and crawling waves of the moonlit beach appearing as meaningless as my life felt. The waves drew me in, hypnotically, arriving one after another, in and out, in and out, until the ebb became indistinguishable from the flow, and the waves appeared to roll backwards into dark nothingness.

I saw my life reflected in that black hole before me, my hopes, my dreams, my desires sucked away, draining into oblivion. It was an optical illusion, reality flipped upside down, but what was real? What was an illusion?

◆

We pressed Dorian hard, but two nights before his decision day, my mother called up to me. "Jake, phone."

I went into my parents' bedroom and lifted the receiver. "Hello," I said.

"Hello, Jake," a sharp voice answered. "My name is Forrester Alexander. I am the head of the Bainbridge alumni association. I have one question for you. How would you like to attend Bainbridge for the next four years?"

"I don't think I can," I said without hesitation.

"Why not?"

"My parents can't afford it."

"Maybe they can," he said. "I… we can offer you a half scholarship."

"What is that? How much is that?"

"It's a half scholly, but basically, your parents only pay what they can afford."

"I'm not sure."

"It's well worth it for the chance to attend one of the top prep schools in the northeast. What d'you say?"

"Well, thank you. Thank you very much," I replaced the receiver, and walked down the stairs in a daze.

"Mom, Dad, guess what? I just got a half-scholarship to Bainbridge."

"Congratulations!" My dad swatted my back. "This is going to be great!" Suddenly, my stomach began to churn, and a hollow feeling struck my heart. The more excited my dad was, the more scared I became.

"It's still a lot of money," I tried to temper their enthusiasm. "I don't want you sacrificing that much for me."

"Don't worry about that. We'll find the money," Dad said. "You don't realize how much this is going to change your life."

◆

We visited both schools the next day. Bainbridge didn't look like a typical high school. No yellow buses lined the front. No rusted chain link fences enclosed the perimeter. Shiny sports cars and over-sized SUVs filled the parking lot. Small trees and flowered bushes lined the campus grounds. The floors were vacuumed, not mopped.

"Isn't this great?" My father beamed at everything we saw. "Tremendous, outstanding, excellent," he repeated again and again.

Bainbridge was an easy choice. Cathedral was a high school. Bainbridge was a country club. But I was still hesitant.

"This looks like a college," my mom said, in a whisper.

"It's too much money," I told my parents.

"You don't pass this up," my father told me. "This one decision will change your life. You'll get everything you want. You go to Cathedral, you'll end up at a state college. You go to Bainbridge, you'll go to the Ivies." I never questioned what Bainbridge could do for me. I only worried what it might do to me.

◆

The day after we decided to go to Bainbridge, I heard, "Jake Pearson, please report to the principal's office. Jake Pearson please," rumble out of the PA system.

I sat in front of the Sisters again. Both of their voices were more confident, angrier. "I heard you decided to go to Bainbridge," Sister Maureen said.

"Uh-huh."

"Are you excited, looking forward to it?" There was an edgy tone to her voice.

"Yes."

"Bainbridge can do some great things for you in your life."

"I guess so."

"It would be a shame if you weren't able to go," Sister Margaret

Mary said.

"Probably," I nodded.

"So, I think it's best if you admit what you did, so your new school doesn't find out."

"Find out what?"

"What you did. What you're capable of. Who you are. That you would lie."

"I don't know what you're talking about."

She let her glasses slide down onto the tip of her nose and stared at me over her frames. "Michael Bailey told Sister Maureen here, that he saw you in the parking lot that night of the basketball game messing with some cars."

"Are you still talking about this?"

"I'm giving you a chance to save yourself." Her eyes screwed tight into mine. "Save your future." I looked right back at her without a word.

"Well. What do you have to say for yourself?"

"It wasn't me," I pleaded. "It must've been somebody else."

"So, you're here telling me that you weren't at the game?" She asked.

"I was at the game," I said.

"So, Mr. Bailey was telling the truth. He did see you there," she said.

"He probably saw about a hundred other people there, too."

"He said he saw you out in the lot, with some other boy."

"I don't know what he saw." My voice quaked. "I was there at the game. I was in the gym. You can ask Dawn. She saw me there. I swear."

"Well, Michael Bailey swears, too," she said. "And he doesn't have a crush on you."

"What are you talking about?" I stood up abruptly. I wanted to admit what I did. I wanted to get this all off my chest. I was tired of the hiding and lying, pretending I was someone I wasn't. I didn't care what the punishment was. I looked right at her. She smiled at me smugly like she knew what I was about to say. "I... I... didn't do anything," I said and walked out of the office.

◆

Chapter 13

After school, I was shooting baskets at the far corner of the playground near the church, when Mitch walked up to me. He didn't say a word. He grabbed the ball, and his short beady eyes riveted into mine. I stood there frozen. I didn't know what to say. He stepped toward me. I could feel heat and sweat emanating from his body. I shook my head. "To my grave," I whispered. He nodded, turned and bounced the ball into the bushes surrounding the statue of the Virgin Mary. I walked over there and noticed the bushes were smoking. A deep, hearty laugh floated out of the greenery like the gray smoke rising from smoldering shrubs.

I stepped around the bushes and through the haze. "Hey, Jake, you ever see this before?" Gregg Taggart held up a magazine that unfolded in three levels, and broke into a sinister laugh. She was lying atop pink, silken covers. Her body was curved in an "S" with her arms above her head. My heart paused, as my virgin eyes ran to and from places they had never been before, and had not even known existed.

"Look at him," he laughed, as I stared at the glossy page. "He's in shock. He's never seen poon before."

In school, we learned about a tribe of Indians who believed that a picture steals the soul. As I stood before them, I wondered what I had stolen for allowing my eyes to see that picture.

Gregg held out a smoldering butt to me. "Take a hit." I stood petrified as he placed the butt in between my fingers. I put the moist end to my lips and inhaled. My lungs filled with a warm tingling. My neck muscles became very weak, my head began to sway. Then my lungs exploded into a purging cough. I fell to my knees coughing and stared at the grass until my head stopped spinning. I crawled from behind the bushes and leaned against the basketball pole. My eyes were fixed straight ahead, my head floating above my body.

"Goddamn amateur." They laughed.

There is no good in the world, I concluded.

"Last Friday, I glommed a fifth from the old man, and went to Danielle's, her rents were gone." Taggart's hissing laugh sizzled.

"Got her all oiled up, and I just slid my hand down in there." Taggart said casually. "I kept exploring. She didn't stop me either. She just let me do it, like she liked it. I didn't know what I was touching, but it was awesome."

My flesh quivered. *There must be something more to life than that*, I thought, or maybe I just hoped there was. I concluded that all of the world's problems were somehow rooted in that conversation.

I pushed myself up and walked across the parking lot. For some reason, anger was boiling inside me.

I spotted him unlocking his bike. "What are you doing?" I said as I walked up to him.

He didn't respond.

"What are you doing, Bailey?" I said again.

"Nothing," he tried to slide his bike pass me.

I don't know what came over me. Michael Bailey wasn't a bad kid. But when I looked at him, and I saw his skinny arms, his concave chest, his hairless face on top of his long crane-like neck, I was disgusted. I stuck my leg out and caught the front tire of his bike. He straightened up and bowed his concave chest at me.

I smiled at him, "You like ratting me out?" I kicked him and his bike to the ground. "Making up lies about me?"

He scrambled to his feet. "I didn't say anything."

"Don't lie." I threw out a jab and my fist hit him square in his bony chest. It felt good. It felt powerful. It felt like I could keep hitting him and hitting him. "Sister told me what you said."

"I don't know what you're talking about."

I looked at him. "You're lying again." I threw another firm jab and struck him again. He glared at me with the hollow look of fear in his eyes. I struck him again with another jab, and his fear continued to grow.

"I didn't say anything to anybody." His voice was weak like him.

"Shut up." My fists hit his left rib cage, his left shoulder, and then his upper back. He kept cowering away and away until his back was turned completely to me, his frail, boney body was coiled into a fetal-like ball, whimpering.

I stopped, sickened by his frailty. "Are you gonna rat me out again?"

The next thing I saw was his fist raining down from the clouds, the moment before it struck my eye. I could see his crooked bony knuckles on impact. His skeletal fist spun me halfway around. When I looked up, through my blurring eyes, I saw him sprinting across the parking lot toward the front of the school. I ran after him with a salty, metallic liquid running down my face. I didn't know if it was blood or tears.

I sprinted and sprinted until I tackled him on the thick sidewalk. We skidded across the cement. He tried to get up, but I threw him against the sidewalk, and pinned him there with the weight of my body.

I punched with such a fury that I don't remember if I struck him a hundred times or ten. I pounded him and pounded him until I was out of breath. I stood up. His face was streaked with blood. He rolled over, covered his face and wailed.

"You're not gonna tell anyone about this," I said firmly. "Nobody. You understand?" The back of his head nodded. "Take this to your grave." I walked away, and just left him there, face down, crying and bloody.

I went straight to my room when I got home. I knew he would tell, so I sat on my bed, trying to piece together some story, some plausible argument that would justify what I did, but there was nothing, no reason, no rationalization, no elaborate fiction to mitigate my guilt. I don't even know why I did it, but I did. I knew it was wrong the moment my fist first struck his flesh, but I couldn't stop myself, so I was just left with the consequences, expulsion from school, no Bainbridge, public high school. I sat on my bed all night, and waited and waited, preparing for a call that never came.

Bailey missed school the rest of that week, but returned on Monday with a black eye, and a story of an Evel Knievel-like bike jump that failed, and suddenly, he didn't appear as weak and frail to the rest of the class. Our eyes made contact one time the rest of the school year. I didn't apologize. I didn't say a word. He just looked at me knowingly, and in that brief instant we both realized our silent lies were better than the spoken truth. He kept my secret, and I kept his.

Chapter 14

"You're living in a fool's paradise if you think you can breeze through and still graduate. Tomorrow's test counts 50 percent of your grade," Sister Margaret Mary said at the final bell on the last Thursday of the school year. "If you don't pass, you'll be back with me next year. Ask Mr. Coakley, he'll tell you." I knew she couldn't keep me back, but I also knew an "F" could cause Bainbridge to rescind its offer.

Most of the eighth grade had stopped doing schoolwork weeks ago. They spent their nights at the beach, enjoying the newfound wonders of the opposite sex. But from the moment I arrived home that night, my nose was pressed in the thick book. Numbers, fractions, equations scrolled through my mind like a computer screen on the fritz. *What if I don't remember how to find the least common denominator? What if I forget to invert the fraction before multiplying? What if I fail? I have to pass. I have to get into Bainbridge.* So, I stayed in my room all night with my nose pressed in an Algebra book under a hazy yellow light.

I could feel the thumping music, and hear their playful screams and shrieking laughter down on the beach. Out my window, I saw the distant shadows of kids filtering in and out of the cabanas at the club.

I scanned the pages of the textbook. I understood the concepts, but I didn't trust my brain to remember them. My breathing became louder. I flipped the pages. Compound Fractions. My heart beat quickened. *I don't know any of that.* Multiplication of Compound Fractions. Sweat beaded up on my forehead. No recognition. My mind had become a fog of numbers, letters, broken windshields and bloody faces, and the silhouette of girls in the moonlight. My panting breath got faster as my eyes skimmed the pages. I could identify the letters, the symbols, and the words, but the way those words and symbols fell in line next to each other felt like a foreign language. I don't know any of this. I slammed the book shut.

I slid a small piece of paper in front of me, and in the tiniest, the most delicate writing, I wrote "LCD," "Inv. Fract," "Foil," and a list of other reminders, equations, definitions, on that tiny piece of paper that fit neatly in the palm of my hand. I was prepared.

I didn't know how late it was. I walked down the stairs gently trying not to creak the old, wooden steps. Under the sole light in the far corner of the living room, my mother stared out the window at the changing lights of the empty street corner. The tint of her hair changed with each snap of the light. But her expression remained constant. Her pained face would only change when a car rumbled up the driveway.

What horrors could she be thinking of? Was there an accident? Would a police car roll up the driveway instead of our green Civic? Or, would no car come at all? I would never make her feel that pain, I promised myself. Nothing out there could be so important.

"What are you doing?" I flipped on the light.

"Waiting," she rubbed her eyes.

"Joanne?"

Her red eyes nodded.

"You shouldn't wait in the dark, Mom. It'll hurt your eyes."

"I really didn't notice it getting dark," she looked at her watch. "Why are you up so late?"

"Studying math."

"Oh," she smiled. "The last test of eighth grade. It must feel good. You must be so excited about Bainbridge next year."

I slumped on my right hip. "I'm not sure it's the right place for me. It may be too hard. I have a tough enough time at St. Francis."

Her eyes flickered. "You'll blossom. You're such a smart kid. You have so much potential. Why you waste it on that damn baseball, I'll never know." She glanced out the window not looking for the car, but for a new thought. "You'll learn so much."

"I don't know, I think I'd do better at Cathedral, it's a lot easier," I confessed.

"The eagle complained he could fly much faster if not for the wind in his face," she told me. "Until he realized if there was no wind, he couldn't fly at all."

◆

The next day, Sister Margaret Mary paced around the classroom passing out the tests slowly, enjoying our angst, holding the test above our desks like she was trying to decide who would be the lucky recipient. It was one of the few times we ever saw her smile.

She placed the test on my desk, and I read the first question. The solution lined itself up immediately. I knew exactly how to solve the problem, and the next one, and the next one, all of them. The answers came easy. I did not use the notes. I didn't need them. I did not benefit from them in anyway, except maybe knowing they were there, easily accessible, freed my brain to retrieve all the information inside.

I finished the test, and I had remembered everything. I did it all by myself. But as I handed her my test, her thick heavy hand grabbed my leg and pulled out the small piece of paper. She held my note in her hand loosely, within my reach, tempting me. "I knew I always had to keep an eye on you. I knew I'd catch you sooner or later."

She walked to her desk, and loudly slid her left bottom drawer open. The room silenced. Everyone knew that sound. Every eye was locked in on her. No one made a sound. She stared at me. Her mouth was a thin horizontal line, her jowls hung loosely. All I could see were the pulsating black pupils in her eyes.

"Assume the position." She pulled out a thick, white piece of wood that looked like a sawed-off canoe oar. I walked to the front of the classroom, bent over and placed my hands on the metal chalk rail. The wait for it to begin was as agonizing as the first strike. The heels of her black shoes ticked firmly against the linoleum as she paced back and forth, back and forth. I felt her sinister smile. I could hear the firm clap of the wooden paddle against her open palm. Her heels clicked louder. Her strides quickened. Then the clicking stopped, and so did my heart. The wood stung my upper thighs and buttocks as she drove the paddle through to the back of my pelvic bone. My forehead banged against the blackboard. The pain spread down my legs and up my back, and the reverberating crack rung in my ears.

She struck me again, and the pain shot down my legs like scalding water. She hit me again, and again, and again with ten clean whacks. She hit me with so much force I thought she was trying to drive me through the wall. My hands squeezed the metal rail until my palms hurt as I tried to keep my face from bouncing off the chalkboard. The stings mounted until my buttocks became so numb I did not feel the pain of the strikes. She paused before the last strike until I relaxed, and then she struck me so hard the paddle broke at the handle and her shoulder bounced off the chalkboard.

Her nostrils flared like a raging bull. A gray swatch of hair streaked with black fell out of her habit and hung delicately across her left eye. For a solitary moment, a hint of femininity flashed before the class. That distaff moment revealed that her students were not the only ones trapped by her hideous form. I did not cry. I refused to give her the satisfaction of one tear, but I could not turn around. I knew if I saw their faces, every drop would fall.

She tucked the hair under her habit. "We'll just keep this episode to ourselves," she said, then turned to the class. "Line up for church."

I clung to the chalk rail as if it were keeping me from falling until the stampede of eighth grade feet rumbled out the door. Only then did I find the strength to fall in the back of the line, and march down the hall and across the schoolyard to the church. Tears clung to my eyelashes, but none fell.

Both eighth grade classes made the long trek across the yard to the enormous stone church to receive the Sacrament of Reconciliation. The school wanted to purify us, liberate us of our sins, so they could send the graduates out into the world untainted. We walked through the wooden doors, and passed beneath a cardboard sign that read:

ONLY SINNERS WELCOME

The church was dark except for the dancing of devotional candles in the front. Scattered along the edges, the disembodied heads of white marble statues floated in the faint light above the pews. Their white faces were smooth and unblemished, like the faces of children. And the face of Jesus hanging on the cross expressed a peaceful anguish, a contented acceptance of his plight.

The statue of Mary in a flowing blue robe intrigued me. She was human, not much different from me, but we prayed to her as if she were a God. Mary was never just Mary, she was always "The Virgin Mary." The word "virgin," spoken with such reverence, became more her name than her actual name. She was the only person to whom the word "virgin" was a compliment, and maybe the reason why we prayed to her.

Our gods are from a time incomprehensible to us. They wore sandals and robes, and Jesus hung from a cross wearing a loincloth. We don't fight their battles or dream their dreams. How can we understand their philosophy, and fully embrace their faith? How can we consume the bread of life, if we have never spent a hungry day in our lives? What did all of this mean to me?

The building was so quiet I could almost hear the silent prayers of two decrepit ladies kneeling in the front pew. The overpowering silence was broken by whispers and snickers from the back pews, and by Sister's wooden heels striking the marble floors as she marched back to shush the girls and boys. I kneeled in the darkness, unable to sit on my throbbing muscles, waiting for my turn.

I stepped into the dark and cramped room, filled with the smell of sweating cedar. I pulled the door shut and fell to my knees onto the cracked leather of the kneeler, tripping a fuzzy light. The room was quiet except for a low murmur of sins seeping through the walls from the adjacent confessional. I stared straight into the blank window. The wooden door of the window slid open with an elongated hiss, and a speckled light shot through the lattice divider outlining the head of the priest.

He groaned to announce his presence. Father Rochester was old, senile. We would see him in the alley behind the church minutes after mass, smoking cigarettes and flicking the burnt ashes at squirrels.

"Forgive me Father for I have sinned," I performed the sign of the cross. "It's been one month since my last confession."

The round shadow bobbed. "What are your sins, my son?"

I thought for a second. "I lied to my mother," I guessed. "I became angry with my sister. I took the name of the Lord in vain... I... I... committed sins of omission." The usual innocuous sins rolled out of my mouth thoughtlessly. "I disrespected..."

"Blah, blah, blah, blah, blah..." The harsh monotonous sounds broke through the screen.

"Huh?" I was confused.

"Blah, blah, blah!" he said louder.

"Uh," I muttered. "I'm trying... What's... going on? I..." The words stumbled out. I didn't know how to talk to him. I wanted to throw the door open and run.

The screen in front of me opened. The foggy light poured in. There he was before me, hunched over, our noses inches apart with nothing in between. No door, no screen, nothing. I felt completely naked.

"Why don't you tell me your real sins?" he said.

"I am." I was afraid to look at him. "I am telling you my sins."

"No, you're not. You're giving me the canned sins. The same sins I get all the time, from people too afraid to tell me their real sins." His face was so close it didn't seem real. "These are the same sins you said last month. Tell me your true sins, or are you too scared?"

"I'm not scared of anything," I straightened up.

"Well, let's get to your real sins, then. Tell me what you did in the parking lot in March."

"The parking lot? How d'you know about that?"

"Know about what?" he asked.

"Nothing," I mumbled.

"Let's just say I have certain vices which allow me to observe the happenings on the school grounds."

"Why didn't you bust me, then? You could've saved Sister a lot of trouble."

"I was waiting to see if you would own up to it, at least to God."

"I tried to pretend it never happened," I said weakly. "I'm sorry."

"Do you think that's good enough, Jake?"

"What am I supposed to say?" I squirmed.

"Nothing. It's what you're supposed to do. It's easy to say you're sorry. It's hard to act sorry."

"How can you act sorry?" I asked.

"Make amends," he said. "Repay those you sinned against. Pay the price for your sins. Own your sins."

"OK," I nodded. "I'll try."

"Don't try. Do it!" he barked. "Tell me what happened this morning in class."

I hesitated.

"Tell me what you did last week in the yard," his eyes looked through me.

"What?" I stammered.

"Next to the bike racks."

I knew what I did, but admitting it, made it real and forced me to face my true nature. "I beat up Michael Bailey for no reason," I blurted out.

"Why?"

"I told you I did it for no reason," I explained.

"You know why. Tell me."

"I hated him," I confessed.

"Why would you hate him?"

"He was weak, and I hated him for that." The words flew out of my mouth without consideration.

"Why would you hate someone for being weak?" he asked.

"I have no idea," I was broken. "But I did."

I hadn't been sorry for all those things. But at that moment, I was. "I am sorry." I pleaded. "I don't want to be that way."

"I know you don't, and you don't have to be." The top of his head leaned toward me. "It's up to you."

"How?" I said.

"Jake," he paused a moment. "The reason I never turned you in was I wanted you to come to me. When you confess a sin, you admit to yourself that you are better than that, that you expect more from yourself. I see you for the man I know you can be. I don't want you trapped being the kid you are right now." He reached up and closed the screen. I kneeled there, shivering. I didn't speak.

"Jake, I absolve you from your sins," he fashioned the sign of the cross.

"What's my penance?" I asked meekly.

"In the prayer book on page 264, 'The Prayer of St. Frances.' Read it. Say it every night for a month without fail. Take the book with you, tear the page out if you have to. Say it slowly and listen to every word." He reached up to shut the wooden door.

I knelt in a pew next to a withered old man staring at a fresco image of Jesus' lifeless body being taken down from the cross, and in that dark church I saw myself for the first time, honestly. All my internal lies had been cut away. I saw who I truly was, and also who I really could be.

As the lines of students outside the confessionals dwindled, the low lights surrounding the apse rose up off the floor. The altar boys walked in from the wings on top of the glow and placed a Bible, a chalice, and the wine on the altar.

My classmates filed in and out of the wooden doors. "What did you get?" they asked each other. "What did he give you?"

"Four-two-one," which meant four Hail Marys, two Our Fathers and one Act of Contrition. "Two-three-two," "One-four-one," and so on, as if it were all a game.

What are these guys doing? I said to myself. *What are their sins?*

Father Rochester stepped to the podium at the beginning of mass, and read, "Do not love the world or the things in the world. If anyone loves the world, the love of the Father is not in him. For all that is in the world — the desires of the flesh, and the desires of the eyes, and pride in possessions — is not from the Father but is from the world. And the world is passing away along with its desires, but whoever does the will of God abides forever."

I sat in the church throughout mass that day, staring at the other kids in my class as they whispered and laughed, and I thought, *I'm just as good as these guys. Maybe better.*

At that moment I had my revelation. It wasn't a light from heaven or a voice from above, nor did it feel like I was struck by lightning. It was simply an understanding, a clarity, figuring out in my mind what everyone had been talking about all along. A slow, cool awareness seeped across my being. It all became clear. All the clutter in my mind suddenly lined itself up, like I was finally let in on the secret.

My whole life, I've been trying to keep up with all these kids who were better than me, smarter than me, faster than me, better looking, funnier, more popular. As I saw all the kids who have been beating me in everything, filing out of the confessional doors and kneeling down to pray. I realized they sinned, just like I did. They had things to confess and penance to do, no different than me. I concluded *I can be better than all these kids. I'm going to pray every morning and every night. If prayer takes away your sins, then the more I pray, the purer I'll become, and I could go back to when life was good, pure, like being born again, assuming a fresh unblemished sheen.*

I made up my mind in the darkness of the church that from that day forward, I was going to be better; not just than myself, but than everyone else. I was going to be the best person in the world.

NW

Chapter 15

GOOD LUCK – CLASS of '95 was stretched across the front of the gymnasium. Green and orange crepe paper draped from the ceilings, and the hard dance music pulsated across the building.

Tonight, I start a new life, I said to myself as I sat in the corner on a steel folding chair thinking about my life, all the things I wanted to go back and change, bad choices, missed opportunities. I thought of how much better my life will be. How much better a person I am going to be. What I wanted was simple. I just wanted to be happy, nothing more, and now I thought that finally being good, would bring me happiness.

Then, she was there. Hovering above me like an angel, holding her hand out to me. Dawn's face was radiant and her hair floated around her head impervious to gravity. Her white dress hung off her shoulders tenuously, like the crepe paper hanging from the rafters. The delicate material silhouetted her slight curves. I hesitated. She smiled at me softly. "C'mon."

I rose and met her tiny hand. She led me through a pack of laughing, shoving boys to the middle of the dance floor, turned, and faced me. I stood flat-footed, frozen and inept. She stepped toward me, and we fell into an awkward embrace.

I pulled her dainty body and soft dress against my polyester blazer, clutching her in my sweaty palms. We danced but didn't speak. Her deep eyes peered up at mine with a look that said she was exactly where she wanted to be. She rested her head against my shoulder, and her slight body pressed softly against my chest.

She felt so fragile. I was afraid I would break her ribs if I squeezed too tight. It was one of the few times I had noticed my own masculinity, my own strength.

For those brief moments, we lived together in a world separate from the noise and clatter of the outside. We danced our deliberate circular steps, and I felt as though suddenly, the world was spinning around us. The gym, the streamers, the other kids became a blur, and the music became a low din. I heard her breath and felt her quivering body. I could see her face, smell her strawberry hair, and keep beat to her pulsating heart. An ineffable feeling of tranquility spread over every cell of my body. I had never felt so content.

I didn't want to let her go. She was the only girl I knew who liked me. Maybe she had seen something in me no one else saw, the very best version of myself.

Our bodies finally parted after the third song, I stepped back, but held both her hands. We were too scared to utter a sound; afraid our words would demystify our moment. I clutched her hands, afraid to let go. Her eyes held the depth of infinite virtue. I didn't think I could live up to that look. I was not worthy of her eyes yet, so I let go of her.

I walked to the far side of the gym, sat against the wall, and watched her dissolve into the sea of girls. For those three songs, we were caught in a higher existence, separate from the rest of the world. When I came off the dance floor, I had to re-acclimate. Like a newborn child, my eyes had to learn how to focus and my ears had to decipher sounds again.

I walked outside and down the cement steps into the sweaty night. Next to the building, behind a green bush, a bright white blazer smothered a pastel flowered dress. The two wriggling bodies froze at my footsteps as I stopped and stared, and then they resumed writhing against each other vigorously. I ran back into the gym and searched for her in the crowd, but she had disappeared. Maybe that's all I'll ever get, a few brief moments of happiness. Maybe I don't deserve anymore. Or maybe it wasn't even real. Maybe I dreamed it all.

◆

When I got home, I sat on the end of my bed and thought about my life, my future. I pulled out a clean piece of paper, and in my neatest, straightest penmanship, I wrote with much care and precision, as if I was writing my own personal Declaration of Independence; my own Ten Commandments.

Today I begin a new life. Today I become the person I was meant to be. The person no one else is. I am going be good. I am going to be great at being good. The best.

+ I will reject sin. It's simple: Do what is right, and don't do what is wrong. Don't lie. Don't steal. Don't cheat. Give, don't take. Love, don't hate. Help each other.

+ I will purify my mind. I will stop watching TV, stop reading the newspapers. They are pollutants. No impure thoughts. I will stop thinking and saying bad things about others.

+ I will purify my body. Hard work purifies. The harder I work, the purer I'll become. I will work harder than everyone else. If I can't beat them, at least I will outwork them.

+ I will never indulge the pleasures of the flesh. Physical denial cleanses the body, frees the spirit, and sharpens the mind to see truth. No alcohol or drugs. They poison the body, pollute the mind and paralyze the soul.

+ I will never kiss a girl before marriage. What could be more pure than to marry the only girl I've kissed? And that pure kiss will be proof of my true love, and make me worthy of that love, and if I was worthy of it, then maybe I could find it.

+ I will reject material things. I must stop worshiping the false gods of money and things. Self-denial is the path to enlightenment.

+ I must separate myself from everyone else. If everyone else is a sinner, I must reject the life that everyone has chosen, and choose the life that everyone has rejected.

+ I will separate myself from myself, I must reject the person I was, so I can become the person I know I can be.

Today I become a new person, the best person.

I had finally found something I could be great at, and there was no competition. In a world that competed for everything, no one competed to be the best person. I didn't need to know algebra to make the right moral choices. I didn't need a quick bat to choose right over wrong. I decided to be different, and that singular decision would affect every decision I made for the rest of my adolescence.

Everything made sense now. This was it. I found my purpose for being. I had been searching for the one pure thing to justify not only my existence, but all existence, and I realized at that moment, the ever-elusive purity of life, that one totally pure and good thing could in fact be me.

I believed if I freed myself from sin, I would find the perfection that would give my life eternal significance, and I could live in my own private nirvana.

NW

~ Part II ~

Chapter 16
(Summer 1995, age 14)

Own your sins rattled in my mind as I rode my bike to Michael Bailey's house the day after graduation. *Make amends. Repay your sins.*

It was the first step on my long journey to fulfilling my revelation. I would have to make amends for my sins, so I could purge my soul of inequities and become worthy of my revelation. Revelations reveal more about the self than they do about some inscrutable truth of the world.

As I rode along the winding streets, I thought that maybe somehow, through all that had happened, we could be friends. He could see that I was a good person, and I could somehow help him.

He lived on a street that bordered Galilee and Sea Haven, in a white, two-story house with black shutters, and a red brick chimney hugging the south side.

I walked up his front steps and gently knocked on the screen door. A baby cried out of the darkness, a low voice rumbled, and the fuzzy white outline of a woman's face appeared behind the dark screen. She was small, with narrow hips, an angular build, no curves, no flowing feminine form. She had a full head of thick black hair that rolled down her shoulders, and on her slight hip, a diapered toddler clung.

"May I help you?" she asked with sweet formality.

"Is Michael here?" I sputtered.

"Mickey! Mickey!" she called out sharply. "You have a friend," she smiled at me with tempered excitement. Moments later, Michael Bailey appeared next to her.

"Oh," he turned his insipid eyes away.

"Would you like to come in, dear?" his mother offered, and then turned to Michael. "Ask your friend in, Mickey."

"Uh, no," he glowered at me impatiently.

"Mickey, that's not…"

"That's OK," I told her. "I just came by to tell him something."

She pulled the baby up on her hip and looked at me with guarded anticipation. "What do you want to tell him?"

We stared awkwardly at each other. "I just, I just came by to say, to say I'm sorry about what happened at school last week."

"What happened at school last week?" Michael asked impassively.

"You know," I nodded. "The thing that happened at the playground... next to the bike racks."

He shook his head. "Nothing happened at school," he quivered uneasily as his mother wrapped her arm around his shoulder. "Nothing happened in the yard. Nothing happened at the bike racks, and nothing happened on the sidewalk."

"Is there something you forgot to tell me, Mickey?" She looked down at her frail son.

"Nothing Mom," his black pupils rolled to my eyes.

"Well, I'll just leave you two to talk about whatever it is that didn't happen." She gave her son a firm kiss on the top of his head and walked into the dark house.

"What are you doing here?" he seethed.

"I want to apologize."

He shook his head. "No. You don't get to apologize. If I have to live with this, so do you."

"But, I'm just..."

"I don't want your apology. I don't want anything from you. Go away."

"I thought we could be friends," I offered weakly.

"Friends? I don't want to be your friend!" he snapped. "Leave!"

I took a step back, paused, and looked straight in his eyes.

He stared right back into mine. "Please," he said, painfully. "Please, leave."

I rode home, in and around the cars that rolled through Galilee, and I saw my reflection in those car windows. I thought of the 23 shattered windshields in the dead of winter and I decided to make a list of all the names of the people whose windshields I destroyed. Each car belonged to friends of my parents, or parents of my friends, or simply friends of friends. I managed to find 21 of the 23 names. I vowed to pay each person 200 dollars cash.

Early the next morning, I pushed myself out of bed, and stumbled across the street to the ocean. The day broke and I was there. The waves crawled in peacefully, quietly. The sun peered just above the horizon and rolled out its golden carpet across the shimmering blue satin, all the way from heaven down to my feet. It felt like the post-mordial ethereal road, lined with aimless souls searching for eternity. I believed

I could take three steps and touch God.

At the north end of the beach, a shadowy figure plodded through the sparkling sand with two metal bars on his back like a mule, dragging a wiry metal sieve through the sand, separating out the broken shells and bits of crab.

Dorian stopped and pointed to a similar instrument, leaning against the rocks. "Grab that one." He pivoted back down the beach. "We got about 20 more passes."

It took us two full hours to clean the beach that day. But the next morning, just as the red sun peered above the blackened water, we were back at it, marching up and down the continent's edge with those steel poles on our backs.

"There's just as much junk as yesterday," I complained. "It's like we were never here."

"We clean up our beach, then New York," he pointed to the ambiguous north, "dumps its garbage in its water and we have to do it all over again."

"That's not fair that we got to clean up their junk, too!"

"We clean what washes up on our beach," he told me.

"There'll be just as much junk tomorrow, and the next day, and the next day."

"Whatever we don't pick up stays or gets washed down to Asbury or Spring Lake. Someone's got to stop it."

We cleaned that beach every day the entire summer, and I made $2,980 dollars. I put $142 into twenty-one envelopes with the solitary word "sorry" written across the front, and placed one envelope in each of their mailboxes. A strange sense of empowerment grew inside with each envelope I delivered, not just from giving, but in knowing I could do without. It wasn't enough, but it was the best I could do.

◆◆

I went home that night, and packed every frivolous diversion in my room, my TV, stereo, and video game system into big cardboard boxes, leaving only my clothes, my books and my baseball gear. That's all I needed. When I looked over my barren room, I felt liberated.

I carried the boxes downstairs. "What's all that?" my mom asked.

"Just some stuff I'm giving to charity."

"What stuff?"

"Just some video games and things. I don't need anymore."

She looked at me with surprise and pride. "You're giving away your video games and TV?"

"Uh-huh," I nodded.

"That may be the best thing you've ever done, Jake. I'm proud of you." She gave me a hug.

"I don't want Christmas or birthday presents anymore, either," I told her.

"But we like giving you presents, making you happy. That makes us happy."

"Give my presents to some poor kids, to someone who needs it. That would make me happy."

"Jake, be careful, don't go overboard. It's great wanting to be good, but there's nothing immoral about receiving a present."

"Jesus was the greatest Christmas present, and my life is the best birthday present. Accepting man's gifts weakens God's gifts."

"I know your heart's in the right place," she told me. "But there's always a danger when you try to prove to the world how moral you are. Sometimes, you end proving how moral you aren't."

◆◆

I stopped at the church to see Father Rochester to tell him how I was making amends for my sins.

"The money's a nice gesture," he told me. "But if you really want to do some good? Don't just give your money, give yourself.

"I did. I gave up my whole summer making that money."

"If you want to make an impact on the world, make an impact in someone's life. Meet them, get to know them, let them benefit from having you as a friend."

"I tried and I got a door slammed in my face."

"You're gonna to give up that easily? There are people, all over, needing someone, anyone. They don't need your money."

◆◆

I took the bus to Sea Haven and walked into the county's social services department. It was in a crumbling pale brick building, next to an abandoned firehouse. I squeaked open the glass door clinging to a misshapen door frame, and stepped in. The inside was hotter than the outside. Two fans labored in the corners, recycling the dingy hot air.

"Hi." A dark-haired woman with steel framed glasses looked up at me. "How can we help you?"

I dropped the box on the counter. "I want to donate this."

She peered into the box. "Great! That's so nice," she lugged the box to the back. "Is there anything else?"

"Yeah, I was thinking of, you know, helping some way," I said.

"You want a job?" she asked. "You're a little young."

"No, I want to, like, volunteer for something."

"Oh." She grabbed a stack of pamphlets. "What types of things are you interested in?"

"I don't know, ma'am," I told her. "It doesn't really matter so much."

"First, my name is Ms. Hathaway," she held out her long, thin, unadorned hand.

I clumsily grabbed it. "I'm Jake. Jake Pearson."

"It's very nice to meet you, Jake Pearson. I appreciate you coming. But this is a serious place. Everyone here legitimately wants to help people," she removed her glasses and stared me straight in the eyes. "If you're here on a whim, you won't be helping."

"I really want to do good."

"OK," she pried a pamphlet out of the stack and handed it me. "Go here this Saturday. They always need someone. If you have any questions, feel free to give me a call. My number's right there." She circled a ten-digit number on the front.

◆◆

I turned the knob slowly, and the 10-foot oak door rumbled open, sliding effortlessly in a well-worn groove in the stone floor. I stepped inside as if into a distant past, or my far-off future. The building looked a hundred years old without a hint of modernity. The halls were narrow, the ceilings were high, many layers of paint blurring the original design of the wood molding, and the windows were fogged with a yellow film. It was as if the facility didn't want to alienate those it cared for by being newer, fresher, and displaying more hope than they possessed.

I followed two gray-haired ladies in their wilting flowered robes as they inched along the matted carpet and shuffled past slightly opened doors. I saw every stage of old age; two withered men playing cards, a woman dancing in a circle, catatonic eyes staring at a TV screen, a nurse spooning oatmeal into a toothless mouth like a mother feeding her baby. There were screams and moans and long refrains of gibberish emanating through the walls, and with each door I passed, I felt like I was nearing death, glimpsing the future, my destiny.

His room was second to the last at the end of the long corridor. I knocked gently, but there was no answer. So, I slowly pushed, and the unlatched door opened. The room was small and cramped, and smelled of eucalyptus and mothballs, like my grandmother's attic. There was a steel framed bed in the corner, and a 19-inch television bracketed from the ceiling. The rest of the room was warmed with well-worn remnants of his previous life; a Barcalounger, a corduroy loveseat, two mismatched chairs, and a scarred wooden rocker. Books and magazines were arranged in uneven piles throughout the room.

He was sitting in a faded green velvet chair in the corner.

"Hello," I said.

"Who's that sneaking around?" he called out without turning. "Who's there?"

"Uh," I mumbled.

"Speak up," he crackled.

"Me," I said.

"Who's me?" His back was still to me.

"Jake," I said, confidently.

"Gray who?"

"Not Gray…"

"Get the hell out of here," he yelled. "How long do I have to live before I can spend 20 minutes without someone barging in?"

He turned sharply as I stood frozen in the doorway. His white hair was thick along the sides, but thin on top. He had gray bushy eyebrows and untamed white hair sprouting out of each of his orifices. His pink skin was translucent, splotched with bright red webs and dark black spots.

"Who the hell sent you?"

"Miss Hathaway," I said.

"What are you doing here?" He eyed me suspiciously.

"They said I could help."

"Help me? I don't need help. I didn't ask…"

"Well, they said…"

"Who is this they you keep talking about?"

"I told you, Miss Hathaway."

"Miss Hathaway isn't a 'they,'" he said. "She's a 'her.'"

"Well, her, she sent me to help you."

He pressed his large, swollen hands firmly against the arms of his chair, and with a tortured groan, pushed himself to standing. "Let's say I do need some of this so-called help you keep speaking about. What makes you so sure that you are the right man for this very important job?"

"I don't know," I said. "I'll try my best."

"Trying ain't good enough boy," he flashed a decrepit smile. "What'd you do?"

"Do?" I asked.

"How bad did you screw up to get sentenced here? What'd you do wrong?"

"Nothing, I'm just here…"

"Nothing? That's worse. What kind of crazy kid would waste a summer day with some old fool who's gonna be dead in six months?"

"I just want to help you."

"Who do you think you are, that Tim Robbins guy, some sort of Maharishi? You come here once and solve everybody's problem. Is that you?"

"I'm gonna be here more than just once."

"No, you're not," he snarled. "You won't be back, never."

"I will, too."

"No one ever comes back."

I stood in his doorway, unnerved by his raw callousness.

"Get the hell out of here. Let an old man live in peace, will ya. Let him die in peace. I don't want some crazy kid visiting me."

◆◆

"I'm not going back," I told Miss Hathaway on the phone as

soon as I got home. "It's too hard. He doesn't even want me around, or anybody."

"Too hard?" she said incredulously. "That's not a reason not to go back. If it were easy, we'd have a million volunteers."

"I know, but he's mean."

"If he weren't mean, he wouldn't need a volunteer to visit him now, would he?"

"I know, but I don't know how to talk to him. He's yelling at me all the time. Everything I say, he throws it back in my face."

"Is that what you thought, that it would be nice and easy?" she asked. "Helping people is hard. If you don't want to go back, don't go back. No one's got a gun to your head."

Good, I thought to myself as I hung up the phone. *He's gonna be dead in six months anyway.* But then I thought about Father Rochester's words about my responsibilities to the world. *I gotta go back. Or, do I?*

NW

Chapter 17

"What's the point of life, if everything's given to you?" Quinton sized up Bainbridge the moment he stepped off the bus the first day. "Look at 'em. They think driving daddy's Benz makes 'em special."

The Bainbridge Boy stood at the front of the school, motionless, taking a step forward, carrying a stack of books under his left arm, and a ball wedged under his right, his vacant eyes watching the students walk through the thick glass doors, focusing on nothing, but seeing everything.

INTEGRITAS, FIDELITAS, ONUS are etched on the base of the statue; the cornerstone values of the school: Integrity, Loyalty, Responsibility.

◆◆

A tall, thick man with a sharp gray crew cut stepped to the podium that first day. "Simply by walking through those glass doors," Headmaster McGovern motioned toward the front of the school, "you have an advantage over the rest of the world. But advantages come with a price. Each of you," he pointed his right index finger vaguely in my direction, "must carry the burden of expectation, the expectation to be the best. Last year, we were, in fact, the best."

He rattled off a litany of championships, awards and distinctions from the past year. Quinton turned to me, "Yeah but they never played St. Benedict's or CVC, so all of this is a bunch of bullshit."

Mr. McGovern removed his glasses. "We don't expect you to achieve what you achieved last year; we expect you to achieve more. You are the best, and we accept nothing less than the best."

He looked out over the student body. "There's a young man starting his first day with us today, class of '99, who will help us do just that." He motioned at Dorian, and he rose nervously with his head down. The students gave him obligatory applause.

"This young man proves that we are only about one thing that transcends culture, creed, color, class, and that one thing is excellence." I basked in the glow of Dorian's excellence.

"But with excellence comes responsibility," he continued. "The responsibility to those who are not privileged to walk through those glass doors every day. Success is not an end unto itself, but a means to a greater end. You have a choice. You must choose whether to use your advantages to improve yourself or improve the world. Your vision must be greater than that of the self. Integritas, Fidelitas, Onus; these three words pounded into the cement walls of this building are the three pillars of this school, of those privileged to call this institution theirs."

My heart quickened. His words spoke to me. These words that I had never heard before, crystallized my revelation. It all became real.

I left the auditorium and walked through the halls to my first class. Success dripped from the walls of the school like blood. Awards and plaques were displayed every 10 feet, ingraining a culture of superiority and divine purpose into the students every day.

Mr. Addler walked into my Algebra class, first period. He was tall, boney-thin, pasty-white, whiter hair and a pale thin mustache outlining his pink upper lip. "We are going to have a test every Friday," he announced. "These tests will make up 33 percent of your grade."

He tapped the blackboard, covered with small white precise numbers and letters. "This is your homework, copy it down, and turn it in completed first thing tomorrow morning. Homework will be graded every day and will also count 33 percent of your grade."

I creaked open the textbook, and the smell of the crisp new pages leapt out at me like all of my fears and inadequacies. I slammed the book shut, I was afraid to look at the perplexing web of numbers, letters and symbols waiting to ensnare me.

"We will have a final exam, which will be cumulative. For those not yet enrolled in an SAT course, that means the test will cover the entire trimester. It will also make up 33 percent of your grade. For those of you not used to this type of accelerated curriculum, who think they can just show up and pass my class because you can throw a baseball, this is your wake-up call. Get used to it or get out. Any questions?"

Quinton's hand shot up. "What makes up the final one percent of our grade?"

"Not asking smart-ass questions." Mr. Addler answered.

My heart and mind were racing. "I can handle this," I tried to calm myself. "This is the one tough class everyone gets."

Mr. Kaufman handed us the syllabus to *Western Civilization I* as we walked through the door. A stack of books waited for us on our desks. My eyes ran up and down the list of books and page numbers. I quickly calculated we had at least a hundred pages of reading per night.

"You are to do the reading every night, without fail," he told us. "We will discuss it the following morning. For those who think they can B.S. their way through, you will be pleased to know that you are to write a one-page synopsis of the reading every day. It will count 30 percent of your grade."

◆◆

Bainbridge was a mistake. It was completely different than St. Francis. I met people with last names like Weinberg and Goldman; Nguyen and Suzuki. I was suddenly thrust into this place where people's beliefs, philosophies and lifestyles were different from mine, and I was forced to reaffirm my own views of the world every day.

We were the outsiders. I felt the eyes of everyone staring at me, judging me, thinking they were better than me. Each loud voice echoing down the halls told me I was not welcome. Each shrill of laughter did not include me.

I hated the school. I hated the people. I hated the blue carpet, the clean walls, the tall trees and the green grass. I came to Bainbridge to give myself a chance at a better life. It was a wish, not a guarantee. Only a fool exchanges his soul for the hope of a dream.

I sat in my bedroom that night staring at a pile of books on my desk under a solitary light in the corner. I had so much in front of me I didn't know where to begin. I picked up a small paperback on Ancient Greece. There were no pictures, and the words were smaller than the *New York Times* print. I shut the book and tossed it on my desk.

My father burst in. "Hey, how did it go?"

"OK," I muttered.

"I'm sure you did great." He bubbled with enthusiasm.

"Dad." My eyes slowly filled up. "I don't think I can do this." Tiny drops began to roll down my face. I tried not to look at him.

"You'll do great, just great," he said.

I shook my head. He walked over and grabbed a book off the stack. He opened it and scanned the pages. He ran his thumb along the edges, as the drops of water ran off my chin.

"I don't think I can do this," I repeated.

He snapped the book shut. "You're right. Maybe you can't do

this. Maybe you're not smart enough. Maybe you'll fail out. Maybe they are better than you." He leaned over my shoulder. "Maybe you aren't even good enough to play there."

I looked up at him, water running off my cheeks.

"There is only one way to find out, and it's not sitting here in the dark, crying. Open those books, start reading. It's not going to be easy."

I turned to him with drops of tears clinging to my eyelashes.

"You know what I think?" he continued. "I think you will rise to any occasion. You will meet any challenge... *if*... if you have any guts."

"It's hard." Tears rolled down my face.

"Of course, it is," he roared. "I thought you had more balls than that. If you want easy, go to the other place. One phone call and you're there. Easy. You'll spend the rest of your life working for someone else. You want hard, try spending your life doing other people's work. A pawn in their dreams. It's your choice. It's your life." He slammed the door and left me sitting there alone marinating in my self-pity, under the sparse light.

◆◆

"Look at these damn preppies." Quinton strolled through the halls fearlessly. "They'd be nothing without daddy's money."

"Hey, new kid." Carter Alexander yelled toward the lockers. Carter was a self-ascribed rebel, the stereotypical non-conformist, the echo of our generation. He always had a new gimmick; an earring, a non-trendy haircut, alternative music, a calculated rebel, predictably unpredictable, conventionally unconventional, always the opposite of the expected.

He sat in a wooden chair, surrounded by five others. "New kid," he called out. "New kid," he shouted louder and louder until Quinton finally turned his head.

"Is there a problem?" Quinton walked toward him.

"There's something wrong with your clothes."

"I'm wearing the same stuff you're wearing."

"That's it. You're wearing our clothes; you're trying to speak our language. But you'll never be one of us."

"I wouldn't want to be one of you limp dicks for all the money in your trust funds."

"Nice language. See what I mean?" Carter turned to the others. "You can take the boy out of the ghetto, but you can't take the ghetto out of the boy."

Quinton pressed up against Carter. "What did you just say?"

"You heard exactly what I said."

"You want ghetto, I'll give you ghetto."

Dorian stepped in. "Is there something wrong?"

"Yes," Carter said. "Here's a black guy who wants to be a white guy."

"Which white guy does he want to be? Him or him or him?" Dorian pointed at random white faces. "This guy, that guy. You?"

"Hey," Carter pointed to Dorian. "You're our savior," his voice laced with sarcasm. "You must think you're something special."

Dorian shook his head. "No. I'm just like everyone else around here."

"You'll never be like us. So, stop trying. You're acting like a dolt."

"I am the only one acting like an adult," Dorian replied.

"A dolt," he snapped back. "Not adult."

"Dolt?" Dorian asked. "What's a dolt?"

"If you don't know, you are one."

Dorian shook his head and walked away.

NW

Chapter 18

"Don't hold your breath, Seth," Quinton said to a short, thick senior with round black framed glasses as I walked up. "On second thought," Quinton backed away, "do hold your breath, please. Or try brushing your teeth once in a while."

"I don't get you, brother," the boy shook his head and walked away in disgust.

"What's going on?" I asked him.

"They keep asking me to join the B.U.S."

"Why not? What's the matter with the B.U.S.?" I asked.

"Black... Unity... Society," he spoke each word very demonstratively, drawing out their meaning, "is a contradiction in terms. Unity? How can we unite the school if we segregate ourselves? It should be called the Black Separate Society."

"Some white guys join."

"Who joins? You?" he asked. "Just some white dudes looking for college grub join."

"Ya know, I hate this black and white stuff. I wish we all could be just shades of gray," I told him.

"Then the light grays would hate the dark grays," he concluded. "And the dark grays would hate the light grays."

"Well, I wish there were no colors at all then."

"We'd still find some other reason to hate each other," he said. "And we wouldn't be able to appreciate a sunrise."

◆◆

"I was playing golf last weekend," Carter loudly told two other boys. "And there was this foursome in front of us. They were wearing those pants that come down to here," he cut his right hand just below his knee. "You know the pants that come here."

"Were they knickers?" one boy asked.

"No, they were white guys." The three burst into laughter.

Carter saw Quinton, "Sorry, I didn't think one of you was here."

"I'm gonna kill 'em." Quinton moved toward the three. "I'm gonna kill 'em."

"No," I stepped in front of him. "You'll get kicked out."

"I don't care." His fists were balled so tight I could see the whites of his knuckles. "I just want to pound 'em."

"So do I, but we can't."

"The circus is in town. The circus is in town." Carter shouted as Jay walked to his locker. "I bet when he opens the door, 50 more just like him climb out."

"Why don't you just leave us the fuck alone," Quinton shouted.

"Why don't you just leave us?" Carter answered.

"Make me." Quinton stared right into his eyes.

"I don't make trash, I burn it."

"Trash?" Quinton balled his fist.

"Don't listen to 'em Q," I grabbed his cocked arm. "Don't fall into their trap. We're better than they are."

"I ain't gonna take their shit," Quinton said. "I knew we shouldn't have come here."

"That's the only smart thing you said all day," Carter chimed in.

"They're miserable people," I shouted. "And they want to make everyone else miserable, too."

"Was anyone talking to you?" Carter walked up to me. "It's none of your damn business."

"It is my business, if I want it to be," I told him.

"Who the hell do you think you are?" He stood nose to nose with me. "You've been here for a day."

"You damn preppy," I pressed my chest into his.

"You're here for free," he sneered. "My dad pays for your tuition. So you should be more thankful."

I pushed his chest and he banged against the lockers. He lurched at me, but I grabbed his neck and cocked my fist. The blood boiled inside of me as I bit my bottom lip. I wanted to drive my fist through his skull.

"Delaney, Delaney!" the pack of boys shouted.

Coach Delaney grabbed my collar and slammed me into the lockers. "What is this, Jake? Did I bring you here to beat up the other students? Huh? Did I?"

"But he—" I tried to explain.

"But he nothing." Delaney shot back. "What does he have to do with what you were doing?"

"Coach Delaney," Carter spoke up. "I was minding my own business."

"Shut the hell up," Delaney snapped. "I don't know who started it, and I don't give a damn. Both of you, vacuum the entire school every day for the rest of the week."

"I didn't do—" Carter started to say.

"It's an amazing physical phenomenon, Jake," Delaney said, voice rising. "When you open your mouth, your ears close. When you close your mouth, your ears open."

He pulled me aside. "You better start doing something other than fighting around here. Start contributing. They don't give guys like you two chances."

I turned to Quinton. "This is why you gotta join the B.U.S."

"No," he replied. "This is precisely why I don't."

◆◆

I wandered through the maze of halls, confused, when I found myself in the athletic wing and saw the long rows of wooden plaques, with the names of every sports' captain and every MVP, dating back to the 1800s, lining the walls. My eyes scanned the precisely etched names. I wondered about those boys. *How were they different from me? How were they like me? Who they were, what they were like, how special they must have felt?*

In huge glass cases, there were championship trophies, fossilized balls, and woolen jerseys displayed. Each was a story of victory, accomplishment, immortality.

In the middle of the case, a certain ball intrigued me the most. It was brown from age and looked hard as a rock. But in faded writing barely discernible to the naked eye, it read:

BAINBRIDGE - 4
MERCER PREP - 3
MAY 13, 1916

My father wasn't even alive when that game was played, but its memory still lives in that protected case. I wondered if any of the boys who played in that game were still alive, and if they were, did they realize when they stepped on the field that day, that that game would live on forever.

I read the names and studied the artifacts, protected there for eternity. I imagined that someday I could achieve something worthy of living in those glass cases. This was my best way to beat them, to prove my superiority, as an athlete and as a person, to show I didn't need their money. I didn't need their lives.

NW

Chapter 19

"I told you I'd be back." I stepped into his room and was struck by the thick fog of eucalyptus. He sat in his Barcalounger with his head down, reading a thick book.

He looked up, his eyes blinking, trying to grab sight of me. "Who the hell are you?"

"Jake."

"Gray who?" he snarled.

"You know, I was here last Saturday."

His eyes studied my face. "Ah, you," he waggled his finger at me. "Didn't I make myself clear? I don't need any of your help."

"I just thought..."

"Why do you insist on wasting your time on an old fool whose gonna be dead and forgotten real soon."

"We all will," I said.

He nodded. "That's the first thing you've said that makes any sense."

I smiled.

"Don't be too proud of your damn self," he told to me. "If you're gonna be here, what the hell do you want to do?"

"I don't know. Talk?" I shrugged.

"Talk?" he pushed himself up and reached into his desk drawer. "Don't need to talk." He pulled out a black box and fell back into his seat. He turned the box over, and white rectangles splattered loudly across the table.

"Bones?"

"What are bones?" I asked.

"What kind of kid are you? When I was your age, we played bones all the time. This is all we did in the army."

"I don't know how to play," I admitted.

"Don't know how to play bones?" He shook his head. "And he's here to help me."

He slapped a white rectangle down with a reverberating crack and slid it to the middle of the table. "Six."

I stared back at him blankly.

"You got a six?" he demanded.

I lifted up a domino and carefully placed it next to the first one.

"It doesn't take a genius," he said.

His pink-knuckled fingers tenuously turned the white domino over and over in his hand, running all the possible moves through his brain. He raised up and firmly smacked it down, jarring the table.

The dominoes uncoiled in front of me like a white speckled snake. I placed one down on the table and slid it into position.

"You play like a goddamn woman!" he barked. "Smack 'em with confidence."

I picked up the domino and slapped it on the table, with a disappointing thud. He shook his head. "He's here to help me."

"How are we doing today?" A big round nurse walked into the room bubbling with feigned excitement. Her hips and chest shimmered with each step as the strained buttons of her uniform quivered.

"I'm 87 years old. How the fuck do you think I'm doing?"

"You know how we feel about that word," the nurse said, smiling.

"You don't fuckin' like it."

"If you can't control yourself..."

He looked right at her. "Fuck, fuck, fuck, fuck, fuck, fuck, fuck."

"Don't say that," I said. "Especially to a woman."

"Well, if I can't do that to a woman no more, I should at least be allowed to say it to one."

She smiled and shook her head. "Don't be so sure. You may have a little life still in you. You may surprise yourself."

He looked at her. "If you get rid of the kid, we can test your theory." He arched his eyebrows at her.

"Myrtle O'Connor, 15A, would be thrilled to take you up on your offer."

"Ah, she's too old for me. I don't want a withered prune, Gray. I want a plump juicy melon."

"You really know how to romance a lady." She lifted a tiny cup to his face

He brushed it aside with the back of his hand. "What's that?"

"You know very well what that is."

"I ain't taking it. I don't even know what it's for. They're trying to poison me, Gray."

"It's for your heart," she lifted the small cup up to him again. "We don't want to have another episode."

He shook his head.

"This is going in one hole or the other." He tilted his head back, and she poured the pills into his tightly opened mouth.

He chased them with a cup of water as she walked out of the room.

"I'll give her a fuckin' episode," he seethed.

◆◆

"This place is bullshit, Jake, bull... shit," Quinton fumed as we walked toward chapel the following Monday. "I got detention."

"What for?"

"Cutting class."

"You can't... "

"It's a set-up, man. They're trying to get the brother kicked out of here."

"You're paranoid."

"Am I? Get this. On Friday, I told Kaufman I had to take a piss, so he tells me to go to all the way to the science wing."

"The science wing, from history?"

"Yeah, man. It's a 10-minute walk, each way. And then he busts me for being out of class."

"Why'd he send you all the way to the science wing?" I asked as we sat down in the auditorium.

"They don't want a brother pissing next to their white boys in their fancy bathroom. I gotta use the bathroom that's not been cleaned all year. It's segregation, man. Separate but unequal. Bull... shit. Like they did down South. My piss is as yellow as yours, Jake."

"Actually, I drink eight glasses of water a day, so my piss is a lot clearer than yours."

"This ain't funny, Jake," Quinton said.

"Don't blame me. I didn't do anything. I don't like using the school's bathrooms anyhow. This doesn't make any sense. He sent you all the way there from the History Wing?"

"Yeah, he told me straight up, go to the laboratory."

"The laboratory? I don't get it?"

"You don't believe me?"

"Hey, I'm on your side."

Derek Cox leaned back, and said, "It's a lavatory, you idiots, not laboratory."

"What the hell's a lavatory?" Quinton looked back at him.

"Another name for a bathroom," Derek said. "He just told you to go to the bathroom."

◆◆

"To whom much is given," a tall, thin boy stood in the middle of the stage, "much is required. We were all born on third base."

"Third base? I wasn't even born in the dugout," Quinton whispered.

We have been given lives that the rest of the world can only dream of. Occasionally, we're asked to give back." He placed a large wicker basket at the foot of the stage. "That time is now. Give up that ski weekend or dinner at The Green. Dig deep, give to a worthy cause. You're not required, but those who can, should. Follow your conscience." The boys around us rose and filed into the aisles. "Our goal is to raise $10,000 for Heritage House this year. I believe in our school. Saving the children is the first step to saving the world."

Quinton turned to me. "Aren't the people who are screwing up the world former children?"

The parade of boys shuffled, zombie-like, to the stage, dropping wads of cash or thin checks into the basket.

Mr. McGovern grabbed the microphone, "No school in this state will raise more money than we will. We will be the most generous school in New Jersey."

Quinton and I sat there amid rows of empty seats with empty hands and pockets, and we could feel contemptuous eyes cutting into us, looking down upon those who never knew the pleasure of painless giving.

"It's bullshit that we have to pay more," Carter complained as we walked out of chapel, "and these scholarship kids get a free pass."

There was nothing I could say, so I accepted their contempt with silent indifference. They didn't know me. Their moral superiority wasn't earned. It was bought and paid for like everything else, but I resolved to never let them outdo me, especially in good works. So, I volunteered for everything: the turkey drive, toys for tots, meals on wheels, helping hands. And I went back to see Mr. Sullivan every Saturday like I had something to prove. He was the same each week: suspicious, cantankerous, angry, going on and on about letting him die in peace, and then we played bones.

"What are you doing for Thanksgiving?" I asked.

"What's it to you?" he growled.

"I was just wondering, since you don't have any family."

"Who said I didn't have any family?"

"I figured nobody comes…"

"You figured wrong."

"Why don't they visit?" I asked. "Are they…" I stopped.

"Assholes. You can say it, they're all assholes."

"I wasn't going to say…"

"When my kids were born, I thought they were gonna be special. You know, president or cure cancer or something great. I never thought my kids would become assholes. I was wrong. Mine are assholes, certified, which means I must be an asshole. Apple trees make apples, right?"

"You're not an asshole."

"Thanks, that means a lot coming from some weird-ass kid."

"What do your kids do?"

"Retired. I'm so damn old, my kids are old enough for the old folks' home."

"You should call 'em."

"Haven't spoken to any of 'em in 20 years."

"Twenty years? Why? What happened?"

"Nothing," he shrugged. "We just stopped calling. They forgot about me."

"You should call 'em before it's too late."

"Too late for what?"

"You know."

"I don't mind dying alone. Been alone my whole life. It only makes sense."

"You're not alone," I tried to reassure him. "I'm…"

"We all are alone. We just don't think we are because there are always people around. Babe Ruth, Elvis, Rockefeller, all died alone. Even the President of the United States is alone. Why should I be any different?"

"You shouldn't be alone on Thanksgiving."

"I was alone last Thursday and no one gave a crap. Why does it matter if I'm alone this Thursday?"

◆◆

The following Monday, I was paired with Clay Anders, a short, thick, physically mature senior. He was built like a man with broad shoulders and riveting muscles. He shaved every day, had a five o'clock shadow by three. "I drive," he stated in a hard-resonating voice. "I stay with the car. Freshmen lug the birds to the houses. I've done my time as a pack mule."

We drove in what he called his secondhand car because he didn't trust his Benz in the 'hood.

He turned the car onto a street with several boarded-up houses and vacant buildings, weaving around potholes and abandoned cars, driving like he knew exactly where he was going. He stopped next to a sagging, broken house, and turned to me. "I wonder what their HOA dues are?"

I stepped out and felt the warmth of white wisps of smoke rising above a rusted trash can. I carried a 10-pound turkey and a cardboard box filled with rattling cans of vegetables and boxes of dehydrated fixings up a flight of stairs and knocked at the first house. The screen door rattled loudly against the rotted frame.

"Hello," my voice quaked into the empty blackness.

"Just leave it on the porch and go," a voice shrilled from the depths of the bare house.

"I need to make sure..."

"Leave it and go!" the voice screamed louder as it closed in on me.

I slowly creaked open the door and peered into the living room. "Leave it on the steps!" The house shook as a thick, broad-shouldered black woman burst out of the darkness wearing a flimsy white night gown, stomping right at me.

"Put it down," Clay shouted from the sidewalk. "Get the hell out of there!"

I dropped the box on the porch, and sprinted down the stairs, a step ahead of the crashing door and pounding feet. I looked back and she stood on the porch flailing and screaming.

"Self-preservation, man," Clay told me as we jumped into his car out of breath. "If they say leave it, leave it. You don't have to shake their hands or talk to them, nothing. Avoid them as much as possible."

"I just want to make sure the people who deserve it, get it."

"Deserve?" He recoiled at the concept. "What the hell are you talking about?" His sarcastic voice was laced with anger.

"This stuff should go to those who deserve it, right? Ya' know, the less fortunate."

"Less fortunate? If you're poor in this country, it's your own damn fault. This is the richest country the world's ever known. Most people who were ever born lived in abject poverty and died an agonizing death. These deadbeats are doing better than 99 percent of human beings who ever walked." He looked at me, as the tires squealed. "They're doing damn good just being in America."

"Apparently not, or we wouldn't be bringing 'em food."

"All we're doing is feeding their laziness."

The next few houses I simply placed the turkey and the box on the front step and walked away. I didn't knock. I didn't speak. Finally, as I was placing the food on a front step, a woman said, "It's all right, you can bring it in." Her voice was not intimidating, so I pushed the door open and slowly entered. I stumbled on the shag carpet, almost spilling the box of food. I placed it on the kitchen table and put the turkey in the sink. The woman was tall and thick, with a high-pitched voice. Her meaty hands rummaged through the box inspecting the labels. "What happened to the Ocean Spray Cranberry?" She read the ingredients on the back of the can. "Too much sugar here. And what's this 'no name' stuffin'? We want Stove Top."

"I don't know," I said in a muffled voice.

"Yeah, you don't know nothin', just work here, right?" She picked up a can of green beans. "Must be cuttin' back. Too much preservatives." She tossed it into the box disgustedly. "Like they're trying to kill us. Maybe that's what they want."

"I think they're doing the best they can," I said.

"The best they can. If we was white folks, we'd have Stove Top, believe you me."

I shrugged. She cut sharp glances at me, inviting me to leave, but I couldn't escape the awkward silence.

I looked into the far room in the back corner of the house, and I saw it, a leather sleeve with leather laces interwoven in and out of the metal eyelets, and sprouting out of the top was a shiny, silver hook, lying next to a heavily worn baseball glove.

"Does Stephone..." I began to say.

"Jake, what are you doing?" Clay poked his head through the screen. "C'mon, we gotta go."

We trotted down the front steps. "Bitching about Stove Top," he sneered. "I want to tell that fat bitch that beggars ain't fuckin' choosers. It's always the same."

He punched the pedal and we shot away from the house. "Ch-ching," Clay said. "One step closer to Yale. Colleges eat this shit up. They eat it up faster than those mamelukes eat up that turkey and stuffing we just gave them."

"Don't you have any compassion for them?"

"Compassion? What you call compassion, I call capitulation."

"Capitulation? What's capitulation?" I snapped, knowing that somehow, he had just insulted me.

His head rolled slowly toward me. "How did you get into this school?"

I went home that night never expecting to feel bad about doing something good, but nothing about that day felt right. It felt all dirty.

NW

Chapter 20

"This book will change your life." Mr. Kaufman waved a blue paperback in front of the class on the first day of spring trimester. "It will change the way you look at the world. The way you view other people, the way you treat people different from you." He handed me *Night* by Elie Wiesel.

That night, I opened the small, unimpressive looking book, and read it in one mesmerizing sitting.

> *"We believed in God, trusted in man, and lived with the illusion that every one of us has been entrusted with a sacred spark...I did not deny God's existence, but I doubted his absolute justice...In this place, there is no such thing as father, brother, friend. Each of us lives and dies alone."*

With each word I read, my firmly held beliefs were challenged, and once again I began to question God, my revelation, my striving for perfection. What was the purpose of all this? What was the meaning of existence, not just mine, but all of existence? Are we all destined to recede into history, forgotten?

"I know the Holocaust was bad and all, but it happened so long ago. Why do we keep harping on it?" Quinton asked the next day.

"Those who fail to study history," Rob Silver said, "are bound to repeat it."

"Those who fail to study *accurate* history," Mr. Kaufman clarified, "are bound to repeat the mistakes of the past."

"There's never going to be another Holocaust," I predicted.

"Let's not be so sure, Jake," Kaufman warned. "There are some bad things going on in the world, even today."

"Like what?" I asked.

"The Middle East," Rob jumped in.

"Yeah, but that's been going on for thousands of years," I said.

"Yeah, and it all goes back to the Christians' persecution of the Jews," Rob explained. "The Christians burned down the temple, they slaughtered us during the Inquisition, and the Holocaust. We've been persecuted for two thousand years. We needed our own homeland. And now that's why the Muslims hate us. It's all because of you Christians."

"I didn't persecute anyone. Don't blame me."

"No one's blaming anyone," Mr. Kaufman told me.

"Silver is."

"Inaction can be just as bad as action."

"There's nothing I could do to stop the Holocaust now."

"Yes, but what would you have done? Would you've acted like Chamberlain?"

"Wilt?" Quinton asked.

"Neville," Mr. Kaufman looked right at me. "If you knew in 1938 what you know today, would you assassinate Adolf Hitler?"

"I would put a cap in his Kraut ass," Quinton blurted out.

"What about you Jake?" Mr. Kaufman turned to me. "Would you kill Hitler?"

"No," I shook my head.

"So you're OK with six million Jews getting incinerated, Neville?" Silver asked.

"No. But killing the leader of a country is wrong."

"That monster murdered half my family. You have to do whatever you can to stop him," he said.

"Are you OK with someone shooting our president?" I responded.

"Who's the president?" Quinton asked.

"Hitler doesn't fall under the same rules as everyone else," Silver argued.

"I don't know," I said. "If you kill Hitler before he did anything bad, isn't that what he did to the Jews? Wouldn't you just be proving Hitler right?"

"So, you agree with Hitler?" Rob challenged me.

"I didn't say that," I protested.

"We know," Mr. Kaufman broke in. "But you have to be careful what you do say. Words are powerful. And the more careless you are with your words, the more dangerous what you say becomes."

"I hate this," I said. "It's all just a bunch of semantics."

"C'mon, Jake," Quinton said. "Don't be anti-semantic."

"This ain't a joke, Q," Silver chided him.

"Do you really think if you lived back then you would've done things differently, like you'd have been the one person who went against the crowd?" I asked. "You can't go back in time, and you can't know the future, so all this is a bunch of B.S."

"You may think studying the Holocaust is bullshit, but the rest of the world doesn't," Silver said.

◆◆

That afternoon, I walked in to the soothing menthol smell of Vicks VapoRub.

"You get into a fight?" Mr. Sullivan pointed to a purple circle above my left elbow.

"I got beaned last week."

"Beaned? You're a ball player?"

"Yeah, I play."

"Who's your favorite player?" he asked.

"McGwire, Sosa," I said. "I like Piazza."

"You like the long ball?"

"Yeah."

"No one hit 'em like the Babe."

"Ever see him play?"

"My uncle took me when I was your age," he stated proudly. "He had box seats, third base line, Yankee Stadium. When I walked out of the tunnel and saw the green grass, the blue walls, the white arches of the facade, it was like walking into heaven." He smiled for the first time.

"Did you see the Babe crank one?" I asked.

He shook his head no. "He struck out the first three times up, not even close. Then, the ninth inning, he takes this big whack, and it was the loudest crack I'd ever heard, like a gun shot. The ball goes straight up, higher than the stadium. So high I couldn't see it anymore, and then it dropped out of nowhere, and landed right behind first base, so damn high, they couldn't catch it. When I looked up, he's standing on second base, with that big fat grin on his face. Amazing."

He dumped the bones on the table, and they bounced around, clattering to a stop.

The big round nurse peered her head in. "The father's here if you want to take communion."

"Get the hell out of here with that crap!" he screamed. "Don't ever ask again."

"Don't you believe in God?" I slid a double six into place.

"I've lived 87 years and the one thing I know for sure is... there is no God," he stated unequivocally. "I've never seen the slightest clue that God exists in any form."

"Wait, you've lived 87 years and that's the only thing you know for sure? It's like you don't want to believe in God."

"What does wanting to believe have to do with anything? I used to believe, but what's the point? I still got old. I'm still gonna die."

"But that's just it. God gives you a chance at an afterlife."

"It's a comforting thought, Gray," he smiled. "But that don't mean it's true."

"Doesn't mean it's not true."

"Listen to me. You're gonna die, too, and all this wanting to believe in God means nothing when you're under the ground. And all this time you've spent here with me means nothing. It's not gonna get you to heaven. Your body doesn't go on living, neither does your soul, neither does your memory. You get one chance to live for a short time, make the most of it while you still have it, 'cause when it's over, it's over. You're forgotten."

"So, no one goes to heaven?"

"I don't believe in hell so I can't believe in heaven," he said. "If I believe in God then I must believe in heaven, and then in hell. And if I believe in heaven and hell, then I know I ain't going to heaven, so I'd rather die and disappear into nothing than spend eternity in hell."

"Why are you so sure you're going to hell?"

"Because you're here," he grinned. "There ain't another S.O.B. in this world that wants to spend a second with me; no friends, no relatives, no kids, no grandkids, only some pansy ass kid. Why would God want to spend a second in heaven with me?"

◆◆

Heaven and hell, God and death were fixed in the front of my mind the rest of the day. I couldn't fit them in their tidy little compartments any longer.

"Read the batter's swing," my father yelled at Andy Pettitte that night. "He's late on the fastball. Throw it again. Force him to speed up his bat, start his swing earlier, then come with the change." He looked over at me on the couch, and I nodded agreement.

"You can't throw a curve on that count," he screamed at the TV as the white dot bounded down the first base line. "You even know better than that, Jake." He turned to me as Nomar Garciaparra slid into third base.

"Throw him the high heat out of the zone. Change his eye level, Jake, then bring the splitter down. That's called setting up the hitter."

"Shouldn't they play in?" I asked.

"Never seen it work. Play halfway, charge any hard-hit ball. You get your glove on more balls. Prevent the big inning for chrissake."

"I can't remember all this!" I confessed. "I'll never be as good as them."

"Being as good isn't good enough. You have to be twice as good as the next guy."

BANG! BANG! BANG!

"Jesus Christ, what's going on?" my father screamed, and my mother rushed to the front door.

Uncle Roth strolled through our front door, wearing a Panama hat and carrying a pizza box. He walked up to my mother and kissed her on the mouth. She stepped back, on the verge of a blush.

"How you been, Marie?" His pupils danced at the sight of her.

"Oh, fine," she brushed her hair away from her face.

"You're as beautiful as ever," he said.

"You always say that."

"You always are," he smiled.

He then held his right hand in front of my nose, like a king, and I inspected his truncated right hand.

"What the hell? What's going on?" my dad finally walked over to him. "Where's Sarah?"

"Ahh," he hemmed, "she couldn't make it."

"How'd you get here?" my mom asked.

"Drove."

"All the way from Orlando?"

"Eh, it wasn't bad," he said, looking out the window. "Twenty hours, made it in one shot."

We sat down at the dining room table. My dad turned his rocking chair halfway toward us, so his right eye could watch the Yankees, and his left ear could hear the conversation.

"I see he's as sociable as ever," Roth winked at me.

"Have you seen this Jeter kid play, yet?" my father shouted.

"Yeah, this spring in Tampa. He's excellent."

"He plays like you," my father said. "Great instincts. Great feel. Great hands."

Roth rolled his eyes and peeled a slice of pizza out of the box.

"Why were you the one who picked up the grenade if there were five other guys on the chopper," I asked him.

"I don't know. Instinct? I just grabbed it without thinking. Ya know, I wasn't the only one hurt. Sully and Smitty got it a pretty bad."

"Do you ever get mad that you never got your chance to play in the majors?"

"No guarantee I would've made it," he said calmly. "It's funny, I run it through my head over and over again, like when you make an error to lose a big game. Actually, I moved to it pretty good, fielded it cleanly, good transition, I just wasn't quick enough." He smiled to himself, then his eyes stared right through me.

"My dad said you were better than him, and he played in triple-A," I told him.

"Oh no," Roth shook his head. "Your dad was excellent."

"But you missed your chance. Doesn't that kill you?"

"If I were good enough to play in the majors, then I would've been quick enough to get that thing out of the chopper. At least, that's what I tell myself," he said.

"Not every play is makeable."

"But, if that grenade didn't blow up in my hand, I probably would've been killed over there, anyway."

"I would've been so scared," my mother said. "I would've been praying all the time."

"I didn't need to pray, Marie. My gun was my prayer. And I didn't need to be scared. I thought I wasn't ever coming home. I was gonna die there."

"Did you kill anyone?" I asked.

"Roth, you don't need to…"

He looked down and ran his good hand over his face. "Nine," he admitted. "I killed nine V.C."

"You did?" I was intrigued.

He nodded. "Nine human beings. Nothing to be proud of, Jake. Most of 'em were kids, my age, probably a lot like me with hopes and dreams, except they were born on the other side of some politician's line, and we had better guns. When my nightmares come, I don't see this," he ran his gnarled hand slowly along the side of his scarred face. "And I don't see Sully or Smitty. I see the faces of those boys I killed, every single one of 'em. Their cold, lifeless eyes'll never see their families again. This," he wiggled his stubbed fingers, "is good. The finger that pulled the trigger doesn't exist anymore. This was God's way of stopping me from killing."

"Jake's starting catcher for his high school," my father called into the dining room.

"Congrat—"

"JV," I clarified. "JV."

"Nothing wrong with that. Michael Jordan got cut from his high school team. You never know."

"Yeah, but I don't have a 42-inch vertical."

◆◆

While I played on the junior varsity that spring, Dorian became the first freshman in school history to start every varsity game. My dad did not see my mediocrity as a roadblock to his dreams, but as an opportunity, a reason to continue our batting practice sessions, as his hopeful determination for my baseball greatness morphed into a zealous obsession.

"Quicker, quicker!" He screamed from 45 feet away, after each full-speed pitch. "Quick hands, quick bat," he repeated, as he inched closer and closer toward home plate. "No one can beat you. No one can throw it by you."

"Quick hands, quick hands," I told myself as I stepped to the plate with runners on second and third with two outs trailing by one in the last inning against Mercer Prep's JV. I pictured a line shot in the alley or a double down the line. I felt it in my hands, and in my bat.

The first pitch sailed down the middle of the plate and I snapped my wrist through the ball trying to drive it down the third base line. But the moment before contact, the ball cut in on my fists, struck the handle of my bat, and shot up fluttering toward right field. I sprinted down the first base line, trailing the flight of the looping ball. The second baseman dove fully outstretched at the dying quail, his body parallel to the ground. The ball stuck in the webbing of his extended mitt, but fell out when his left shoulder bounced off the right field grass. I touched first base and turned in time to see Jay sprint across home with the winning run.

The entire team swarmed Jay, as I stood there watching without the urge to sprint to my teammates and celebrate. The Mercer centerfielder trotted by and scoffed, "Cheap ass hit."

I looked up, but I was too embarrassed to respond. He was right. It was a cheap hit. It was luck. I grabbed my bag and walked toward the school.

"Atta baby! Atta baby!" Roth's head popped out of my dad's car. "Mr. Clutch. Way to go, baby."

"Cheap hit," I confessed, almost embarrassed as I climbed in.

"No way," Roth screamed. "You took that inside pitch and slapped it to right, just like Rod Carew, baby."

"You did what you had to do," my father added. "Never ever apologize for a hit. They're too hard to get."

My father and Uncle Roth rode in the front seat while my mother and I sat in the back. "Roth, you have to get Sarah to fly up," my mom suggested. "I haven't seen her in years. It would be like old times. She's so much fun."

"I don't know, Marie." He looked out the car window.

"Call her," she begged. "I'll talk to her. I'll get her to come."

"She'll never come here."

"Why not?" her voice spiked.

"We're separated," Roth answered.

"Oh, dear!" my mom shrieked. "You two were perfect together."

"Separated? What the hell are you doing here, Roth?" my father demanded. "You need to get in your car, drive back home and make your marriage work. I'll drive you there myself."

"We're not getting back together," he stated.

"Therapy," my mom suggested.

"She left me," he blurted. "She's seeing someone else. There's no going back."

The car was silent.

"I don't believe she's seeing somebody," my mother said weakly.

"It's true. You know how I knew Sarah was seeing someone else?" he asked. "There were no anonymous phone calls, no unexplained absences. I didn't catch 'em doing anything."

"How'd you know?" my mom asked timidly.

"Her eyes. Joy had returned to her eyes. The same look she had in her eyes when we first got married, but it wasn't for me." He peered out the window. "I was driving home from work one night when it hit me, like someone came up and whispered it in my ear. Everything became clear. I drove around for two hours, trying to convince myself it wasn't true, but the harder I tried to prove I was wrong, the more I convinced myself I was right. When I got home, I didn't say a word. I just looked at her and she confessed everything. The funny thing, though, no matter how much it hurt? Knowing she felt that way again made me feel good. It became too hard seeing her unhappy day in and day out. So, the best thing that I could do was to let her go."

"Bullshit." The car screeched to a stop. "The best thing to do is fight for her. She's your wife, goddamnit, and you're just giving up? Get your ass on the next plane to Florida. I'll pay for it. You're gonna let some jackass steal your wife?"

"I would've just made her unhappy if she'd stayed. And she would've stayed, if I'd asked."

"Make her happy," my father screamed. "That's your responsibility. That's your job as a husband. Don't ever give up."

"I didn't give up, Jack. I gave her her happiness."

◆◆

Uncle Roth didn't go home. He stayed until the Fourth of July and was with us when a jagged streak of white sizzled across the sky and set the Mason's roof on fire that summer.

"We are now three away!" my dad declared ominously.

"Do you think we'll get hit?" I asked Roth as we watched the firemen smother the Mason's flaming porch with water and foam.

"I don't know, Jake. But there's nothing we can do about it."

NW

Chapter 21

"Prejudice has no place in this institution," Mr. McGovern told the entire school at chapel the first week of sophomore year. "I'm sure everyone is aware of the egregious incident that occurred in the parking lot last evening."

It had taken Mr. Kaufman about 10 seconds to figure out what he was looking at as he reached for his door handle. It was not big. It was not obvious, but it was real. And it shook him to his core. No more than three inches high, just big enough to let him know it was there. Etched into his door was a deep, thick swastika. He shuddered at the realization that evil walked among us, in and out of the classrooms, being taught by his lectures, but unable to learn the true lessons of history.

"I ask the guilty party to take full responsibility," McGovern continued. "Show the school you have a semblance of self-respect. Come to my office by the end of the school day and admit your guilt. If no one accepts responsibility, then all extra-curricular activities will be suspended. Games will be canceled, plays will be called off, and everyone will be required to do work-service until the perpetrator owns up for his actions."

First period, Mr. Addler filled every inch of every black board with algebraic problems in his neat white print. "This is your homework," he said tapping the board. "It will be like this every day until the jackass owns up for what he did."

"You know they did it," I heard Carter say over the lockers later that day. "We never had a problem like this before."

"Exactly," Silver agreed. "They went to Catholic school. Catholics don't like Jews. Ever hear of the inquisition. Hell, last spring, they were defending Hitler and making anti-Semitic jokes."

◆◆

At the end of the week, Mr. Armour pulled me out of Western Civilization and brought me to McGovern's office. I sat down in an oversized leather chair surrounded by tall wooden shelves filled with leather bound gold-leaf books.

"I have a great understanding of where you came from. Ninety-five percent of the boys at Bainbridge are lifers. They've been taught tolerance, acceptance, respect for other people, different cultures, from day one. This is all they know. A real Bainbridge boy would never do something like that. Never. I don't know what they taught you at St. Francis."

"Do onto others as you'd have done onto you."

"So, you'd like having your car vandalized?"

"We didn't do that," I said coldly.

"We?" he asked.

"Well, I know I didn't do it."

"So, you're saying, the others could have?"

"No, that's not what I…"

"So, you're saying," he surmised, "you don't know that they didn't do it."

"I don't know who did what," I said. "I just didn't do that."

His eyes screwed tight onto mine.

I couldn't contain my smile.

"Do you think this is funny?"

"No, I think it's a joke. I didn't do it. I'd never do anything like that."

"Never?" He smiled. "You've never done anything like that?"

"Do what you want. Kick me out. I don't care."

"Look, I like you Jake. I don't want your life ruined because you grew up in an unenlightened orthodoxy. So, stop making it hard on yourself by denying everything. You will be expelled. But if you admit what you did, you can take a week suspension, pay to get Mr. Kaufman's car repaired and you'll understand what prejudice is all about."

"Yeah," I nodded. "I think I do understand." I stood. "It's like getting accused of something without evidence simply because you're different." I walked out.

◆◆

"I wish they would just let me die," Mr. Sullivan complained the following day, rubbing the double six domino between his thumb and forefinger. I found an eerie solace in his morbidity.

"Don't talk like that," I said weakly.

"I'm like that ugly old plant that no one waters until it's all yellow and withered and about to die, and then they drown it with water and bring back to life just long enough to forget to water it again."

"But when you die, it's over, it's permanent. You're gone for good. You never come back."

"Thanks for scaring the hell out of me."

We played several games of bones without saying very much, just silently sliding our pieces into place. In the middle of the third game, he peered up at me. "Why are you here? Why d'you always come?"

"I just want to…"

"Don't give me that crap about helping."

"I don't know," I shrugged. "I like it?"

"Like it? How the hell can you like this? You're a weird kid. If I was you, I'd be running the streets, chasing puna."

"Not everyone thinks like that," I said.

"Of course, they do."

"I don't."

He studied me, and then turned his head like he caught a pungent odor. "You're not one of those?"

"One of what?" I asked.

"You don't like girls, do you?"

"Yeah, I do," I said quickly.

"Of course, you do," he gave me a slight wink. "That's why you're here with an old turd on a Saturday. Just my luck. They send a Mary-Jane to keep me company."

"I'm not a… You just like having me here," I told him. "So, you can win at something."

"I win every day. Every morning I wake up, I win. They gave me six months to live, like a prison sentence. But you know what? I'm going a year, maybe two, just to chap their ass for never leaving me to die in peace."

"See? They want you to live."

He shook his head. "They don't want me here. Every morning, I see the disappointment on their faces when I finally open my eyes."

"Six months," I whispered to myself.

"Six months, six years. What's the difference?" he grumbled. "We're all dying. If you can live happy knowing that, that's something."

◆◆

I sat on my bed that night staring at the silver waves of the moonlit beach. Although I had plenty to be happy about, deep down I was sad. It was not a jump-off-the-Empire-State-Building sadness, but a persistent gnawing at the core of my soul, taking the edge off my joy and keeping happiness at arm's length. I didn't know where this sadness came from. Was it an outward expression of my inner self, or an internal response to external realities?

Quinton burst into my room. "This is bullshit. It's all bullshit!"

"What is?" I asked.

"It's bullshit what they're doing to us," he said again.

"Who did what to whom?"

"That Alexander dude. He did it, and they're blaming us."

"What?"

Quinton sat down and looked right at me. "He tagged Kaufman's car."

"How do you know that?"

"Pickles told me."

"Pickles? The janitor?"

"Yeah. He said he saw that dude, Carter, that night messing with cars in the teachers' lot."

"Why didn't he tell anybody?"

"They'd fire his ass if he ratted out the one of the brass' kids. He only told me 'cause he heard they were trying to pin it on us." He stood abruptly and shook his head. "I'm telling. I'm gonna expose that rich sonofabitch."

"You can't. His dad gave us our scholarship. You'll get thrown out."

"I don't give a damn."

"I do. They'll throw us all out."

"I want to blow this hell hole up." Fire was in his eyes. "I don't give a damn what happens to me. I just want to expose his ass."

"That's crazy. That'll only hurt yourself. Let's just keep our mouths shut and think about our future."

"Why are you so weak?"

"Yeah, and you'll be the bravest kid at community college."

"I'm gonna get that prick, believe me. I'll take him down, one way or another."

Quinton didn't say a word to anyone, and neither did I. We protected our futures with our silence. No one was suspended or expelled, and the crime slowly faded into obscurity. Bainbridge gradually went back to normal, games were played, plays were performed, final exams were taken.

They couldn't convict us, so they punished us by pardoning us and claiming the moral high ground. "It's better to set four guilty men free, than punish one innocent man," Rob Silver said, dangling their virtue over our heads.

◆◆

I pushed the door to 13B like I had done every Saturday for the last year and a half. It swung slowly open. The room was empty, and the eucalyptus smell was gone. His bed was made, his clothes folded and stacked neatly. A nurse walked in, carrying a crisp bundle of white bed sheets.

"Where is he?" I asked.

"You can't be in here," she snapped.

"Yeah I can," I told her. "I come here every week."

"You his kin?"

"Kin? What's that?"

"His grandson, nephew, cousin?"

"No, I just been... Where is he?" I asked again.

"He's not here," she dropped the stack of linens on his bed.

"Where'd he go?"

"I can't tell you that. You're not his family."

"Family? I'm the only family he's got. I'm the only one to tell. If you don't tell me, you tell no one."

"I'm not supposed to."

"Is he alive, or dead?" A chill ran over me as I thought about that word.

"I'm not authorized."

"You're not authorized to say whether he's dead or alive?"

"He's at the hospital," she finally relented.

"What is he doing there? Why didn't anyone tell me? What does he have?" I bludgeoned her with questions.

"Well, there was an issue," she began. "We found blood in his urine. We ran tests and found a malignancy in his testicular region.

They removed the malignancy."

"What did they do to him?"

"He's old."

"I know he's old. You don't have to tell me he's old. I'm the only one who comes here. I'm the only one who knows him."

"His body's breaking down. All they can do is fix what's broken and keep him one step ahead of the inevitable."

◆◆

I rode my bike the five long miles to the hospital. He laid in the cold, steel bed with tubes running out of his nose, and each arm. I walked in cautiously, afraid to startle him. His head popped up, and his eyes grabbed hold of my face. I stared at him, trembling.

"How you doing?" I inched toward his bed.

"How the fuck you think I'm doing?" He said in a hoarse whisper. "I have more tubes sticking out of me than a still."

"Hang in there," I grabbed his forearm. "You'll be fine."

"I'll be dead."

"Don't say that," I told him. "You'll get through this; we'll be back playing bones in no time."

"You're the only one," he rasped. "I got one foot in the grave, and they still don't show."

"They'll come."

"No, they won't."

"It doesn't matter anyway, I'm here. You'll never be alone. I'll be here every day," I promised. "We'll get through this together."

"Gray," he motioned to me, and I leaned toward him. "You never know how hard life is until they cut your balls off."

I stared at him silently stunned.

"Who am I fucking kiddin'?" he forced a pained smile. "They haven't worked in years."

"Hang in there," I squeezed his hand.

"I am." He looked right at me and whispered. "You gotta be a tough motherfucker to get old."

◆◆

I went back to see him the next day. I didn't want him to be in there alone. I pushed open the door and the sun's white light shone on a freshly made bed. My heart stopped. There was a pristine emptiness to the room, like he just vanished from existence.

"Where is he?" I sprinted down the corridor. "Where is he?" I demanded of the nurse behind the reception desk.

"Where is who?" the nurse asked.

"Mr. Sullivan!"

She flipped through some papers on a clipboard. "We have no Mr. Sullivan."

"He was in that room yesterday." I pointed down the hall. "3-A."

"They must have transferred him."

"Where?" I sprinted back down the hall to his empty room. "Where is he?"

"Mr. Sullivan passed away last night," another nurse said placidly from behind. I stepped back away from her. "I'm terribly sorry. There was nothing we could do." She placed her hand on my shoulder. "It was just his time to go."

"Was he alone?" I wriggled my shoulder free.

"Well..." she hesitated.

"Was he alone?" I asked her again. "Was someone with him?"

"He died in his sleep," she stepped toward me.

"No one was in there with him?"

She shook her head.

"Where were you?" I barked.

"I was at my station," she fired back, but then softened her voice. "There are 15 patients on this floor. I can't be everywhere."

"You could've been with him. You knew how sick he was." I walked over to his bed and sat down. "I should've been here. No one should die alone."

"He was old. He lived a long, full life. I wish I live that long."

"No, you don't," I said. "No, you don't."

◆◆

I went to the home later that day. The big round nurse came up to me.

She studied me. "Are you Gray?"

"Gray? Yeah, I'm Gray."

She went into the closet and walked back to me carrying a small shoebox. "I found this with his things," she held out the box with *To Gray, from Gene* on it.

I took the box from her. "Thanks." I pulled it to my chest, and didn't say another word.

"Well, I'll be at my station if you need me."

I carefully opened the lid. Inside, there was our box of dominoes, an old baseball, and a piece of paper. The ball was grayish yellow with faded red and blue interwoven stitching. And on the paper was a message scratched out in blue ink:

Gray,

The Babe didn't hit one out, but he did foul one down the 3rd base line that day.
Thank you for being there.

Your friend,

Gene

P.S. - Don't let the bastards grind you down.

I smiled. *That's one ball that's not going into Dad's bucket.*

NW

Chapter 22

"Though I walk through the valley of the shadow of death, I will fear no evil: for thou art with me." The priest spoke these words as they lowered Mr. Sullivan into the frozen ground.

My mom and I were the only mourners at his funeral. No family. No friends. No one else showed up. It was just us, the priest and an altar boy. They lowered him into a rectangular hole on the edge of a sparsely filled, snow-covered cemetery. I trembled as the wind swept across the gray head stones lifting the dusty flakes into the sky as if the souls of those buried there were rising to heaven.

"Are you OK?" my mom asked, hugging me as we walked away from his gravesite.

"What was the point of helping him, Mom?" I asked. "He still died."

"Did you think you were going to save his life?"

"No, I just thought I could help him, but I couldn't."

"You did. You brought happiness to a dying old man. You were probably the best time he had in years."

"But what's the point in helping anyone? It's all gone, forgotten now."

"I think that's the best we can give to each other, just brief moments of temporary happiness."

◆◆

I closed my eyes in bed that February night, drifting off to sleep as I pictured him in that box, under the ground, all alone for eternity.

I was jolted awake by a sharp "tick" sound in my bedroom, and I opened my eyes just long enough to read **1:02** on the digital clock. Just as the weight of my eyelids threw me back into blackness, I heard it again, and then again and again, bouncing me between light sleep and dreamy consciousness.

I finally pulled myself out of bed and stumbled to the window. My bleary eyes peered out over my backyard into the frosty night. A vaporous white body floated in the snow-covered yard like a ghost.

I pried the window open. "What are you doing?" I whispered loudly down to him.

"C'mon." Dorian waved me down.

"What going on?"

"C'mon down," he waved again.

I threw on jeans and a sweatshirt, crept through the kitchen, and slipped out the back door.

"My mom threw me out." Galilee was emblazoned in red across his chest. He was wearing his summer league baseball uniform with black high-tops.

"What did you do?"

He shrugged. "I was born."

I laughed. "Why do you got your uni on?"

"She told me, I could only leave with what I owned, and this is all I got."

"C'mon inside," I said turning to my house.

"No," he shook his head. "I'm out of here. I'm leaving."

"Where?" I asked.

"Vero Beach," he announced. "The Dodgers are in spring training."

"You're going to Florida? Right," I mocked.

"Why not? I got nowhere else to go. It's winter break, we got a week off of school."

"Let's just go inside," I grabbed his arm. "You can sleep in my room. Everything will be good tomorrow."

"Everything will be the same tomorrow." He pulled his arm free and turned toward Ocean Avenue. "I'm going. I got to."

"What about Karen?" He straightened up. "You can't leave her. She needs you."

"I'm doing this for her. When I sign my big-league contract, the first thing I'll do is get her the hell out of that place."

"What contract?"

"Dodgers are having an open tryout Monday," he explained. "And they're gonna sign me. They sign 16-year-olds all the time."

"If you're Dominican," I joked, but he was right. If they saw him, they would sign him.

"You can't hitch all the way to Florida by yourself, you'll end up on the back of a milk carton."

"Then come with me," he said. "You can try out, too. We'll be Dodgers together."

I knew that was a lie, but it made me feel good anyway. "I can't come with you, this is crazy."

"Fine, I'm going with or without you," he said. "I can't take it. I can't live in that house anymore."

"You're gonna to get picked up by some nut job and killed."

"I don't care. I'm getting in the next car that comes by and heading for the sun. I'm gonna sign my contract and be done with all this."

He walked toward the street, and I stood on my porch. He turned, "You coming, or what?"

"What," I said, and watched him walk away.

Back inside, I watched from my kitchen window as cars zipped by him, one after the other, exposing the foolishness of his plan. But then, an 18-wheeler hissed to a stop next to him. This was actually happening. I ran to the laundry room, threw some clothes in a paper bag for him, grabbed all the money I could find, and sprinted out the door.

◆◆

"Where you headin'?" an unshaven face asked as I ran up to them.

"South," Dorian said.

"How far?"

"Vero Beach, Florida," Dorian stated dramatically.

"What for at 2 a.m.?" The blacks of his eyes rolled up and down us.

"I got a tryout with the Dodgers," Dorian said.

"No, you don't." the driver shook his head.

"Yeah he does," I blurted out.

"I'm no scout," the driver said. "I just think if they wanted you, they'd have put you on a plane."

"The tryout's on a contingency basis," Dorian answered.

"Contingent on what?"

"If I show up, they give me a tryout."

He peeled his hat from his head and curled the brim. "How old are you?"

"Eighteen," Dorian said.

The man looked at me. "Eighteen," I said.

"Where do you go to school?"

"JCC," Dorian replied.

"I'm not bringing you down for spring break, am I?"

"Look at the way I'm dressed," Dorian said.

"Alright, I can take you as far as Savannah." The man relented with a smile. "After that, you're on your own."

Dorian climbed up the steps to the cab and turned to me. "You coming?"

I looked at him, then back at my house, and then I followed him into the cab.

I knew going with him was wrong, but the thought of him being alone out there, anyone being alone, was more wrong, so I convinced myself that the right thing was to go with him, to help him make his life better. It's amazing how easy it is to talk yourself into something.

His muscular hands squeezed the steering wheel through a turn, and the veins in his forearms popped out. His square chin hinted at a beard while his dark hair was combed across his forehead and curled in a loop.

"I'm Marcus," he reached out and shook our hands with his eyes still on the road.

"I'm Dorian," he pointed his thumb at me. "That's Jake."

"What position do you play?" he asked Dorian.

"Any position he wants," I chimed in.

"Center field," Dorian nodded.

"Are you trying out or just along for the ride?" Marcus looked at me.

"I play but I'm not trying out."

"I played in high school," he said. "First base. I was pretty good, actually, second team all-district. I could've gone pro, but I blew out my arm." He up-shifted.

"That sucks," I said.

"No big deal," he shrugged. "Baseball's passé anyway. It's a dying sport. The games are too long. Too slow for modern America. It'll always be around, out of tradition, but it'll never be like it was."

◆◆

The three of us, an unlikely trio, stared blankly into the dark night as the foggy headlights cut through the blackness at 80 miles an hour. The burst of air from northbound 18-wheelers hurtling past us shook the cab.

"You'd think there'd be more crashes," I said.

"The lines," Marcus said, "keep us safe. They're powerful. Those thin strips of paint are the only things keeping me from turning this truck into the oncoming traffic." He snaked the wheel left, then pulled it back straight, and the tail of the truck whipped into alignment.

"The only things?" I said, as I casually pulled my seatbelt over my shoulder, locked it in place, and gave a sharp glance at Dorian.

Marcus nudged me. "Don't worry kid, I'm as sane as they come."

"That's what crazy people say," I whispered to Dorian.

I tried to sleep with one eye closed and the other peering at the road until I gradually drifted off.

We drove south on I-95, over the Delaware Memorial Bridge, through Baltimore and around Washington, D.C. We saw the Lincoln Memorial and the Pentagon from the highway at 75 miles per hour, continuing through Richmond, Raleigh, toward Savannah.

The eastern sky was turning light blue. Someone somewhere was seeing the sunrise. There was no sound except for the whistling of the wind through invisible cracks in the cab. Dorian's forehead leaned against the side window, his eyes fixed on nothing I could see.

"What are you looking at?" I yawned.

"The mile markers."

"That's not going to get us there any faster," I told him.

"If I can keep my eyes locked in on the numbers as we drive by, I'll be able to lock in on the spin of any 80-mile-an-hour pitch."

I locked in on the round white reflectors running down the middle of the road, and imagined they were fastballs coming at me one after the other, picturing myself hitting those imaginary pitches until I drifted off again.

We made our way south as the sun rose above the Carolina Mountains, and the clouds floated by like smoke from a stack. The highway was carved into the mountains, the dark gray rock lopped off its side like a large slice apple pie.

Although we were driving south, I felt as though we were driving toward the sun. The temperature rose with each passing mile. And we neared a consciousness not felt in New Jersey in late February, a feeling of total emancipation, we drove toward summer.

◆◆

Later that morning, Marcus pulled the truck into a dingy diner just off the highway, the diner you'll find on the edge of every small town, skirting America's interstates, the oases of the highway deserts.

A vast assortment of rootless people filtered in and out, all from different places, going in different directions, with different pasts and different futures, their lives converging at that time and place for a few brief minutes, exchanging a nod, a smile, or a few words. These generic people made up our world for that moment in time, never seen or even thought of again. But while they were there, they were as present as anybody in our lives.

She emerged out of this random conglomeration of humanity and smiled at us. I looked up and beheld her soft, pristine face. "Where are you fellas headed?" she asked. Her beauty was painfully misplaced, and rarely noticed among the vague transients.

"Florida," Dorian answered.

"You're so lucky," her voice bubbled. "I'd love to go to Key West one day and watch the sunset from the southernmost point in America."

"You can also visit Hemingway's house," Dorian added.

"Is that where you're going?"

"No, Vero Beach." Dorian said

"You're the strong silent type." She turned to me and winked.

"Not so much."

"Not so much strong or silent?"

"Both," I answered.

She etched our orders in her mundane little pad as a bright stare of dreams beyond this diner flickered in her eyes so vividly I could almost see them. She floated from table to table, tediously chronicling the random desires of temporary people with unwarranted earnestness. She listened intently to one man tell his tale of travel loudly for all to hear, even though she had heard the same unique story a hundred times before; nodding and smiling until an old waitress with a blank stare of dreams that died long ago reproved her for her kindness.

As we rose to leave, from across the diner, her eyes locked with mine. We were caught in a moment so hopeful, yet so fragile. She smiled demurely. I saw in her what everyone has been overlooking her entire life, and she looked at me in a way I had rarely been looked at before. And in that fleeting moment I felt all the possibility of the world, that this person who I've never seen before could be my future, she could bring me happiness if only we were born in a different time or place.

Instead, I let her walk out of my life without a word, without any sign of that frail hope taking root in my heart in that fragile moment. She disappeared into the pack of transients to live her life, chase her dreams without a second thought of the hope we offered each other in that moment. I walked out of the diner as my waning desire dissolved into that place in my heart reserved for unfulfilled dreams.

◆◆

Marcus pulled the truck onto the highway, and the enormous machine roared down the road, plowing through the green sea of pine trees as if it were forging these great concrete corridors itself.

"Thirty years ago," he looked off into the empty woods. "You hitchhike on this road, you end up on a chain gang."

A faded red Ford Dually pickup pulled out in front of us spraying dirt across our windshield. Only the letters "O" and "R" were still visible on the pinkish tailgate. Three shirtless men, brown from the sun, sat amid bundles of tarps and stacks of woven baskets, the orange and black stocking caps on their heads bobbing up and down.

"Migrant workers. Labor's cheap around here, 70 cents an hour, and they're glad for it." He looked right into my eyes. "Try telling them how hard your life is."

Marcus lifted a small black tape recorder and whispered into the top end.

"What's that?"

"Just something I do," he said as he stuffed it under the seat.

"You keeping a log?" Dorian asked.

"Something like that."

A white, steely-eyed possum darted into the highway in front of us. "Watch it!" I slammed my foot into the floorboard. We didn't slow or swerve. We simply plowed straight ahead, and I felt a small thump as we crushed him into the cement.

"You just splattered that thing all over the road," Dorian screamed. "You could've at least tried to slow down."

"Can't," he shook his head.

"Yeah, you could've," Dorian said. "You had time."

"Against company policy."

"What kind of company do you work for?" I bristled. "You get a bonus for each kill? A hundred for a possum, two hundred for a fox?"

"Nope. There've been too many accidents swerving from animals. People killed. Lawsuits. A mess. So they told us, it's either us or them. What can you do?"

"Quit?" I suggested.

"Can't," he said.

"Why can't you?" Dorian asked.

He reached under his seat. "Here." And dropped a stack of papers on my lap.

"What's this?"

"My manuscript."

"You're a writer?"

"Not yet. But, that's why I drive this truck. I get to see the country and meet all sorts of people. I look for people following their heart. That's why I picked you guys up. You're following your heart. At least he is." He looked at Dorian. "Few do."

"Is that what the tape recorder is for?" I asked.

"I'm writing a book, or rather I'm talking a book. There's a lot of time to create stories in this cab. A lot of great material out here."

"Have you ever been published?" Dorian asked.

"Sort of," he said, hesitating.

"How can you sorta be published?" I asked.

"Have you ever heard of *Hunt for Red October*?"

"Yeah, sure," Dorian replied.

"I saw the movie," I added.

"I wrote that book," he stated with cool seriousness, oblivious to the absurdity of his claim.

Dorian slowly looked at me, his jaw clenched tight, straining to repress laughter.

"I thought Clancy wrote that?" Dorian finally asked.

He looked out the side window. "I wrote that book."

"You were like a ghost writer or something?" I asked.

"No," he said calmly. "I wrote that book. It took me eighteen months. I sent the manuscript to the publisher, and they sent me a rejection letter. Six months later Red October comes out and goes right up the bestseller's list. I picked it up in a bookstore one day and started reading. I knew in the first chapter it was mine. Same story, same publisher. It's not word-for-word, but my idea, my storyline, my plot, my characters, my book."

"*Red October* was pretty good," I said.

"Mine was better. Mine was about a sunken nuclear sub in the Atlantic, and the race between the Soviets and the U.S. to find it. It paralleled the nuclear arms race, spoke to how winning wars is not determined by who's right or wrong, but by technology, resources, wealth, luck. Victory's connection to moral superiority is dubious, at best."

The more he explained himself, the more frightened I became of a man so absolutely certain of his own delusions, holding our lives in his hands.

"The only thing he did better was the name, *Red October*, a pertinent reference to the October revolution."

"You should sue," I suggested.

"Same battle, same war," he scoffed. "It's not who's right. It's who's got the best lawyers."

"Hasn't Clancy written like five other books?" Dorian asked.

"He didn't write them, either." Marcus snapped. "He's got friends at the Pentagon, and they just feed him all that information."

"Have you published anything else?" I asked.

"I don't want to be published. That's not why I write. I don't try anymore. I don't even send out my manuscripts."

"What's this book about?" I asked.

"A truck driver who picks up two teenage boys one night and leaves them on the side of the road for dead. I'm doing research right now," he winked.

He spun the radio knob, blipping past the stations catching random words that fell into an extended sentence of gibberish. He stopped the dial on a discussion of a suicide bombing in Israel.

"Those people are crazy over there," I observed.

"It's the fringe that causes the trouble," Marcus said. "In Israel, a Jew lives in this house, a Palestinian in that house. A Jew here. A Palestinian there. Living next to each other, peaceful. But we're never told that. All we hear is the fringe."

"Didn't they all used to be the same people?" I asked.

"We all used to be the same people," Dorian said.

"It's God's fault. There've been more wars, more killing in the name of God, than everything else put together," Marcus said.

"They must believe in a different God than I do," I said.

"What if there was no god?" Marcus mused. "What if there wasn't a heaven? Or a hell?"

"Thanks, John Lennon," I said. "Imagine all the people living…"

"No, I'm serious. What if this is all there is? What if when you die, there's nothing else? Huh? Would the world be more peaceful?"

I thought about Mr. Sullivan. Was he in heaven? Or hell? Or just in the ground? "No, 'cause we could do whatever we want, then," I said.

"Is that the only thing that's holding you back?" He asked. "God?"

"God's pretty powerful," I said.

"If there were no God, then people would become our gods," Dorian said. "The politicians, the president."

"If I were president…" I started.

"If you were president what?" Marcus challenged. "You'd be different? You wouldn't be corrupt? You'd make the world a better place? Feed the hungry? End war? What arrogance. That's what everyone thinks, but nothing ever gets better. What makes you so special? What makes you different from anyone else? You think you're incorruptible?"

I shrugged.

Marcus shook his head. "Everyone's crooked. The only difference between Nixon and the rest of 'em, is that Nixon got caught. The only thing he did wrong was not smashing those damn tapes. He just erased the bad stuff. That's what got him. Eighteen minutes of blank tape. You know, we all have our 18 minutes of blank tape, 18 minutes of infamy."

NW

Chapter 23

"When you sign your big league contract," Marcus winked at Dorian, "you can pay me back." He handed Dorian an envelope with two bus tickets as we stood on the side of the road in a one stoplight town just north of Savannah.

"We can't take this." Dorian pressed the crumpled envelope back into Marcus' chest. "It's too much."

"Take 'em," he climbed into the cab and leaned out the window. "If I ever hear about you two hitching again, I'll kick both your asses." The truck rumbled away and disappeared from our lives forever.

◆◆

An hour later, we climbed aboard the bus and rode south on Route 95 through Jacksonville, and then Daytona, until the sputtering bus rumbled underneath the blue and white sign welcoming us to Dodgertown around ten o'clock that night. Every street corner, restaurant and drugstore in Vero Beach was adorned in Dodger blue. We stayed that night at a Kingston Inn off the main drag. $19.99 per night for a double bed.

We hitched to the field the next morning and arrived just after sunup. A light mist rose off the dew-covered grass and floated toward the glow of the morning sun. Scores of different baseball uniforms milled about the field. The tryout was very businesslike. They separated the players into three groups, pitchers and catchers, infielders, and outfielders.

"What are they gonna do?" I asked a leathery, tanned woman writing names and addresses into two large binders at a wooden table.

"Cookie cutter," she dismissed me.

"What do you mean cookie cutter?"

"Speed, arm strength, power," she stated. "There's a threshold of physical ability you need to play pro ball. That'll weed most of 'em out."

They weighed and measured Dorian, timed his 60-yard dash, and watched him throw two bullets from right field on one hop to the middle button on the catcher's jersey. An overweight man with a clipboard gave him a white jersey and a blue Dodgers' cap and told him to come back after lunch.

That afternoon, only 20 players returned, all wearing a Dodger's jersey and hat. It looked more like a team, than a tryout.

A weather-beaten batting practice pitcher threw 10 straight fast balls down the middle of the plate that Dorian sprayed on a line to all corners of the field, blazing streaks of white against the deep lush green of the outfield. His swing was beautiful, a seamless melding of form and function. It was the first time on a baseball field that he looked like he belonged, like he fit in. This was his level, and he was the best one out there.

The men lining the fence scribbled furiously into their notepads with increasing intensity after each searing drive. After his ten pitches, a man in the dugout motioned to him. "Stay in." That's when he really found his rhythm. The balls leapt off his bat, and then the scribbling stopped as the men just watched, knowing. There was nothing more to write.

◆◆

As Dorian was shagging flies in the outfield, I walked across the complex toward a cluster of bright baseball diamonds. I heard him before I saw him. In five-second intervals, a sharp, definitive "thwap" echoed across the fields, followed by a steady thrumming. I was drawn to that sound. "Thwap!... Thwap!... Thwap!" And then I saw him in the cage on the far field. Mike Piazza stood as big as life, in a sleeveless Dodgers t-shirt, blistering line drives with such ferocity that even the pitcher behind the protective screen looked uneasy.

His bat struck the ball so cleanly, so purely, that contact appeared predestined, and the ball flew to the far reaches of the field so effortlessly. I could hear the hum of the ball cutting through the air. There was not even a hint of wasted motion. His swing was flawless. Every movement, every muscle contraction, had the sole purpose of directing all of his power to the point where the barrel meets the ball, exploding in one riveting and beautiful instant. And no one else was there to see it. Unseen beauty is as prevalent as it is rare.

The man with the clipboard shoved his hairy arm in my face. "Take this card and tell your buddy to give me a call in two years after he graduates."

"How did you know?" I slid his card into my back pocket.

"It's my job to know who Dorian Childs is. We didn't have five straight Rookies of the Year for nothing," he told me. He turned to walk away, then stopped. "When we were 16, we used fake names."

◆◆

"We should go back," I told Dorian.

"I know," he agreed. "But we've come this far, I don't want to turn right around and go home."

"I know, but my parents are probably going nuts," I said.

"We have $51.28," Dorian said as he stacked the coins in neat little piles on top of the bills. "That should last about a week," he said. "Winter break ends next Monday."

We found an all-you-can-eat lunch buffet at the nearby Ho-Jo's for $3.99 a piece. We ate once a day, and our $51 bought us six days of sustenance. We were like camels, stuffing ourselves until we couldn't force another bite down, hoping it would last for the next 23 hours. We snuck dinner rolls under our shirts that we ate at night, and slept on the beach underneath an overturned rowboat.

We stayed on the beach all day, swimming, running, sunning, like the summers of old; six carefree days without worry, without competition, without confrontation, without the outside world infringing upon us.

I stood on the beach and looked north at the sand stretching on forever, and although I was a thousand miles from home, I felt as though I was standing on the same beach that I grew up on, and I only needed to walk around the bend to see the red brick chimneys of my house.

I looked out over the ocean and wondered about the first footprints. The people who first stood here must have thought that thin blue line separating the sea from the sky was the end of the world. They didn't know there were worlds beyond, worlds filled with people not much different than they, people who lived and died, laughed and cried, hoped and prayed, dreamed, loved, killed, for they did not understand the difference between what you see and what you know. Their eyes were their only barometer of life's truths.

"The stars are all out of place," Dorian said as we stared up at the thousands of stars glimmering in the oily sky. The razor thin crescent moon hung in the heavens like a celestial hook dangling the earth tenuously off an invisible wire.

"Yeah, the Big Dipper's supposed to be over there," I pointed to the northern sky.

"Sometimes, they scare the hell out of me," he said, his eyes fixed on the white speckles.

"How can you be scared of stars? They're so far away."

"That's what scares me. They're so far, and so many," he said. "When I look at them and think of the billions of stars and planets and other worlds, I feel small, like nothing, and my life is a fraction of a second on a speck of sand in the vast sprawling universe."

"Do you believe in God?" I asked.

"What do you mean?"

"I mean, like, do you believe that God exists?"

"It's not that I don't *believe* in God. I just don't believe *in* God."

"Well, that clears things up."

"I believe in God. I just don't believe in the promise of God."

"You gave up on him?"

"I didn't give up on God. God gave up on me."

"God nev—"

"My whole life, I did everything He said, but nothing changed."

"What did you want to change?" I asked.

He snapped his eyes at me like I should know that answer. "Everything, anything."

"You ever think that God is just made up, so we'll do what they want us to do?" I asked.

"I've thought about it, but I never think it," he said. "Sometimes, I think the people who don't believe in God are as delusional as those who do." He rolled on his side and fell asleep without another word.

I awoke the next morning to the sound of the waves licking the morning sand, and the sun peering over the horizon. Dorian strolled out of the surf, emerging from the bright morning rays with golden droplets falling from his bronze flesh like miniature suns.

"If you can look at the sunrise and not believe in the Maker," he said as he approached, "you're a better man than me."

NW

Chapter 24

"All good things must come to an end," I said as I counted out the remaining $11.38.

He leaned against the boat. "We had fun, right? It was worth it." His skin had grown so dark that his white teeth glowed, and his blonde curls bouncing in the breeze made his head look like it was on fire.

Two girls stretched out on a blanket and chairs no more than 15 feet from our boat. They wore sunglasses, one-piece swimsuits and a half bottle of suntan oil. The blonde girl sat facing us with her left leg wrapped around her right, and the brunette sat with her back to us, her bent knees spread. Their glossy pink nails flipped the shiny pages of their magazines. They whispered, giggled and broke into exaggerated laughter.

"What are you reading?" I called over to the girls. The blonde one flashed the cover of *Glamour Magazine* at me.

I nodded, and we sat in uncomfortable silence.

"Are you here on spring break?" I finally managed to spit out a question.

"No, we live here," she replied. "We waitress just down the road." She pointed in an ambiguous direction.

"We hitched all the way from Jersey," I said.

"You guys on spring break?" The blonde put on her sunglasses and pulled her hair back over her ears.

"No, we came for a tryout with the Dodgers," I told them.

"Really? Impressive. How'd you do?" the blonde asked.

"Great. He was the best one," I pointed at Dorian.

"So, you're gonna play for the Dodgers," the brunette turned to Dorian. "That's awesome. We love the Dodgers. Maybe we'll see you play someday."

"I don't know," Dorian said.

"Didn't they take you, draft you, or whatever?" The blonde asked.

Dorian shook his head. "Nope."

"Oh, that's a shame," she smiled. "Maybe next year."

"Maybe," I said hopefully.

Dorian hopped up and walked toward the water, leaving the three of us idle.

"Sorry," I told the girls.

"That's OK," the dark-haired girl said. "He's probably upset about the tryout."

"We should go to Key West," the blonde said. "We'll drive all night. We can watch the sun rise."

"I don't know."

"Why not? You hitched from Jersey. You might as well go all the way."

"We go back tomorrow," I said.

"Why?"

"I don't know," I hesitated. "I think it's just time for us to get going."

"Well, you should come by the restaurant tonight, before you leave, anyway. It'll be fun," she offered. "We'll give you free food."

"OK," I said, and she gave me directions to the bar.

◆◆

I walked down the main drag that evening by myself. Dorian refused to go. From the outside, the restaurant did not appear to be much, a scarred wooden door with the *The Salty Dog* carved above the frame. Opening the door, the fading sunlight gave way to a dingy haze. The lights were low and the music lower. There was a television flickering in each corner. A balding gray-haired man in a trench coat sat at an empty table in the middle of the room. The brunette stared at the soundless glow of the television. I was glad she was by herself. I didn't go there expecting something to happen. I went there because I did not want nothing to happen again.

"You never told me your name," I sat down at an empty table. She smiled. "I kinda figured you weren't coming." She wiped the table with her graying dish rag.

"I told you I'd be here."

"Where's your friend?" she asked.

"Couldn't make it. Yours?"

"She's off tonight."

"I guess it's just you and me."

"Well, then, what can I get you?"

"Coke," I said. "Coke's fine."

"I like that," she smiled at me.

"You still haven't told me," I said.

Her dark hair was pulled back into a French braid and she wore a dull pink sleeveless shirt cropped halfway up her back. "What?" she asked.

"Your name."

"You haven't told me yours," she smiled.

"Jake."

Her light blue jeans hung just off her curved hips, exposing her subtle cleft and a flowering infinity sign embroidered into her white skin. She turned around and her pink nails placed a short glass of popping soda on top of a square napkin in front of me. "How's that?"

"You don't like your name?" I took a sip.

"Of course, I do. I'll tell you," she said, "when you're ready."

I slowly felt myself inching toward a line I swore I would never cross. But that line became more alluring the nearer it got.

◆◆

She took her break early and we went to the back room of the bar. She handed me three darts and said, "Let's see what you got, mister baseball man." I stepped to the line, aimed, and as I released the first dart, a loud cough exploded out of her mouth, and my dart pierced the board inches below the bullseye.

"C'mon," I cut my eyes to her.

"Can't you handle a little pressure?"

As I cocked the next dart, she quickly lifted the front of her shirt up and down, and my dart stuck in the wooden paneling to the left of the board.

"You can't do that."

"I can do whatever I want," she walked over and stood behind me, so close that I could feel her warmth. She pressed her front tight against my back. Her right hand slowly slipped over my shoulder, and under my shirt until it rested on my left pectoral muscle. I froze for a moment, but then spun around, and stared into her eyes.

Marvin Gaye's voice slid out of a juke box in the next room. *"Wake up, wake up, wake up, let's make love tonight,"* his silky voice slowly filled the room. *"C'mon, c'mon, c'mon, 'cause you do it right."*

"I love this," she said, pulling me out into the open floor. She wrapped her arms around me and flung her head back. *"Baaaa-by, when I get that feeling, I need sex..."* she looked right into my eyes. *"...u-al healing."* She leaned back, closed her eyes, and pursed her lips. I stood like a statue, and held her in my arms, swaying rigidly until Marvin Gaye's voice faded away, and the music dissolved into silence. She stepped away; our hands parted.

She looked at me. "I'm going to put another quarter in the juke box," she pulled a silver coin from her front pocket, "and play that song again. But this time when we dance, kiss me." As the soft smooth music seeped over the small room, she fitted into me.

"Wake up, wake up, wake up, let's make love tonight," she sang into my eyes. *"'Cause you do it right... when I get that feeling, I need sex..."* She tilted her head back and stared up at me wantonly. I slowly inched my lips toward hers. My body tingled with anticipation.

"You came two thousand miles for that?" The booming voice startled us, severing our sultry connection. "You're worrying your poor mother to death over her? You can get that in any seedy bar along Ocean Avenue."

"Your mother?" The girl backed away from me.

He stood in the doorway with a wry smile as he reached up and massaged his chin with the nubs of his right fingers.

"How'd you find us, Roth?" I said.

"Dorian called Johnny. Johnny called your old man. And he called me."

He pulled two first class train tickets out of his jacket pocket and crammed them into my open palm. "Next time you get it in your mind to come to Florida, you're staying with me."

◆◆

Dorian and I rode the Amtrak up the eastern seaboard without speaking most of the trip. One of us was either sleeping or trying to sleep most of the way.

"My dad spent nine years riding on trains and buses like this," I said, somewhere between Washington and Baltimore.

"I bet it was worth it." He stared out the window.

"A lot of miles, a lot of motels," I said.

"A lot of at-bats."

"You know," I said, "if you want to stay with us when we get back, you can."

"Nah, I'll go face the music."

"What are you gonna do about your mother?"

"I'll survive," he said. "I always do. She's probably forgotten all about it. What about you? You may be in big trouble. I'm sorry."

"I'd do it all over again. It was worth it. I'll never forget this." It was then that I really started thinking about the repercussions of our journey. "I'll just tell 'em the truth. They say I'm always OK if I just tell the truth."

◆◆

The Amtrak dropped us off at the Sea Port station and we rode a Greyhound the rest of the way. I stepped off the bus on the corner of Ocean and Main, in front of the big white club, and stared up at my house. It looked so warm, so big, so close. And yet, when the light turned green, Ocean Avenue looked like an impassable chasm. I paused, and with one step I began my long journey home.

I stepped inside the front door and they both rushed at me.

"I'm not putting up with this," my father seethed.

"You had us worried sick," my mom screamed.

"We thought you were dead," my father said.

"Running away is never the answer, Jake," Mom chimed in.

"Did you stop to think what you put your mother through? Huh? Worried sick, staying up all night. Is this what we can expect from you?" Dad asked as he walked to the window. "That door's closed to you if you pull another stunt like this."

I stood in front of them silent as they tore into me. I didn't offer up an excuse; no mitigating explanation, no equivocating arguments. There was none I could offer, and none they would accept. I took their tongue lashing with quiet equanimity for I knew they were right, and I was wrong, and that was the truth, and the truth is liberating even when it proves you were wrong.

And then in the middle of all the yelling, a calmness swept over me because seated in their anger and their passion was love, and unwavering care and concern for me that released me momentarily from myself.

My dad walked up to me and said, "If you don't know right from wrong by now, and don't know to do the right thing, there's nothing we can do for you. You're on your own."

My mom then hugged me and kissed my cheek. "I'm glad you're home." And went into the kitchen to make me breakfast as if I were the prodigal son.

"I'm sorry," I told my father. "Nothing like this will happen again."

His eyes rolled up and down me, and then he nodded. "I believe you." He stared at me with a fallen look and we were locked in an awkward silence. I did not know what else to say. He did believe me, but I didn't know if he still believed in me.

Dad finally broke the impasse by asking, "Did you see Piazza?"

"Yeah. I watched him take BP," I said, and we went into the kitchen.

◆◆

It hurt to see the pain I caused my mother. It hurt to see how much I let them down, and how much I let myself down. I had to make up for this. I had to prove that I deserved their love and they could still believe in me. So, I doubled my efforts. I did extra chores around the house, and I went to the social services office and volunteered for the food drive, the blood drive, the shoe drive, the book drive — any drive they had. I was driven to make amends. I spent my summer days volunteering, and my summer nights playing baseball. No time for the beach, no time for friends. I had no other option.

But I began to wonder if maybe the life I was pursuing was not possible. Maybe the world was too tempting, too contaminated, and too ambiguous to produce the purity I was searching for. It was a tedious, tenuous balancing act to always do the right thing. I realized I may have painted myself into a moral corner.

NW

∼ Part III ∼

Chapter 25
(March 1998, age 16)

I felt trapped. As I entered my junior year, the segments of my life — school, baseball, my revelation, my future — were closing in on me. I was caught in the unenviable place between who I was, and who I wanted to be. I was trapped; trapped by time, trapped by my unattainable moral pursuits, trapped by my wants, my desires, my needs, trapped by my inadequacies. There was no escaping me.

How I envied those free souls unfettered by the constraints of this arbitrary world, embracing life outside the boundaries, living without a thought, without a care, without a concern for another, who believe their existence was sufficient remuneration for their freedom. I thirsted for their soul, I hungered for their carelessness.

But there is a freedom within the cell of self-denial when the soul sinks to the bottom and roots itself in the nothingness, soaking up the void, purifying in the cold black emptiness. All is cut away: want, desire, need, greed, envy, and the infinite soul emerges. It is only in the nothingness where freedom resides without a price.

I believed that spiritual purity determined success. A strike out, a pop up, a failed test, were not the result of a physical weakness or a mental lapse, but a direct consequence of a spiritual failing; a corrupted thought, an evil intent, a lack of purity. My sins were to blame. And I believed hard work and good deeds were the only way to purify my life, my soul.

My father and I continued our batting practice sessions every day, without fail. But no matter how many balls I hit, no matter how far, how hard, or how many times in a row, I never felt any closer to him. Each time I swung, I wasn't simply hitting a baseball, I was striking an invisible barrier between him and me, trying to smash it to pieces so he could see me for who I was.

But the only things I accumulated from my life of hard work and self-denial were regrets, failure and condescending pats on the back. I began to hate baseball, not because of my father, but because of me. No matter how hard I tried, how much time I spent practicing, how much I sacrificed, I was average. I began to hate baseball for exposing my mediocrity.

◆◆◆

I walked through the tall glass doors of the administrative wing and into the college admissions offices. I knocked on the second door and entered slowly. There she was. My heart hesitated. Her long, silky legs emerged from her tight skirt, folded around each other as she sat.

"I believe," Ms. Vivaqua said as she stared disappointedly at my SAT scores, "that all your outside activities will have to make up for your scores not being exactly where we need them."

She was young. I didn't know how young, but behind her fully mature body, I could see a gleam of youthfulness, a trace of innocence. All the boys at Bainbridge knew who she was and were always devising ways to speak to her, glimpse at her, or even just catch a whiff of her perfume.

"I didn't really think about that," I said.

"Jake, you've worked so hard. You deserve credit for it." She slid her glasses on and quickly flipped through my file. The dark oval-shaped frames made her appear more mature, more intelligent and exquisitely attractive.

"Let's see," she said as she read the contents. "Food Drive, Blood Drive, Toys for Tots, Meals on Wheels, Turkey Drive, Helping Hands. Wow, you've done a lot." She pulled off her glasses and her brown eyes locked onto mine. "This is quite admirable for a young man like you."

I shifted uneasily in my seat. "I don't know."

"This is much more than the typical college grub, I see."

"I guess," I looked up at the ceiling, intimidated by her soft brown eyes. A black, wiry-legged spider inched down a thread as it weaved its gray web in the far corner.

"We need to dress up your file as much as possible, so they don't only focus on the scores. You should go see Coach Delaney. See if your baseball can help. I hear you're excellent." She stood and shimmied her skirt straight. She gathered a pile of books in her arms. "He knows a lot of people. See if he can make some calls for you and then come back and see me. You can come by anytime you like." She smiled. "Anytime. I'm usually here pretty late."

◆◆◆

"Choice!" His sharp voice startled me as the lone word bounced off the cement walls of his dimly lit office.

He was wearing a gray shirt with the word **COACH** written in block letters across his chest. He wore a metal watch on his right wrist and a black sports watch on his left. His receding gray hair was sheared in a tight crew cut, de-emphasizing both its color and scarcity. Brown patches marked his face, and hard crevices were carved around his eyes. I could almost count the number of years he coached by the lines on his face.

His workouts were legendary, running five miles a day and bench pressing more than most of the seniors. It was rumored that he was on the beach when we raised the flag at Iwo Jima.

We called him The Bone, because as Quinton observed once, "Delaney doesn't see the glass half empty, he sees the glass as bone dry." Coach Delaney was misunderstood, though. He was not a pessimist. He was just an optimist who had lived too long.

"Choice is our single most important possession, Jakie. Use it wisely," he said to me.

He was hard, and abrasive, not because he saw the bad in us, but he knew the good in each of us. He cared too much to allow himself to be well-liked.

"I ran around that track 20 times," he said looking out the window. "And I ran into the wind the whole way. North, south, east, west. It didn't matter."

"That sucks," I said.

"It's better than having it at my back. It makes me stronger."

"Just makes it harder."

"Yeah, but you know what kept me going, Jakie?" he asked. "Choice. Every step of the way, I had a choice, stop or keep going. It wasn't just one choice, but choice after choice after choice."

"What was the verdict?" I asked.

He held up his black watch and said, "37:32"

"Slowing down," I said.

He nodded. "It's a crime to get old, Jakie. But the body lets everyone down, eventually. Why should I be any different?"

"You need to take a break once in a while."

"I'm like an old Buick. If I stop, you'll never get me started, again." He sat back down.

I sat down in front of him. "I met with Ms. Vivaqua this morning."

"Uh-huh." he uttered.

"She wanted me to see if any college coaches have called about me."

He looked away. "It's still early. Have you gotten your scores back?"

I shook my head. "They weren't very good. I don't know what to do."

He studied me. "I do." He pointed right at me. "Go and have one hell of a season. Force those colleges to take notice. You can play at any school in this country. Show 'em!" He spoke these things with such belief and raw vigor, it was as if he was trying to will me into believing in myself. "If we make it to state, there'll be 50 college coaches there. We have a chance with you, Dorian and this new kid from Massachusetts."

The "new kid" existed mainly as a rumor. He arrived after Christmas, junior year, and floated in and out of the lockers and halls in the school anonymously, like a ghost, heightening his legend. I thought I saw him once coming out of shop class.

"I've seen him around. He's big."

"He's good." Delaney nodded. "Real good."

"Dorian good?" I asked.

He grinned. "Close. He's a phenom. He's got four of the five tools. He could keep me here, at least for another year."

"Why did he come mid-year?" I asked quietly.

"His mother's sick. She's seeing some specialist in the city. They wanted him at a school close to her."

"Any offers yet?"

"Princeton." That name struck me like a dagger. "He's smart, too."

I shrugged. "He must've gotten thrown out or something?"

"He's a nice kid," Delaney assured me. "I met his dad. He's good people."

"He probably got caught cheatin', or something," I said.

Delaney leaned forward. "Jake, suspicion doesn't look good on you. Stop worrying about others and start worrying about Jake. Why don't you go get ready for practice? You're a leader. Set a good example, be the first one out on the field today. Shorty's in the cage."

♦♦♦

"Hamlet sucks." Quinton tossed his book into his locker. "All he does is bitch and complain. To be or not to be. I say shit or get off the pot."

We dressed for practice mechanically, peeling off our slacks and Oxfords, and pulling on our stirrups and jerseys.

"What'd you write for the third essay?" I asked Jay about our Western Civilization test that day.

"It was easy. I just threw in a bunch of stuff about oppression, exploitation, disenfranchisement. Kaufman'll eat that shit up. I even used transcendence a few times—"

Crack, crack, crack. The violent claps of his meaty hands silenced the room. Everyone froze. His broad shoulders cast a thick shadow across the center of the room. The ghost had come to life.

"This place is a goddamn morgue!" Cullen's voice boomed. "This is baseball, for chrissake. It's supposed to be fun."

He walked over to me and extended his massive hand. "I heard some great things about you," his thick fingers engulfing mine. "Can't wait to throw to a catcher who knows how to handle the dish."

Each of his features was oversized. The enormity of his head, his hands, and his forearms made me feel small. We were the same height, but I felt I was looking up to him, and I couldn't stop staring at him.

"I've heard some great things about you," I returned his compliment timidly.

"I'm just looking forward to playing with you guys."

"We really need a player like you."

He looked at me square in the eyes. "Let's stop stroking each other," he said bluntly, and then turned to Jay. "Hey, what are you doing tonight?"

Jay looked around. "Nothing," he answered. "No plans."

"Good," Cullen smiled. "They're having a midget throwing contest, and I want you to be my partner." He then snatched up Jay by an arm and leg and swung him back and forth. "One... two... three..."

NW

Chapter 26

I emerged from the skeletal woods and beheld the three pristine diamonds unfolding before me in the valley below, cut razor sharp into the woods, sitting there untouched by the wilderness like they were in a glass dome.

I walked down to the varsity fields, and Jay was already sitting in the dugout adjusting and readjusting his wristbands.

"How'd you beat me out here?" I asked.

"I'm always the first one, on the first day. It's good luck."

Everything was connected in Jay's eyes, and he believed he could control the fickle nature of baseball through a hard set of rituals. He did all the usual stuff: same bat, same batting gloves, same socks after wins, never stepping on the foul lines, but always touching first or third base when running on and off the field.

"Do you actually believe any of those things you do have any effect on the game?" I asked him.

"If they didn't," he lined up the wristbands. "I wouldn't do them."

◆◆◆

"Hitting is an art form," Coach Delaney said, pacing in front of us that afternoon, grasping a bat. "Each one of you are artists. You can learn the techniques, master the fundamentals, but that'll never be enough. You must dig deep, find the artist inside of you." He swung the bat at the air gracefully. "Express who you are through your hitting."

"We can hit any way we want?" Quinton asked excitedly.

"Yes, push your limits, expand yourself," Delaney challenged.

"I'm expressing the switch hitter inside of me this year," Quinton announced.

"We want artists: Rembrandt, Michelangelo, Picasso, not Jackson Pollock."

"Who's Jackson Pollock?" I asked.

"He played for the Brewers," Quinton said.

"You go to Bainbridge and you don't know Jackson Pollock?" Delaney leered at me. "I even know Jackson Pollock and I went to trade school. Your parents deserve their money back." He whacked the mud off his spikes with the bat. "Nobody knows who Jackson Pollock is?"

"He's the guy that splattered the paint," Jay spoke up.

Delaney pointed his bat at him. "Exactly, I don't want incoherent paint splatters. I want beautiful strokes filled with meaning, so there needs to be discipline within your freely expressed art."

"But didn't Pollock say he controlled how the paint splattered?" Jay asked.

"If he did, he's a better man than me."

We sprinted out to our positions.

The sound of baseball is eternal. There is an unceasing murmur to the game; the crack of the bat, the whiz of the ball, the scratching of spikes, the incessant chatter. You can close your eyes, and the images of a double play or a double in the alley can be envisioned simply from the sounds.

Wally Waymer stepped to the plate wearing only his undershirt because his jersey could not button around his bloated torso.

The bat looked like a twig in his hands. He swung all wrist because his massive stomach blocked his full swing. He flicked the bat at the ball, and it exploded off his bat.

"Go ahead, Wally," Jay yelled, as he watched Wally drive a ball down the left field line.

"Wally ain't lying," Cullen shouted from the outfield.

Quinton fired six straight fastballs down the middle of the plate that Wally rifled all over the field.

"Don't hurt us," a voice rang out.

The last pitch Wally flipped toward right center, and Dorian, on a full sprint, scooped it up on one hop, and fired to first base before Wally stumbled past the bag.

"That's the most pathetic thing I've ever witnessed in my 45 years of athletics," Delaney yelled as he charged down the first base line. "Thrown out from center field? You're a disgrace." Delaney stood over Wally as he gasped for air, his hands on his knees. "Absolutely pitiful."

◆◆◆

Dorian stepped into the box, scratched the dirt, and pivoted on his left foot. He stood poised as Quinton started his windup. His hands slowly worked in a slight circular motion, and the split second before the ball sped toward him, his hands cocked slightly back, like the hammer of a pistol, waiting, waiting, waiting, until the ball was so close. And then, at the last possible moment, he uncoiled with a fluid suddenness, and his barrel intersected the ball and sent it out on a line. A sturdy whoosh, a firm crack. It was the sweet sound of baseball, the pure sound; the sound of excellence, wholeness. And he stood, watching the ball fly, uncoiled, yet perfectly balanced.

His bat cut through the next ten pitches, like a magic wand redirecting the balls on a sharp line toward every part of the field.

"Goddamn," Delaney screamed. "Save some of those hits for the game."

"There's only one at-bat." Dorian stroked a piercing liner over the second baseman's head. "None yesterday." A blue dart to left. "None tomorrow." A line drive in the right field alley. "Only now." He drove the next ball into the L-screen protecting the pitcher.

Cullen thundered balls off the tee into the fence as Dorian sliced his last pitch down the left field line. It faded, and landed softly, inches in fair territory. "If I hit like him," Cullen announced disgustedly, "I'd wear a dress."

Dorian looked at Cullen, then turned to Quinton. "One more pitch."

Quinton fired a strike on the inside half of the plate. Dorian snapped his hips open and dropped his bat head on the ball. The ball leapt off his barrel and flew in a high arc, carrying through the crisp cool air until it landed on the infield of the JV diamond. He placed his bat against the fence and trotted to the outfield.

◆◆◆

Cullen stepped inside the cage, and we all stopped to watch. "What's that hat doing next to second base?" he yelled at Jay.

"Hey, Cullen," Jay shouted back. "Big man, little stick. Little man," he grabbed his crotch, "big stick."

Cullen's hands squeezed the bat so tight that his forearm twitched, and his knuckles turned white. He stared at the pitcher's mound. As the ball was released his left foot rose and fell heavily, his hips snapped powerfully, and his bat swooped in a perfect arc across the plate. With a loud crack, the white ball rocketed high in the air toward left field, sailing and sailing until it disappeared beyond the fence. He leaned back on his heels and his eyes caught mine staring at him. He gave me a quick wink. Like a robot, he swatted seven of the next ten pitches to the same place, seven lightning bolts. He looked like something you would find in the Research and Development Department at Louisville Slugger, testing the performance of aluminum bats. Each swing was the same perfect arc, a beautiful symmetry. And with each successive drive, the pairs of eyes on the field met knowingly, and as the last ball fell beyond the fence, a buzz of anticipation swelled throughout the team and I began to picture the state finals in my mind.

◆◆◆

After I struggled through my series of groundouts and pop flies, I stood in the outfield as Curtis Snow stepped into the box with the confidence of a 10-year major leaguer. He swung fearlessly, flailing at every pitch, high, low, inside, outside, ball or strike. It didn't matter. There were no good or bad pitches to him. His bat attacked each one with the sole purpose of striking it with all of his force. A rogue smile crossed his face as he watched the balls fly hard and fast through the air.

Coach Delaney walked up behind me. "I have one word for you," he said with muted authority. "Let."

"Let?" I said.

"Let… the ball come to you. Let… your swing work."

"Hitting's an aggressive act," I pointed at Curtis. "I have to attack the ball."

"It's your life," he shrugged, walking away.

◆◆◆

After practice, as my teammates trudged up the hill, my father strolled down it carrying a bucket of balls in one hand and two rolled up imitation Persian rugs over his other shoulder.

"If I took as much batting practice as Jake," Wally declared. "I'd lead the shore in hitting."

"That, or you could stop stuffing your face with Twinkies," called out a voice in the pack.

My father stretched out the two rugs on the mound and in the batter's box, and then threw ten violent warm-up pitches that clanged loudly against the backstop. Then, adding to my embarrassment, he barked, "Batter up!"

He stood on top of the carpeted mound, like the ugly offspring of failed dreams. He hurled the ball toward home plate hard and fast, and as the balls ricocheted off my bat, Dorian chased after each one with childlike exuberance, like he was having fun. But for me, this was strictly work. The more swings the better. It was simple mathematics. I had to take more swings than anyone else to get where I wanted to go. The road to the major leagues was paved with sweat, on lonely fields.

How many times did I have to hit his pitches before it was enough? I wondered.

"You can never get enough B.P.," he smiled as he refilled the bucket.

"Can't we take a break?" I pleaded.

"You have to perform a technique 10 thousand times before you master it. Repetition smooths, refines."

"When I take too many swings, I get tired, fall into bad habits."

"Fatigue doesn't cause flaws," he barked at me. "It exposes them."

So I kept hitting, and hitting, until my hands started cramping and my bat felt heavy. I do not know whether it was fatigue or some hidden desire, but I dragged the bat through the zone and hit the ball before I snapped my wrists. It flew off the bat and right at the pitcher's mound. My dad could not have been more than 40 feet away and bent over from his follow through. The screaming liner struck him on top of his head and shot straight up in the air. A dull thud reverberated across the fields. He stumbled forward. His legs wobbled, but he fought to hold the ground, not wanting to give me the satisfaction of seeing him fall. He took two awkward steps to the left to right himself. The ball fell a couple feet in front of him. He picked it up, stepped back on the mound and pitched the same ball to me, hard and fast. I swung and missed.

I stepped out of the box, leaned back and studied him. He stood, crouched in his ready position. "What are you waiting for? Let's go," he snapped, and proceeded to pitch me the rest of the bucket.

We drove away from the field. I never asked him if he was OK, and he did not want me to ask.

"It's a humbling game," he mused. "Only fools have egos in this sport. Hall of Famers fail seven out of 10 times. In any other business, you'd be a failure."

Failure was one aspect of baseball that appealed to me. Failure is acceptable. But I needed to find a way to ensure that successful rate of failure to guarantee my three out of ten.

"Did you see Cullen hit?" I asked.

"Yeah, he's OK," his eyes remained fixed on the road.

"OK?"

"He didn't hang the moon."

"Cullen's the best hitter on the team."

"Dorian's better." He peered at him through the oblong glass. "You're better than Cullen." He turned to me.

"You kiddin' me," I laughed.

"He's got too many holes in his swing," he said.

"Holes?"

"First, his swing's too long, pound him with fastballs in. Second, he's off balance, throw him off-speed stuff away." He peered over at me. "And most importantly, he swings at pitches out of the zone, so you don't have to throw him a strike to get him out. You should know all this."

"Well, I think he's good."

"Let me tell you something. I went off to rookie ball three days after my high school graduation. After the first practice, I looked around and thought, I'm just as good as these guys." He smiled to himself. "The first month, I was hitting four hundred. I thought I'd move right up, Double-A, Triple-A, maybe the big club in September."

"I know, I know. You were good."

"No, they kept me in Rookie Ball all season. It wasn't good enough to be just as good as the next guy." He stared right through me. "There's a level of play, a standard I had to reach to become a big leaguer. It didn't matter how I compared to anyone else. It was only about me. I never looked over my shoulder again."

"Did you ever play in the big leagues?" Dorian innocently asked my father.

"Couldn't hit the fastball." My father summed up his career quickly as if it were his epitaph.

"That's it?"

"I had my chances and I didn't get it done. I wasn't good enough. I have no regrets." My dad looked in the rearview mirror. "That's the beauty of baseball. Everyone gets their time at bat, to take their cuts. It's up to the individual. If you played the field and you did the work, you deserve the chance to hit."

"What about the D.H.?" I asked.

"The D.H. is un-American," he growled. "Guys get to hit that didn't earn it. It's communist."

After my dad dropped Dorian off at his house, I looked up at him and said, "I don't want you coming to pitch to me anymore."

"But you need it. There isn't a baseball player out there who doesn't like B.P."

"It's embarrassing. You're embarrassing me," I said. "I don't like it. I don't want it. I don't need it."

I don't know why I said those words because they weren't true. They just exploded out of me from years of bottled up resentment of his unsolicited dreams for me, and once they escaped, I could not recapture them. I wasn't good enough to live up to his expectations, his idealism, no matter what I did.

"OK," he said passively. He did not say another word, and just stared straight ahead.

I knew from his eyes that I shouldn't have said what I said. I could deal with the mockery of my teammates, but not the look I put in his eyes. Deep down, I did want him to come and pitch to me, but I didn't know how to tell my dad I was sorry.

NW

Chapter 27

"We're going to start from the ground up." Coach Delaney stood in the middle of the gym, wearing nothing but a pair of gray shorts. He held up his black metal spikes. "Your cleats will be black with black laces. Shined and polished for every game." He pulled on his long white socks. "Everyone will dress exactly like this. Exactly. It's a uniform. A uni-form. Uni, meaning one. Form, meaning... form. One-Form, One-Form. Not any way you want or feel. One way and only one way." The entire team started pulling on their socks and pants like he instructed. "We are one team, not a group of individuals. Separate yourself by your play, not your dress."

"If all that matters is how we play," Cullen muttered, "we should be able to dress anyway we want, right?"

"Respect the game," Delaney pointed his bent finger at us. "You tarnish yourself; you tarnish the game. Everything you do, affects how you play. If you approach the game like a Big Leaguer, you'll play like a Big Leaguer. And if you approach it like horseshit, you'll play like horseshit."

He pulled up his pants and fastened his black belt.

Wally strained in the corner, vainly trying to close the top button of his pants.

"What the hell's your problem, son?" Delaney turned to Wally, red-faced.

"There's something wrong with these pants," Wally snapped. "They don't fit."

Delaney walked over to him. "They," he looked at Wally's misshapen body in disbelief, "don't fit. They... don't fit," he repeated. "Listen, son. God gave you a gift. You have something in your swing. The ball jumps off your bat. I never had that. There are guys in the bigs that don't even have that. But what do you do with your gift? You sit around playing video games, eating Hostess cupcakes, turning into a big blob of fat cells."

Short bursts of halted laughter ricocheted around the group. Delaney paused and scanned the rest of us. "It's not funny. It's sad, very sad." He turned to walk away but stopped. "From exertion comes wisdom. From sloth comes ignorance." Echoes of his words faded in the silent rafters as he walked away.

♦♦♦

"I don't think we would've won a game if we didn't know how to put on a uniform," Cullen said as we walked toward The Commons. We sat on the ledge in front of the lockers at the same time every day, engaged in the same recycled conversations, hoping something new would stroll through those big glass doors.

"This Holden Caulfield dude is an annoying mother fucker," Curtis said. "All he does is bitch."

"It's a book about teenage angst," I said.

"Angst going to prep school? You want to see angst, try living in the hood," he said. "That's not angst, it's straight up and down scary."

Cullen reached into his locker and tossed a catcher's mitt at me. "Here, this is for you."

I grabbed it and turned it over. It was the Wilson A2000. "This is what Piazza uses." I slid my hand inside. The leather was so soft, it was like touching pure silk. It molded to my fingers perfectly. It snapped shut quickly and smoothly. "No wonder they never drop a pitch."

"You like it? It's yours," he said casually, like he had a locker full of them.

"You can't give me this." I pushed it back into his chest.

"What do you mean I can't? I can do whatever I want with it."

"It cost too much."

"You'll catch me better with it."

"Thanks, man." I pounded the pocket with the back of my fist. "My dad caught in the minors and never had a glove like this."

"Don't worry about it."

"Freshmen," Wally walked up. "They're dumb and lazy." Anger oozed from him like sweat.

Cullen turned to him. "You know what they say about people who live in glass houses?"

"What's that s'posed to mean?"

"You know exactly what it means, cupcake," Cullen stood up.

"Yeah, but I want you to tell me," he thumped Cullen's chest with his forefinger.

"Relax," I stepped in. "Nothing to get bent out of shape over."

"How can he get bent out of shape when he's amorphous?" Cullen asked.

Dorian turned to Cullen. "You know what they say about people who don't live in glass houses?"

"What do they say?" He was annoyed.

"They shouldn't throw stones."

◆◆◆

The noise and the bustle stopped as Mrs. Vivaqua strolled down
the stairs. All heads turned simultaneously as she stood on the landing
and fixed her tight skirt. She stood overlooking the boys staring at her.

"She thinks she has all the answers," Wally stood up. "I can ap-
ply wherever I want!" he shouted. "You're overreaching! You're overreaching!"

"I heard she spread easier than butter in high school," Cullen
smiled.

"Now she walks around here with her nose and her ass pointing straight toward the sky," Derek said.

"She's not as hot as she thinks she is," Wally sneered.

"Yeah, she is," Jay said.

"I'll bet it doesn't require a lot of persuasion to get Sylvia in the
rack," Cullen added.

"You know she graduated top 10 from Vassar," I offered.

"I don't care," Cullen dismissed me.

"I don't care that you don't care," I said weakly.

"She doesn't know what she's doing to us," Jay's eyes followed
her.

"She knows exactly what she's doing," Cullen replied. "Why
d'you think she teaches here? She likes 50 boys having a chubby right
now because of her. Just give me 15 minutes. I'll give her an entrance
exam."

"It's against the rules," I said.

"Fuck the rules," Cullen said and then turned to Dorian. "You'd
tear that ass up, wouldn't you, stud?" He winked at him. "Bring the high
heater?"

"No," Dorian said plainly. "That's not what I want."

"You're just saying that," Waymer snapped, "because you've
never been with a girl."

Cullen looked at me. "Flaming."

He turned to Dorian. "What do you want?"

"Nothing," he replied dispassionately.

"Not even that?" Cullen gestured at Ms. Vivaqua.

"No, I'm not in love with her," Dorian replied quietly.

"We're not talking about love, we're talking about sex," Cullen said, annoyed. "Love's not even part of the equation."

"It's the whole equation," Dorian said.

"Who are you, the Pope?" Waymer snarled.

"I just don't want what you guys want," Dorian shot back.

"So, you like dick?" Cullen asked.

Dorian cut a stare so sharp he could've decapitated him with a flick of his eyes.

"You're telling me, you don't have the same physical desires as the rest of us?" Waymer said. "Like you're better than us?"

"How can you talk about love when you've never been laid?" Cullen added.

"How can you get laid, if you're not in love?" Dorian answered.

"I could love her," Cullen snickered, "for about 15 minutes."

"More like three," Jay added, "...seconds."

"Whatever dude, as long as I get my rocks off." Cullen then leaned into my ear: "Something's wrong with that dude. I think he bats from both sides of the plate."

I looked at Cullen. "He's a lefty."

"You know, he likes it from the other side."

"I don't think so. I've known Dorian my whole life."

"Exactly!" he bellowed. "Think about it. Have you ever seen him with a girl?"

"He's just shy."

"Have you ever heard him talk about a girl?"

"I've never been with a girl," I argued.

"I worry about you, too."

Quinton poked his head into our group. "I hear what you're saying, D. For me, I, too, choose quality over quantity."

"You call Fiona Miles quality?" Curtis asked.

"I never laid a glove on her," he said, turning back to Dorian. "Like I was saying, being with one good woman is better than being with a hundred women that a guy like, like... Jake could get."

"Oh yeah," I responded quickly, "I don't get any women."

The mid-morning break bells bonged, and Wally hopped up and walked toward the dining hall.

"Pavlov's dog," Cullen said. "Hey cupcake," he called. "Grab me a couple of donuts while you're at it."

Wally returned to the lockers, carrying two donuts in each hand.

"That's what I'm talking about, cupcake," Cullen clapped his hands. "Teamwork, spread the wealth."

"Get your own damn donuts," Wally snapped.

"You don't need all four donuts; believe me, you don't." Cullen tossed a dollar bill at Waymer. "Keep the change."

Wally stared at him, lifted a Boston Cream to his mouth, and took a large bite. The white cream spurted out and the dark chocolate dripped over his lips and down his chin that he left there, mockingly.

Cullen eyed him. "Those who eat alone, die alone."

Wally smiled. "I'd rather eat soup with a friend, than steak with an enemy."

"So, I'm an enemy?"

"You ain't a friend."

"Give me a freakin' donut!" Cullen lunged at Wally.

Dorian jumped in between them. "Friends, enemies, we're all a team."

"I don't need a lecture from Mr. Perfect." Wally pushed him.

"Relax!"

"Make me," Wally snapped.

"I'm not making you do anything," Dorian said.

"You only feel good when you're showing everyone up," Wally shouted back.

"You don't want to be shown up? Do something about it." Dorian pointed at the half-eaten doughnut. "You're an athlete. Eat right. Get in shape. Coach wouldn't be on your ass if you could button your pants."

"I have a medical condition," Waymer said.

"Yeah, it's biological process," Cullen said. "You stuff your face with a bunch of crap and your body turns it into fat."

"It's not how much I eat. I have a glandular problem."

"A glandular problem?" Quinton scoffed.

"Yeah, I could eat nothing and still not lose any weight."

"I bet you never tested that theory," Cullen said.

"Glandular problem? Answer me this, Waymer," Quinton asked. "Were there any fat people at the Holocaust? Think about it."

Wally stood up. "We're gonna settle this right now," he walked up to Dorian.

"I don't want to fight, man," Dorian's eyes calmly locked in on Wally's.

"Oh, is Mr. Perfect scared? I'm not gonna hurt you, that bad," Wally seethed.

"I don't want to fight, man," Dorian backed away.

"What are you, a pussy?" Cullen shouted.

Dorian flipped his palms up in the air. "Yeah, I guess I'm a pussy," he said and walked away.

We all stopped as plaid skirts and cardigan sweaters slowly flowed through the glass doors and swayed down the hall. The soft curves of the exchange students from the local all-girl's schools melted the hard, rigid lines of the cold corridors. We were captivated by their bare knees, smooth calves, milky-white arms, and soft red lips.

"All-boys schools suck," Derek lamented. "It'd be nice having that around all day."

"You don't want it. Believe me. I went to a co-ed school for two and a half years," Cullen warned. "It's a lot better not having to deal with them all the time. Just 'cause they grow some bumps and curves, they think their God's gift to the world."

"Cullen," Wally said, "I thought you were God's gift to the world."

They walked in front of us, our eyes casually locked in. "I did that. I did that. I did that." Derek Cox motioned to each girl as they walked by. "I did that, I did that, I did..." He paused for a moment. "No, no, I stand corrected, she did me." He pointed to the last girl. "And I will do that before the end of the year."

I silently listened to their depravity with a hint of delight. Their impurity seemed to purify me.

Our eyes reflexively followed the swarm of girls buzzing up the stairs. Their scent hovered in the air like sweet honey. We stared at the empty steps until their lingering perfume dissipated.

Just then, Laticia swept through the glass doors with two other Catholic school girls. She walked urgently, her eyes straight ahead, her lips tight together. She didn't look like any of the other girls that came here. She had short, straight, dark hair, an angular build with narrow hips, and no make-up.

"I've never seen her before," Dorian eyed Laticia as she walked toward us.

"Stay away from that chick," Derek Cox warned. "She's a bucket."

"Yeah, she's been under more sheets than the KKK," Quinton said.

She veered left and walked straight to me as I sat on the steps pounding my new mitt. She stopped in front of me. Her long, lean legs were spread slightly at my face.

"Hi Jake." She pressed her bare knees together.

"Hi." I slid up the column to standing.

"Where's the attendance office?"

"Just go up those steps." I pointed my chin across the common area. "Take a left at the top, and you're there."

"Thanks." She smiled and walked toward the stairs.

"What they hell was that? Getting some nookie on the sly?"

"I went to grade school with her," I felt obligated to explain.

They looked at me suspiciously.

"She was nice. She's not that bad looking," I said without thinking. "I'd go out with her."

"Jake, you've never been on a date," Quinton reminded me. "You'd go out with Mrs. Holloway at this point."

"I wouldn't kick her out of bed," Derek said.

"No one has," Quinton said.

"Jake," Cullen shook his head. "I wouldn't touch that with a 10-foot condom."

"I don't know," Dorian pondered. "There's something about her. Something…" He eyed her as she ascended the stairs. "I think if she was with the right guy."

"I thought you were only interested in looove?" Cullen said. "That's the last thing on that chick's mind."

"Stay away, D," Quinton shook his head. "Once a ho, always a ho." He turned to Curtis. "There ain't no ho rehab," they said in unison.

Laticia continued up the stairs, pretending not to hear, as her skirt flapped dismissively at us.

One of the other girls peeled off and sat down on the landing with an open book. Her modest looks and slight figure blended easily among the puberty-stricken boys. There was something familiar about her.

"Her father's a murderer," Curtis said. "He offed some guy about 10 years ago."

"I'm calling B.S. on that," I protested.

"It's true. She goes to Rahway to visit him. My cousin works there," Curtis explained.

"Works there?" Cullen asked, "or is housed there?"

"Don't turn it on me. It's the honest truth."

I could feel someone staring at me. I subtly cut my eyes at the girl on the ledge, and she looked away. "I don't believe it," I said.

"You know, you gotta respect her," Quinton said thoughtfully. "I wouldn't go see my old man if he were in the can for offing some dude."

"He didn't kill anyone..." Derek said. "He got busted selling drugs."

"Whatever it was, she's bad news. The apple don't fall far from the tree," Cullen said.

I looked over at the girl again and she looked away. We traded furtive glances, and each stolen look drew me to her. I walked over to her and crept along the landing while her face was buried in her thick book.

She peered up, and her long thin lashes fluttered in front of her large brown fragile eyes. "We've danced before," she said with a slight giggle.

"St. Francis graduation dance," I declared.

"I didn't think you'd remember." Dawn smiled vaguely.

"How could I forget?" I looked around. "It was my last dance," I lied. "I didn't think you would."

"Of course," she smiled. "I had the biggest crush on you." Her white front teeth pressed into her glistening red bottom lip.

"Really? I kinda liked you, too."

"I never would've known."

"Well, you, you've changed. You got so much bigger."

"Thanks," she laughed. "That's so nice of you to notice."

"No, I mean, you're, you're like a woman." The words stumbled out of my mouth.

"That's very observant, Jake," she looked down and inspected the front of her body. "How could you tell?"

"You know what I'm saying, you're a woman now," I fumbled around again.

"I don't know. I think I'll always feel like a 12-year-old girl," she said.

"Yeah," I sighed. "That's exactly how I feel."

"Really?" She laughed again. "That's good to know. I'll have to make a mental note of that."

"No, I mean, I'll always see myself as a 12-year-old kid." I looked down at my feet.

She flashed a demure smile.

"Do you still?" I mustered the courage to ask.

"Still what?" she replied sharply.

"You know, have a crush?" I looked away again.

"Hmm, not so much," she smiled into her thick book.

"Why'd you leave that night?" I asked.

"What night?"

"You know what night."

"You left. I went to the girls' room and when I came out, you were gone. Me and Michelle went down to the beach that night looking for you, but I never saw you again."

I leaned against the cement wall. "It's funny how we can live so close and never cross paths."

She shut the book loudly and looked up at me. "We're crossing paths now."

"So we are," I smiled at her. "So we are." My heart started pounding. I didn't want this to end like the dance, so I took a deep breath. "Would you, um... sometime, you know, if you want, would you like to, I mean want to, I don't know, uh, go out, you know, sometime with, uh, me. I mean, I don't know..."

"Are you done?" she said, smiling.

"Well."

"Say it!"

"Say what?"

"Say what you're trying to say."

"OK."

"But in six words or less."

I took another deep relaxing breath. "Maybe I can give you a call sometime," I said casually.

"That was eight."

"Can I call you for a date?"

"Seven."

"May I call you?"

"Yes, maybe you can." She closed her book.

"What's your number?" I asked.

"You know my last name." She stood and walked away.

NW

Chapter 28

"There are coaches all across New Jersey today talking state championship," Coach Delaney told the team in the dugout before opening game. "Every coach is giving this speech and every player believes these words." He looked down and scratched the dirt with his spikes. "But what happens to all this promise? This potential? Every team, every player, will confront some adversity. Being a champion is hard. The world is filled with also-rans, second place, those who traded their dreams for excuses. There are only a few champions. Which one will you be?"

"His pitch selection is indiscriminate, but his motion is impeccable," Mr. Fulbright proclaimed as he walked into the dugout with his scouting report. Unlike the rest of the team, I listened to him intently, soaking up every ounce of information. The more I knew the better.

"What's he got?" I asked.

"His curve approaches the plate with much alacrity," Fulbright spread his wiry fingers, "but his fastball is quite dubious."

His fastball is dubious. His fastball is dubious, I repeated to myself. I didn't know what dubious meant, but it didn't sound good.

At that moment, I decided to hit the first fastball I saw. Curveballs, sliders, off-speed pitches, were too hard to hit. If I attack the pitches, I knew I could hit any fastball I saw. I was determined to put my bat on the ball — put every ball in play. I refused to strike out. That was the ultimate embarrassment. So, I attacked everything, disguised my fear with false aggression.

◆◆◆

The season started well. The first pitch was a fastball that I quickly turned on and drove into the left center alley for a double. I went 3-for-4 in an 11-2 win over Burlington. We were good. I could see it the first game. We were a complete team, very few holes.

"That's the way to open the season, right?" I sat down next to Delaney as he tallied the scorebook.

"I'm always happy with a win," he closed the book, and gathered his pitching charts.

"You don't seem happy. We're on our way."

"On our way to the trash heap," he snapped.

"Trash heap?" I was confused. "Weren't you at the game today? Bainbridge versus Burlington? I thought I saw you there?"

"We're horseshit," he sneered. "Burlington's just more horseshit than we are."

"We played good."

"You're happy about the way we played today? The way you played today?"

"Three for four," I smiled with satisfaction.

"If that's the only thing you can say, then we really are horseshit," he flung the equipment bag over his shoulder and walked to the shed.

◆◆◆

We won the next five games, but I struggled. I squeezed out an infield single and a bloop over second, but nothing solid. Something was not quite right. I couldn't find my timing. I was swinging at balls and letting strikes go down the middle. Nothing felt right. My mitt felt strange in my hand, like I had never worn a one before. My bat felt thick and heavy. My fingers could sense every minute bump, groove and imperfection. I tried everything, a new stance, a different swing, searching for comfort.

◆◆◆

"I'm dropping you to seventh," Delaney told me before the next game.

"Behind Jay?" I asked. "I'm just in a slump. I'll work my way out of it."

"Swing your swing," Delaney said to me.

"What does that mean?"

"You try something new with each at-bat," he said. "You become a different hitter every time up. Swing your swing."

"I don't know what my swing is anymore."

He scratched his speckled scalp. "My wife dragged me to buy a washing machine last week," he said. "The guy showed us 10 different machines, all the bells and whistles."

"What did you get?"

"A Maytag," he nodded.

"Why?"

"Most washers have at least 14 moving parts, but Maytags have only six." He held up six fingers.

"So, what?"

"They don't break down. Less moving parts, less chance of something going wrong, more efficient. Like your swing, the more moving parts, the more chance something will go wrong, and the slower your bat. Simplify. Increase your bat speed by decreasing motion."

"Major leaguers aren't efficient," I countered. "They move all over the place."

"The swing's the thing. Major leaguers do all that pumping, hitching, but when the pitcher's here," he cocked the ball next to his right ear. "Every good hitter is just like this." He folded into a perfect hitting stance. "All that crap before is meaningless. Everyone takes a different path to get here." He stood in the perfect batting stance. "The paths, no matter how crooked, are unimportant. It's where you end up that matters."

"Some of their swings are ugly," I said.

He nodded. "They're ugly. But they perfected them. The only thing that matters is where you are the moment the pitch is thrown, or more precisely, at the moment of contact, one inch before you strike the ball and one inch after, everything else is meaningless. Master that one inch."

◆◆◆

The next game, I was standing in the on-deck circle, embarrassingly watching Jay rip open the Velcro straps and readjust each glove one finger at a time between pitches.

"If he spent as much time studying the pitchers as he did worrying about those damn gloves, he'd lead the shore in hitting," Delaney said.

The front spike of my right cleat drew numbers in the clay, determining my value, my worth, calculating my batting average if I got a hit, or made an out, using mathematical probability to ensure my acceptable rate of failure.

Numbers don't lie. They tell you who you really are. That's what I loved and hated about baseball. The game is honest. The game tells the truth. But that truth bore the seed of my doubt. I doubted myself and I doubted the world. Doubt is more destructive than hate, more debilitating than fear. Doubt held me like an iron fist. Doubt answers its own question with an unequivocal no.

I studied the pitcher's windup and release as he worked at a quick pace to Jay, timing up his motion with each pitch.

The first pitch he threw me was a fastball low and outside. The pitch I was looking for. I threw my bat head at the ball and the bat handle rattled. The ball bounded high in the air toward the shortstop. I sprinted to first base, head down, arms pumping. *I can beat this, I can beat this*, I told myself as I raced down the line. I could see in the corner of my eye the shortstop scoop the ball, and I feel the ball closing in on me as I raced to the base. The ball snapped in the first baseman's glove a half a step before my foot hit the bag.

I spiked my helmet. "I can't buy a hit!" I screamed. I stood there, my helmet at my feet, completely lost, not wanting to move.

"He hasn't gotten a hit since Moby Dick was a minnow," a voice sneered as I walked back to the dugout.

I sat on the steel bench gasping for air, watching the vast expanse of my future slowly dwindle into oblivion.

"Jake," Delaney put his arm around my shoulder after the game. "It takes two thousand frowns to make a wrinkle. At the rate you're going, you'll look like me by the end of the week." He turned toward the dugout. "Smile. When you're playing well, you're having fun; when you're having fun, you're playing well. This game doesn't owe you a damn thing."

"I'm not having fun."

"If you're so miserable," Delaney snapped, "quit!"

I shook my head.

"Your old man will still love you, even if you're not a ball player." He walked away.

I stood alone in the middle of the diamond surrounded by the green grass and unfolding trees, bathing in the waves of the sun. I shuddered at the placid solitude of where I was in the world at that very moment. I was all alone. The prospect of quitting had never entered my thoughts since the first day of Little League. It's something you don't do. Quitting is never an answer.

NW

Chapter 29

"Let's get the hell out of here," Cullen brushed past me on the stairs as the faint bong of the fifth period bells still hung in the air. "I can't take another bite of turkey tetrazzini. C'mon, I'll buy." I followed at his heels, gathered up in his energy.

"We can't."

"Why not?" he laughed. "We're not hurting anybody."

"We can't leave the school grounds," I pleaded.

He looked right at me. "Life's short, man. Live on the edge. This isn't about a better meal. It's about a better life. You only regret the things you don't do. Ten years from now, you'll remember us going out to lunch today."

"Maybe, if we just ask Fulbright. He'll let us go." I grabbed his shoulder.

"It's better to beg for forgiveness than ask for permission."

"This isn't right." I stopped walking.

"Everything's either right or wrong with you. There is no right or wrong, just strong and weak."

"Quinton," I thought out loud, "takes attendance. Let's ask him to let us slide."

"You're such a goddamn pussy. You never do anything because you just want to. Start living your life on your terms. Who cares what other people think? If we get caught, we get caught. Deal with it, we'll survive."

I followed him through the athletic wing, out of the doors, to the student parking lot. Porsche 911 was scrawled across his small trunk. We climbed in and pulled away, leaving the lot full of shiny cars. We roared down the long winding black top, through the tunnel of tall oak trees that led to the main road, top down, sun in our faces and hair flapping in the breeze. And for the first time in three years, I felt free.

"Goooo!" His voice splashed against the windshield, as he wriggled the car behind a long line of crawling brake lights. "How can the light be green for two fuckin' minutes, and we don't move an inch, then it turns red and we start moving. It makes no sense. You wouldn't believe how much gas is wasted in this country at stoplights alone."

"I told you we shouldn't go," I reminded him. "We're gonna be late."

"If we're late, we're late. I could care less."

"I care."

"You know what your problem is?" he mused. "You live like you hit."

"What's that supposed to mean?"

"You're too passive. Attack the ball. Attack life," he pressed the accelerator and the car lurched forward. "Push your limits. Don't worry about balls and strikes, right and wrong. Hit their mistakes, make 'em pay for their mistakes. If he throws a hanger out of the zone, hit it. He's hoping you don't swing. Exploit their weaknesses. There's no time to wait. Your physical limitations are mental."

"Don't hold back, tell me how you really feel," I said.

"Only a real friend would be this honest," he said, giving me a wink before screaming, "Goooo!" again, this time at a beat-up hatchback sputtering along in front of us. "Look at this girl! Fixin' her hair. Doing her make-up. Idiot." We pulled up beside her, and he craned his neck to put a face on her ineptitude.

"Not bad, I'd take a pop at her," he said as we passed.

"Why'd you transfer to Bainbridge?" I asked him.

"My dad wanted me to be close to home."

"How long were you at boarding school?"

"Since I was 10."

"Ten? Why would he bring you home now, if you've been gone for eight years?" I asked.

"He wanted me home." He shrugged.

"Yeah, but why in the middle of the year?"

"What is this, the damn Inquisition?" he snapped. "My mom's sick. She wanted me living at home."

A gray truck lumbered in front of us, and Cullen peered the nose of the car over the double yellow lines, waggling it back and forth. "This guy's breaking the land-speed record. You should have to take an IQ test before you get your license. There's so many damn retards on the road." He looked out his window, and then abruptly pulled the car across the yellow lines and pressed the accelerator. The car jumped forward, and roared into the open road, as we pulled beside the truck. The square red outline of a car appeared above the horizon. The blank eyes of its headlights stared right at me, growing bigger, rounder, brighter with each second as we accelerated right at it.

"Cullen, Cullen!" I screamed as the red car closed in on us.

It grew bigger and bigger until it was so close, I could read its license plate, *PLZ 137.* "Cullen!" I grabbed his shoulder, and with one whip-lashing jerk, the car lurched back to the right, jumped across the yellow lines, inches in front of the truck and millimeters before the on-coming red car. He wrenched the steering wheel back to the left and the car righted itself between the lines of the right lane.

"Are you nuts?" I screamed.

"I had it the whole way. Where's the trust?"

"The trust? I was almost the most trusting kid at the morgue."

"It wouldn't have been 'cause of me. This is a god honest fact, more accidents are caused by slow drivers driving in the fast lane than anything else."

"How many are caused by driving on the wrong side of the road?"

"It's like the Autobahn. They go 120, 130, no problem. There are fewer accidents there than any highway in the world. I've driven on it."

"That may be true," I said, "but when they get in an accident, it's instant death."

"What's wrong with that? It's better than being in a fucking wheelchair your whole life. And I bet there's no chick doing her make-up on the Autobahn."

◆◆◆

We sat at the Samurai hibachi. A short, slight Japanese man with a wispy goatee and a tall white hat, stood before us. He slid his long, thin silver knife and pointy fork out of his holster and clanged them together. He sliced and diced the chicken and steak, the shrimp and lobster with minute precision. He flipped cut shrimp out of the flames, across the table, landing perfectly on plates and in unsuspecting shirt pockets.

"I told you you'd like this," he said. "What are you doing two weeks from Sunday?"

"Nothing. I mean, I usually go to church," I groped for the appropriate answer, unsure of his intentions.

"You still go to church?" he asked incredulously.

I looked down. "Yeah. Why not?"

"You mean like, you're still a Catholic?" He studied me.

"You're born a Catholic, you stay a Catholic."

"I know, but you still do all those things, the ashes, incense, holy water, all that crap?"

I shrugged.

"You still follow the Pope?"

I nodded.

"Why? He's old, out of touch. Nobody follows what he says anymore. Catholics are having pre-marital sex, abortions, birth control, getting divorced. It's a joke."

"Then they're not Catholics."

"And you still go to that medieval ritual every Sunday?"

"It's not like someone's putting a gun to my head," I said.

"Good, 'cause we're going to the Yankee game that Sunday. All the other guys are in." He smiled. His teeth were so packed in his mouth that the front four began to overlap and it appeared that he had too many in his head, like a shark's mouth. I imagined if one tooth fell out, another would move up to fill in the space. "We're all set. VIP treatment. My dad'll fix it."

"I don't know. If it were a night game..."

"How can you still believe in God with all we know about evolution? Charles Darwin? Survival of the fittest. The strongest, the smartest, the most aggressive."

"But didn't Darwin say that it's not the strongest or the smartest, but the most adaptable that survive?"

He leered at me. "The strongest and the smartest are the most adaptable."

"But there's no virtue in being the biggest, the strongest, the smartest. What about humility and compassion? There's virtue in being humble."

"The meek don't inherit the earth," he shook his head in disgust. "The meek only survive because the strong let them. Think about those weak saps back at school choking down turkey tetrazzini. All you need is a little initiative to get on in this world. Take this guy," he motioned toward the little man in the tall white hat flipping the sliced shrimp onto our plates. "Look how fast he is, how precise. He's the star. He's the only reason people come here. Survival of the fittest. The nice slow guy in the back is washing this guy's dishes. There's no virtue in that."

Chapter 29

Cullen took the check from the waitress, said, "Arigato," peeled a hundred off a wad of bills, and left it on the table for a $42 check.

We made it back with four minutes to spare. As we parted in the athletic wing, I turned to him, "Hey, Cullen, thanks a lot," I said. "That was fun. I'm glad you talked me into it."

"You needed this."

I did need that. I needed to know what it felt like to go after things I wanted, even things I didn't know I wanted. I could no longer surrender to tentativeness. I would try harder and attack more. I was going to will myself into success.

NW

Chapter 30

"I can get used to this," Quinton said as we stretched out on the soft black leather seats, consuming as much luxury of the long, white limousine as possible as it navigated through a maze of residential streets. "This is bigtime."

"You gonna be OK today?" Cullen turned me.

"What d'you mean?"

"You'll be able to contain yourself? You're not going to cream all over yourself when Piazza steps out of the dugout."

"Shut up, man."

"This must be a predominantly white neighborhood," Cullen observed as he stared out the window.

"Why d'ya say that?" Curtis straightened up.

Cullen pointed to a white rectangular sign that stated proudly: **DRUG FREE ZONE.**

"Yeah," Quinton agreed. "It is all white." He tapped his window at a yellow triangular sign warning: **SLOW CHILDREN.**

NEW JERSEY, THE SAFEST STATE greeted us in bright white letters as we pulled onto the Garden State Parkway.

The heat billowed off the pavement as our long, white car weaved around slower, smaller cars racing north at 80 miles per hour.

"Damn, we're cruisin'!" Quinton stared at the smaller cars choking on our fumes.

Jay turned to Cullen. "Who pays if this guy gets a ticket?"

"He should. He's the one that's doing something wrong," I argued.

"Speeding isn't wrong," Cullen said.

"Really? It's not wrong to go faster than the speed limit," I said sarcastically. "That's kinda the definition of 'speed' and 'limit.'"

"We have to speed."

"Where's that written?" Quinton asked. "Traffic code, 15.3-8, the said driver must, at all times, drive his or her said vehicle at a speed not less than fifteen miles per hour faster than the designated limit."

"If everyone obeyed the law, and went the speed limit, no one'd get anywhere," Cullen said.

"Speeding's like the leading cause of preventable death," I told him. "More lives are saved by slowing down, than like, you know, curing cancer."

"It doesn't work," Cullen shook his head. "We have to speed. Speeding makes our highways work. Back in the '70s, two guys in California drove up Route 1 side-by-side going exactly 55 miles an hour. It caused a traffic jam a hundred miles long. Speed limits are guidelines. Each driver decides his own limits."

A sharp, caustic odor stung our noses as we crested the Driscoll Bridge, and rolled down into north Jersey. The light gray smoke pumped out of the tops of large cement cylinders, and disappeared into the blue sky, leaving its invisible sulfuric gas to seep through the hidden cracks of our sealed car. Rows of enormous white oil silos rose up on both sides of the turnpike like a field of giant mushrooms.

With each passing mile, the verdant state dissolved into a murky gray, as the bright Big Apple blossomed in the distance.

"That's exactly why everyone busts on Jersey," Quinton tapped the glass at the gray pulsating factories, pumping black smoke into the blue sky. "That's all the world sees. They never see the beaches, the farms. There's a reason why it's called the Garden State."

"It's better this way," Jay said. "Then everyone would want to live here. New Jersey's like Iceland."

The silhouette of the Manhattan skyline pierced the blue sky to our right as we inched along on the final arm of the Turnpike.

"Next time, we'll take B.P. My dad'll set it all up," Cullen thought out loud.

"Yeah, I'm going yard in Babe's house," Quinton boasted.

"What about that, D.C.?" Cullen asked. Dorian simply nodded.

"You don't talk much, do you?"

"Don't know," Dorian shrugged.

"See there, all I get is monosyllabic answers," Cullen flipped his hands in frustration.

"'Don't know,'" Quinton corrected him, "is actually two syllables."

"You gotta watch out for the quiet ones," Cullen whispered loudly. "They're the ones that go postal. That's what they said about the Unabomber. 'He was quiet.' 'He was a loner.' They're practically reading your M-O, D.C."

Dorian looked up, "Just because I haven't talked to you much doesn't mean I don't talk to anyone."

"Ya gotta learn to open up. Enjoy life. Live on the edge. Have fun. That's the secret to life." Cullen flashed his toothy grin. "I enjoy every moment of my life."

The limousine rumbled over the George Washington Bridge and carved its way through the sweat soaked streets of Manhattan, along Harlem River Drive, and veered onto the ramp to the Bronx. We waited in traffic on the top of the ramp overlooking a small baseball diamond with a skin infield. Boys of different hues played vigorously in partial uniforms and ragged jeans, sprinting, diving, sliding, as if this anonymous game was the only important thing in the world.

As the limo rolled down the ramp, the cathedral stadium grew up out of the graying streets of the Bronx, dwarfing the decaying buildings of its home city, as if the high white stadium walls that rose up from the crumbling sidewalks, in fact, propped up the decrepit town and prevented it from imploding into an ashen heap.

We stepped out of the limo and the Bronx hit us in the face. The street was dirty, and the people worn out. A middle-aged man leaned up against a tree growing out of the sidewalk. A layer of filth was painted on every inch of his exposed skin. He wore a grayed and frayed Yankees cap with a tattered overcoat draped over his bony body. He stretched out his hand and his grimy fingers wriggled, begging me.

I reached into my pocket and grabbed a couple of loose bills.

"What are you doing?" Cullen slapped my forearm and pressed it against my hip.

"I'm just helping the man out."

"No, you're not," he said.

"It's just a couple of bucks."

"Just a couple bucks," the grimy man echoed.

"If he's scamming me, he's scamming me," I said. "I don't care. If I get ripped off 10 times, but help the eleventh one, I'm fine with that."

"Jake. It ain't about you," Cullen shook his head. "Never give money to beggars."

"That's cold blooded, man." Quinton laughed.

"Have a heart," I wrested my arm free and handed the man the bills.

"You have a heart. You ain't doing him no favors. The reason this man's on the street is because of big-hearted people like you. It's the same reason you don't feed your dog off the table. The man goes where the money is. You're paying this man to live on the street. You're subsidizing his poverty. If there's no money on this street, he wouldn't be on the street. He'd go get a job."

"Or he'd starve to death," Quinton said. "Six of one. Half dozen of... "

◆◆◆

The 80-foot Louisville Slugger with *George Herman "Babe" Ruth* scrawled on its barrel sprung forth from the dying ground, standing erect, like baseball's Washington Monument, casting a long shadow against the high walls of the vast building, waiting there, expecting two giant hands to reach down from the heavens, to raise it up one last time, and swing for the fences.

We walked through the deep blue fence and along the brick wall where the bold names and youthful faces of Babe Ruth, Mickey Mantle, Joe DiMaggio, were etched in bronze and enshrined, frozen in time forever. Only their spirits live on, woven in the aura of the stadium like the smell of rosin and tobacco, and they rise up out of the green with the steady beat of the game, giving those lost souls life, a chance to play again, to echo their deeds across this verdant field for eternity.

"His last season was '39," Dorian said as he ran his fingers over the raised letters of Lou Gehrig's name, "and he was dead in '41. Two thousand, one hundred and thirty games in a row, and was dead two years later, 16 years to the day after he replaced Wally Pipp."

"Who replaced Gehrig?" I asked.

"Babe Dahlgren," Dorian answered like it was common knowledge.

"Who would you rather be," I asked. "Wally Pipp or Babe Dahlgren?"

◆◆◆

We sat two rows behind the third base dugout. The field unfolded before us, its sharp lines and edges were carved into the green and orange, and its white lines stretched along the edges to meet the high blue walls. Above the blue, a speckled conglomeration of faces of every color melted together into a shadowy mosaic rising and falling with the ebb and flow of the game.

The hard lines of the diamond define the game, give it meaning, and are as unforgiving as they are immutable. Almost never counts in this stadium. You are either in or you're out. An inch is as wide as a mile within these walls.

"Unbelievable," Dorian said as he studied the Yankees' infield practice. "The ball looks like a marble in their hands. Third to first is nothing."

The coach hit a sharp ground ball to the right side. Chuck Knoblauch slid over, scooped and shoveled the ball with his glove toward second base where Derek Jeter intersected it as it hung over the bag, and in one seamless motion, fired it on a perfect line to Tino Martinez.

"Amazing." Dorian grasped the railing, staring out at the field with a wide-eyed smile. "Incredible," "tremendous," "unreal," passed through his lips as easily as the white ball passed through their gloves.

Cullen nudged me. "The All-American kid's happier than a punk at boy's camp."

A boy with a crisp Yankee hat and a stiff, shiny jacket sat two seats from us wearing a kid-sized leather baseball glove, and the starry-eyed fascination of his first big league stadium.

"Even if the ball was hit to him," Cullen asked loudly, "does he actually think he could make a play on it?"

"My dad brought his glove to every major league game he's ever been to and has never caught a ball," I said.

Good afternoon, ladies and gentlemen, and welcome to Yankee Stadium. Bob Sheppard's iconic voice rolled down from the rafters. *Attention. Please rise for the singing of our national anthem.*

We all rose to our feet and removed our caps, like we have been trained to do. I placed my right hand over my heart and stared intently at the flapping flag above center field. The voice started off low without the accompaniment of music. A middle-aged man stood next to the dugout with his chest out proudly, still wearing his Yankees cap.

"Look at that asshole with the hat on," a man sneered from behind me.

"Hey buddy, take the hat off!"

Oh, say, can you see, by the dawn's earl—

"Take the hat off," a voice called out toward the man in the hat.

What so proudly we—

"Show some respect, buddy!" a thick Bronx accent railed.
At the twilight's last gl—
"Hey, buddy take the hat off!"
Whose broad stripes and bright stars through the peri—
"Someone tell that guy to take the hat off."
O'er the ramparts—
"Take it off!"
...were so gallantly stream—
"Take the damn hat off!"
And the rockets' red—
"Hat's off, buddy."
The bombs bursting—
"Hey retard, you in the blue!"
Gave proof through the night that our flag—
"Show some respect."
O! say does that star-spangled ba-a-a—
"Hey, asshole, take the goddamn hat off!"
O'er the land of the freeeeeeeeee—
"Take the mother fuckin' hat off!"
and the home of the braaaaaave.
The man sat down and removed his hat.

◆◆◆

Two men sat down in front of us, a beer in one hand and a cigar in the other.

"Steinbrenner's a fuckin' idiot," the first one chomped his cigar. "He'll screw up a wet dream. His big move, trade for this Brosius guy."

"What about Strawberry?" asked the second, smoke streaming from his mouth.

"Another genius move. The guy hit .103 last year, and we break the bank on him. Stick a fork in his ass. All the talent in the world, too fucking lazy." He pressed the flame from his lighter to the end of his cigar.

"There's a six-year-old three feet away!" Dorian said loudly at the back of their heads.

The boy pounded his mitt with a closed fist, so intent on the icons on the field that he was oblivious to the idiots in front of him.

"It's a free country," Cullen told him. "This is the collateral damage of the First Amendment."

The Yankees burst out of their dugout and branched out across the field to their positions. "Best unis in baseball." Dorian's voice raced. "Look at the pinstripes. No team should have the names on their back." The game came to life in three full dimensions before my eyes. It was not the two-dimensional confluence of multi-chromatic flickering pixels on display in my living room every night. This game was real. The players human. The action close, tangible. I felt I could reach out and touch the players. I could feel the game, hear the ball hum through the air and crack against the bat, and feel its sting as it popped in the glove. My heart was pumping.

The game is a symphony of sweet, sharp sounds of purposeful action. Every action has an intent, every sound has a purpose. And woven into all those sounds is silence; slight moments of calm which provide a rhythm that shapes and defines the game as much as the sound.

◆◆◆

Mike Piazza's broad shoulders emerged from the dugout as he stepped onto the on-deck circle.

"Hey Piazza, you suck!" one of the men with the cigars blurted out.

Piazza slid two metal donuts onto his barrel and his powerful forearms swung the bat effortlessly in a circle above his head.

"Hey, Piazza how's your boyfriend?" the other man joined in.

Thick pads covered his aching knees as he stepped into the batter's box. His right spike scratched at the dirt, and he twisted on the ball of his foot. With his head down, he took a powerful swing, and then turned toward the pitcher, his eyes locked in on the ball. He carefully watched the first two pitches sail by, one strike and one ball. "Swing the bat, you faggot."

He swung hard at a change-up, and the ball bounded high in the air, and for a moment, it was coming right at me. I popped to my feet with great hope, that undeniable belief that your moment is at hand. But as quickly as it rose up, it faded, the ball petering out in front of the dugout, leaving me with an empty void of inadequacy to be quickly filled and emptied with the next fleeting glimmer of false hope.

"Relax," Cullen said, "you're embarrassing me. Stop trying to catch every foul ball. Act like you've been here before."

Piazza stepped out, knocked some dirt off his spikes and reset his feet.

Andy Pettitte reached his arm back and scorched a fast ball toward the outside edge of home plate. Piazza cocked his hands, strided toward the ball and uncoiled. His arms reached full extension at the moment of contact; a gunshot rang across the field as the ball whistled through the golden rays of sun and bounded on the soft green grass of the right field alley. Piazza rounded first and loped toward second like a newborn foal taking his first gallop.

"He runs like a queer," one of the cigar men said.

Piazza stopped gingerly at second base ahead of the throw.

"Fuckin' homo," his friend agreed.

Two innings later, Jeter stepped to the plate. He dug into the box, his piercing eyes looked in with a high purpose, following each pitch all the way into the catcher's mitt or onto his bat. The crack of the ball striking his bat snapped my head toward home plate. The ball caromed high off the dirt in front of the third base line and raced towards us. I could not gauge its speed or angle. The ball appeared still, hanging above me, simply getting bigger and bigger and bigger. My heart skipped when I realized it was coming right at me. A rush of sweaty humanity pressed against me and flooded my eyes with their hopeful hands. I hopped on top my seat and shot my hands up to meet the growing ball. My gaping fingers reached toward the sky. I could see the spinning red seams through the swarm of tentacle-like fingers. The moment the ball struck my outstretched hands, a distinct, purposeful jab in my back shocked my body forward.

The ball ricocheted off my hands and bounced into frenzied fingers snapping at it like a pack of snakes fighting over a mouse. My eyes followed the ball to the ground and the side of my face hit a cement step. The ball rolled away, and I clawed after it between and around trampling feet, down the aisle until I hit a wall. Dorian's broad shoulders. The shiny white ball rested in a small vacuum in front of him, motionless, as if it were resting in a glass container. A tiny hand reached down, grasped the ball, and pulled it to the NY emblem on his jacket. The boy then thrust the ball high in the air to a mixture of cheers and boos at his beaming face flashing on the center field screen.

"You let a little kid with a plastic glove take that ball from you," Cullen shook his head at me in disgust, as I sat on the cement aisle covered in beer-soaked popcorn and peanut shells, the tiny hand pounding the ball into the pocket of his glove, the boy grinning at his father.

◆◆◆

"Look, its Pepperoni Piazza again." He stepped into the on-deck circle the next inning, and lifted the bat over his head, swinging it in tight, fast circles.

"You're gonna need those knee pads when your boyfriend comes over tonight." The man proudly streamed smoke from his lips. Piazza tossed the two metal doughnuts to the side and walked to the plate. He stepped in the batter's box and dug in.   He took two quick strikes.

"Take a seat, pretty boy."

Piazza then watched two searing fastballs pop into the catcher's mitt inches outside the black. "Swing the bat, you homo!" He proceeded to slap a curve, a change-up and an outside fastball into the seats along the first base line. A cold, hard determination was chiseled on his face, his eyes skewered in on the pitcher as the ball whipped out of his hand, and screamed to the plate.

The ball struck his bat with a thunderous crack and shot into the outfield like a beam of light. Bernie Williams galloped to the right field alley, and Paul O'Neill glided back to the blue wall toward the shrinking sphere. The ball carried through the length of the blue sky and disappeared into the vast mosaic of the bleachers.

I watched Piazza proudly, like a father at a Little League game, as his frail knees carried him in a long, labored circle around the bases and across home plate. He looped around behind the catcher and trotted along the screen slapping fives as he approached the dugout. He was 10 feet from me. I could see the sweat rolling down the sides of his face. The stadium fell silent. Everything seemed to stop.

I stood up. "Way to go, Mike!" I called out to him.

He stopped, took a step back. His head snapped up and he looked above the edge of the dugout. His dark eyes screwed tight into mine. My heart stopped. I froze in anticipation. He leaned towards me. "Fuck you!" he barked and ducked into the dugout.

◆◆◆

The game continued with a steady cycle of foaming beer pouring into the two men's mouths and vulgarity spewing from their lips.

"Purchasing a ticket," Dorian said, "does not buy the unalienable right to demoralize any player."

"They're drunk," Cullen said to Dorian. "They don't know what they're doing. Let it go."

"Drunk is no excuse."

"Who's this Brosius guy?" one of the men scoffed as the third baseman struck out. "He'll never do anything for this team."

"That Knoblauch," Quinton chided in an exaggerated voice as the player dug in for the pitch. "A pure professional. Heart and soul of the Yankees."

"Knoblauch, you suck!" the second man screamed, after Knoblauch popped up to short.

The first man stood and cupped his hands along the sides of his mouth. "Hey, Chuckie, I got some career advice for ya." He waited. "Fuckin' retire."

Dorian leaned forward toward the two men. "Excuse me," I heard him say in an overly polite voice. "Can you do me a favor?"

"What do you want, Junior?" the fat man on the right bristled.

"Grab a bat and stand in the batter's box, and try to hit just one pitch, just one." Dorian held up his left index finger in the man's face. "Please reserve your judgments until you can do that one simple thing."

"Maybe, Junior," the man stood up, "I'll take that bat and crack you in the head with it."

Dorian stood eye-to-eye with him and smiled.

The other man stepped toward Dorian. "Just sit down, Sonny, before you get hurt."

Dorian stood his ground.

The man sprung at him, and in one quick snap, Dorian shot his hand out toward the lunging man, snatched the base of his Adam's apple, and squeezed it between his thumb and his forefinger. The man gasped silently. "If you even breathe," Dorian said coolly applying pressure to the man's esophagus, "I will rip your throat out."

The man stood paralyzed, his stiff body hanging from his Adam's apple. A painful breath squeezed out of his mouth. His friend stood next to him, paralyzed by fear. "Let him go."

Dorian carefully pressed his fingers together and the man gagged for air. "You have two choices. Sit and talk quietly, or leave."

The two men sat down without another word, and we enjoyed a Yankee 5-4 victory.

NW

Chapter 31

"He can't hit his way out of a wet paper bag," an unknown voice from the stands summed up my season as I walked to the plate. The eighth game of the season, in the midst of an 0-for-10 slump, I finally managed to connect with the ball, but just as hope sprung up inside me, it was quashed by the leather glove of the third baseman who snared the line drive in his webbing.

"Put that down as a hit," Delaney ordered as I walked into the dugout.

Fulbright looked up. "But coach, the third baseman caught it."

"Put it down as a hit," he demanded. "He couldn't have hit it any better."

That was the problem. I couldn't have. But I didn't need his charity. It just made everything worse. Letting me win, like they did in Cap League. Everyone gets a trophy, everyone's a winner. Pretending I'm better than I am. I was on the verge of giving up, acknowledging what I long feared: I'm not good enough. It was like I was on a cliff holding on for my life. And I realized that the pain of hanging on was worse than the pain of letting go.

"I can't catch a break, coach," I told Delaney. "The ball just doesn't bounce my way. It isn't fair."

"Too many bloopers fall in for hits to feel cheated when our line drives get caught," he said.

I was the only player on the team who failed to hit safely against last-place Farley, so Delaney left me in at right field with a nine-run lead to try to pry me out of my slump.

The pitcher kicked his leg and tossed two straight pitches that I just watched float in for strikes. His next pitch started in flat and down the middle. It came in so slow that I could almost count every stitch on the spinning ball. I froze. My mind locked as I watched the ball split the center of the plate. It passed so slowly, I could have reached out and caught it with my bare hand. I stood paralyzed, locked in my batting stance.

The ump looked at me, almost disappointed, and solemnly called strike three. I fired my bat at the backstop, and the field fell silent as the aluminum rattled down the length of the chain link fence.

Dorian flipped me my glove, and I loudly tore open the Velcro straps of my batting gloves as I strolled toward right field frustrated.

"Thirty-one! Thirty-one!" A voice bellowed from our bench. I continued walking to the outfield with my head down. "Thirty-one!" I stopped at the edge of the grass.

"Get over here!" Delaney waved at me furiously. I didn't move. "Get over here!"

I walked directly to our dugout, my head down and away from the disapproving leers behind the fence. Delaney stood on the lip of the dugout, his eyes locked on me. My walk turned into a half-hearted jog.

"What the hell are you doing? You're walking around here like it's the Champs-Elysees," his voice boomed across the valley of fields. "You're embarrassing yourself; you're embarrassing the team. There's only one way to play. Sprint out to the outfield like a real ballplayer."

I turned to run.

"No," he grabbed my jersey. "Do it the right way." And slung me toward the bench.

The entire field was silent, staring at me. Even the Farley players stopped and watched. I sat back down on the bench and waited for a satisfactory moment. "Run!" he barked. I jumped up off the bench and sprinted to the outfield.

◆◆◆

"It's easy to trust the guy who never screws up." Delaney paced in front of us after the victory. "We all love the teammate who bats .400, never makes an error, gets the game winning hit. The true test is to trust the guy who doesn't always get the key hit, who doesn't always get the bunt down, who doesn't always hustle." All eyes were on him, but I felt the corners of each eye on me. "We must trust each other, even the guys who don't deserve it. Trust is never earned, it's always given. It is only when we give each other our trust that we become deserving of it."

◆◆◆

I sat in the back seat pretending to fix a broken lace on my mitt, and I could feel my dad's eyes studying me in the rearview mirror. "With great hitters," he started dramatically, "when they put their bat in the bat rack, you can't tell if they just struck out or hit a home run."

I nodded quickly to stop the lecture. I knew Dad wanted for me what he had failed to achieve. He spent a decade of his life riding on buses from one one-stoplight-town to the next chasing a fantasy, believing that connecting enough of those dots on the map would eventually draw the picture of his dream. But, the towns in which he plied his trade were, like himself, not quite big enough, fast enough, or refined enough for the big leagues, so I was his last hope to fulfill his life's pursuit.

As his hands pulled the wheel through the turn, I noticed we have the same right thumbs. The tips curled up at a 90-degree angle, and the bottom joint is double the size of the left thumb. Both of our right thumbs are identical except that he broke his in the minors. Somehow, I inherited my father's broken right thumb, along with his failed dreams.

As we drove, my thoughts unfolded like the road before me; a mixture of hate, envy, and fear boiled inside me as I thought about my life, maybe I was just kidding myself, maybe I was searching for a meaning that doesn't exist, striving for an excellence that I will never achieve, looking for a significance where there is none.

"I played for 11 teams in nine years," my father said. "I was cut a half-dozen times, traded in the middle of a doubleheader. I went anywhere they wanted me to play." He told me his story again and again, trying to convince me, or himself, that there was something heroic about a decade chasing something that remains forever beyond his grasp.

"But you never got to the majors," I reminded him.

"No, but there were times when I picked a guy off first, or lined a double off some bonus baby, and for that moment, I was as good as anyone in the world, I was a major leaguer."

"Why weren't you ever called up?" I asked him bluntly.

"I wasn't good enough." He looked out the side window.

"But you just said there were moments."

"Those moments were too few and far between. I reached for the stars, Jake, and failed. I have no regrets. I'd rather fail at excellence than succeed at mediocrity."

"Why didn't you just give up after a few years?"

"It's hard to give up your dream," he said wistfully.

"But all that time and never making it, is a waste."

He ran his fingers through his wavy hair. "Some dreams are so great they're worthy even if you fail. When I had my dream, there was always a part of my life that was perfect. I used to close my eyes and visualize my dream, and see what life could be, what it should be, perfect. My dreams were real because I pursued them. It was a great 10 years. Not because I achieved my dream, but because I had my dream. It wasn't a waste; dreams make this all worthwhile. When I put my mitt away, my dream died, and I don't know what perfection is, anymore."

"You must hate us," I said without thinking.

"I love you so much, I'd give up perfection for you." He slowed the car down. "My dreams are gone. I can handle that. What bothers me, what hurts the most, is that when I look at you, I don't see a dream inside of you."

"So, if I become a major leaguer, your life will be worthwhile again?" I asked sharply. "I'm not good enough to play in the majors, Dad."

"That was my dream. If you follow someone else's dream, you will fail. If you follow your own dreams, you'll succeed more than you could ever imagine. But if you have no dreams, you'll be nothing."

"I have my dreams," I told him. "There are things I want to be. Goals I want to reach. Standards I want to live up to."

The car lurched to a stop in our driveway, and before I could get out, he looked at me in the rearview mirror and said, "Good. I hope so. It takes courage to have dreams."

I nodded, slammed the door, and walked inside.

NW

Chapter 32

"You're afraid." Delaney pointed his decrepit finger at me before the next game.

"I'm not afraid of nothing."

"You're afraid to hit."

"No, I'm not," I said. "I'm swinging at everything."

"You're so scared of striking out that you hit the first pitch you see, his pitch," he said. "Never settle for anything less than your pitch, not even with two strikes. Success always courts failure."

"I'm being aggressive to get out of my slump. The more balls I put in play the more chance one will fall in."

"You're aggressive because you don't know the strike zone."

"I know the…"

"Not just balls and strikes, but which strikes you can handle and which ones you can't. Look at Clayborne." He pointed at Cullen hitting soft toss.

"I can't hit like him."

"Good, 'cause you're better than him."

I laughed. "He has 10 home runs already."

Delaney stared right into my pupils. "He doesn't know his strike zone. He doesn't care. He swings at balls out of the zone all the time."

"He swings at bad pitches because he wants to hit their mistakes," I said.

He shook his head. "You can't get to heaven on the sins of others."

"It works," I said.

"Yeah, just enough to keep him swinging at bad pitches — pitches he can't hit consistently. He's tempted too easily. The lure of easy success gives the pitcher his out pitch."

"How do I know what's a good pitch and what's a bad pitch?"

"Wait. I'd rather strike out waiting for my pitch than ground out swinging at his. Wait, and let it happen."

◆◆◆

"Get in." Cullen's car screeched to a stop next to me as I waited in front of the school after another oh-for-three game. He kicked the passenger's door open. I climbed in, and we pulled way.

Curtis was standing alone, waiting for a bus with his gym bag slung over his shoulder. Cullen rolled up next to him, "Ya need a ride?"

Curtis opened the door. "You sure you want to do this?"

"Buckle up," I warned.

We raced up the school's undulating driveway, slicing through the darkening woods, and pulled out onto the main road. With each turn through the streets toward Curtis' home, the houses became less bright, the landscaping less colorful, and the streets in need of more repair.

"You know who lives around here?" I remembered from the turkey drive. "Stevonne...uhm..."

"Simpson?" Curtis said.

"Yeah," I nodded. "I played Little League against him."

"You know what happened, right?" he said.

"No." My stomach tightened up. "What?"

"I guess it wasn't big enough news for the white papers."

"What wasn't?"

"Last summer, his dad," Curtis said, his voice mixed with intrigue and sadness, "came home one Sunday morning and shot Stevie, his sisters, and then their mom," Curtis put his index finger to his temple and crooked his thumb. "While they were sleeping. They found his pops a couple weeks later in Kentucky living in his car."

"Why?" was the only word I could manage.

"Life sucks," he shrugged. "Maybe his old man probably finally figured that out."

"He was a good pitcher."

"He was a good dude," Curtis nodded. "Stevie was my dog. His little sister, Traynice, used to play with my sister all the time. It's a damn shame. I never figured Stevie's pops would do something like that. He wasn't a bad dude. He was just like everyone else."

"Not like my dad," Cullen objected. "My father would never do anything like that."

We drove on for a few miles in silence.

"Things like that happen a lot around here?" I asked.

"They happen everywhere. You think white dudes don't do crazy shit?"

"I don't know. I don't see skin color," I said.

"Everyone sees skin color."

"I didn't mean I don't see skin color," I said. "I just see skin color the way I see hair color or eye color. It's there, but it doesn't mean anything."

"That's an insult, Jake. That's easy to say for a white dude," Curtis said, and then pointed to a drug store on the corner. "You can just let me out here."

"You don't have to get out," I said. "I didn't mean anything by that."

"Yeah, we can take you home," Cullen told him.

"I know. It's not that. It's just that you can drive into my neighborhood," Curtis said, pulling on the door handle, "but it's 50-50 you're driving out."

"If it's that rough, why don't you just move?" I asked.

"Move?" He sneered. "Where?"

"Anywhere, other than here. At least try," Cullen said.

"Try? Why d'you think I'm at Bainbridge? Why does my ma work two jobs? We're trying our asses off."

We dropped him off at the corner, and he walked down the street with his gym bag hanging from his left hand and his blazer slung over his right shoulder. He stepped out of the car a Bainbridge student, but with each step he took, he blended into the background of his neighborhood, until he looked just as natural walking those cracked cement streets as he does walking the bright carpeted halls.

Cullen wrenched the wheel to the left and punched the accelerator. The car leapt out across two lanes and the double yellow lines, in a perfect arc, and into the oncoming lanes in front of squealing brakes and booming horns, and fit snugly between two sedans at full speed.

"What the hell was that?"

"Relax," he said. "They got brakes."

"Yeah, I heard them."

"It's called living on the edge."

"More like dying on the edge," I said.

"Jesus Christ!" Cullen shouted. "When are you going to stop being such a pussy?"

"If you want to live on the edge that's your business, just don't bring me along."

Cullen pulled over. "Fine, take the wheel," he said, flinging open his door, "if you're such a goddamn expert." He walked around the car. "It's like driving with a chick."

I pressed the small, thin accelerator and the car jumped forward. It practically drove itself. Everything in the car worked too easily, too well. The pedals and the steering wheel were overly sensitive, and the car slid left and right, but it always seemed to right itself without me doing anything.

We roared down the highway, flying past the other cars effortlessly. The power, the speed was intoxicating. I felt I could do anything.

"So what's going on with that Dawn girl?"

"I don't know," I shrugged. "I'm thinking of asking her out."

"Thinking? Strap on a set of nuts, go over to her house right now, and ask her out."

"I don't know."

"What's there to know? I've never known a girl who didn't want to be asked out."

"OK, OK. I will," I told him. "Just not now."

"If not now, when?"

"I'm working on it."

"Working on it ain't getting it done. Let's go."

I gunned the engine and drove aggressively down the back roads towards her house and screeched to a stop at a red light hovering over an empty intersection. The bright white lines stretched out into the black nothingness. The purring engine was the only sound on the vacant street. We waited and waited and waited, our lives suspended by a red light glaring down at us with disdain.

"You'd think they'd change the timer at night," I said.

"Just blow it off." His white knuckles squeezed the armrest.

"I can't."

"It's broken, just go."

"I don't want to break the law," I said.

"Fuck the law. There are no cops around." He looked over his shoulder. "It's only wrong if you get caught." He pressed his left hand down on my right knee.

"Stop."

"We're not waiting all night, staring at a red light like a couple of idiots."

"Jump out and hit the walk button," I told him.

He didn't move. "Then I'll do it," I reached for the door handle.

He jammed his left foot on the accelerator. The car shot out into the intersection as the red light turned green.

"If we would have just waited two more seconds."

"I'd never get those two seconds back. Two seconds can change your life."

I finally pulled up to the sidewalk next to Dawn's house. I took a deep breath and waited. My right leg started to shake.

"C'mon, let's go," he prodded.

"I don't know."

"If you don't get your ass up to that door, you're walkin' home." I froze.

"Grow a sack," he said. "This is about more than a date with some chick."

I got out of the car slowly and looked back at him as I shut the door. I walked up the path to her front door.

"Yes," her mother peered through the chained door.

"Is Dawn here?"

"Isn't it a little late to be calling on someone?" Her eyes studied my face.

"I guess," I shrugged. "I just need to ask her something."

She shut the door and walked away. I was about to leave when the door cracked open, and Dawn's eyes appeared in the sliver opening.

"Oh, it's you." A faint smile crossed her lips. "What do you want?"

I smiled and held up both hands balled into fists, and raised my index finger as I said, "Do," and raised one finger for each successive word: "you-want-to-go-out-Saturday-night" until I was holding eight fingers in front of her.

She held up her right fist. "Yes," as she raised her index finger. She smiled and closed the door.

NW

Chapter 33

"His curve is acute but his fastball's obtuse," Fulbright said as he walked into the dugout before the next game. "His repertoire is fraught with problematic obstacles. Extremely treacherous."

We were 10-0 in the month of April, when our toughest challenge stepped on the mound. His six-foot-six-inch frame perched atop of the 18-inch mound made him appear eight feet tall. He reached his hands high above his head, almost touching heaven, as his tattered shirt sleeves, extra-long glove strings, and bouncy black hair flailed distractingly.

Each movement, the arch of his back, the turn of his shoulder, his high leg kick, were necessary parts of a series of movements designed to put his arm in the optimal position to hurl the ball visciously at me.

The ball flicked out of his hand like a Frisbee and flew to a point six inches outside the plate. I held my bat firm on my shoulder as the ball tailed back in crossing the black for strike one. His next pitch zoomed straight down the middle, and I snapped my bat at the ball, just as it faded and faded outside the plate, and bounced into the catcher's mitt as I waved my bat at the air for strike two. His third pitch jumped out of his hand and flew right at my ear close enough to hit me. My knees buckled, just as the sideways spinning ball cut sharply down, and popped in the catcher's mitt for strike three.

Cullen walked by me on my way back to the dugout. "What's he got?

"Everything," I said. "He's got everything."

"Hitting him is tougher than Chinese arithmetic," Delaney said as I sat on the bench.

My next two at-bats, I flailed vainly at the slithery serpent as it dipped and dove and slid in all directions a millisecond after it splintered in an unreachable path across the plate.

"What do you do when you're facing a power pitcher?" Cullen grabbed me after my third strikeout.

"Move back in the box."

"Exactly. What is this guy?"

"A junk-baller," I told him. "Curves, sliders, change-ups..."

"Use your brain," he tapped his temple. "Move up in the box. Hit the ball before it breaks. Turn every pitch into a fastball. Squeeze the hell out of him, give his junk only 55 feet to work. Attack him. Put him on his heels."

My fourth at-bat, I placed my left foot on the front line of the box. The first pitch started low, straight and hard, and by the time I realized it was a fastball, I only had enough time to weakly offer my bat at the ball before it snapped in for strike one. I then half swung at a curveball in the dirt, and a slider a foot out of the zone, for my fourth strikeout of the game.

As I meekly walked back to the dugout, an anonymous voice rang out, "That's seven runners he's left on." I looked up to find the voice, but it didn't really matter. How can I blame someone for speaking the truth? I snapped on my catcher's gear at the end of the inning and picked up my mitt. On the inside thumb in red small capital letters, was written:

OLD CHINESE SAYING:
FALL DOWN SEVEN TIMES GET UP EIGHT.

We were down by two going into the last inning. I was due up sixth.

"Look for the dot on the ball." Dorian's right forefinger drew a small circle in the air. "The last three at-bats, he got you out on sliders. If he gets two strikes on you again, he's going to back to it."

"I know, I know."

"If the spin is away from you, it's a fastball. To you," his fingers twirled forward. "It's a curve, but if you see a dot on the ball, it's the slider."

"I know," I said, "but I can't think about all that in a split second."

I walked over to Delaney. "If my turn comes up, you should pinch hit for me," I told him.

"Why would I do a foolish thing like that?"

"'Cause I can't hit this guy."

"Whether you think you can or think you can't, you're right," he said. "Now, grab a goddamn bat."

There were two outs and two on when I stepped into the on-deck circle. I was hoping Curtis either homered or struck out, and I cringed when the ball popped into the catcher's mitt and the ump awarded him first. Every eye at the field was locked in on me.

I stood frozen in the on-deck circle. "What if I strike out? What if I look like a fool? What if I lose the game for the team?" Self-doubt flooded my psyche as I meandered to the plate.

Dorian grabbed me. "Don't think," his eyes riveted into mine, "just see the ball."

"Why don't they pinch hit for him?" I heard a voice whisper as I stepped into the box.

I tapped the sides of my cleats with my bat, adjusted my batting gloves and rearranged the dirt in the box – delaying the inevitable, thinking, "There's no way I'll ever hit this guy."

His first two pitches, a ball up and in, and a strike on the outside corner, I just watched sail by with no intention of swinging. I couldn't tell which pitch was a strike and which one was a ball without the umpire's call. I stepped out of the box, leaned back and stared up at the blue sky. There wasn't a cloud up there. The blue was so deep I felt I was staring into forever. And then, my mind emptied, all the clutter cleared away — sucked into the vacuum of eternity.

I looked back at the pitcher, the only thing I saw was the ball. I didn't see his distractions. The crowd, the umpires, the fielders faded away — all I saw was the ball. I could see it turning mechanically through his fingers inside his glove. I followed it through his motion and picked it up at his release point. The red dot in the center of the ball drilled down at me. The next thing I saw was the ball growing smaller and smaller into the deep blue as I drifted down the baseline. When my foot hit the bag, the ball ricocheted off the left-center wall, and I sprinted toward second base. The center fielder gathered up the ball and threw it in a long arc toward the infield. My right foot bounced off second base and propelled me toward third. I slid into the base ahead of the cut-off throw. As I stood up, Jay lassoed my neck, and pulled me to the ground. Dorian and Quinton sprinted toward me, and then every member of the team leapt on top of me, smothering me in the grass.

"How does it feel, Jakie? How does it feel?" Delaney thrust his arm around my shoulders after the mob dispersed.

"I don't know," I shrugged.

"You don't know?" He pulled me close. "Enjoy this. Savor it. You won't get many of 'em."

"I just... That hit was luck," I confessed to him. "It surprised me."

"Everyone's surprised when they get a hit," he patted my back. "But the good ones are just as surprised when they make an out."

◆◆◆

"I feel kinda weird, you know, coach giving me the game ball, everyone slapping me five," I admitted to Dorian as we walked to his car.

"That's the burden of being the man," he said, tossing his bag in the trunk. "You deserve it, you won the game."

"I struck out four times. Left seven runners on base. I almost lost the game."

"But we won."

"It was a lucky hit," I confessed.

"Lucky?" He climbed into the driver's seat. "There are no lucky triples."

"But I didn't do anything. I don't even remember swinging."

"Because you didn't swing," he pointed at me. "You did."

"What is that supposed to mean?"

"I think you know."

We drove on in silence. I didn't know. My mind was churning. Finally, as we were pulling down his street, I looked at him. "How do you hit like you do?"

"I treat each at-bat like it's my first." He thought for a moment. "And my last."

As we pulled into his driveway and got out of the car, a pink flash scampered across our beaming headlights like a small, scared animal, and embedded herself into Dorian's hip, clinging tightly. The screen door banged, and the silhouette of a hunched angular woman stood on the porch, "'Bout goddamn time," bellowed from the dark porch swarming with mosquitoes. "You come and go as you please? You think this house revolves around you?"

He stared right at his mother and ran his fingers through his sister's hair.

"Answer me! Where the hell have you been?"

Dorian just stood there staring at her in silence.

"We had a game," I finally said.

"A game? I'm getting sick and tired of this goddamn baseball. I'm gonna call that school and tell 'em you're not playing."

"You can't," I said.

"Why the hell not?" she snarled. "I'm still his mother."

"He's on scholarship. He's gotta play."

"You stay the hell out of this," she snapped. "This is none of your damn business. He can go to public school."

"He can't..." I caught myself in mid-sentence.

"What's wrong with the public school? Is he too good for public school? I went to public school. Your old man went to public school."

"It would be a waste if he left."

"He needs to do something useful in his life. Get a job. Start pulling his weight around here, not playing a goddamn game."

The headlights flashed across the front of the house blinding us, and the car skidded to a stop at our feet.

"Hey guys, how did it go? How'd you do against that big gorilla?" My father leaned out the window, smiling. "You get one hit off of him and you're way ahead of the game."

"Hello, Jack." The cold voice floated down from the porch.

"Hey, how you doing, Tina?" my father brimmed with unfounded enthusiasm. "The kids are having a great season, aren't they?"

She stood silent and still.

"Baseball's a wonderful game. There's nothing like it," he rambled on. "It's so good for the kids. It teaches them so much. It keeps them out of trouble. It gives th—"

The screen door slammed behind her.

"Hang in there, man," I whispered in his ear. "Thirteen months, and you're out of here. You'll be playing pro ball somewhere. You'll never have to spend another night under that roof again."

"I won't." He petted his sister's head. "But she will."

◆◆◆

My father and I drove home. He didn't say a word about Dorian's situation, but then turned to me. "You know the difference between the guy that makes it and the guy that doesn't?" He looked at me like I should know.

I shrugged.

"The fourth at-bat."

"The fourth at-bat?"

"Yes, both guys will go oh-for-three, or three-for-three, but what you do with your fourth at-bat is what defines you. The guy who makes it can't wait for his fourth at-bat, and the guy who doesn't is either too scared or too satisfied."

"Which one were you?" I asked, the words barely leaving my mouth before I regretted them.

He didn't respond, other than to say, "Never give away an at-bat, Jake. Never."

NW

Chapter 34

Everything's luck, I concluded. How could I go from striking out four times to hitting a triple, if not by accident? Hitting a round ball with a round bat could not be anything but luck.

I replayed that last hit over and over in my head, reliving that feeling, trying to ingrain that sensation into my nervous system so I could reproduce it whenever I needed it. But when I stepped back into the cage the next day, I was back to my old self, nothing had changed; the same pop-ups, the same weak grounders.

As April came to a close and my season creeped by, my goals were slipping away. I knew the lack of extra batting practice was hurting me. I needed the extra work. But I couldn't go back to my father. I wasn't afraid to ask; I was afraid of his answer.

"Help me," I pleaded in a loud whisper.

Delaney nodded. "Stay after practice tonight," he said, and walked away.

◆◆◆

When the field was empty, he sat me down in the aluminum bleachers and looked out into the field.

"Baseball players are flawed," he slowly turned to me. "If you want to be a great hitter, you must accept that you will fail and fail often."

"I don't want to accept failure," I said. "I want to be great."

"More people go to Hell for trusting in their own goodness," he pointed at me, "then succumbing to their own badness."

I was already regretting this. "Aren't we gonna do some drills, or something?" I stood up, but he placed his bat against my chest and pressed me back down.

"Patience. The first thing you learn is the hardest thing to change. So, we must begin the right way." He lifted the bat and took a long methodical swing. "Hitting is not simply a physical act."

"I know, I know. It's mental."

He shook his head. "It's a state of being."

"I don't need a philosophy lesson," I told him. "Mickey Mantle said, 'You can't think and hit at the same time.'"

"Exactly," he nodded. "You're thinking right, when you're not thinking."

"That doesn't make any sense."

"Do you know the difference between a line drive and a pop-up?" he asked.

I shrugged.

He held up his right hand pressing his thumb and forefinger together. "A millimeter, one millimeter."

"Then it's all luck," I muttered. "One millimeter is so arbitrary."

"No," he shook his head. "Great hitters control that millimeter."

We climbed down off the bleachers and walked over to the batting cage. "Let's start at ground zero. Pick a stance and stick with it." He slipped into a stereotypical batting stance. "You change your stance every game, every at-bat. Why'd you open your stance last game?"

I dug in next to the tee. "I figured if I opened my stance and moved closer to the plate, I could hit the inside pitch and still cover the outside corner."

"Whichever way the wind blows," he shook his head, "the grass leans." He placed a ball on the tee in front of me.

"Why don't you just pitch me some balls? Tees are for five-year-olds."

"Tees teach you how to hit the ball properly... from every location. They close all the holes in your swing."

He pointed to the tee. "Hit the ball," he said.

I took a stride and threw the barrel of my bat at the ball. A hollow "ting" sounded, and the ball nosedived into the dirt. He casually placed another ball on the tee. "Again." I swung harder and produced the same result, "again," and "again," and "again."

After each mishit, he simply replaced a ball on the tee, and watched me swing. The balls shot in every conceivable direction, and I could feel his eyes watching my swing, noticing every glitch, every misplaced movement, every flaw, without a word.

"Why do I have to do this?" I asked as the sweat rolled down my forearms, soaking my batting gloves. "I'm practicing for practice?"

"Just keep hitting."

"Can't you tell me what I'm doing wrong, something, anything," I begged him between swings.

"If you hit off the tees enough," he said quietly, "the picture of how to hit will appear in your mind's eye much clearer than any words

I could come up with."

We hit this way for an hour, hundreds of swings, striking a ball into the green net. And just as the top edge of the sun disappeared behind the trees, he calmly said, "That'll do." And walked away.

♦♦♦

Dawn and I walked down the boardwalk that first night beneath the neon lights of dingy arcades and the foggy glow of greasy hamburger shops. I stared out over the flowing waves at the surfers grabbing one final ride before sunset, gliding in on the low moon beams as their white boards cleaved the glassy black water.

"I can't believe it's been almost three years since our dance," she said. "It feels like such a waste."

"I took this movie class at Bainbridge, once," I told her. "Blow-off. They showed these avant-garde movies. None of 'em made any sense. So anyway, for our final, we had to watch this whole movie on a Saturday, six hours long. The entire movie was just a single shot of the Empire State Building." I could feel my voice filling up the dark night air. "Am I talking too much?"

"No, no, you're great," she leaned into me as we walked.

"Anyway, the same shot, same camera angle, same everything, for six straight hours. Guys came in and out. Quinton brought in a pizza, but I stayed the whole time. And then, after about five hours, a light on about the fiftieth floor snapped on. The whole place went nuts. Yelling, screaming. It was the greatest thing I've ever seen at a movie. That one light made the whole five hours worth it."

"And...?" her eyes twinkled in anticipation.

"You're that light."

She squeezed my hand tight.

"I don't know why I told you that. I think I was just trying to make you think I'm smart."

"On our next date, you can solve some calculus problems for me," she smiled, and looked at me through the tuft of hair that cut across her right eye. "You don't have to try that hard."

"Today's special is the Pepperoni Deluxe," the short, round waitress said gleefully, her white smile creasing her red lips. "A large deluxe for the price of a small." Like her broad face, her ripe voice was ready to burst into laughter with each sentence she spoke.

"Do you want pepperoni?" I looked at Dawn hoping she did not.

She studied me nervously. "Do you want pepperoni?"

"Yeah, sure," I lied.

"OK, that'd be fine," she quietly stared down at her plate.

We sat there, silent, occasionally catching a glimpse of each other and smiling. I glanced down at my watch nervously.

"You have another date?" she asked.

"No."

"Why do you keep looking at your watch then?"

"I'm trying to see how long I can go without noticing how beautiful you are."

"Yeah, right," she smiled. "I'm sure you use that on all the girls."

I shook my head. "Just the pretty ones."

The waitress set the pizza down and served us each a slice without asking.

I studied my slice trying to figure out how to extract all five slices of singed pepperoni, unnoticed. "I bet you're beating the guys away with a stick."

"They keep their distance whether I have a stick or not." She picked at her pepperoni with the tip her fingernail. "You and girls?"

"Don't have much time for girls," I tugged at the edge of the crispy disk with the tip of my fork. "I spend most of time on baseball."

"Baseball?"

"Don't you like baseball?"

"Sure, why?"

"Most people either love it or hate it." My fork pried two slices off the crust. "Which one are you?"

"Both," she replied.

"You hate it but pretend to like it because you think it's un-American not to."

"No, it's too political."

"Baseball's not political."

"It was for me," she said.

"You think the D.H. is communist?"

"What's the D.H.?" she asked.

"Why is it political?"

"I played baseball when I was 10," she said with subdued pride. "With the boys. My mom sued the town of Long Beach. I played the whole season. The summer of '92."

"That was you?"

She nodded. "My mom made me play. It was horrible. Everyone was always yelling for me or at me. I divided the whole town."

"What did you hit?" I pulled two more disks of pepperoni off of the melted mozzarella, and set them on the plate.

"I really don't remember. Too much pressure. Every time I batted, I wasn't just trying to hit the ball. I was proving some point. I hated it. I just wanted to go to the beach in the summer."

"Why didn't you quit?"

"One time, I hit a single, and when I was standing on first, I saw the mother of the pitcher in the stands cheering for me. The whole thing didn't make sense."

We ate in silence, each furtively examining the other. There was something alluring about the way she took delicate bites and gently chewed.

"You're amazing," I said.

She closed her eyes and turned away.

I quickly peeled the remaining three pieces of pepperoni from the melted cheese and hid them beneath my napkin. She turned back to me, reached down with her bright red fingernail and pried the remaining four pepperoni slices off her pizza. "I don't like pepperoni either," she reached over and put her hands in mine.

"Thanks for the effort, but next time, honesty is the best policy."

"Next time?" I smiled at her, and she nodded.

NW

Chapter 35

"A free society is not free." Fulbright looked down at the class. "We must have laws. We must restrict freedom to protect freedom." His voice became sterner. "Can anyone give me an example?"

"Killing?" Jay shouted.

"Murder!" Fulbright pointed sharply at him. "Murder's good. Every point of law is the determination of rights. What are the two rights involved in murder?"

"The right to life?" I said.

"Exactly," he pointed at me. "And the opposing right?"

"The right to kill," Cullen said.

"Precisely. The right to kill versus the right not to be killed. Which one prevails?"

"The right not to be killed," the class agreed in unison.

"What do we do when someone kills someone?" he asked.

"Throw 'em in jail."

"If I'm president," Cullen said as he rose up, "every murderer on death row? Dead. Like in the old days. You're found guilty on Tuesday, you're swinging from a tree on Wednesday. Do ya think there would be any more murders after that?" He looked around for approval. "We waste 90 G a year keeping just one of those idiots alive."

"Don't those idiots have rights, also," Fulbright started to say, "or more precisely, don't we have an obligation to give those idiots, their souls, a chance for redemption?"

"They have no souls!" Derek Cox shouted.

"What about the guys who didn't…" I started to say.

"If you're innocent," Cullen cut me off, "I know, set a hundred guilty people free to save one innocent …da da da da da…. Dead! The innocent just gotta take it for the cause."

"How can you decide to execute someone if you don't care if they have a soul? Dorian asked.

"Great question," Fulbright jumped in. "Never give a sword to a man who can't dance."

"That's Confucius," Jay said.

"That's confusing," Quinton quipped.

Fulbright turned to the other side of the room. "What's another issue where two rights conflict, that boys your age may confront?"

"Abortion," someone called out.

"Abortion's wrong." The words shot out of my mouth instinctively.

"Why do you say that?" Fulbright asked me.

"I'm Catholic, that's what we're taught."

"That's not good enough, Jake. If you don't know why you hold a belief, you have no claim to it."

"It's killing. Killing's wrong." Emotions boiled up inside of me. "I'm against killing, the death penalty and abortion, we should protect all life."

"Doesn't the mother have a right to decide if she wants to be a parent?" He looked at me directly. "Shouldn't she have control over her own body?"

"The right to life is stronger than the right not to have a baby." My words bounced off the quiet walls.

"The mother's a citizen, protected by the constitution," Wally offered. "The baby has no rights. It's not even human. It's just a blob of cells."

"You're just a blob of cells!" I snapped. "How can she be a mother if it's not a baby? You're OK with abortion, Wally, because you are already born."

Fulbright massaged his chin, letting the silence become thick. "Some believe life starts at birth…"

"Life starts at conception," I blurted.

Fulbright lifted his hand at me. "And some people believe life starts at conception."

I looked to Dorian. He just sat there in the back of the room, quiet, disinterested.

"The Supreme Court says life begins at six months," Cullen stated dispassionately. "After conception."

"A baby doesn't know from months," I said.

"It's fetal viability," Derek said. "Supreme Court said you can abort a baby up until it's viable outside the womb, which is six months. So you're smarter than the Supreme Court, Jake?"

"How do we know if the fetus is viable outside the womb, if we kill it inside the womb?" I asked.

"We must draw the line somewhere in that murky time between conception and birth," Fulbright said.

"The line is already drawn," I growled. "At conception."

"You want to redraw the lines," Derek accused me. "A woman shouldn't be forced to have a baby if she doesn't want it."

"So, a life should only be protected if it's wanted, but we can kill it if it's not? You better watch out Cox, 'cause no one wants your ass around."

"It's important," Fulbright nodded introspectively, "that these discussions remain on an intellectual level. When we inject emotion, personal attacks into academic discussions, we arrive at poor conclusions."

I did not speak the rest of class. I didn't care what they thought. I knew what was right, and what was wrong. I left quickly and trotted down the colorful carpeted stairs and straight to my locker. I needed to get out to the field early for B.P. with Delaney.

◆◆◆

"Who does he think he is with his high and mighty bullshit?" rumbled over the metal lockers. "Like he's better than everyone. If that prissy little Dawn turned up pregnant, I bet he'd have her at his daddy's doctor's office so fast it would make your head spin."

I wanted to climb over the lockers and pound them, but I didn't. I just quietly put my books away.

Derek Cox walked up to me. "You actually believe in God?"

I hesitated, and then I thought about Peter. "Yes." My voice wobbled.

"You actually believe there's some invisible old man living in the clouds that controls everything, and he's going to throw you to Hell if you do bad things?"

"Yeah."

"How can you believe in something you can't see?"

"I can't see the wind, but I believe in it."

"Yeah, but I can feel the power of the wind, feel its warmth."

"I can feel the power and the warmth of God."

"How do you know it's God?"

"The same way you know it's the wind."

"If God exists, and he's a loving, compassionate, all-powerful god, why's there so much suffering in the world? Why doesn't he just snap his fingers and cure disease, feed the hungry? Just fix all the problems of the world? Because, if he's loving and compassionate, he can't be all-powerful, and if he's all-powerful, then he's not loving and compassionate."

I stood in front of him perplexed. I had no answer. I didn't know why God didn't free the world from all its suffering. I didn't know why people starved to death under his watch. I had no answer for him.

"Huh? Why doesn't he? I'll tell you why. Because God doesn't exist."

"I wouldn't want to live in a world like that," Dorian said, stepping out from behind the lockers.

"You wouldn't?"

"The world's exactly the way it should be," he said. "Suffering's a good thing."

"I know, I know," Derek mocked, "suffering makes you stronger. That which doesn't kill you..."

"Suffering makes life worth living," Dorian corrected. "If there were no suffering in the world, I'd put a bullet through my head."

"People put bullets through their heads because they are suffering."

"If there was no suffering," Dorian went on, "no pain, no hunger, no death, life wouldn't be worth living. The refrigerator would always be full. We'd get As on all our tests. We'd all bat a thousand. Every day would be Christmas. We wouldn't know what love is because there'd be no hate, no loss. No one would die. We wouldn't be human. Everything that makes us special would be lost. There would be no human greatness, no triumphs of the human spirit. If God stopped the pain and suffering in the world, life would be a horrible, miserable existence."

I walked away without a word to the athletic wing, dressed quickly, and walked through the woods out to the field. My mind was still buzzing. Maybe that voice from the lockers was right. I didn't know what I would do in that situation. I had never thought about it for me. It always seemed like someone else's problem. I began to wonder. What were my beliefs? Why did I hold them?

Delaney was already at the cages waiting for me. Each of my batting practice sessions with him was like the first, hitting hundreds of balls off a stationary tee.

I mustered the courage to ask him, "Why do I have to do the

same things over and over and over again?"

"It's like you have a big jar of black marbles. Each black marble represents one bad swing you accumulated over the years," he explained. "With each good swing, you replace a black marble with a white marble. The more white marbles you have in your jar, the more good swings are at your disposal when you're at bat, so let's keep replacing your bad swings with good ones."

"Ain't that the way," Quinton called out from the dugout. "The bad thing's always black, and the good thing's always snow ass white."

No matter how many white marbles I put in the jar, I still hadn't made solid contact in weeks.

"We work and work and work on those tees, and I haven't gotten a hit in five games." I asked him before practice one day, "Can't we move on to something else, something real?"

"If you rush, you will fail," Delaney told me. "Trust the process. Don't let something as meaningless as not getting hits allow you to question what we're doing."

"Meaningless? The only reason why I'm doing this is to get hits."

"I thought you were doing this to become a hitter."

◆◆◆

After that practice, Delaney dragged the tee to the field, and put it directly on home plate.

"Hit the ball to right." He told me, placing a ball on the outside peg of the tee.

I took my stride and uncoiled at the ball, but only managed to graze the top half causing it to topple down a few feet in front of the plate.

"Hit the ball to right field," he placed a new ball on the tee.
I swung hard with the same result.

"Again." A dribbler to the pitcher's mound.

"Again." A pop up in front of home plate.

"Again." A slow roller to the left side.

He placed ball after ball on the tee and I tried again and again, but I failed to hit the ball to the right side.

"I can't do it," I protested. "I'm a dead pull hitter. I can't hit the other way."

"If you can't, you can't." He placed a ball on the tee.

I locked into to it, closed my left shoulder, and swung. The ball shot out over the infield, and I watched it rise over the left-center alley, and short-hop the fence. I stared at it in admiration.

"What are you doing?" he shouted.

"Looking at the ball I just hit for a double."

"The ball," he said incredulously, "is not your concern. You can't tell how well you swung by looking at the ball."

"How else can I tell?"

"When you know that, you'll be a hitter." He walked off the field.

◆◆◆

"All that extra work is a waste," Cullen told me as we drove away from school. "You either have the natural abilities or you don't."

He lurched the car to the right lane. "You can't take a left turn in this goddamn state. You have to take three rights to go left."

We drove on, and the red taillights became closer and closer, stacking one on top of the other.

"This Puritan work ethic of yours is bullshit."

"What Puritan ethic?" I asked.

"It's the work of the devil. You work and work and work, but it doesn't build you up. It tears you down, makes you weaker, and that's when the devil goes to work to show how weak you really are."

"I need it."

"If it's so helpful, why are you oh-for-April?"

"I got a couple hits the first game."

The cars in front of us slowly stopped and filled up both lanes. We inched along, hemmed in by red taillights. He slammed his hands against the steering wheel. "Some idiot got into an accident and screws up our night."

"How selfish of him to inconvenience you with his death," I said.

The shrieking sirens startled us, as the red and white lights pulsed hard in our mirrors. I looked back and saw an ambulance roaring through a narrow path of cars on the highway.

"Good." Cullen inched the car to the left and crept forward like a cheetah stalking its prey. He eyed his mirror. The lights grew bigger and the sirens blared louder. As the ambulance sped past, we shot out into the road, and fell in behind the flashing lights, racing down the highway.

"You can't do this!" I screamed.

"Can't? I am." He turned to me with a crazed liberated smile cut into his jaw. "I take advantage of every opportunity."

We stayed with the ambulance, weaving through the maze of cars stopped by the same lights and sounds that liberated us.

"That's the difference between you and me. You see an obstacle; I see an opportunity. You'd have just followed the rules, stuck behind 400 other saps just like you, sucking on each other's exhaust."

We sped along in the wake of the pulsating lights and blaring siren until the ambulance began to slow. Ahead in the distance, I could see red and blue lights flickering slowly in a solemn circle. The ambulance pulled to a stop on the left shoulder. On the side of the road, there were white sheets draped over two bodies.

"I take advantage of my chances," I growled.

"When? When have you seen something you wanted and taken it for yourself?"

"It's happened."

He flashed a condescending look. "Don't bullshit me. It's not you. I know you better than you know yourself."

"I just can't think of any specific examples, right now." I looked out the window at the two sheets.

"'Cause you don't have any. You're always worried you're doing something wrong. I've seen guys like you my whole life," he said, sitting high in his seat. "They're the ones I'm usually stepping over when I'm taking what I want."

"So what? I'd rather live with a little honor, character."

"Why? What does that get you? You act like this is forever. You never know when this shit ends. Look at those dudes over there." He motioned to the white sheets. "One day you're fine, the next day, who the fuck knows? You gotta live this day like it's your last."

"Really? What would you do if today was your last day on Earth?"

"I wouldn't live any different. I do everything I want every day. I make the most of my life. The real question is," he said, rolling his eyes at me, "what would you do?"

I didn't know. I shrugged.

"Have you nailed Dawn yet?"

I looked away, embarrassed.

"Are you kidding me? What the hell are you waiting for? What d'ya got to lose?"

"I'm hoping for something," I said.

"Hope's nothing. If you got hope in one hand and your dick in the other, you'll just be left holding your dick."

"I don't want to go too fast. I don't want to make any mistakes."

"Make mistakes. Life is slipping away," he told me. "If you were lying over there next to those two dudes, would you be happy you banged Dawn or didn't?"

"I'd be pissed I was dead."

"Exactly, you only live once. Live for the moment."

I turned to him. "I'm not much; not rich, not good looking. But one thing I am is a good guy. There are no trophies for that, no statues. And it may not mean a damn thing, but you know what? It's more than I can say about most people." The words poured out of me, and for the first time with no consideration for their effect or their consequences. I didn't care.

NW

Chapter 36

Finally, one day, Delaney lugged the bucket of balls out to the mound. "You're up."

I grabbed my bat and dug into the box. He wound and fired a fastball right down the middle. I swung as hard as I could but missed it completely. He threw me four more identical pitches, with identical results.

"Wait!" he howled. "You're out in front of every pitch." He walked toward me. "Why do you stand so far back in the box?"

"It gives me the most time get around on the fastball."

He pressed his lips together. "It's causing you to come forward at the ball. Hitting's a circular motion, not a linear motion. Swivel on your back foot, snap your hips, bring your hands, and then, the bat comes effortlessly. One full circle, not back to forward." He uncoiled his circular swing. "Stand in the center of the box."

"In the center," I protested, "I won't have an advantage on the curve, and I'll be slower on the fastball."

He walked closer. "Advantages create disadvantages. Stand close to the plate, they'll jam you. Off the plate, they'll paint the black. In front, they'll blow it by you. In back, you'll be waving at off-speed stuff. Stand in the center, and you can hit anything they throw."

I stood in the center of the box, but the next 10 pitches were a series of misses or dribblers to the left side.

Delaney pulled the bat from my hands. "You're too anxious. Your bat head's coming too soon." He mocked my swing with the barrel in front of his hands. "You're so worried about being late that you're early, and you hit weak grounders to short. The pitcher's not jamming you, you're jamming yourself. Hitting is timing, hitting is timing. Wait."

"How long do I wait?"

"Until the pitch almost crosses the plate, take it deep in the zone. Wait ... let your hands come first, and then bring the bat head through. Create the proper bat angles." He extended his arms with the bat at a 90-degree angle. "Hands inside the ball. Strike the ball before you break your wrists. You'll make better contact. You'll hit more balls between the lines. Let the ball generate the power. Don't fight it, use it."

He laid the bat diagonally across home plate. The knob intersected the inside front corner and the barrel crossed the outside back corner. "This line is where you must hit each ball at each location. The further outside the pitch, the deeper in the plate you hit the ball, and the longer you must wait. Wait, and adjust the angle of your bat."

"The ball's coming 85 miles an hour, and you want me to wait on it?" I asked. "There's no time to wait. If I wait, he'll throw it by me."

"You'll be quick enough. Trust your bat. Trust your hands. Trust yourself."

"What if I'm too slow?"

"Why can't you just say I mistimed it?" he asked. "Why do you have to conclude I'm too slow or he's better than me? Why do you give each swing that much power over your life?"

"If he threw it by me, then I can't hit the fastball. And if I can't do that, I'll never be a great hitter."

"You can be a great hitter even if you never hit the ball safely," he pointed the tip of his finger at me.

"Hits are the only things that count, the only proof of my worth."

"There's value in an at-bat other than getting a hit," he said quietly. "Sometimes, striking out is better than a hit."

"In what universe?"

"If your process is true and your motive is pure," he glared down at me, "you're on the road to perfection."

He threw me some more pitches, but each time I failed to make solid contact. It was too hard. I was thinking about too many things.

He fired another pitch at me. I swung. The ball shot straight up into the air and dropped weakly to the right of the mound.

"I can't do it." I threw my bat against the fence. "My way's easier."

"Anyone can hit like you, like a caveman."

"There's such a fine line between being too late and too early," I yelled at the trees.

"Narrow is the path that leads to salvation," he said. "Don't expect this game to get easier. You must get better."

◆◆◆

"I'm telling you, you're wasting your time with the old man," Cullen told me as we walked toward the lunchroom the next day. "It's not your swing. It's your approach, your whole approach to life."

"What's the matter with my approach to life?"

"Look at the way you walk down the hall, like a little pussy, stepping out of everyone's way, avoiding guys smaller than you, saying sorry, accommodating everybody. Mr. Nice Guy."

"What am I supposed to do run into everybody?" I asked.

"Yes," he nodded. "You're supposed to walk down the hall like a man. Shoulders back, chest out, you don't move out of anybody's way. Make the motherfuckers move out of your way."

"And what if they don't? Just run into them?"

"Yeah, and then, yell get the fuck out of my way." He flipped his hands in the air. "Show 'em who's in control, who has the power. Every relationship is about power. You're either the fucker or the fuckee."

"I don't want to live that way."

"Then you don't want to succeed in life. Take Dawn. That should already be a done deal, but you're never gonna get anywhere with her because you're passive. Take control. Don't wait for things to happen to you, make them happen for you.

"No, I'm gonna take it slow with her. I'm gonna treat her with respect."

"Where has this good guy crap ever gotten you? Huh? Women don't respond to that bashful, I'm a nice guy shtick. If you want a woman, you have to make her feel like a woman, and she feels more like a woman, the more man you are."

"I'm not like you."

"That's for damn sure."

"I can't pull that off," I told him. "I'd rather get a girl because I'm a good person, not because I fooled her."

He turned his head and took a long look at me. "You're still a virgin, aren't you?"

I froze. I didn't say a word, and my silence told him everything. He shook his head in disgust. "What a waste. You're a good-looking dude. You deserve more. And I'm not just blowing smoke up your ass. There are a lot of guys uglier than you getting a hell of a lot of ass. You're the biggest underachiever I've ever met." He pointed right at me. "My goal is to make you a man."

"Why is it always about sex? Not all men think of women as sex objects."

"If men didn't like sex, the human race would've died out millions of years ago."

My mind was swimming, reconsidering my choices, my life. Where has being good gotten me?

"I don't think women want the same thing as men," I said in a meek defense of my life choices.

"Yeah, they do. Don't let 'em fool you. They're no different than us. Why d'you think they spend 300 bucks on a new dress? Or a hundred on their hair? Why do they starve themselves? It's all about getting laid," he ranted. "Don't let the women tell you it's about love and marriage. That's just their way of justifying sex, legitimizing that animal inside of them."

"Most girls want a nice guy," I tried to convince him, and myself.

"Really? You're a nice guy, how many girls want you?"

I looked at him, silent.

"See? Nice guys finish last. Nice guys always get screwed, but only figuratively."

"I don't even know what to say to a girl," I confessed.

"When you talk to women, look into their eyes. Penetrate their souls. Touch them. Make 'em feel your strength, your manhood. It reinforces their femininity. Every woman wants to feel attractive and desirable to a man. Compliment 'em." He thought for a second. "Just say, 'You have nice eyes.' 'I like your smile.' 'I love your laugh.'"

"I don't want a relationship based on lies."

"Everything a girl does is a lie. They wear make-up, lipstick, false eyelashes, fake nails, push-up bras, hair extensions, high heels. They don't look like they look. But that's what I'm saying. You want them and they want to be wanted. That's not a lie. The actual words are meaningless. The truth is irrelevant. The fact that you thought her worthy enough to lie to is all the truth she needs. It's all part of the dance, the mating ritual. The peacock spreads his feathers and puffs himself up to get a mate. He's not really that big and that beautiful," he told me. "You can have all the women you want if you listen to me."

"I'd rather have one true relationship with a girl than a hundred fake ones."

"You can have both," he grabbed my shoulder. "You can have a hundred flings and then when you're ready, find the one to spend your life with, and have your kids."

"A hundred flings taint the one love."

"You're 17 and you're still a virgin. There are not many good looking 17-year-old girls who haven't already been plucked. You're waiting for something a hundred years ago. It doesn't exist anymore. What's gonna happen when you find out your wife's already been with 10 other guys, and she's your first? I couldn't do that, and you won't be able to either."

"What about Dawn?" I asked.

"Truthfully, you can do better than that. Just do as I say, they'll all melt in your hands. It's so easy. Watch this."

Cullen walked toward the snack bar. She was sitting by herself, as usual, when he casually strolled over, and placed a can of Diet Coke in front of her. "Thought you might need this."

She peered above her half-eaten sandwich. "Diet Coke? You telling me I'm fat?"

"Of course not. Let's start over." He reached out and grabbed her hand. "I'm Cullen."

"I know who you are," her eyes inspected him.

"And I know who you are, Laticia."

"It's Lah—tee—see—ah," she drew out each syllable. "Not Luh—tish—uh."

"Forgive me, La—tee—c—i—a, I thought it would be refreshing to sit with some real people for a change."

"I don't know from real or fake." Her eyes studied him.

"I like that shirt, where did you get it?"

She nibbled at the crust. "Consignment shop."

"It brings out the color of your eyes."

"You really think so?" She forced her eyes toward her plate.

"Do you mind if I borrow a fry?" He slid one off her plate.

"Are you done?" She stared right at him. "You finished?"

"With what?" He remained calm.

"I've had this lunch before."

"What lunch?"

"I get it. The popular kid being nice to the school slut. You talk with me for a few minutes, feel good about yourself and I never see you again. I'll save us both time. I'll give you your good guy credit, if you let me eat in peace."

"You got me all wrong," he stared right into her eyes.

"Why would someone like you want to sit with someone like me?"

"I want to get to know you better."

"I bet you do. Is that what this is? You're looking for a quick pop? Let's go. I'll meet you behind the curtains in the chapel?"

"Give me more credit than that," he placed his hand on her forearm. "There something about you, something special that I want to get to know."

"How?"

"What are you doing a week from Saturday?"

"I have to check my busy calendar," she laughed to herself.

He tightened his eyes on her. "I was wondering, would you do me the honor of going to the formal with me?"

"Uh…" she hesitated. "I don't think so."

"Why not?"

"It doesn't make any sense," she shook her head. "Why would you want to go with me?"

He closed the top end of the straw and lifted it. "This doesn't make much sense either," he said, holding the soda-filled straw above the glass. "But it happens anyway."

"You can go with any girl you want. And get whatever you want from them."

"I know, but my girl, Jenny, can't make it. She has finals, and I don't have a date for the formal. So, I figured I start by asking the prettiest girl I know and then work my way down."

"Where are you at? A hundred and ninety-seven?"

"Two."

She picked at her sandwich. "I wasn't planning on going to any prom."

"You gotta go," he prodded her.

She eyed him skeptically.

"You can trust me." He winked and flashed his all-encompassing smile.

"OK, I'll go," she relented. "What more can I lose?"

He popped up, "Great! I'll pick you up by seven."

"You don't know where I live," she said.

"Yeah, I do."

"What are you doing?" I asked as we walked to the lockers. "You said you wouldn't touch her with a 10-foot condom."

He winked at me, and I sensed something wasn't quite right.

"Does Jenny know?"

"What Jenny doesn't know can never hurt her."

"It's wrong," I objected. "You gotta tell her."

"When my mom dies, you can have her job," he said sourly.

"So, it's all right for you to go out with other girls behind her back?"

He shrugged casually. "You gotta do what you gotta do."

"No, you don't," I said. "So, you wouldn't be pissed if you found out she was seeing some other guy?"

"Of course, I'd be mad."

"You're a hypo—"

"I'm not gonna spend my life worrying what she might or might not be doing a thousand miles from here," he said. "And I'm not gonna turn down opportunities to maintain some archaic guise of faithfulness either. If I get caught, I get caught. I'll deal with it. I don't know what she does, and I don't care to know either."

"Don't you want to know that she cares enough about you to be faithful to you?"

"If she really cared about me, she'd care not to get caught."

I walked away, his words rattling around my brain, challenging my comfort zones. None of it made any sense.

♦♦♦

"Don't eat it too fast, or you'll get a caveman headache," I told Dawn as we sucked on Italian ice at the Lighthouse that night.

"Caveman headache?" she asked.

"Ya know that headache you get when you eat ice cream too fast."

"You mean freezy head."

"Quinton eats these in one gulp just to give himself a headache." She looked up with a purple smile. "He's crazy."

"Yeah, but funny," I said as the red and blue ice bled down my hand.

"Did Cullen really invite Laticia to the prom?" she asked.

"I was there when he did."

"How did that happen?"

"His girlfriend couldn't make it, so he was just being nice. She shouldn't get any delusions."

"Delusions?" She looked at me offended. "You think he's too good for her?

"This is Cullen and you know her... her past."

"Yeah, she went to St. Francis," her voice turned fiercely calm, "just like you and me. She rode on your bus."

"Why are you mad at me?" I asked.

"I'm not. I just feel sorry for her. She's always sitting alone. Not many friends. When I heard about the prom, I got excited for her."

"See, not many friends. There's probably a reason for that."

"Well, she doesn't have the best reputation, but she's always been nice to me." Dawn's voice was measured and cool.

"She's the only child of a single mother. They live in a shotgun house right there by the bay. Her dad's in prison. Not much good comes out of that."

"She could still be a good person. I just want to go up and talk to her. But she's so hard on the outside."

"She probably just needs a friend," I said.

She smiled at me. "You have the bluest eyes," she said. "Like the ocean."

"Is that a good thing?"

She smiled. "Of course, silly.

"What would you say if I asked you to go to the formal?" I asked tentatively as I licked the purple juice off my hand.

"I don't know," she replied, "I can't tell you."

"Why not?"

"I only answer real questions."

"Going to the prom with me isn't a real question?" I snapped.

"Not in the backward way you just asked me, like you were protecting yourself," she said calmly.

"From what?"

"Getting hurt. I guess I'm not worth risking getting hurt over."

I took a deep breath. "Will you go with me to the Spring Formal a week from Saturday?"

"You're being a little forward, aren't you?"

NW

Chapter 37

"Hit the ball back through the center." Delaney pointed the bat at the pitcher's mound. "This will simplify everything."

"The center?"

"The pitcher's mound, the center of the field, is where the ball comes from, where the action originates. Hit the ball back through the center, through the core of the defense. It's like driving a stake through their heart. Simply concentrate on that, everything else will fall into place. If you don't remember anything else in your life, remember this." We spent a half-hour after practice, and I didn't hit one ball back through the center.

"I was better when I was figuring it out for myself," I said.

Delaney stood about 15 feet in front of home plate and held the ball above his right ear. "Just hit the ball back to me."

"Pepper? You want to play pepper?" I asked. "It's another kid's game."

"Hit the ball back to me." He threw a firm pitch down the middle of the plate that my bat intersected and batted on two hops back to his glove. "See, hands in front of the barrel." He threw another quick pitch that I batted directly back to him. "Back through the center. Hands inside the ball." He repeated that with each successful hit. We went back and forth until my swing fell into a groove. "The bat's longer through the zone."

"That works for pepper, but not on an 85-mile-an-hour fastball."

"You know what your problem is?"

I shrugged.

"You're human."

"Well, what's the alternative?" I smirked.

"Human beings are the only animals with a conscious mind," he tapped his skull. "The conscious mind has no place in baseball, Jake. You know the difference between those who make it and those who don't?"

"Talent?"

"No. You have as much ability as they have."

"Hard work?"

He shook his head. "The ones that make it are too stupid to think they can't make it."

"Stupid? I thought we're supposed to play smart."

"Don't think. Great hitters never think about striking out, they never consider failure. They never think about hitting a home run, either."

"What do they think about?" I asked.

"The ball."

"If I'm not thinking, how will I know what to do?"

"The eagle doesn't know how to fly. He just flies."

"I'm not an eagle."

Without warning, he fired the ball at me. My hand flew up and caught it inches from my nose.

"See?" he smiled. "Why do you think you have to think? Did your mind say, 'Lift your hand, contract your bicep, catch the ball?' No, you just reacted. Trust yourself. You'll be quick enough. Don't think, react. Trust your instincts."

"You could've hit me in the face," I said.

"I knew you'd catch it. I trust your instincts more than you do."

"If it's all instinct, why do I have to practice?"

"Think in practice, react in the game. Learned action," he paused, "becomes instinct."

"If I'm not thinking, then I'm not doing anything."

"Why is it necessary for you to do anything?"

"I may be crazy, but I want to get a hit every once in a while. Otherwise, what good am I?"

"Base hits are merely tangible proof of intangible realities," he said.

I don't even know what that means.

"What are strikeouts proof of?" I asked.

"Sometimes, it's better to strike out on 12 pitches than to get a hit on the first."

He's losing his mind, I thought as I stared at him. "How is striking out better than getting a hit?"

"You believe what you do in the batter's box defines you. You can't find the meaning to your life in an at-bat. Your value as a human being does not teeter on each swing of your bat. Stay pure. Tainted motives blur your vision and slow your reflexes. Remove yourself. Disappear."

"If I disappear, where will I be?"

"If you disappear," he replied, "you will find yourself." He walked off the field. He looked old, hunched over. He had an old back, old shoulders, old man legs, and an old man philosophy.

Disappear? I don't understand any of it; his outdated philosophies, his weird sayings. The season's almost over, and I just wasted half of it on batting tees and pepper, old time baseball. It's a power game: home runs, doubles, total bases, slugging percentages, not walks and hitting to the opposite field. I stopped listening to him. I didn't care anymore. Nothing mattered. I was going to do it on my own, just like Dorian did in Little League. I decided at that moment I was going to will my way to success, and the only way was being more aggressive than the pitcher. I'm not waiting anymore. I'm attacking.

I attacked every pitch I saw in the final game of the season, and aggressively struck out the first three times. In the bottom of the seventh, I grabbed my bat and strode confidently to the plate. If we won, we were in the state play-offs. One final chance to prove myself.

Aggressive, aggressive, pounded in my brain as I dug in. I was going to attack any fastball and drive it. I was going to show my way is the best way, the only way. If I was going down, I was going down swinging.

I swung hard and missed the first pitch and drove the second one sharp but foul down the left field line. I let two curves float by for balls, evening the count.

The next pitch was a high fastball. It was there before me, growing bigger and whiter with each nearing millimeter. It was my pitch. The pitch I wanted, the pitch I could drive, my chance to prove myself, so I went after it. I threw the head of my bat at the ball.

What happened next, I was not quite sure at that moment. Something reached up and grabbed my bat barrel, just before it struck the ball. My wrist shook from the *whap* of aluminum against soft leather, and then I felt the customary crack of my bat.

The ball flew, as I drifted down the line, staring at the sky, the umpire leaped up, flailing his arms. "Catcher's interference! Catcher's interference!" Everyone stopped.

The ball hung in the sky like a midday moon and floated and floated and floated until it disappeared beyond the center field fence. I rounded first base as the other players stood like statues, confused. I circled the bases in a dead sprint, not sure if I should even be running. I ran into the dugout, no one knew what to do, so they hesitantly slapped me skeptical fives.

The ump leaned into our dugout. "Catcher's interference, son," he pointed at me. "It's an automatic single. Or do you want the home run?" He paused and smiled when he heard his own question.

"What did you hit?" Delaney kneeled next to me as I gathered up my gear.

"The catcher's mitt."

"What pitch?"

"Fastball."

"I knew it." His face lit up. "The catcher's mitt. The catcher's mitt," he repeated, thoughtfully. "Slowed your bat down. Your hands came first. They had to. The mitt forced you to wait on the pitch. You were still quick enough, and you still had enough power to knock it out of the park."

"It was an accident," I shouted and walked out of the dugout.

"There are no accidents," he called after me.

◆◆◆

"There are five billion Chinamen who've never seen a baseball, who don't give a damn about what happens today," Delaney paced in the dugout before we took the field that Saturday against Middlesex in the first round of the play-offs. "Go play for each other."

I hit weak grounders in my first three at-bats, but Dorian hit two doubles and Quinton allowed one run in six innings. We led by one with two outs and two on in the bottom of the seventh. Quinton's pitch was driven on a line just over Jay's head. Curtis and the runners on first and second broke on contact. Curtis scooped the ball off the top of the grass as the tying run rounded third, and fired it home. I stood at the plate, watching the ball as the runner bore down on me. I put my left foot on the third base edge of home plate and waited. The ball flew toward me, suspended in the air, sailing over the green grass and orange dirt, impervious to the forces of gravity. I waited and waited for the ball to come to me as the runner charged home. The ball hit my mitt as his spikes struck my hip.

I landed chest first on the ground, rolled over and showed the ump the ball. He swept his arms to the side. Safe.

I leaped up. "I held the ball! I held the ball!" I screamed, but then saw the batter take too wide a turn at first. I wheeled and fired a strike to Cullen who caught it cleanly and dropped the tag high on the runner's hip. "Safe!"

"He was out. What are you, blind?" I ran up the line at the first base umpire. "He was out!"

"Jake! Jake!!" The dugout yelled. I turned and saw the second runner sprinting toward home. Cullen tossed a firm ball at the plate as I ran toward it. I dove and caught the ball in mid-air. I dropped my mitt on the runner's sliding knee. I looked up, the man in black stood with his arms wide and to the side. I was immediately inundated with the black celebratory cleats of the Middlesex players dancing around me. I laid face down in the dirt until their frolicking feet dissipated. I trudged into the dugout and hit a wall of infuriated stares of my teammates.

Delaney stood before us. "The hardest part of becoming a champion is, there are no guarantees. You can do all the right things. You can work harder than everyone else, play harder, fight through adversities, leave your heart and soul on the field, and still not claim the prize," he pounded his fist into his open palm. "That's the most difficult thing to comprehend. You can do all that is right and still end up wrong. The dream is never guaranteed, but the champion fights on." He walked toward the bus. "The champion fights on. The champion fights on," he repeated until he and it faded away.

NW

Chapter 38

"Tonight, you become a man!" Cullen bellowed as I climbed into the shiny limo that consumed most of my driveway.

"This is nicer than the other one," I ran my hands across the soft leather.

"Stick with me. I'll have you farting through silk underwear."

"This has got everything." I flipped on the TV.

"Not quite." He opened the wood cabinet of the mini bar. "Empty. But..." He reached into his coat, and pulled out a thin bottle. He unscrewed the cap, tilted it to his lips, and took a quick, painful swig.

"The precious nectar," he said sinisterly.

He handed me the bottle. "Go ahead."

I eyed him as I lifted the bottle to my lips, tilted it, and the tawny colored liquid splashed against my closed lips.

He nodded his approval. "If you like that, you'll love this." He reached into his coat again, pulled out a plastic bag and laid it on the seat, displaying eight white, short sticks with twisted ends.

"What are those?"

"You don't know?" he sneered. "Why do I waste my time with you?"

I remained silent, still unsure of what they were.

"Mojo, you know, wacky weed." His meaty fingers groped inside the bag, grabbed one, and held it out to me with his big, contagious smile.

I was more nervous than curious. "I'll pass."

"Pass? You can't pass. It's a gift. That's insulting to the giver."

"What if the gift's insulting?"

"If I didn't know any better," he leered at me with sheer disgust, "I'd swear you squat to pee."

I turned from him and stared out of the window. The limo driver took a long final drag on his cigarette and flicked the orange butt into my bushes.

"We're not hurting anybody. It's prom night. Have a little fun, for chrissake."

"I don't need that to have fun."

He stuffed the plastic bag back into his coat. "More for me."

I shrugged.

He smiled at me, and then said again, "Tonight... you become a man."

"I don't know," I said. "I like Dawn and all, but I don't know if she's right for me."

"Right for you? Right for you? Does she have a pussy?"

I shrugged. "I assume she does."

"Then she's right for you."

"Why is it all about sex?"

"Because it is. Sex makes the world go around."

"No, relationships do."

"You wouldn't be here if not for sex, if your mom and—"

"I don't want to even think about that," I said.

◆◆◆

I was sitting in the kitchen of Cullen's large Victorian house waiting for him to get ready when Mr. Clayborne walked in. He was big and thick like Cullen, but no longer had the sharp edges of youth. He dropped a big, fat plastic jug of shelled pistachios onto the oval table. "Get these away from me," he said, pushing them at me. "I eat 'em, and eat 'em, and eat 'em. The more I eat, the more I want. It's crazy."

"Maybe that's why they call 'em nuts," I said.

He gave me a dull smile.

"For some reason," he grabbed a handful and funneled them into his mouth, "they taste better when you shuck 'em yourself."

"Everything's better if you work for it."

"Jake, I'm not telling you guys what to do tonight. I'm not Simon Pure. Just remember, you both have great futures. Don't do anything to jeopardize that. I'm not in a position to make moral judgments. I was your age. I felt that pressure, that pain, those hormones."

I didn't answer.

He funneled more nuts into his mouth. "I did everything you guys are doing: staying out, drinking, sex, pot. I'm not saying it's right. But I never hurt anyone, and I turned out fine."

"It's one thing to want to do them and another thing to do them," I said, telling him what I thought he wanted to hear.

"Just don't do anything to hurt yourself, or your future. Don't get me wrong — we would all like to live by a strict moral code, but today, life's too complex to fit into neat little boxes. A hundred years ago, there were real life consequences for immorality. Modern medicine, technology have rendered morality useless. My kids have everything they need. They're protected. Prosperity has made standards and mores unnecessary," Mr. Clayborne said. "It's up to the individual. Hell, even congress is talking about repealing the Glass-Steagall Act. Sometimes, you need to be allowed to make your own rules."

Glass what? I had no idea what he was talking about. "I don't know. There's still a lot of problems out there."

"Yeah, crime, poverty, drugs. The country's divided," he said. "We're losing this country, Jake."

"We will always have our freedom."

"Freedom's a blessing," he said. "And a curse."

"Freedom's a good thing," I responded.

"The best," he agreed. "But it's destroying us."

"How is…"

"Freedom reveals who we really are. Freedom exposes us. We are where we are and who we are because that is exactly where and who we want to be."

I stared at him in silence.

"How is Mrs. Clayborne doing?" I changed the subject.

"She has her good days," he expelled a heavy breath, "and her bad days. She's having more bad days lately, but her bad days aren't as bad. So, I don't know what that means."

"She'll beat this," I feigned hope.

"Hard to beat cancer, Jake. But we're fighting. We'll do anything, go anywhere. I'll spend my last dime. I'm not gonna let her go quietly into the night."

◆◆◆

I climbed the stairs and walked into Cullen's room which was as big as my living room.

"It's unfair that one man can look this good." He preened in his bedroom mirror. "So many women, and just one me."

He turned to me. "Can you grab those black shoes in my closet?"

I walked over toward his closet.

"While you're in there," he said, "you can put on my old tux. It's a lot nicer than what you got on."

"That's alright. This one's good," I said.

"Yeah, mine's probably too big in the shoulders anyway."

I stepped into his wood inlaid closet filled with rows and rows of suits, sports coats, dress shirts, and slacks of every color. I had one jacket and tie to my name. He had a small department store in his closet. He had three rows of shoes on racks, 10 pairs wide. I grabbed the nicest pair of black shoes I saw.

"What are you, new?" he said when I handed him the shoes. "Not the Sperrys, get me the Ferragamos."

"What the difference? They look the same to me."

He cut a dismissive glance at me.

The door swung open and a tall, blonde woman bounced into the room; her scarlet strapless dress could barely contain her jiggling body. She walked straight over to Cullen and pressed her red lips onto his mouth. He leaned her back, her body melting in his arms. He kissed her long and hard as I stood and watched like I was staring at a movie screen.

"I can't wait to go to your little dance," she told him after their lips parted. "Hi, Jake." She walked over and gave me a big, encompassing hug like we were long lost friends. "I can't wait to meet Dawn. I hear she's so cute."

"This is a big night for Jake. Tonight he..." Cullen whispered into her ear, and she burst into a short hysterical laughter.

"Just relax, sweetie," she leaned in so close I could feel her soft warmth. "I can still remember my first time. It's the only one you'll remember forever."

"I think I will remember tonight," I said, grabbing Cullen's arm and leading him into the bathroom.

"What about Laticia?" I whisper-shouted. "You can't bring two girls to the prom. No one can pull that off. Not even you."

"I'm just taking one." He looked at me like I was crazy. "Jenny took her exams early and decided to come." He shrugged. "What's the big deal?"

"Are you going to tell Laticia?" I asked.

"She'll figure it out."

"You can't dog her like that!" I was incredulous.

"I can do whatever the hell I want."

"She deserves to be treated better than this," I told him. "It's wrong and you know it. I don't want anything to do with this."

"Well, if you don't go with us, you don't go at all."

◆◆◆

Through the left side window of the limo, the bleary auburn sun was resting just above the horizon, nestled among the purple clouds like a soft fuzzy peach, shooting streaks of amber across the darkening sky.

"That looks so amazing," Jenny pointed to the surreal confluence of colors.

"How can anyone look at that and not be happy just to be alive?" Cullen asked.

"I am always happy," Jenny declared in a synthetic voice. "It makes no sense to ever be unhappy."

"I'd be happy all the time, too, if I'd won the lottery," I said without thinking.

"What d'you mean by that?" Cullen snapped.

"What are you trying to say?" Jenny's sweet voice suddenly turned sour.

"It's easy to be happy when everything always works out for you."

"Maybe everything always works out for me because I'm always happy."

"You're rich. You're beautiful. You don't know what it's like for someone to look at you without a smile on their face," I told her.

"You want me to apologize for being pretty?"

"No, just have an ounce of understanding for the non-beautiful people in the world."

I stared out the window as the daylight slowly disappeared, being consumed by the blackness as if the devil were pulling all the world's light into the darkness.

◆◆◆

At the same time Cullen, Jenny and I rode in that stretch limousine watching the day end, a girl across town waited for her night to begin. Hope lived in a part of town where it had died far too often, where it had little reason to live.

Laticia never fretted about this night like the other girls. She never thought about it since the day she had her own revelation, the day she realized her unpopularity. She knew prom was supposed to be special. That's why she never planned on going.

But tonight, all the pain, all the loneliness she had endured would be wiped away. She would be the envy of all the other girls. She was going to the prom with the boy all the boys wanted to be and all the girls wanted to date. She had won, even if it was for only one night.

Her mother spent two weeks' pay on satin and lace, and two weekends creating a classic prom dress, a dress for her daughter whose very existence prevented her from ever wearing one herself.

When Laticia glided down the narrow front stairs of her house with her beautiful new dress flowing with each stride, her mother beamed, admiring her daughter, and pushing down the pent-up pain of her own lonely prom night that still stabbed at her.

Laticia sat. And waited. And waited. The clock on the wall could not move fast enough. She wanted to reach up, grab the minute hand and hurry it along. But she waited patiently, listening intently for the bell, watching each minute, each second, agonizingly tick by.

◆◆◆

"What's going on?" Dawn glared at me when she climbed into the limo and saw Jenny instead of Laticia.

"I don't know," I shrugged.

"Yeah, you do," she said.

"I didn't know this was happening," I whispered.

"I don't like this," her voice barely audible. "I don't want to be a part of this."

"You're not. We didn't do anything wrong, and there's nothing we can do now."

"Yeah, there is," she grabbed the door handle. "Stop the car," she shouted to the driver.

"No, this'll ruin our night," I whispered.

"No, going with them will ruin our night," she whispered loudly. "I don't want to be any part of this."

The car eased to a stop on the side of the road. Cullen leaned toward us. "Is there a problem?"

"Yes," Dawn said. "I can't do this."

"Do what?"

She turned to Jenny. "I'm sure you are a very nice person, nothing against you, but I can't go with you under these circumstances." She pushed open the door and climbed out.

I looked at Cullen. "Sorry," I said, and followed her out onto the street.

"You may be OK with that, but I'm not," she started walking back to her house as the limo pulled away. "I'd rather take a cab than be a part of that."

"I'm sorry. I know it was wrong. I told him that. There was nothing I could do to change it."

"You're right, you couldn't change it," she told me. "But you didn't have to go along with it."

"I don't care about Cullen, and I don't really care about Laticia. I just care about you. I just wanted us to be together tonight."

"I care about her," she said. "It hurts to think of her sitting at home, all dressed up, all alone. That's plain cruel," she said. "At some point you have to stand for what's right, Jake."

◆◆◆

"He will be here soon, mija," Laticia's mother assured her every few minutes. And each time she said, "He will be here," the realization that he would not became more real.

After a time, with each barren second rolling past, the hands on the clock began to move too fast. She wanted to reach up and stop them, stop time. She sat on the lonely couch and watched the television through the reflection in the window facing the street. No one came.

The shadows in the living room grew longer and longer until they disappeared into blackness. She feared, and hoped, he'd gotten lost or into an accident, but deep down, she knew. She gave up. Hope died, murdered by its creator. She didn't shed one tear, not willing to waste a drop on something as foolish as this.

She walked up to her room, shut the door, and unceremoniously removed the dress and carefully spread it on top of her bed. She pulled on an old pair of pink sweats and flopped down in a rocking chair in the corner. She rocked slowly, deflated without the strength to hope any longer when a knock came at the front door.

Her mom hurried to the door and slowly opened it with hopeful trepidation.

"Mija," she called out, her voice cracking, "you have a friend." Laticia didn't move. She closed her silent eyes, and rocked back and forth, hugging a doll she had not held for 10 years.

Her mom poked her head into her room and whispered, "Mija, someone here to see you."

Laticia pushed herself up and dragged her body to the front door. Before she could look up, she heard, "I don't have anyone to go to the dance with." He held a small white naked flower in front of her.

"That's really funny," she said, not smiling. "I'd expect this from the other boys, but not you." She was exhausted.

He continued, "I was wondering if you could do me a favor, the honor, and go to the prom with me. We don't even have to dance. We should go, just as friends."

She leaned on her right leg, shaking her head, wondering if he was for real, or simply the prelude to another cruel joke. "I can't take a whole gym laughing at me."

"If they laugh, they laugh. We can't let that stop us. We can't give them that much power over us." She stared at him and waited. She couldn't decide whether she had too much pride to go, or too much not to go. She looked over her shoulder and caught the hopeful eyes of her mother peering around the corner, giving her a nod of encouragement.

"That would be very nice, Dorian," she finally said. Her face flushed. "I would love to go with you."

"Hope Johnny's car's OK. It's no limo, but it'll get us there."

"It's perfect." She smiled and ran to her bedroom, hope reborn.

◆◆◆

"That's some bullshit right there," Derek Cox said as Cullen strutted in with Jenny on his arm. Knowing whispers and muffled laughter spread across the gym.

"What the hell's going on?" He turned to me. "What happened with Laticia?"

"I don't know."

"Yeah you do. He blew her off, didn't he?"

"How does it affect you?"

"Her life's messed up as it is, and to do that to her?" his date, Michelle, said. "Nobody deserves that."

"Not even her," Derek added.

"I know. That's why we didn't go with them," I told him. "We took a cab here because we didn't want to be part of that."

"Well, good for you," Michelle told me. "You guys can ride with us if you want."

I leaned against the punch table, watching the girls flock in and out of the ladies' room as the band kicked into *Livin' la Vida Loca*. A tiny hand grabbed mine from behind.

"You're not going to stand like a statue all night?" I spun around and gaped at the tall, thin woman holding my hand. Her perfume swept over me, penetrated me, filled me like a shot of adrenaline. "This is a dance," Ms. Vivaqua said, pulling me to the center of the gymnasium, "so, let's dance."

She twisted and turned me all over the floor. Her fiery eyes stared into mine and her white teeth sparkled as she laughed and smiled the entire song. My heart raced each time our bodies brushed against each other. But the only thing I remember is how warm her hands felt. When we finished, she leaned into me, "You're a great dancer, Jake. We should do it again." She walked away and disappeared into the crowd.

Kurt Cobain's voice pounded out of the oversized speakers. *"Come as you are, as you were, as I want you to be, as a friend, as a friend, as an old enemy..."* when Dorian walked through the doors with Laticia under his arm.

Everyone stopped and stared. Laticia looked at Dorian with the giddy innocence of a newlywed. He led her to the middle of the floor, and as they passed, the dancers resumed, awkwardly trying to catch up to the music. I had never noticed how pretty she was.

"Good for her," Michelle said.

"It's all about true love, right?" Cullen said, with no hint of remorse. "I may have a little more respect for my boy, after all."

Dawn walked up to me with a proud smile on her face. "Dorian has restored my faith in humanity."

I smiled and led her onto the dance floor. I pulled her toward me and she fell into my arms. I held her next to my chest and the same strawberry smell I'd inhaled three years before was still there.

We danced the same awkward steps and she felt the same in my hands, so soft, so fragile. It was as if no time had elapsed between the two dances, like we had stopped and taken a break for a couple of songs and came back together again.

◆◆◆

Dawn and I walked out onto the balcony overlooking the oval lake.

"I'm so happy for her," she said.

I nodded.

"They're perfect together."

"I guess it all worked out in the end," I said.

A large harvest moon rested just above the milky water, consuming most of the dark sky, stealing all the light from the stars.

"The moon looks so beautiful." Dawn grabbed my hand and leaned into my chest.

I leaned toward the pressure of her body, supporting her. "Sometimes, when the moon is that big, if you look real close, you can see the flag that the astronauts planted up there."

"Really."

"Yeah," I pointed to the sky. "It's right there at about two o'clock by that round shadow."

"Yeah, right." She knocked my hand out of the sky.

◆◆◆

I slid next to her soft, supple body, and she rested her head on my shoulder in the back of Derek's limo. "Thanks for bringing me," she whispered in my ear, her warm breath tickling the hairs on my lobe. Her sweet smell wafted around us and an edgy serenity washed over me. I wanted to get lost in that invisible cloud, protected and safe in that pure, unsullied moment.

My forehead glistened, my heart pounded, my body tingled at the slightest touch of her silk gown, her soft skin, her tantalizing scent. The sweet innocence of anticipation swept over me, enticing me, and if left untasted, would linger for eternity as the succulent bitterness of an unfilled desire.

Derek wrestled with Michelle. He slid his right hand between silk and skin. Her dress slipped off her shoulders, and the pale white skin of the side of her right breast glowed like a small moon. Watching their half-naked bodies wriggling in unison, and moaning in erratic ecstasy, I felt cheated. I felt robbed.

Maybe my adolescent proclamation of purity has deprived me of what all teenagers have a right to enjoy, a need to enjoy. Why should something I promised myself when I was a boy dictate the decisions I make as a man? Maybe it was too idealistic, too childlike? What's wrong with a little fun? It's only natural. Everyone does it.

Maybe the human body is not meant to remain totally pure. Maybe it needs to taste sin, to breathe immorality, to touch decadence along the way, or it will slowly wither and die.

I pulled Dawn to me. "You sure you don't want to go to the party?" I whispered into her strawberry hair.

"Of course, I want to go," she pined, "but my mom would never let me out again if I don't get home by midnight." She pressed into me.

I tilted my head forward and our lips met. Her lips were soft, too soft, delicate, receiving. Her mouth opened and closed mechanically, like a baby bird being fed by its mother. She was even less experienced than I was.

I slid my hand down the small of her back, but she intercepted it. "No, Jake."

I turned my body square to hers. My lips reached toward her lips, and with both arms pressed her shoulders back on the leather seat. Her breath expelled audibly as I laid on top of her small, stiff body. I slid my hands up her thighs and lifted her dress.

"Stop, stop," she cried out. "Stop!" She pushed on my chest, but I was too heavy for her. "Jake!" she cried.

I popped up quickly. "Sorry, sorry," I said, holding my hands up like a caught criminal. "Sorry, sorry. I don't know what I was thinking. I'm sorry. I'm sorry."

She stared at me, readjusted her dress and ran her fingers through her hair.

"Will you guys keep it down," Derek rebuked us.

"Just take me home, Jake," she said plainly. "Tell the driver just to take me home."

We sat in the car looking out the window without speaking a word. *What have I done?* I thought. *I ruined it. The only girl stupid enough to go out with me and I do that to her?*

I felt her eyes steal a quick glance at me. I looked over. She smiled, and I smiled back. She closed her eyes slowly and opened them at me. She finally reached out and slid her hand into mine.

Her porch light snapped on and the kitchen curtains fluttered as we pulled into her driveway. "I really liked dancing with you," she confessed as I helped her out of the car.

"I've improved since the eighth grade."

"No, you haven't," she laughed and flipped her hair out of her face.

"It's not the skill, it's the partner." I squeezed her hand.

"You can't improve on perfection," she placed her hand on my back, and I leaned in. The kitchen curtain opened and closed quickly. She ran up the steps to her front door, looked back and called out, "I still do."

"Still what?" I said.

"Have a crush."

◆◆◆

They both stared at me as I slithered back into the limo. "Strike three?"

"What does it look like?"

"At least you went down swinging. It wasn't the smoothest move, but I give you props, you swung for the fences."

NW

- 274 -

Chapter 39

A *m I the only kid in America alone on prom night?* I thought as I
closed the door to the limo and watched it drive away. I stood on
my gravel driveway and looked at the empty highway, everything silent,
no cars sped by. I felt comfortable all alone, hidden in the black night
on the edge of the world. I was drawn to the emptiness of it, as if I were
filling some mysterious void. The heels of my shoes ticked against the
asphalt until I stood on top of the double yellow lines of the thick black
road, looking up at the empty sky.

My shoes then crunched against the gravel of the club's parking
lot.

"Sweetie, sweetie," I heard in the distance. "Over here, dear." A
dim light from an open glove box of a rusted Buick glowed in the corner
of the lot casting a slight feminine shadow. She was sitting in the front
seat with her bare legs dangling out of the open door. I approached
slowly.

"What's your name, sweetie?" her syrupy voice asked.

"J-J-J... Jake," I said nervously.

"James."

"No, no, Jake," I inched closer, but keeping a safe distance from
this stray woman, like I would a stray dog.

"Jake, honey, can you help a stranded lady?"

A frayed flower sundress clung to the contours of her body. A
white lace cross hung around her neck and rested lightly in the crevice
of her chest. Her hair was greasy, her face was hard, and the edges of her
teeth were gray.

"I'm not going to hurt you," she flashed a gray smile at me. "I
just need some money to eat, sweetie. I drove all the way up from Carolina today. I'll pay you back as soon as I get my first check. I promise,
darlin'. I start working at that Holiday Inn down the road tomorrow."

I looked at her, and then down at my feet, and then back up
at her. I slid a five-dollar bill from between a pair of twenties from my
wallet and placed it in her open palm.

"Thank you, love." She crumbled it into a ball in her fist. I
turned and walked toward the gate. "Jake," she called out. "I really need
your help, sweetie."

I stepped back toward her. "If you could just use that credit card, to get me a room at that motel, that would sincerely help me." I reached for my wallet but stopped. "I will pay you back before it shows up on your card."

"Well..." I didn't know what I was supposed to do. What was right? "This card is only for emergencies."

"This is an emergency, darlin'. I start work tomorrow. I'll pay you back. I swear to Sweet Jesus."

I paused.

"I can repay you in other ways too," she smiled and shimmied her meager chest at me. "I'm no whore. I'm just a stranded lady who needs help. You can do whatever you want to me. I promise I'll be a good woman to you. I just need a place to lay my head."

I walked away without another word, through the gate with my head down, toward the back of the building. "Please, Jake, please!" Her voice faded into the dark night.

I climbed up on the dumpster and used the metal brackets of the downspout to scale the side of the building. As I reached the top of the wall, I thought about that woman. I knew there must be more to her than that desperate, discarded soul I just spoke with, but to me, she will always be that person, frozen in time with no past, and no future.

Was she born like that, I wondered? Or was she like everyone else at one time in her life? She must have had a future once. What were her hopes? Her dreams? They had to be greater than the front seat of that rusted Buick on the side of a beach road on that dark morning. How did she get there? What series of events caused her to end up in that place and time? Maybe that seat was the final destination of failed dreams, or possibly the logical landing place of a dreamless soul?

Did she ever go to her prom? What was her first kiss like? What was her mother thinking right now? Where was her father? Did she have a brother, a sister, a friend, anyone who loved her, who cared that she was in that car that morning?

When she was born did her first shrilling breath of life bring incomparable joy to the ears it touched. And when she dies, will her final stifled gasp for life bring equal amounts of sorrow? Or will it fall upon deaf ears, or apathetic ears, or no ears at all? Her final faint plea for mercy is like the final gasp of the lonely tree falling dead in the woods; if no one is around to hear it, there was no plaintive sound to hear.

I climbed onto the roof and looked over the Jersey shoreline.

The moon didn't look any bigger than it did from my driveway. The black night was fading. The tip of the bleary sun peeked above the horizon, and the red of a new day seeped over the ocean and bathed the shore in blood. The purple sky rose out of the dark water and unfurled over the world.

The sun that sank ten hours ago on the other side of the world was rising again. That break of light gave me the feeling that life is not a series of days that flow into weeks which fill up the years, but life is just one long, continuous day, and night is a blink of the eternal eye.

The lazy waves quietly folded into themselves as the sun continued to rise over the horizon, spreading its dazzling light across the black water as if God was pulling the light out of the darkness, once again separating the white of day from the black of night.

I climbed down off the roof and sat under the arch between the big two-faced clock that overlooked the beach. It read 5:26.

◆◆◆

Out of the waves, two figures emerged, the yellow sunbeams bouncing off their glistening bodies. Dorian and Laticia walked up the beachhead. Two thin strands of cloth hung Laticia's slip tenuously over her shoulders, and the salty water pasted it to her burgeoning chest and faint hips. They climbed the warped steps, and at the top, Dorian bent down and rattled the knob of the spigot. Water gushed out across the walk, and he lifted each of her feet, washing away the sand.

He wrapped a white blanket around her, and she curled her arms inside, wriggled her body until her slip fell around her feet. She pulled the blanket tight and sat next to him on the wooden bench under the clock.

"Why did you come for me tonight?" Laticia asked.

"I took a chance he wouldn't show."

"What would you've done if he did?" she asked.

"I'm just glad he didn't."

"So am I."

"It wasn't right what he was doing to you."

She turned to him. "You knew what he was doing?"

"I knew he would let you down, one way or another." He reached out and took her hand in his. "Why'd you come with me?"

"You're not like the others." she said.

"I'm not?"

"That's a good thing. There's a stillness to you, a peace. You know what I mean?"

"Yeah, when I saw you in school, there was something about you. Something I haven't seen in anyone else," he said.

"There are things you don't know about me," her voice softened.

"I know all I need to know," he shook his head.

"You need to know about my past."

"I don't believe in the past."

"The past creates the present, and the present dictates the future," she said.

"It's all the present to me," he leaned over the railing. "The past doesn't matter."

"Doesn't it bother you what the other boys say?"

"No, it doesn't. I see you with my own eyes," he told her. "I don't care about your past."

"I need you to care. I need you to believe in me, not just overlook me," she told him. "I'm going to tell you anyway."

"Don't," he turned away.

"Then, I'm just gonna tell it to the ocean," she said.

"It doesn't matter."

"When I was a freshman, I became close with one of my teachers," her voice cracked momentarily. "He was brilliant, but mainly I liked that he paid attention to me. We'd talk for hours… about art, politics, current events, whatever. He taught me so much. He opened a whole new world to me. He took me to plays, and concerts. Things I never would've done. He was like the father I never had, but I always kept my distance."

"You didn't trust him?"

"I trusted him, but he was a teacher," she said. "Anyway, one day I was in his classroom after school. I'd been alone with him before. But this time, I don't know. It was different. It all happened so fast. He didn't say a word. His hands were all over me. He'd been so good to me; I would've done anything for him. I couldn't say no to him. I didn't feel like I had the right to say no to him. It was all over so fast.

"The only thing I remember is running down the hall crying,

trying to button my blouse, hoping no one would see me."

She gathered herself and waited. "I ran into the girl's room, into a stall and just cried and cried. I was bleeding. It wouldn't stop, so I just stayed in there, I don't know how long, until the bleeding and my tears stopped. I never told anyone, not even my mom. I just thought if I didn't say anything then it didn't happen." She didn't say another word for a couple of minutes. They just sat there looking out over the water.

"He didn't even acknowledge me after that, so I just blocked everything out. I thought I could just erase that whole thing from my life. But slowly, people started talking. I didn't care. I was already an outcast."

"Why didn't you say anything?"

"No one would believe me." She stood and leaned against the railing. "I felt so ashamed, like I did something wrong, like I let happen."

He wrapped his arms around her. "You did nothing wrong. You were perfect. I hate that you went through all that."

"I'm so dumb. I would have done anything for him, so he just took what he wanted, and tossed me aside. I should've known better. I'm so dumb." Her body curled forward as if in pain.

"Who's dumber?" he asked, "the girl who finds a rock and treats it like a diamond, or the man who finds a diamond and discards it like a rock?"

She turned back to him. "Sometimes, I think God looks down at us and laughs."

"He wouldn't laugh, would he? He probably just shakes his head in disbelief."

"You won't believe this, but that was the first and the last time I've done that with a man," she whispered loudly.

He bent down and drew in the scattered sand covering the boardwalk.

"He was the only man I've ever trusted." She looked right at him. "Until now."

They sat there just looking at the water.

"At the end of the year, he took a teaching job in the Midwest and I took four months off to have my baby. My mom told everyone I had mono, but they knew. The worst part is there are girls at my school who've been with so many boys, but they never got pregnant. So, they're still pure, still treated like queens, and I'm the school slut."

"You could never be that."

"I am that."

He turned to her. "What happened to the baby?"

"She's doing better than me. A couple from Maine adopted her, a lawyer and a doctor. I couldn't get rid of it. I knew the moment I felt that little life inside me, I loved her."

"You're amazing," he shook his head in awe.

"I remember holding her the day she was born. She was wrapped so tightly in this white blanket, so helpless, like a perfect little lamb. All I could see were her big blue eyes, looking around, absorbing everything like little sponges. I held her in front of me as long as they let me. I thought if she looked at me long enough, she would remember me."

"She'll remember," Dorian said softly. "She'll remember, even if she doesn't know it."

"The next day, I had to let her go. I cried and cried for two days straight. I fell in love with her the minute I held her."

He stroked her hand lightly.

"Still," she said as she gazed out over the rolling waves, "I feel guilty bringing her into this world, where the worst thing you can do is be accepted. I want to go back. I want to be a kid again. Everything's happened too fast."

Dorian brushed her dark hair away from her face and they held each other.

She looked up at him. "Do you think God punishes us for our sins?"

"Like, does God make us pay for our mistakes?"

"I don't know," she said. "Like send us to Hell, or purgatory, or some awful place?"

"The thing that makes God, God, and us, human, is that God loves everyone, even the worst of us. He even loves the murderers, the rapists, the selfish jerks, all of us. So, I don't believe you'll be judged on the mistakes you've made, or even your sins. God will judge you solely on how you love."

They sat next to each other, looking at the rising sun and the bluing sky. "Thanks for bringing me here. I love it here. The ocean erases everything."

They walked down the boardwalk and strolled through the parking lot. They stopped at the stranded Buick and stuffed a wad of bills into her hands, as if they were paying their toll for their moment on the beach.

♦♦♦

    I marched past my house and continued west on Main Street. The town was slowly awakening as the streetlights dimmed and the houses and storefronts stirred to life. I walked until I stood before the big red door of the small white church. The door opened with a long, loud groan, and there were four old bent ladies kneeling in the first pew, as still as statues in front of the flickering devotional candles waiting for mass to begin.

    "Forgive me, Father, for I have sinned." I performed the perfunctory sign of the cross.

    "What are your sins, my son?"

    "There are too many to recount, but one I must confess," I said.

    "Go on."

    "I've had impure thoughts about a girl. I think about her in a bad way. I try not to, but it just happens. It's like my mind has a mind of its own."

    "I see, my son," he said. "What is your sin?"

    "I tried to make this girl do something she didn't want to do, and I know we shouldn't do."

    "It's good you know you shouldn't do it." His deep calm voice tried to reassure me. "That's the most important thing."

    "I know but it seems like I'm the only one in the world that thinks that."

    "Your girl thinks that," he said. "Do you care for this girl?"

    "Yes."

    "Have you done anything with her you shouldn't do?"

    "No," I said. "I mean, we've kissed. Barely."

    "Good. You may not be able to control your thoughts, but you can control your body, and if you control your body, your mind will follow. This isn't your fault, you're a teenage boy. It's normal."

    "Sometimes I hate being a teenage boy."

    "Enjoy it while you have it." He leaned toward me. "I want you to say 10 Hail Marys, 10 Our Fathers and one Act of Contrition."

    "I thought it wasn't my fault."

    "The penance is for all those sins that are too numerous to recount."

I shut the thick wooden door with a thud and kneeled in the pew behind the old ladies. When I finished my penance, I walked to the back of the church with my head down, the clicking of my tux shoes echoing off the marble floors. As I approached the large red door, I saw it. I had never seen one before, and never thought I would see one in a place like this. I'd heard it called many different crude names and innocuous euphemisms, but I couldn't recall its actual name as I tried to process what I was seeing. What must have occurred last night for something like that to have been left there? It was long, translucent, and shriveled. I approached hesitantly. It didn't belong there. As I reached to pick it up, I saw the small round tip was filled with a whitish fluid. I backed away and sidestepped out of the door.

◆◆◆

I turned the handle to our front door. It was never locked. There wasn't even a key that fit into the keyhole. Anybody could have walked right into our living room at any time, day or night. The door rumbled open and I crept into the living room.

"How was your night?" my mother asked at the dining room table, the low rays of the morning sun rolling over her shoulders.

"It was OK," I told her.

She looked up at me through the steam rising from her oversized coffee mug. "I'm sure it was more than OK," she smiled. "You should've had a wonderful time." She sipped the coffee gently. "This is the time of your life, enjoy it."

"I don't know, Mom. Things just don't work out for me."

"Maybe you don't want them to work out."

"I do. I want to enjoy life, but nothing falls right for me."

"I look at you," she sighed heavily, "and you won't believe this, but you're more like me than your father."

"You never played sports."

"I know. You and your father have a lot in common, all that baseball, but you're more like me." She carefully placed the mug on the table. "He's a dreamer. He follows his heart in everything he does. You're more cautious, like me."

"I don't want to make mistakes. I don't want to have regrets.

Dad lives life like there's no such thing as regrets."

"He has regrets. There are things he wishes he'd never done."

"See, I don't want to live life filled with regrets."

"If you don't have regrets, you haven't lived."

"What about you?" I asked. "What are your regrets?"

"My only regret is I have no regrets." She placed the mug to her lips.

◆◆◆

"I'm sorry about what happened in the limo," I told Dawn over the phone later that morning. "I don't know what came over me."

"I'm always going to be a good Catholic girl," she apologized to my apology. "You know how I feel about you, Jake, but I'll never be like that girl Michelle. Never. I want you to be happy, but I won't change who I am to make you happy."

The line fell uncomfortably silent and my mind raced from thought to question to explanation, and then the words "why not" seeped through my closed lips, trickled into the holes on the mouthpiece of the phone, raced across town, and struck her ears. I could almost see the stunned expression on her face through the phone lines.

"Why not?" she said severely. "If that's what you want, by all means, go and get it. There are plenty of girls that'll give you that. I want you to be happy, Jake. I want you to get what you want. So, if that's what will make you happy, go get it, but remember you'll never find anybody who cares for you as much as I do."

"That's not what I want," I stated firmly. "I just want, I mean, what I want is... I don't know what I want," I conceded.

"We have so much ahead of us, Jake," she said. "Let's not ruin it. That'll be in our future. I know it will. And we will be incredible together, you and I, but not right now. We're not ready." The line was silent except for the soft crackle of static. "Do you know how old my mother is?" she finally asked.

"Forty. Forty-five?" I guessed. "My parents are in their 50s," I added.

"She's 34 years old. I," she emphasized the singularity of that word, "was a prom baby. My mom was 17 when I was born. My dad was barely 18. They never went to college. They never held a good job.

They've never made any money, and they never had another baby. So, I'm waiting until I'm ready. You're not ready at 16, at least, not me."

That summer, Dawn and I saw each other almost every day, but we were rarely alone together. She kept her distance, purposefully avoiding another limousine episode, asking me to be patient, reminding me that we will be great together one day.

I spent most days lazily at the beach, and most nights playing or watching baseball. Nothing exciting happened until the Rogers' front porch exploded from lightning one morning at three o'clock. Everyone in town started looking at us differently. They knew we were next.

∼ Part IV ∼

Chapter 40
(Fall 1998, age 17)

"One man's garbage is another man's dinner," Cullen observed as Dorian and Laticia strolled down the hall toward the athletic wing. "Pussy's undefeated, Jake. I'm tellin' ya: Un...de...feated."

Dorian and Laticia were inseparable and they floated through the school as if they lived in a self-contained world immune to the slings and arrows of the outside. They radiated a pure happiness that was felt by anyone who longed for it, and she glowed with the aura of newfound innocence.

It was the first time in my life that I didn't feel the slightest tinge of jealously for someone who had something I didn't have or might never get. I felt something that perfect must also be so exceedingly fragile that it would break under the weight of something as petty as jealousy.

How did they get so lucky? I wondered, not green with envy, but blue with sadness. They affirmed that what we long for does exist, for all, if we are patient enough to hold onto the innocence, the purity given to us at birth. I had failed to see their hope, but I see it now. I see everything now, but it's too late.

They parted at the athletic wing. He walked through the glass doors toward the gym, and she glided down the corridor, her plaid skirt wagging side to side.

"Laticia!" Cullen called out, but she continued walking, pretending not to hear. "Laticia!" His sharp voice stopped her.

She approached cautiously cradling her books against her modest chest.

"You're looking very nice," he observed, subdued.

She stared at him, cool and silent.

"I understand why you'd hate me but..."

"You understand..." she snapped incredulously.

"What happened..." he began.

"I don't want to hear it!"

"You should be thanking me." His meaty hand pawed her slender shoulder. "Think about it. If I didn't do what I did, you and Dorian wouldn't be together."

She slipped under his hand, and her sweater drooped below her shoulder.

"You're right. I should thank you for not showing up. I'm so glad you didn't." She walked away without another word.

I looked at him. "Why don't you just leave her alone?"

"Hey, if it weren't for me, they wouldn't be together." He then slapped me on the back. "Now tell me what's going on with Dawn?"

"I don't know," I shrugged.

"C'mon, you can tell me. She was pretty damn good, wasn't she? She's got a little tomcat in her?"

"Nothing happened," I had to admit.

"Let me get this straight. You've dated her all summer, and nothing happened? That's a damn shame." He shook his head.

"What? We're…" I squeaked.

"You've probably only kissed."

"So, so what?"

"You know what you are? You're her security blanket. She has you until someone else comes along and makes a woman out of her."

"You're wrong," I argued. "I think she loves me."

"She doesn't love you. If she did, we wouldn't be having this conversation. She would've already given it up."

"Maybe I don't want to do that."

"Everyone wants to do that," he said.

"I don't," I blurted.

"What are you trying to tell me? You like dudes?"

"No, I just don't go around screwing anyone with a pulse like everyone else. I'm better than that."

"You think you're better —"

"Jake! Jake!" cut through the clamor. I followed the sound and saw Ms. Vivaqua waving me over from the top of the stairs. I followed her into her office and sat down. "I was going through your file this morning, and even though you have fabulous extra-curriculars, maybe we're overshooting a little bit. There are other options that may better fit your academic profile."

"Like what?"

"State."

"I don't want to go to state college. My dad's not paying all this money for me to end up at state. I would've just gone to Cathedral."

◆◆◆◆

I drove home with Dorian after school in Johnny's '65 Mustang. "Doesn't it bother you what all those guys say about Laticia?" I asked him.

"Nope," he shook his head.

"How can't it?"

"Remember when Mrs. Armstrong took me to get my glasses?" he asked.

"Yeah, what does that got to do anything?"

"Laticia is like those glasses. When I'm with her, I see things I never saw before. It's like my life was black and white, and now it's all full of colors."

We turned into his driveway and his mother's new rusted car was docked next to the garage. She was back. Dorian's car skidded to a stop. He jumped out and sprinted up the steps to his house. When I pushed the screen door open and walked in, the walls were vibrating. The garbled shouts from in the back room shook the house. I sat down at the wooden kitchen table. Johnny pried at a hinge on the pantry door.

"I guess they're at it again," I said.

"Yeah, yeah," Johnny nodded as he examined his drill. "I just bought this." He tossed it to the side. "It's already broken."

"Should've gone to Walmart. They replace anything, no questions asked."

"Everyone's doing that now, unfortunately."

We heard a smoke-ravaged snarl of "You've gotta be shittin' me!" cut through the air.

"It's true," we heard Dorian fire back. "I never felt like this about anyone."

"He's a little crazy about this girl," I told Johnny. "He thinks he's in love."

Johnny looked at me. "There's nothing purer than a man's love for a woman."

"How would you know?" I asked.

"I was in love... once..." his words trailed off into a hazy memory.

"Really?"

"You don't think I'm capable of being in love?" He unscrewed the bottom hinge.

"I didn't say that."

"I was..." he pulled the door off the frame. "She was beautiful, the kindest woman I've ever met. And she loved me, too, if you can believe that."

"What happened?"

"She died." The words cut right through me like a knife. "It almost killed me. We had our whole life planned out. All the things we were going to do just disappeared. I didn't speak to anyone for months. I walked around like a zombie. I lost everything: my job, my wife, my life. I'm not ashamed to admit there were times when I thought of putting a bullet through my skull. But just when I was about to quit, I met Tina here, and she saved me." He leaned the door up against the side of the refrigerator.

"Tina?"

"I know no one gets why I'm here," he said, as small pools of water rested on his bottom eye lids. "But I had this love inside of me going to waste, and they had nobody to love them. I take care of their needs, and they take care of mine."

He lifted the broken door. "Sometimes, I feel like I'm doing this for her, too." He looked up.

"Like I owe it to her, more than Tina and the kids. Like, she's staring down at me and I'm trying to make her proud."

"I could care less about the little tart," she rasped as she stormed into the kitchen and sat at the table, Dorian at her heels.

"You don't know her. No one knows her like I do."

"Do you know who her father is?" She blew a stream of smoke that rolled over Dorian's face. "Do you?"

"Her father is insignificant," he coughed.

"Is he?"

"I don't love her father, I love her. She's like me, she doesn't have a father," he paused, looked across the room, and regrettably lifted his open palm. "Sorry, John."

Johnny nodded at him.

"Find out who her father is, and you'll stop loving her," her gravelly voice predicted. "Believe me, you will."

"You don't understand," Dorian stood powerfully, pounded his fist, knocking the table into her lap.

She leapt to her feet. Her bony hand struck the side of his face with a sharp clap, knocking him back to his seat. "Don't tell me I don't understand. I used to wipe your ass."

He just sat there unfazed.

Then, the slightest smile creased his stone facade. "Nothing will ever stop me from loving her." He pushed himself up and rushed out the door.

"Just remember, Jake," she turned to me after a long silence. "He will spend the rest of his life paying for someone else's sins."

◆◆◆◆

I caught up to him and we walked along the craggy road in silence, his shoes kicking the loose pebbles and broken asphalt.

I finally broke the silence. "Do you ever want to smack her, just smack her back?"

He looked at me. "You don't hit your mom. Nobody hits their mom," he said with such assurance that if I'd tried to remind him of what had just happened, he would have stared at me with the same look and said, 'Mother's don't hit their kids. Nobody hits their kids.'"

"What are you going to do about Laticia?"

"I don't care about her father, and I don't care about my mother. I'm not going to stop seeing her."

◆◆◆◆

"The last days of summer are always so sad," Dawn said that night as she and I sat under a green umbrella, licking rainbow ices and staring out over the ocean. The red, white and blue ice turned our lips purple, as we raced to consume them before the warm September night did.

"You're eating it too fast," I tried not to laugh. "It's better to take things slow."

"But not too slow," her voice was pained, "or it'll melt away. Last time I was here," she added between licks, "Bruce rode up on his motorcycle. He just walked up and bought a pistachio ice."

"Springsteen did not get pistachio!"

"I swear to God he did."

"Did you say anything to him?"

"No, I was too nervous, but it was so cool, Jake. I wished you were here."

"You did?"

"Of course," she smiled at me like I were a child. "I would've loved for you to be here."

"Really?" I looked right at her. "No one's ever wished I was anywhere."

She smiled at me. "You are the most beautiful man I know."

"You must know a lot of ugly people then." I placed my left hand on her back and leaned my lips toward hers. She dropped her right shoulder and turned her head. My lips landed on her right cheek.

"Ya know, sometimes it is better to take things slow," she stepped away with a demure smile.

"But not too slow," I laughed.

She pressed the slushy ice to her lips and smiled a mouthful of colors.

NW

Chapter 41

"Failing to do good is as sinful as doing bad," my mother said when I told her I was considering not doing the turkey drive. So, I volunteered for the fourth year in a row, but this time I was in charge, breaking in an idealistic freshman.

"You're lucky," I told Gage Turner, the gangly freshman as he climbed in the car. "It's a beautiful Indian summer day."

"Don't say that," he reproved me. "It's racist."

"I didn't mean any..."

"It doesn't matter what you meant. It's still offensive."

"It's just a common express..."

"Don't rationalize your racism with me." He looked away like he couldn't stand the sight of me.

We drove away from the school, and he leaned his head against the passenger's window. "What do we got to do?"

"You don't got to do anything," I told him. "We have the opportunity to bring Thanksgiving dinners to people who need it."

He rolled his head away from me and stared out the window without a word. I parked in front of a crumbling house with a sagging porch. Dispirited angry eyes glared out of dark windows and followed us walking from the car to the front door.

"We're not gonna get mugged or something?" he asked.

"Maybe we will, maybe we won't," I said, knocking on the crooked door. The hinges screeched open. Two white eyes peered through the open sliver. His face was shrouded by the blackness.

"Oh," he slid the door open.

"Hey, aren't you..." Gage pointed at him.

I grabbed his arm. "I thought you lived... You live here?" I asked.

"Uh, no." Curtis said, and looked down. "This is my aunt's house." He stepped back behind the door. "You can just leave that stuff there. I'll bring it in."

"Are you sure? We can take it..."

"That's OK. I got it," he slowly closed the door.

We placed the box and turkey on the porch and trotted down the steps to the car.

"Doesn't that kid go to Bainbridge?" Gage asked.

I looked him square in the eye. "Don't tell anybody what you just saw."

"Why can't..."

"Don't say a word," I barked.

"I don't understand..."

"Yeah, you don't understand, so keep your mouth shut!"

The next house pulsated to the driving beat of a thumping bass. My door-rattling knock could not penetrate the pounding beat. I looked in through the side window, and all I saw was the low flickering lights of a stereo. I knocked again. No answer.

"Let's just leave it and go," Gage whispered.

I turned the knob and pushed. The door creaked open. "Hello?" I leaned into the room. Prince's oversized, pixilated head was singing on the far wall, projected from the oversized TV.

Then, the music screeched to silence. "What the fuck are you doing here?"

My arms flailed, knocking the door wide open. Gage dove to the ground, face first into the balding carpet. "Who the hell are you?" he demanded as he gripped the thick, black baseball bat, cocked and ready above my head.

Every muscle in my body locked up, as I stared at his rippling forearms. "I'm just, I'm just..."

He cocked the bat higher. "I'm gonna smash your fuckin' face in."

"Turkey drive!" Gage screamed. "Turkey drive!"

I held out the cardboard box. His bloodshot eyeballs rolled down and peered inside. He grabbed it with his free hand and tossed it across the room. "Now, get the fuck off my porch before I smash your skull in." He pressed the bat against my chest and pushed me back out of the house.

We stumbled across the porch and sprinted down the steps to the car. "His TV was bigger than my dad's. He should be bringing us turkeys," Gage said as we squealed away.

"I appreciate the way you backed me up," I quipped.

"Fuck that. I'm not getting my skull smashed in for this shit."

I parked in front of the last house.

"I'm not going," Gage said.

"C'mon, let's go. I'm not bringing it all..."

"I'm not going! I don't give a rat's ass if they get this food or not."

"Fine." I loaded the box and grabbed the turkey.

From the outside, the final house didn't look much different than the others, a broken porch light and a bent storm door. A young woman with a thin, well-defined face, leaned against the frame.

She pushed the door open and her long thin arm waved me in without a word. She was tall and spindly. A yellow housedress hung off her razor-sharp shoulders and lightly outlined her thin waist and narrow hips. Her large white teeth sparkled, accentuating her deep blackness. I could see every bone, every tendon, every ligament of her joints. Her hair was darker than her skin, short, straight and pulled back. Her eyes drooped around the edges and the whites were tinged yellow.

I walked through the door and she quickly turned away. A couch and a table with four mismatched chairs were arranged haphazardly and were surrounded by blank walls and bare floors.

From hidden rooms and anonymous corners, five children appeared like apparitions. They were all cut from their mother's cloth, tall and lean, with long white teeth, full round eyes and jet-black skin. They huddled around her, touching and clinging to her wispy frame. The tallest reached up to her hip and the smallest just above her knee. Not one of the five wore an article of clothing that was whole.

I placed the box and the turkey on the table. "Is this OK?" My voice shuddered at their indigence. She took a step to help me, but nervously backed away.

"Thank ya so much, sir," she said, almost apologetically. She was barely older than my sister and seemed as helpless as her children. Their wide eyes and open mouths followed my every move, like I was Santa Claus himself. "Never see so much food in ma 'tire life," her voice shimmered in awe. She lifted the turkey with both her hands. I feared that her boney arms would snap under its weight. "It's a biggun. Lass year, turkey ma husband brung, we ate on it a whole three week, this one's gonna git us to Chrissmas, think?"

I nodded.

"Wish I could pay ya," she offered regretfully. "Not much money, since Donnie gone."

"Where is he?" I asked without thinking.

"He with Jesus," the tallest boy spoke up.

"Really?" I bent down to him. "I'm sorry."

"Ain't nothing you done," the mother said. "Theys shot him."

"Who shot him? Why?"

"Don't much matter now, do it?" A sad smile crept across her face. "God's will, God's will," she said, content to sublimate her grief with an empty platitude.

"I hope this food helps," I said and shuffled back to the door.

As I turned to leave, her long bony arms lassoed my neck, hugging me without a word, my body stiff, my arms dangling. She pressed her full, moist lips next to my ear, and held the kiss uncomfortably long.

"Maybe now you'll have a Thanksgiving," I told her.

"We always have Thanksgiving," she said blankly. As I shut the door, I saw five little kids standing around their wobbly table, their buoyant eyes watching their mother unpack cans of peas, green beans and cranberry sauce.

Pulling away toward Galilee, I looked back over my shoulder at the crumbling neighborhood, tugged by my empathetic guilt.

"We didn't do a thing," I told Gage. "We did nothing."

"I'm glad I gave up my entire Saturday then."

"We didn't. Do we really think that a turkey and some canned foods does anything to actually help anyone other than making us feel good about ourselves? It helps us more than them."

"You can change the world after you graduate from Yale," he said.

◆◆◆◆

"I didn't get in," I told Ms. Vivaqua the following Monday in her office as I handed her my first rejection letter.

She flashed a reassuring smile. "I think they were probably looking for something with a little more punch." Her voice was hesitant, searching for the answer. "Class president, editor of the school newspaper. Something with a significance." She pulled her skirt straight as she opened my file.

"I just thought if you worked hard and did the right things, everything would work out," I said.

"That's a lovely thought, Jake, but it's not reality," she sighed.

"I guess my volunteer work didn't mean anything?" I looked

away embarrassed.

"It means a lot," she said, "but sometimes in life, just being good isn't good enough. Or maybe, they were just interested in the numbers."

"What do I do now," I said, leaning toward her, "Ms. Vivaqua?"

"You need something that stands out." She ran her hand through her thick blond hair. "Something that jumps off this page that says, 'You need me at your school.'"

"Like what?"

"I don't know, sweetie, but we'll figure that out. It's still early," she smiled. "You still have six other applications out there. Don't be discouraged."

"That's easier said than done." I walked out of her office and down toward chapel with my head down, hiding the shame of my rejection, but knowing everyone could see it and feel it. I sat down in my embarrassment. Mr. McGovern stepped to the podium, and invited Cullen, Jay, Carter Alexander, Derek Cox and three other seniors to come on stage.

"These boys," he swept his arm at them, "have all been accepted early to some of the most prestigious universities in the country: Princeton, Dartmouth, Yale, MIT, Georgetown. Let's all give them a round of applause for their hard work and achievement."

The world suddenly felt twisted and misaligned. I was better than all those guys, and I knew that these schools that didn't want me will never understand the mistake they were making.

◆◆◆◆

That afternoon, the unseasonably warm day lured me across the street, and I sat on the boardwalk, searching for answers, with the mist of the crashing waves floating around me. The beach had the barren, unkempt look of winter. The waning sun sat low behind me in the darkening sky, and its flaxen rays spread out over the shimmering water, catching every ripple, every imperfection, glittering like a sea of gold.

There must have been one wave for each grain of sand, I thought as the waves poured in with assiduous ease.

"The waves look like in a painting," Dawn said as she sat down next to me. "Your mom said you were here."

"I think there's gonna be a full moon tonight."

"Why?" she asked.

"The moon makes the waves."

"No, the wind makes the waves."

"There's no wind today," I said.

"You never feel the wind that makes the waves," she told me. "The waves are made from the wind of some storm thousands of miles away, in Africa or Antarctica."

At the far end of the beach, two shadowy figures, shrouded in the sun's rays and the ocean spray, walked toward us, side by side, and then stopped. Laticia wrapped her arms around Dorian in a big hug, and buried her head in his chest, clinging to him, then she pushed away, and ran toward the boardwalk with her head down, hands over her face. Dawn squeezed my hand twice as Laticia stumbled up the steps and ran down the boardwalk. Dawn looked at me, and then ran after her.

I climbed down onto the beach and walked toward Dorian. A white gull pecked at the insides of a clam, and another sucked the meat out of the underside of a crab. "They'll never need a food drive here," I said, walking up behind him.

Dorian casually bent down and picked up a clam as it rolled in with the waves. "The birds don't sow or reap or store away in barns." He held the clam in his right hand, studying its chalky shell. His shoulder muscles flexed inward, and in one smooth motion he pried the shells apart. He scooped out the raw meat and stared out over the water. "And God feeds them all." He launched the meat into the air and a gray gull swooped down, snatched it, and flew away like they did this every day. "Who of you by worrying can add a single hour to this life?"

"You OK?"

He nodded unconvincingly. "Why wouldn't I be?"

"You're talking crazy."

"I'm OK," he said.

"She didn't seem OK."

"She will be." He shook his head. "It's just that her father... her father is... her father is..."

"Screw her father," I said. "I don't care what he is, or what he did. I don't even know why she visits him in jail, anyway."

"She doesn't visit her father," his voice collapsed in exasperation.

"Where does she go on Saturdays, then?"

"She visits people."

"Who?"

"All kinds. She goes to old folks' homes, hospitals. She'll spend an afternoon holding a crack baby. Anybody who needs somebody."

"Is that what you like about her?"

"You know when you hit the ball just right?"

"No, never," I smiled.

"So perfectly, that when the bat cuts through the ball, you don't even feel like you hit it, but the ball takes off anyway, and you feel all-powerful. That's how I feel when I'm with her." He walked away, his feet sliding along the sand, leaving me alone on the empty beach.

I looked out over the beach and wondered what this was like before we got here. *It must have been paradise, with sand so white and water so blue. What will it look like a hundred years from now, a thousand years from now, buried beneath the sea, forgotten forever, like all of us?*

I climbed the stairs and walked across the boardwalk in the direction of my house. I noticed a book with a brown paper cover sitting on the bench. I picked it up and a sky-blue envelope fell out. The handwriting on the envelope against the blue sky, rainbow and white clouds, had a distinct feminine script. I carefully slid the letter from the envelope and slowly unfolded the rigid piece of paper.

Dear Dorian,

If a wish could bring you happiness, then I wish a thousand wishes for you, and if just a little love would free you from your pain, then I would love you a million times more. If I had a magic wand, I would order the sunshine to dry up your tears and return the happiness to your heart. Of course, I don't have any of these special powers. All I can offer you is my friendship. Know that I will always be here for you.

We are not monsters or bad people. Don't let anyone doubt the innocence of what we shared. No one can understand unless they know about the forests and the waterfalls, and the colors and the magic, and only you and I will ever truly know about all of that. You are the most special, decent person I know. Try not to feel guilty about being human.

There's a place for people like us, hidden in the forests where waterfalls flow and rainbows end. Always follow your heart.

Love always,

Laticia

I hid the book in my jacket, and never told Dorian I had it. I kept the letter. I didn't really know what it all meant, but I knew no one would ever write a letter like that to me.

◆◆◆◆

"What did Laticia say?" I asked Dawn as we walked down the pier that night. I wanted to show her the letter, but it wasn't mine to show.

"She was very upset," Dawn told me. "She kept crying and crying about how they can't be together, something about her dad, and I guess his mom is being... "

"Yeah, think about this one: She smacks Dorian and Karen all the time, leaves for weeks at a time, and then she's gonna judge Laticia because her father got busted for something. Believe me, no one's nominating Tina for mother of the year."

She grabbed my hand. "It'll be OK. Everything will work out for them. His mother can't keep them apart. Nothing can."

That night, we sat down in the carousel on the boardwalk and the tinny music spun us around and around. Until that moment, I wasn't sure if I liked her, or if I just liked that she liked me. But a dull ache had slowly begun to fester in my soul, fluctuating between a self-affirming bliss and a gut-wrenching pain every time I thought of her.

"I think I will remember the name Suzie O'Malley the rest of my life," she said as our sleigh peaked and valleyed around the carousel.

"Who's Sally O'Malley?"

"Suzie." She pointed toward a gold sign at the top of the sleigh: *In Loving Memory of Suzie O'Malley.*

"No one will ever put up a plaque like that for me," I said.

"You don't want that."

"Why not?"

"Because you have to be dead."

"I wonder who she was, what she was like, what she did to have her name up there."

"All I know about her," she said, "is that I can tell my grandkids I was sitting in her sleigh when I first realized I loved their grandfather."

NW

Chapter 42

"I would have thought that we would've found you a home by now," Ms. Vivaqua said as she looked over my six new rejection letters. I stared at the unfastened heart-shaped button on her sheer blouse, and wondered if it was undone on purpose, or had fallen open naturally.

"It doesn't add up." She removed her glasses. Her big, brown, impassive eyes peered into mine.

"It does add up," I told her. "I'm just an average white kid. The world's full of me. There's nothing unique about me. Nothing that people really want. I guess I'm just not that deserving."

"Don't talk like that." She perched her glasses on the tip of her nose and scanned my file one last time. "You are special, Jake. Don't ever forget that. Your uniqueness just can't be seen in here," she shook the folder in front of her face. "Can't be measured by raw numbers. Just don't be discouraged, dear. I believe in you."

"Thanks, Ms. Vivaqua."

She smiled. "Jake, please, call me Sylvia."

"I... I don't know," I almost laughed. "I don't know if I can do that."

"Don't you like my first name?"

"I lov... I like it a lot. It's just, you know, you're a teacher."

"I'm your advisor, Jake," she cut me off. "We," she pointed her finger back and forth between us, "work together to help you. We're both adults." She removed her glasses and looked into my eyes. "You know, really, I'm not that much older than you."

"OK, I'll try," I said nervously.

She leaned back in her chair, her chest arching forward, straining the buttons. "Jake, I'm always here for you whenever you need anything." She pushed herself up. "Don't give up."

I rose. "You need some help with that?" I motioned to her stack of books.

"That would be very nice, Jake." Her smile cut right through me. She set the books into my hands, her soft silk sleeves slid across my tingling arms, her delicate fingers grazed my bare palms. I walked behind her down the hall, my eyes fixed on her skirt, hugging her flowing hips. We turned into the conference room, and I placed the books on the round table. "Do you need anything else?" I paused. "Sylvia?"

Her long white teeth burst from her full red lips into an all-consuming smile. "No, that was perfect."

I left the room. "Sylvia? Sylvia? Oh, Sylvia!" mocked me from behind. "What's that all about?" Quinton laughed, his round head bobbing, his white teeth shining. "I like your instincts but that ain't getting you into any school. She doesn't have that much power."

"I was just trying to be nice," I told him.

"Nice don't get you in either, son," he shook his head.

◆◆◆◆

I went straight to the athletic wing. I wanted to get a head start on the season. Baseball was my only hope now. I burst through the large black metal door to the locker room and was hit in the face by the thick, stale air of fermenting sweat like the jolt of smelling salts to a punch-drunk boxer. As I walked toward my locker, my eyes caught two boys huddled in a corner feverishly copying passages from a stack of wrinkled papers into bright blue exam books.

"What are you guys doing?" I peered around their meaty hands.

They dropped the exam books. "Nothing, we're just copying some study notes," Cullen said calmly.

"Why are you putting them into those? Why not regular notebooks, so you can keep 'em all together..." My voice trailed off as our eyes locked, both realizing what I just realized. "You can't..."

"Why the hell does it matter to you?" Cullen picked up the exam book defiantly, snapped it open and began scribbling again.

I slid past them, and long stepped it to my locker with my head down without a word.

"He's not gonna say anything. He doesn't have it in him," Cullen's voice echoed over the lockers.

I sat on the wooden bench, my heart pumping so fast that I fumbled with the dial to my lock like I was all thumbs.

I was sick to my stomach, not at their crime, but at the courage demanded of me to confront it, courage I wasn't sure I had. I stared at my lock, wishing I could unlock this problem as easy as spinning three numbers on that dial. I wanted to relive the last five minutes, walk backward through that big black door and erase it from my memory.

I knew what the right thing to do was. I knew what I was obligated to do according to the Honor Code, and I knew my culpability if I failed to report what I had just witnessed. I also knew that I did not have the strength to do it. I wanted to pretend I never saw what I saw, then maybe it didn't happen. I sat on the bench, simmering in the stench of human exertion. I couldn't move. I wanted to remain hidden there, but I knew I couldn't. So, with one big breath, I summoned all my courage and marched back to them.

"I never pegged you as a cheater," I said, as I walked up to Cullen. He was scratching the remaining notes into the exam book.

"I'm not a cheater. I'm an opportunist."

"What's the difference?"

"Everybody needs a little help once in a while," he winked.

"No, they don't," I replied.

"You mean to tell me you never looked on someone else's paper? You never asked for an answer? You never wrote a crib? Ever?"

"Never," I said unwaveringly.

"Never?" he repeated. "At least we're honest with ourselves about what we're doing."

"You don't look very honest."

"What are you going to do about it?" Cullen rose. "When are you gonna lose this boy scout act?" He moved so close to me I could feel his warm words and his pounding heart.

"It's your life," I said indifferently. "You're gonna pay for this. One way or another, it all evens out."

"I know, I know... we are only cheating ourselves, right," he laughed.

"No, you're cheating everyone. You signed the honor code."

"We're not breaking the honor code." Wally said, pointing to his exam book. "Look at this." On the cover in a hasty script, he had written: *I pledge my honor that I did not violate the honor code on this exam.*

He ran his thumb along the edge of the empty book exposing the blank sheets. "See? I didn't violate the honor code on *this* exam book." And then with his thumbnail, he pried out the staples, removed the blue covers, then quickly exchanged them with the different book he had written in and carefully pressed the staples closed. "The honor code was true when I wrote it, so it's still true."

"That doesn't even make any sense," I tore the books from his hands. "You're too stupid to come up with a believable rationalization."

"Give 'em to me!" Wally flung his arm at me and snatched them back. "When I wrote the honor code it was true, so it's still true."

"Don't do this, Wally," I pleaded. "Just throw the books away and take the test the right way. It's wrong."

"I don't give a damn what you think," Wally said.

"What are you going to do when you're out in the real world? Cheat your way through your job?"

"You don't think people in the real world cheat? You don't think those motherfuckers on Wall Street are cheating every day of their lives? What about politicians, lawyers, journalists? You don't think they cheat? You don't think they lie? You're the one not living in the real world with your goody two shoes crap. This," Wally held up his blue exam book, "is preparing me for the real world."

"Look," Cullen stepped in, "there is no right or wrong, Jake. You'll learn that sooner or later. Plus, it's scientifically proven that the human mind retains only 10 percent of what it reads, 20 percent of what it hears, but 70 percent of what it does. I'm learning more by writing it out than I would by reading or studying, and isn't that what school's all about? Learning, not what grade you get?"

"At least your rationalization makes some kind of sense," I said, almost laughing. "But now that you wrote it out, take the test for real."

"That's double work. That'd be stupid."

I took a deep breath. "If you guys do this, I got no choice but to go to Armour." I walked out the door, and down the athletic corridor. Shorty was pushing a mop across the floor. I inhaled deeply, fully imbibing the acerbic smell of disinfectant, like I was trying to sanitize my mind, my soul, from what I had just witnessed. I stared at the pictures on the wall and read the names of all the baseball most valuable players dating back to the turn of the century.

Shorty mopped his way over to me. "Help me with something?" He walked toward the back exit. I followed. He stopped at a closet next to the exit and rattled his keys into the knob. He looked over at me. "If I had a dollar for every time I saw what you just saw, I wouldn't be mopping these floors."

The door swung wide, exposing a closet piled to the ceiling with misshapen boxes. He flipped the switch and the hazy orange of the naked bulb glowed. He reached up, pulled a large box off the shelf, and dropped it into my outstretched arms.

"Downstairs," he stumbled out of the door, hugging his own

awkward box.

I followed him down the cement stairwell, the oversized box clanging with each awkward step. At the bottom of the stairs, I placed my box on a rolled-up wrestling mat, while he hunted through his thick ring of keys.

"What's in these things, anyway?" I tugged at the clear tape holding the flaps together.

"Don't know," he riffled through the keys.

"If you don't know, why are you moving it?" I asked.

"Been there for 10 years, can't be all that important."

I peeled the tape back and the long flap popped open. Resting crookedly on top was a large, black cup. I pulled it out, and rubbed my finger along the base, removing the tarnish covering the engraving.

1946
NEW JERSEY STATE BASKETBALL CHAMPIONS
BAINBRIDGE
18-2

I dug through the box, and found a plaque.

1953
MOST VALUABLE PLAYER
TOBY VAN HUTTON

I pulled out an old baseball and a deflated football with faded writing on them. The box was filled with black balls, bent trophies, tarnished plaques, all representing a moment of athletic achievement of the school. I took out each piece and carefully set them along the top of the wrestling mat.

"What are you doing?" Shorty asked.

"There's some mistake. Do they know about all these?"

"Does who know about what?"

"McGovern, or someone, know these are here?"

"All I know is they've been here forever, and no one's wanted 'em."

"Can I keep this?" I held up the black state championship cup.

"Ain't yours to keep, or mine to give."

I placed each piece back in the box in a neat meaningless order and stashed the box in the back of the damp storage room behind a broken basketball backboard, my eyes the last to see these fading remnants of high achievements.

◆◆◆◆

I stepped out into the shifting cold of early spring with my catcher's gear slung over my shoulder and walked along the winding path through the woods to the athletic fields. A streak of warmth flowing in the bitter air hinted at the unspoiled promise of spring.

"What the hell've you been eating, fertilizer?" Delaney walked up from behind and swatted my back with a thud. "You're as stout as a mule. What's happening with you? Any news on college?"

"Universally rejected." I looked away. "I'm gonna be stuck at some directional school, or just go to community college."

"Nothing wrong with that. A lot of great men went to community college."

"I'll be the only kid in America who'll go to college closer to his house than his high school."

"The man makes the college, Jakie, the college doesn't make the man. You'll get more out of JCC than a lot of these rich SOBs will ever get out of Harvard. Trust yourself. It'll work out."

"I don't know. Maybe I should've just cheated my way through. It seems to work for everyone else."

"Jake, you're better than that," he admonished me.

"Apparently not."

"You don't realize how fortunate you really are," he said.

"Well, that's kinda hard to do when I'm standing next to Princeton and Harvard wearing a Western Connecticut State sweatshirt," I told him. "It doesn't seem fair."

"If this is the great injustice of your life, you're way ahead of the rest of us."

"I just want to go someplace decent."

"Listen," he said in a low voice as if it was a secret, "Ed McPhee's a friend of mine. He scouts this area for the Mets. He's seen you play. I've talked to him about you. If you have a big season, they'll draft you."

"I want to go to college not the minors," I told him. "I'm not getting stuck in A-ball for 10 years like..."

"If you get drafted, the colleges will call," he said. "That's why it's important to have a great season."

I shrugged.

"Trust me, and smile for chrissake," he said. "You use more muscles to frown than you do to smile."

"I'm doing neither so I'm wasting nothing," I replied and walked away.

◆◆◆◆

"You're either getting better or you're getting worse." Delaney paced in front of us before our first practice. "You never stay the same. What we did last year means nothing. We're back at ground zero. You can never assume anything in this game, in this life. The hay is never in the barn. Never."

He paused, took a step back, looked us over. "Success is only achieved through hard work. And no team on our schedule will be better prepared than us. You can't cheat success." He stared right at me. "If we don't outwork our opponents in practice, we don't deserve to beat them in the games. Nothing in life is free. America's full of opportunity. You always get what you deserve, if you pay the price."

You get what you deserve? You can't cheat success? Those are lies. I was angry, not at any one thing in particular. I was angry at everything.

I stepped into the cage, gripped my bat, and hit 11 of my 20 batting practice pitches over the left field fence, more than both Dorian and Cullen, and I flipped my bat against the cage in defiance.

But after practice, Delaney set the tees up anyway.

"We're back to these?" I asked. "I'm way past these."

"You feel pretty good about yourself, don't you?"

I shrugged.

He placed a ball on the tee. "Hit the ball!"

I threw my bat head at the ball and drove it into the net. He placed another, and I drove that one too. I hit every ball he put up there with as much ferocity as I could muster. I didn't care anymore. *If he wants me to hit a thousand balls off the damn tee, I'll hit a thousand balls. It doesn't matter anymore. I'll never get what I deserve. Never.*

NW

Chapter 43

Everything's fake, I told myself as I dropped my calculus exam on the teacher's desk the next day. I daydreamed through the test. I wrote down the first thing that came to my mind, randomly filling in blanks. I didn't care. *What good are grades and tests? They're fake, just like everything else.*

"Jake," Mr. Alexander walked toward me, "we have some things to discuss." He grabbed my arm and ushered me into an empty classroom. The room was dark except for the light flowing in from the hallway. He sat on the top of the teacher's desk, looking down on me. "A little bird told me about an incident in the locker room yesterday?"

I nodded.

"It appears you have a big choice to make."

I nodded again.

"Sometimes when you have a decision like this, you have to look at the big picture," he began. "Ask yourself if this school is ready to deal with a scandal of this proportion. You know the tradition, the reputation that's at stake here."

"But isn't what they did against the traditions, the honor, the reputation of the school we're trying to protect?" I asked.

"Yes, if what you're saying is true, but it's your word against theirs. Who will they believe?"

I just stared at him. "I know what I saw."

"Yes, but with no other evidence, it will come down to personal character. Everyone already knows that you vandalized Mr. Kaufman's car."

"I didn't do it. It was Cart—"

"But do they know that you got caught cheating at St. Francis..."

"No, I wasn't—"

"Or smashed the windshields of 20 cars, and stole money from a charity carnival?"

"That's not—"

"All of that will come out if you bring an inquest before the honor committee, so think about it. Do you really want to put yourself through this? Put the school through a scandal? Do we really want to lose Cullen? Or Wally? How will that affect their future? How would it affect the team? The chance at states? Nothing good will come out of turning them in. You won't just be punishing Wally and Cullen. You'd be punishing Jay, and Quinton, and Curtis, and Dorian. You're punishing the whole school. Do you really think your character can hold up against Cullen's?"

I didn't say another word.

"I can count on your honor."

I nodded, unconvincingly, and left the classroom.

Quinton walked up from behind. "How'd you do on calc? When in doubt, look about, huh?"

"Who cares? I'm gonna end up at community college anyways. They take good students. They take bad students. They take honest kids. They take cheaters. So, who gives a damn?"

I marched straight down the steps, across the main foyer, through the front doors and out the iron gates. I walked along the side of the road, heading east, toward the beach. Cars zipped past, spraying billows of invisible fumes in my face. I walked and walked until I made it to my old Little League field, chewed up by bright yellow bulldozers. I leaned against the rusted fence looking at the bulldozers perched on the edges of the field poised for action like they were waiting for the coach to send them in.

Cullen pulled up in his car and walked over to me. "There you are. I could've given you a ride."

"I wanted to walk," I replied.

He extended his right hand, and I left it dangling in mid-air. He stuffed his hand in his pocket. "I was scrambling," he said. "If I get an 'F', Princeton may pull my acceptance. I wasn't prepared. You know, with the season, my mom, everything. Haven't you ever been in that position? I couldn't fail."

"You did fail," I told him.

"You know, my dad knows a lot of people." He grabbed my arm. "Important people. Give me the list of the schools you want to go to, and your test scores. He'll get you in someplace good. He's got a lot of stroke. I promise."

"Really?"

"I'm in Princeton aren't I?"

"He would do that?" I looked up hopefully. "I mean, he can get me in?"

He laughed. "Within reason, dude. Let's not go overboard. It's not like you're Ivy League material."

"Thanks... Cullen, thanks a lot."

"Is that your old man?" He pointed beyond the heaping mounds of earth, across the wild grass, to a group of kids playing in front of the burnt orange rusted backstop of the original Little League field. A little barefoot boy in faded jeans and a white undershirt held the bat, while a handful of other boys stood in the field.

"Swing at pitches you can hit," the distant echo of my father's voice bounced off the riverbank. "Do it right!" The boys stood mesmerized by his intense passion.

He threw with the same short quick motion I've seen a million times.

"Yeah, that's him," I said.

"What the hell's he doing?" Cullen asked.

"Why don't you go ask him yourself?"

As I continued to watch, I felt the condescending smirk on Cullen's face. I was proud of where I came from. I just leaned against the fence and watched, and it was at that moment I realized that maybe my dad gave me the best part of himself.

◆◆◆◆

I never turned Cullen or Wally in. I'm not sure why. I wasn't scared of the threats or lured by the influence. I would have turned them in before I took a bribe not to. It just didn't make sense to comply with an honor code that required the innocent to perform the dishonorable act of ratting out teammates. I felt powerful in my silence. I owned the truth, but that was all I had.

NW

Chapter 44

"You made the right decision," Mr. Alexander told me when he shook my hand before the opening game.

"I made the best decision, not the right one," I replied.

◆◆◆◆

"Today, every team is undefeated, and every team is winless," coach Delaney told us before we took the field that day. "Everything we did last year is gone. Past successes do not guarantee future successes. Everything must be re-earned again, and again, and again. And so, it begins today."

We were tied the top of the sixth, but they had runners on first and second. Cullen's curve bounced on top of the plate, and ricocheted off my right shoulder, down the first base line. The runner broke toward third as I scrambled after the ball. I grabbed it and fired it to third from one knee. Curtis snared my chin high throw and dropped his glove in front of the bag as the runner slid into it.

I rose up on one knee and wagged my right index finger at the runner. "Don't do it. Don't do it." I then fired a series of air gunshots at him as he walked back to his dugout.

◆◆◆◆

"A walk's as good as a hit Jake," Quinton's father called out as I stood in the box with the bases loaded and a three-ball count. The next pitch was high, and out of the strike zone. I knew it was ball four. I knew I shouldn't have swung, but it was there before me, alluring, enticing, growing bigger and whiter with each nearing millimeter. I wanted it, so I went after it.

My bat cut right through the zone effortlessly, and if not for the crack of the bat, I would have thought I missed it completely. The white ball streaked across the blue sky, shining and glowing. I stood several steps down the first base line, admiring what I had just done. I wanted to savor every moment. I trotted around the bases with a self-satisfied swagger, slowing down to dramatically touch each bag, holding onto that moment as long as possible. When I approached home plate, I stopped, looked around, pointed to the sky like Sammy Sosa, and then casually touched home before everyone on my team swarmed me.

◆◆◆◆

I waited in the dugout after practice the next day, as my teammates filtered off the field to the school or to their shiny cars. Delaney walked by.

"Aren't we gonna take some B.P.?" I asked hesitantly.

He shook his head. "You have it all figured out."

"What are you talking about?

He looked at me. "You'll never learn. No matter what I do. You can lead a horse to water, but you can't make him swim."

"That doesn't even make any—"

"You're just wasting my time, Jake." He was calm and content. "You don't respect the game; you don't respect yourself."

"I do—"

"He who puts himself on display, does not shine very brightly." He walked away.

"But—"

"There is no but. But is the most dangerous word in the human language." A tint of red slowly seeped across his face.

"I do need your help."

"No you don't. That was quite obvious yesterday. Jake, we are tested in both the deserts and in the oases," he said and walked away.

Fine, I told myself as I watched him walk up the hill. I didn't need him anymore either. No one believes in me, no college coach, no pro scout, and now not even Delaney; no one. But I'm going to prove everyone wrong.

And I did, the next game. I hit two doubles in two at-bats. Quinton's arm was on fire. His fastball was moving viscously, tailing at least six inches through the zone, unhittable. He could put it anywhere he wanted. We entered the seventh inning leading by two.

His first pitch grazed the edge of the black. "Ball one."

The runner on first was taking a daring lead, so Quinton kicked his right leg high, cocked his head toward home, and fired the ball to Cullen at first.

"Balk! Balk!" The umpire burst from behind the plate, pointing the runner to second base. Quinton eyed the umpire indignantly.

His next pitch crossed the plate inches inside the outside corner, but the umpire calmly said, "Ball two." Quinton's beady brown eyes locked in on the umpire as he climbed on top of the rubber. He took a deep breath and wiped his forehead with the back of his wrist.

"Third! Third!" The umpire pointed violently toward third base. "Can't go to your face when you're on the pitcher's plate!"

Quinton stomped off the mound, but the umpire pointed right at him. "One word and you're gone."

His next two pitches caught the corners of the plate but were called balls three and four. Quinton stood at the bottom of the mound, staring defiantly at the umpire for at least 15 seconds as the batter trotted to first.

"C'mon blue, you blind?" shot out from the top of the bleachers. "You're squeezing him."

The umpire peeled off his mask, walked over to the fence, and stared down at Quinton's father sitting in the front row. "What did you say?"

Quinton's father shrugged. "Nothing."

The umpire sneered and nodded arrogantly. "Yeah, I thought so," he said, and strutted back to the plate.

Quinton angrily shook off every signal I flashed. I gave him signs for pitches that he didn't even possess in his repertoire. And then finally, I flashed him the hang loose sign, pitch out. He nodded and a slight sinister smile crept across his face.

Adrenaline pounded through my veins. This was my chance to prove my baseball instincts. As Quinton's arm snapped down, I broke to my right toward the open batter's box, but the ball sped right down the middle. I lunged back at it, but my glove was too late. The ball thumped in the middle of the umpire's chest, knocking him backward with his feet and arms locked straight out. He landed on his back. A cloud of dust mushroomed around him as the runner sprinted to second. Quinton stomped off the mound toward the plate. "How about that? Is that a strike?" he barked.

The umpire, from his back, snapped his index finger ambiguously at the woods. "You're outta here!"

"You're outta here!" Quinton charged at the ump. I grabbed him. "It's not worth it, Q. It's not worth it." He just smiled at the umpire as I escorted him to the parking lot.

"We need you the rest of the season," I told him.

"It's bullshit how he did my dad. Never seen an ump show up some white dude's pop."

◆◆◆◆

Cullen got a quick strikeout, and a popup in relief, but their ninth batter looped a single down the first base line. Curtis charged the ball, scooped it and fired it toward home. The white ball rose up out of the green grass, as the runner rounded third. The throw was up the line and high. I shuffled up the baseline and reached my mitt toward the ball. The hair on my outstretched arm tingled as the charging runner bore down on me.

The moment the ball hit my fully extended mitt, the blade of the runner's lowered shoulder impaled my left rib cage. I felt as though someone had driven a railroad spike into my lungs. I landed on my right shoulder, rolled on my back, and showed the ump the ball. He dramatically punched the runner 'out'.

I couldn't move. Every muscle on my body locked up. My throat seized, wheezing for the tiniest breath. No matter how hard I tried, I couldn't force a molecule of oxygen into my deflated lungs.

Coach Delaney helped me to my feet and half-carried me to the dugout. Slowly, I was able to squeeze more and more air into my lungs, but each breath felt like I was swallowing knives.

I limped out of the training room an hour later, wrapped from the top of my hips to my armpits. The cartilage between my third and fourth ribs had been pulled off the bone. The trainer recommended I sit out at least three weeks.

◆◆◆◆

I lay flat on my back in my bed that night, throbbing, too painful to move.

It's all over, I told myself. *There's no way to get noticed by recruiters only playing half of a senior season.*

My bedroom door swung open and slammed against the wall. He carried a jug of clear liquid with bright red letters *DMSO* across it, a blue cooler, and a huge smile on his face. "This'll get you right." My father's powerful swollen hands popped open the black cap of the bottle, and the smell of rotten eggs spread across the room.

He rolled me on my right side and carefully lifted my shirt. He poured the clear watery liquid onto my left rib cage. "This is the stuff they use at the track on the horses." He pressed into my ribs so hard like he was trying to squeeze all the pain, all the damaged tissue out of me. He then pulled a thick bag of ice from the cooler and packed my left side.

He came in every hour all night long, to reapply the liquid and change the ice bags. "This stuff's magic. My hands feel better already," he said, spreading his thick palms in front of my face. "Tomorrow, you'll feel as good as new."

Around 2:30 that morning, as my father was leaving the room, I readjusted my hips, and my left side lit up like an electric shock. I looked up at him in the thick darkness, "I don't think I can play tomorrow," my voice quivered. "It hurts too much."

He looked down at me and said, "You never miss a game. You never miss an inning. You never miss an at-bat. Everyone on that field tomorrow is in pain."

Before the game started, as I gingerly put my catcher's equipment on, I noticed written along the pinkie of my catcher's mitt:

THE EAGLE BELIEVED HE COULD FLY MUCH FASTER IF NOT FOR THE WIND IN HIS FACE, UNTIL HE REALIZED THAT IF THERE WAS NO WIND, HE COULDN'T FLY AT ALL.

I played the entire game. I played poorly, but I played. Every move felt like a sharp knife stabbing me in the side. I didn't get a hit. I didn't lay the bat on the ball once, but I played every inning.

As the game wore on, the pain became less acute, like a mental callous had formed around the pain, dulling it.

After catching a third strike to end the game, I rolled the ball to the mound and trudged off the field, slumped over, too tired and hurting to remove my gear. I staggered toward the woods, avoiding all human contact. My father intersected me at the bottom of the hill. "You were great," he beamed.

I walked with him to the top of the hill, thinking *he's not an optimist, he's a liar.*

He grabbed my shoulder firmly, "No one, I mean no one on this field today knows what you just did." And then he said something that is still rolling around in my brain. "There's no better feeling than playing in pain."

That one game showed me what I could do, what I could handle and what I could do without. I realized that pain is an excuse. No one lives a pain-free life.

◆◆◆◆

I played every game, every inning the rest of the season. Pain was rendered irrelevant. I fought through it, but I didn't feel comfortable at the plate and I fell into an 0-for-16 slump. But there was no excuse. If I played, I was expected to perform. I tried to stay aggressive, but the oh-for games piled up, and I was fading fast.

Everything I had hoped and worked for was disappearing. I scribbled numbers in the dirt with my spikes before and after each at-bat. My batting average dropped five points with each out but raised ten with each hit, and I realized that success is counted twice as much as failure in this game.

NW

Chapter 45

"This is what you get when you scour the trailer parks," Carter Alexander laughed exaggeratedly loud.

"I feel like I'm living in a Jerry Springer show," Derek echoed his contempt. "I can't believe it."

"I can. Look at where they came from; single parents. That's prime breeding ground for this."

"This is par for the course with Laticia, but Dorian had me fooled," Derek said.

"Well, this just looks bad on the school, on all of us. A good baseball team isn't worth this."

I grabbed Derek. "What's happening? What's going on with Laticia?"

"I thought you already knew," he started to laugh. "Go ask your boy."

"Tell me."

"It's better if he tells you."

I searched the school, but Dorian was nowhere to be found. I knew there was only one place he would be, so I took the long walk through the woods to the field and stood at the top of the hill. There he was, all alone. He sprinted around second base and slid cleats-high into third. He popped up, barely keeping his right foot on the invisible base. He led off, stretching his lead as the pitcher wound and fired a fast ball toward home plate. He paused to allow the batted ball to clear the infield, and then sprinted home. He turned and started all over again.

He stepped in and swung at a high fast ball. The sharp crack echoed across the field as the invisible ball soared into the alley. He sprinted around first and arced toward second. His right foot stabbed at the ghost bag propelling him toward third. He dove headfirst into the base just ahead of the throw.

His movements were so distinct that the other players appeared like painted scenery in the background of a play, making his fantasy game come to life.

I walked down the hill and approached the field as Dorian crossed home after tagging up on a long fly ball. He saw me and nodded.

"What's going on?"

He shrugged and shook his head.

"What's up with Laticia?"

"You haven't heard?" He bent over to catch his breath.

"Heard what?"

"I figured Cullen would've told ya."

"Told me what?"

He looked up at the sky, then down at his feet, and then right at me. "Her dad..." He paused.

"Is a jerk," I snapped. "We know. Get over it, it doesn't matter."

"No. Her dad is…" his voice wavered. "Her dad is..." he repeated trying to build enough momentum to continue.

"Is what?" I prodded him. "C'mon just tell me. There's nothing you can..."

"Is my dad!" he blurted.

"What?... What?... What?..." I repeated, my mind trying to digest this revelation. "That's not even funny. That's something Quinton would..."

"I'm not kiddin," his face unmoved in stone seriousness.

"Wait, her dad is... is your dad?" I said slowly. "Laticia's your..." My mind slowly fit the pieces together.

He nodded. "Sister."

"How?"

"Do the math."

"What are you gonna do?"

"What can I do?"

"You can't keep seeing her. It's wrong," I told him.

"Yeah, but there's nothing in my life that's more right than me being with her," he explained.

"You have to forget her. It'll eat you alive."

"You don't get it," he said.

My mind flashed back to Laticia's letter. *Try not to feel guilty about being human*, she wrote.

"Wait, you've known about this since Thanksgiving?"

He just looked at me blankly.

"You knew she was your sister and kept seeing her."

"You don't understand. I couldn't let her go," he told me.

"You're gonna have to."

"I can't. Everything reminds me of her. Even things that don't remind me of her, remind me of her." He stared straight ahead. "With all the crap in our lives, when I'm with her, I don't know, she makes everything right. It's like... calm, like nothing can touch us. Like we're in the middle of a storm, but we don't hear the thunder, see the lightning, feel the rain, and there's no wind."

"You can't have a relationship with your sister. It's not right. It's illegal to do that with your sister."

"We never did *that*." He walked away.

I watched him climb the hill and slowly disappear into the woods like he was disappearing from my life. I had begun to feel like we were diverging, remaining friends more out of habit. I believed we would always be best friends, but now we were like everything else, simply temporary.

◆◆◆◆

"I can't believe that about Laticia and Dorian," Dawn said that night.

"Yeah, it's crazy, isn't it?"

"I don't know what I would do," she said, "if something like that happened to us. Not being able to be with you would be like torture."

I thought about Dorian and Laticia all night, trying to reconcile the purity of their love and the impurity of them being together.

◆◆◆◆

The next morning before chapel, I sat on the ledge, watching the weak, timid freshmen file into the auditorium like zombies.

"I couldn't imagine doing it with my sister," Carter laughed.

"No one could imagine doing it with your sister," Derek grinned proudly.

"Screw you," Carter growled.

"I guess if you're gonna do it with your sister," Derek thought out loud. "Laticia wouldn't be a bad one to do it with."

I jumped down off the ledge and walked to chapel. Mr. Fulbright intercepted me. "How are you holding up?"

"Why is everyone such jerks?" I asked him.

He stopped. "Let's not paint with such a broad brush."

"Why does everyone treat them like they're monsters? They're not bad people. They didn't know what they were doing."

"Ignorance doesn't absolve people of culpability."

"They didn't hurt anyone, only themselves," I argued. "Everyone's treating them like they're criminals."

"Jake, most people try to cleanse themselves with other people's dirty bath water."

"A lot of people have done a lot worse, and no one says a thing."

He took a step back. "Granted. But you must concede their relationship defies the intrinsic mores of society."

"Why? What's wrong with it? If you're in love, what's the harm in that? Huh? It's discrimination. They just want to be happy. Can't we let them be happy?"

"This is an unexpected stance for you. I thought you'd be on the side of morality."

"I'm on the side of love. What's more moral than love?"

"I didn't think moral ambiguity was your style," he told me. "I thought you were about right and wrong, obeying the law."

"Yeah, but these laws are so arbitrary, so old, like we're hanging onto the past." I stepped in front of him. "They didn't do anything wrong."

"In nature, there is no right or wrong," he said. "Only consequences."

"What are the consequences?"

"Well, the ramifications of inbreeding are dramatic. Genetic abnormalities, inherent diseases, aberrant physical traits."

"But it's only two people, one couple. We're not mountain people. We don't live in a closed society," I argued fiercely. "We don't need these laws anymore to protect us. Why can't we get rid of them?"

"Cicero once said, 'He who does not have a code to live by is like a feather in the wind.'"

"We don't have any code anymore," I told him. "The lines are so blurry and so crooked no one knows which side they're standing on."

I walked toward the stairs against the flow of students. I could not sit through another Chapel. I stood next to the stairs, hidden. As I watched the straggling boys meander into the auditorium, the long foyer turned eerily silent.

The thin bones of her hand grabbed the inside of my left arm from behind. I didn't turn. I just closed my eyes and inhaled greedily. I didn't need to look.

"Why haven't you been by?" Her smell, her soft clothes and her gentle touch led me to the cement corner under the staircase. "I'm worried about you." Her right shoulder pressed in close to mine, so close that I could feel her warmth.

"Yeah, well, things haven't been going so good." My back pressed against the cold wall. My lips were the only thing I could move.

"Well then, what does Coach Delaney say? Do you have a good chance to win a scholarship?" Her voice raced.

"I don't really know," I said hesitantly. "I need to get a hit first before I think about a scholarship."

"You will. Don't worry. You'll get one." She leaned closer. "You deserve it."

"The problem is, the schools I can get into, I'm not good enough to play at. And the schools I'm good enough to play at, I can't get into."

"That's why these next exams are so important. You boys think the spring is a blow off. It's not. Doing well on these exams could get you in the summer admissions somewhere." My eyes locked in on her full pink lips, pursing and touching, and hiding her long, white, healthy teeth with each word.

"I've been studying," I muttered.

"Jake." She leaned even closer. My neck muscles tightened, and my eyes closed. "I'll help you anyway you want," she whispered. "That's why I'm here. Are you having trouble in anything?"

"Well," I breathed deeply. "My worst class is calc."

"Calc, calc," she repeated eagerly. "You're in luck. I minored in mathematics at Vassar."

"You could help me?" I asked feebly.

"Yes. I'll get you an 'A,'" she said. "Come by my office any evening after practice. I'll give you what you need."

"Well," was the only word I could think of.

"I'll be there... waiting."

"OK," I nodded and walked toward the chapel.

◆◆◆◆

"For a preview of next Friday's Variety Show," Mr. Fulbright announced from the podium as I entered the chapel. "I present, the one, the only, Quinton Samuel."

The auditorium erupted as Quinton sprinted up on stage. He grabbed the microphone and tapped the head. "Test, test, test," reverberated throughout the auditorium. He looked up. "Sounds like I'm in Mr. Addler's class."

"I got kicked off the football team this year. I flooded the field," he smiled. "I wanted the coach to send me in as a sub."

"A new study recently found that humans eat more bananas than monkeys. It's true. I can't remember the last time I ate a monkey."

"I've had a tough year. My brother was in a car accident. He got his left arm and left leg amputated." The audience fell silent. "Don't worry, he's all right now." Groans replaced the silence.

"One of my cousins is a dyslexic agnostic insomniac. He stays up all night wondering if there really is a dog. His teachers said he wouldn't be any good at poetry because he's dyslexic. So far, he's made three vases and an ashtray. I shouldn't joke about dyslexia. It affects ten out of two people.

"My uncle is having a hard time. He just found out his other son was gay." Quinton paused. "Yeah, he caught him wearing a Mets' jersey."

A short burst of laughter shot out, and then the auditorium screeched to earsplitting silence. No one was sure if they were allowed to laugh.

My buddy Bernard and I went to the Village last weekend," Quinton continued, unfazed. "We saw this shop with a sign that said for 75 cents, they could turn a brother white for a day. So, we figured, we'd give it a shot.

"Bernard had a buck, but I only had 50 cents. So, Bernard said he'd go in, get it done, and then give me the change. A half-hour later, Bernard comes out, as white as my man Jake over there. So, I go up to him and say, 'Can I have a quarter?' Bernard looks at me and says, 'Get a job, nigger.'"

The echo of the word hovered over us for a tense moment and then the stage lights snapped to black, Quinton's microphone was cut silent, and everything feel dark and quiet. Slowly, veiled laughter floated from row to row and dissipated into feigned outrage. We filed out in stunned silence. I heard a pasty white freshman whisper, "He said the n-word!"

◆◆◆◆

Reaction was swift and predictable. Discussion groups were formed, the official statement was penned. School officials wrung their hands in moral indignation, for they alone had the wisdom and virtue to know which words to say and which ones to keep tucked away in their hearts and minds.

They attacked him with his weapon of choice, words. Mr. Addler paced in front of my calculus class red-faced. "As a minority, Quinton should know better than to make fun of a person with a disability, or other types of disaffected groups. And as much as anyone in this school, he should understand the pain that word he used has brought to so many of his kind. Ignorance is not an excuse. We cannot tolerate intolerance. We, as a school, have gone to great lengths to make him feel as welcome as possible, and now he turns around and ridicules others whose lifestyles he disapproves."

◆◆◆◆

"YOU – ARE – THE – MAN," Cullen proclaimed loudly when I told him about Ms. Vivaqua as we walked out to practice. "She wants you big time. I may have you pegged all wrong. I couldn't even have pulled that one off." He waited and then smiled. "I probably could.."

"Seriously?" I said. "Ms. Vivaqua, a beautiful adult woman, who could have any man in the world, wants a pimply faced, 17-year-old kid?"

"Relax," he said. "You're in like Flint."

"Flint? It's Flynn," I corrected him.

"What's Flynn?"

"You know, Errol Flynn."

"Who the hell is Errol Flynn?"

I shook my head. "Nobody."

"Trust me," he said. "You can forget about Dawn. She's single-A ball. You're in the bigs, now."

"You're smoking crack," I told him. "She's only helping me study to help herself. She doesn't want a directional school on her record, either."

"She wants you. She's probably hounded day and night by these strong aggressive guys and she's sick of it. She wants someone like you."

"Someone like me?" I asked, insulted.

"Yeah, you know why guys like me lose girls to guys like you?"

"The girls have good taste?" I joked.

"No, you're no threat to them," he looked down at me. "You couldn't harm her if you tried. She feels safe with you."

"I don't know."

"What d'you got to lose? If she wants you, great. It's a big-time score. If she doesn't, you study, get an 'A.' Win-win."

"I'm not going if that's what she wants. I'm with Dawn now."

He shook his head. "What a waste. Dawn's not gonna find out. No one will know."

"I will know," I told him.

◆◆◆◆

"Can you believe what they're doing to Q?" I asked Jay at practice.

"Yeah."

"So, you agree with censorship?"

"No, but I can believe they're doing it to him. That's how they operate."

"Yeah, but don't we have free speech in this country?"

"Of course, but you're not freed from consequences of your speech. He said inappropriate things. Funny, but inappropriate. He should know better."

"I don't think they even understood the jokes," I said.

"They don't want to understand."

"What do you think they'll do to him?"

"He'll be fine."

◆◆◆◆

Quinton came up to me during batting practice. "This place is completely nuts, Jake."

"I know. What they're doing to you is ridiculous."

"Yeah, getting expelled for telling jokes, and nothing happens to these white boys for all the shit they do!"

"Can't the B.U.S. use its stroke to help you?"

"B.U.S. don't want me here. I didn't join their little group," he said. "I had my own ideas. I questioned things. I didn't need them. Administration don't want me here, neither. They just want me to do what they want me to do, and I don't dance. Get this. I'm getting kicked out for telling those jokes, but Fulbright just told me I should tell jokes about shitting myself."

"What are you talking about?"

"I'm telling you, it's a set up. They want the brother thrown out of here."

"He wants you to tell jokes about shitting yourself?"

"Yeah, he just came up to me and said, remember Q, the best humor is self-defecating."

◆◆◆◆

I chose not to go to Mrs. Vivaqua's office after practice that evening. Everything around me was falling apart. I didn't know what to think anymore. I didn't know what was right, and what was wrong. I didn't know what was good, and what was bad. I didn't know anything anymore.

What's going on with you St. Francis boys?" Cullen said as we drove home that night. "They're not living up to the standards of a Bainbridge student," he said with a tinge of sarcasm.

"No one ever does," I said. "You and Wally should know that better than anyone."

"It's only wrong if you get caught," he reminded me.

"Or turned in," I replied.

Cullen pulled his car to a stop at a little pub in the highlands overlooking the river. "I can't go in there," I told him. "I'm only 17."

"Yeah, you can." He handed me a laminated card.

"That doesn't even look like me," I said.

"It looks exactly like you."

"I don't have a mustache."

"You shaved."

We sat at the long wooden bar as a middle-aged man behind a medium-sized piano played requests. "Look at those two over there," Cullen said, pointing to two flowing blondes sipping mixed drinks.

"They're ripe for plucking."

"Way out of my league," I told him as he motioned for two beers.

"You kiddin' me?" he said. "I could walk out of here with both of 'em. Go over there, and show 'em what Jake Pearson is all about."

"Pearson," the old man behind the bar snarled as he slid us our mugs of beer. "Are you a Pearson?"

"Yeah," I said.

"You know Jack Pearson?"

"Yeah, he's my dad," I said.

"Jack Pearson is not allowed in this bar for the rest of his life," he declared.

"So we can have his wake here, then?" Cullen asked.

"Not even then, smartass."

"Why?"

"He tore this place apart back in '62." The old man still brimmed with raw anger. "He busted the pool table in two and threw some poor guy through the jukebox."

"Why?"

"Don't know, don't care," he said, snatching the beer mugs from us. "And none of his kids are allowed here, either."

◆◆◆◆

"Your old man must've been a hell raiser, bustin' up the joint," Cullen said as we drove away from the bar.

"I guess so."

"The only thing my dad busts up is billion-dollar companies."

We drove along Ocean Avenue, and I stared up at the dark summer sky, thinking about my dad 37 years ago, long before I was born.

◆◆◆◆

I ended up at Cullen's the next night. The girls were already down in the basement when I arrived. I heard their flighty giggles as I descended the steps. Cullen gave me a cursory introduction to the girls whose names I immediately forgot. They looked alike, except one had light hair and the other dark, but they were the same to me.

Cullen led the light-haired girl to the back bedroom, while the dark-haired girl excused herself to the ladies' room. I sat down in the middle of the large black leather sofa and turned on the TV. The Yankees game hummed to life on the big screen, and Phil Rizzuto's voice grated out of the oversized speakers.

Through the walls of the bedroom came the rustling of sheets, a shrill of laughter, banging of the bed frame, a giggle, a sigh, a moan. I locked in on the game.

She stepped out from behind the big screen, partially obstructing my view of the field. And it was not until after I watched, through and around her body, Jeter slide in front of the tag at second base following a line drive off the green monster that I noticed she wasn't wearing clothes. Her naked body was a fuzzy outline against the flickering colors of the game, but her smooth white skin radiated in the shimmering light.

She walked toward me, like a movie star stepping down out of the screen breaking the fourth wall. Her long curves closed in on me. I felt her warm, soft body with each step. "What are you thinking?" Her soft inviting voice offered me anything I wanted. She stopped halfway between me and the game. Her right hip tilted to the side bearing the weight of her body. "Do you see anything you like?"

Jeter sprinted across home plate to a high five from Paul O'Neill. I looked. Her hands gently rested on her hips. She smiled thirstily at me. Her lips were red. Her hair was flowing. Her legs were long, and her curves were supple. And there was nothing attractive about her.

I rose. "Where are you going?" she shrieked.

"Home, anywhere. I don't want any of this." When I looked at her naked body, I didn't like what I saw. I walked to the steps. There is nothing more defeating than letting yourself down, I realized.

Cullen stumbled out of the bedroom, his pants off, his shirt open. He grabbed my shoulder. "Where the hell do you think you're going?"

"I'm out of here," I pulled away from him and started up the stairs.

"These ladies are our guests." He flashed his hand at the naked girl. "This is not the way to treat your guest."

"I didn't invite 'em."

He yanked me down the steps. "She's beautiful. She's a lay-up and you don't want it?"

"I don't," I said softly.

"What are you, some kinda faggot?"

"I guess I am." I wrested my arm free.

As I walked up the steps, the bedroom door slammed shut. I looked back. She sat on the leather sofa, naked with her legs bent against her chest, and her arms folded around her knees, completely still, watching the Yankees game.

NW

Chapter 46

Dorian's head followed the hum of the ball until it popped into the meat of the mitt. It was there, but the umpire turned his head to the left. "Ball three."

Dorian looked up and nodded, "No that was good. That was a strike."

The ump gave him a crooked stare. "You sure?"

Dorian nodded.

The umpire lifted his mask slowly, stared at Dorian again, shook his head and reluctantly punched his fist in the air for strike three. A buzz swept across the wooden bleachers.

"What the hell's going on?" Delaney exploded out of the dugout. "That was ball three! That was ball three!" He stomped toward home plate eyes ablaze. "That was ball three!"

The umpire walked toward him. "Calm down, coach. It wasn't my call."

"Not your call? What do you mean not your call? You're the goddamn plate umpire!"

"Watch yourself, coach."

"Whose call is it? Explain it to me. The field ump? The catcher? That lady in the first row? Why are we paying you, if that wasn't your call? That's your only call."

Dorian casually placed his bat in the rack, grabbed his glove, and confidently sprinted to the field with his fluid stride. The rest of the team remained in the dugout unsure of what had just happened.

I looked at Cullen, "What the…"

"Fuck," he said. "He doesn't care about this team. He doesn't care about winning." Cullen shook his head. "Last inning, nut-cutting time, and he pulls this shit. What, he's trying to show how virtuous he is after getting busted for banging his sister. He doesn't care about anyone but himself."

I shrugged.

"We're bustin' our ass, and he's goddamn grandstanding."

"Overcome it, overcome it." I called out in the dugout. "It's still anybody's ballgame."

"We can't trust him, Jake," Cullen ranted as I was strapping on my gear. "Delaney should take him right out. How do we know he'll play it straight?"

"He will." I watched Dorian warming up in the outfield. I couldn't comprehend him. I was struggling just to get my bat on the ball, and he was so frivolous with at-bats that he was giving them away, but there was something liberating about what he just did, free from the usual constraints of baseball. The ump no longer had the final say and striking out no longer signified failure. Results did not matter. As I crouched behind home plate corralling Quinton's warm up pitches, an errant voice cried out from the bleachers, "Who is that guy that even the umpires listen to him?"

For the next two innings, we played with one eye on the game and one eye on Dorian. Our diving catches, base hits, double plays were made in spite of him. Our errors, overthrows, strikeouts occurred because of him.

Dorian stepped to the plate two innings later. He saw one pitch. The ball left his bat with a loud reproving crack like the lash of a leather whip against the flesh of some animal. He hit the first pitch he saw. The white ball streamed across the deep blue sky like a shooting star, and it was still rising when it cleared the fence.

We rose to our feet as the ball flew, but we held our excitement and watched silently. No one cheered. Our silence rang in our ears. The only sound was the crunching of his spikes into the orange clay as he circled the bases. He never looked up and his face never hinted a sign of satisfaction. After touching home plate, he quickly gathered his gear and walked to his car. Delaney grabbed him and looked him square in the eye. "Good work, son. Helluva job."

No one else spoke. I followed his easy stride to his car. I was drawn to him and repelled at the same time.

"Why'd you do it?" I caught up to him.

"It was a strike," he shrugged.

"But the ump blew it! What about the times the ump calls balls strikes? Doesn't it all even out? Are we supposed to fix their mistakes?"

He looked at me with his steely eyes. "I took a strike on a 2-2 count. I didn't deserve to stay up there. I didn't deserve another chance."

I didn't know what to think anymore. Everything I thought I knew had been called into question. I wanted to live like him, but I didn't have the strength to let go.

◆◆◆◆

My father picked me up outside the athletic wing that night. I hadn't expected him, but he rolled up beside me like he knew I would be there. I hopped in. We took a left instead of a right out of the Bainbridge gates. I didn't care where we were going. I sat in the back seat and didn't say a word. My mind, my world was spiraling out of control.

"Your grandfather was a great man," my father broke the silence.

"Pops?"

"No, no," he shook his head, "my father."

"Did I know him?" I asked.

"No. He passed away a long time ago."

"How old was he?"

"Let me see now. I was playing in the Texas League at the end of my career. I wasn't a prospect anymore. We were playing a doubleheader in Albuquerque, and I walked into the dugout after the first game, and the manager, Eddie, uh, Eddie Crenshaw, pulled me aside and told me that my father died. I didn't know what to do. So, I played the next game, got two hits, and then got on the next train home for the funeral."

"How'd he die?"

"Shot in the back in an alley in Queens."

"Who shot him?"

"The mob," he said. "He was a police officer, and he wouldn't do business with them."

"I thought he was a boxer?"

"He was," he nodded. "He fought for the welterweight championship in the Garden. The old Garden. November 1st, 1939."

"Did he win?"

"Took a draw," he admitted regretfully. "He didn't get the title, and never got another shot." He smiled. "He used to tell me I was born with boxing gloves on.

"Why didn't you become a boxer, then?"

"He wanted me to box, but I liked hitting a baseball more than someone's face."

"Was he mad?"

"Probably. He wasn't interested in baseball. He never went to any of my games." My dad looked straight-ahead in silence, and then exhaled loudly. "It's funny. You spend the first half of your life trying to earn the respect of your father, and the second half trying to earn the respect of your son."

The hum of the tires against the road became louder.

"Dad, can I ask you something?"

"Anything, son."

"When you were my age, what did you do?"

"I'm sure the same things you kids do."

"I mean like with girls."

"Oh, girls," his eyes glimmered for a moment. "I don't know much about girls. I still even don't understand your mother."

"You don't understand Mom after 30 years?"

"Yeah, like the other night I went to get Chinese food, and she says, surprise me, you know what I like, but I had no idea."

"What did you do?"

"I got two things I thought she'd like, and whatever she picked, I ate the other one," he looked over his right shoulder and changed lanes. "I'm no expert, but I can tell you this." He slowed the car and turned toward me. "How you treat the girls in your life now will affect how much you will respect your wife and daughters, later."

"I try to treat everyone right," I said.

"Good, because one day you'll be driving with your 17-year-old son, and what you decide to do now will determine how honestly you'll answer his questions then."

We pulled up to a vacant lot with the rusted remains of a backstop in one corner and a grass covered mound. "There's still enough light for a quick bucket." He kicked his door open.

I didn't move. Why did it always have to come back to baseball? I knew this was a waste of time. Nothing could save me now. It was too late.

The deep blue sky in the distance was fading into a glowing purple. He peered into the car. "Grab a bat."

I walked to the field begrudgingly.

He marched ten precise paces from home plate, pivoted on his right foot, and turned around abruptly. He gave me a full nod, and I stepped into my normal batting stance. He stood so close that a line drive up the middle would have killed him. He dug his foot into the dirt, wound, and fired a straight fastball down the middle of the plate.

It flashed past me like a laser beam, a brief glimmer of light slicing through the dimming night. The ball crashed loudly against the back-stop and rattled along the side fence.

He nodded again, wound and threw the same pitch. I only heard the whiz cutting the air, followed by a loud crash against the chain-link.

He then fired balls at me frenetically, and I swung at every pitch, a half-swing, a check-swing, a slow-swing, until his bucket was empty. Each pitch crashed against the backstop without touching my bat. He walked straight to me.

"I can't hit those pitches," I confessed. "They're on me too fast. No one can hit them."

"Big Leaguers have less time than that to react," he said, grabbing my bat and stepping into the box. "Watch."

I picked up an armful of balls and trotted to the mound 30 feet away. The first pitch I threw, he missed and as the ball rattled against the backstop, I could not contain a wry smile of satisfaction. His eyes tightened on me. "Throw it again."

My next pitch was harder than the first. He slapped it easily on a line over the shortstop. The next pitch, I threw as hard as I could. He grounded it to third. I threw 10 more of my best fastballs trying to strike him out, and he hit eight of them on a line to the outfield.

"React," he told me when he placed the bat back in my hands.

"React," I repeated to myself. "Forget everything. React." He wound and fired the ball without a thought. My bat flew as if it had a mind of its own, and the white ball shot to the outfield. I reacted to the next 20 pitches the same way, with the same result.

I stripped away the unnecessaries. Nothing extraneous allowed. Physical, mental, spiritual, nothing of excess could seep in. A slight twitch, a random thought, a doubt, were luxuries I couldn't afford. With each successive pitch, I wanted the next one harder, faster.

The next 30 pitches were exhilarating. I was on the proverbial edge. Every move, every thought, every breath, every involuntary reaction had a purpose. All became infinitesimally clear, and I glimpsed not just my purpose for being, but for all being.

My bat striking the ball no longer depended on me, but on my instincts, which were not mine but a gift from eternity, passed down across hundreds of generations, back to the first breath of life. In that moment, I was the culmination of all that had come before me, attuned to the collective unconscious. It was no longer me. I ceased to exist.

We hit and we hit and we hit. He didn't say a thing. He just threw me pitch after pitch after pitch, until it became so dark that I couldn't see the ball, so I listened to it, I smelled it, felt it, tasted it, and then we gathered the balls, and walked to the car without a word.

We drove toward home in silence. That was the first time I knew what it was to be a hitter. After several minutes, he pulled to the side and parked in front of Big Al's Sporting Goods. "Wait here," he slammed the door and trotted inside.

Five minutes later, he emerged from the store carrying a basketball under his arm. "Hold this," he dropped it on my lap, craned his neck, and u-turned the car back in the opposite direction. A few minutes later, we were parked in the same spot we had just left. He grabbed the ball and marched directly toward the basketball courts with the engine still running.

He stepped inside the rusted gate and rolled the ball diagonally across the court. It weaved its way over the eroding asphalt toward the far corner where two tiny hands reached out and grabbed it. The small boy squeezed the ball, caressing it. His little hands spun the ball on one finger, and then shot it toward the metal hoop, under a flickering single streetlight. The taller boy rebounded the ball, bounced it several times, and shot it again. By the time their new ball had swished through the ripped net for the first time, my father was already pulling the car out onto the street.

"It's an absolute crime they don't have a decent ball to play with," he grumbled, apologetically. "Everyone deserves a chance to play."

NW

Chapter 47

"They're scapegoating him," Jay complained as we walked into the auditorium.

A special chapel had been called after lunch the next day, and the entire school was strongly "urged" to "observe" the informal "debate" which addressed what had come to be known as "The Quinton Incident."

"It was just a joke," I said.

"He crossed the line."

"My dad says you can joke about anything as long as it's funny," Curtis said. "But if it ain't funny, it's just plain mean. That was some funny shit."

The lights came up on the stage and revealed three boys seated in wooden chairs to the right of the podium and three boys seated to the left. A makeshift debate was organized to determine Quinton's future. It wouldn't come down to what was right or wrong, but who could argue the best.

Jay stepped to the front of the stage first, and everyone laughed when he lowered the mic to its shortest height. "To live in a free country," his voice started off low, "we must have freedom of speech." The veins of his neck pulsed. "Freedom of speech for everyone, for every point of view, and not just those we approve of. To expel Quinton would be an assault on the ideals that make our country, our school, great, and would permanently damage this school far worse than the peripheral effects of some errant words."

Carter strode up to the podium with his inherited swagger. "Private institutions are not bound by the Constitution. We have the right to act in the best interest of this school. It is a privilege to come here and every student must act according to that privilege. The moment we lower the standards of behavior, we are headed down the public school road to chaos."

Derek walked up to the podium from the left. "How can he argue for rights when the very words he uttered denied certain people their fundamental rights; the right to live a life free from harassment, free from intolerance. We cannot tolerate intolerance."

Curtis crept up to the mic. "We are all sinners, man. No one's perfect. We all want to be accepted, need to be accepted, not just for the good things, but for what isn't so good. The only way we can be accepted is if we accept each other for the sinners we all are."

Quinton never said a word in his own defense. He was not even there.

Dorian walked in from the wings and stepped to the podium. The auditorium fell silent. He grabbed the sides of the lectern, stared down and then looked up. "There is not a better man in this school than Quinton Samuels." He turned and walked off stage.

◆◆◆◆

The next day, as we were warming up for the game, Quinton was nowhere in sight. "Where's Q?" I asked Jay.

"I think he's out of here," he replied. "He had a meeting with the disciplinary committee after lunch, and I haven't seen him since. He wasn't in the locker room."

"That's bullshit," Curtis added. "The way they're doing him."

◆◆◆◆

"His fastball's electric," was the only scouting report that Fulbright gave us before the game. The thunderous pop of the catcher's mitt as he warmed up sent chills down our collective spines.

"That ball has some giddy-up on it," Jay observed.

And as the umpire was sweeping off home plate before calling out, "play ball!" Quinton emerged from the woods in his uniform, and trotted down the hill, almost nonchalantly. We all stopped and stared as he jogged to the field.

"What happened?" I asked as he sat down on the bench.

"Discretionary disciplinary probation," he replied.

"What does that mean?"

"McGovern said if I tied my shoes wrong, I'm done."

"Well, then don't mess up."

"They're the ones messed up, not me"

◆◆◆◆

After watching the first five batters, including Dorian, walk back to the dugout dragging their bat and heads, I looked up to the sky. The small concise clouds were aligned in uniform rows, a symmetry not often found in nature, especially in the ethereal vapors of heaven.

I stepped in the box and eyed the pitcher. I felt unusually relaxed, like what I was doing was both meaningless and significant.

The ball jumped out of the pitcher's hand and accelerated toward me like a beam of light. I don't remember swinging, but I knew the moment the ball left my bat, it was gone. I stared up at the rising ball, reaching for the clouds, flying with a power generated by strength I did not know existed in me, until it disappeared.

♦♦♦♦

From that day forward, the hits came in buckets: 3-for-3; 4-for-5; 7-for-8 in a doubleheader. Like small bursts of lightning, they flew off my bat in all directions. Even the flashes that the fielders somehow snared with their leather gloves inspired a clamor of awe throughout the stands. I played in my own private world. Nothing bothered me. It was as if I could see the pitch before it left the pitcher's hand. But I could not escape the feeling that it wasn't me swinging the bat. Rather, I was being swung by a force greater than myself; a mere instrument, like the bat, used to strike the ball.

I felt infallible. Somehow, I convinced myself I could do no wrong. I closed my mind to the externals, and prevented the truth from seeping in. I stopped thinking. I just reacted. I lived in this fragile existence, easier to get there than to stay there.

For those few fleeting weeks in the spring of '99, I felt what life could really be. I was the player, the person, I had always hoped I could be. Life was quiet. The way it should be. I was free; free from all the angst, no good or bad, no right or wrong. There was no yesterday, no tomorrow, just now. All there was, was existence. That's all there ever is. There was no me, no you, no self. No home team, no visitors, no opponents, no wins, no losses.

Worry, doubt, fear no longer pockmarked my mental landscape. My heart did not raise one beat when I stepped in the box in the last inning down by two with two on, two outs, and our perfect 28-0 season on the line. Failure never crept into my mind, neither did success. I focused solely on the ball. And when it left my bat, I didn't even need to look. It was gone. I sprinted around the bases with my head down, repressing my smile, and pretending like I had been there before. A calmness came over me, as if a walk-off home run had become commonplace, predestined. When I crossed the plate, I was not swarmed by a pack of ecstatic teammates, but greeted by a dispassionate gauntlet of high fives, and fist bumps.

We didn't simply have a feeling that we could do no wrong. We knew we were going to win before the game started. Losing was incompatible with our team's DNA. We knew we would always find a way to win. Individual success measured by numbers, averages and calculations no longer mattered. My focus was solely on the ball.

◆◆◆◆

Last year, we posted the best record in school history at 29-3. As this season rolled into May, we were approaching 30-0. I stared at the glass cases protecting the tarnished trophies and petrified balls marking the history of excellence of the school. I pictured our trophy, unblemished, sitting up high inside this sealed glass case for eternity. *A hundred years from now, students whose grandparents are not even born yet will stare at our trophy and remember what we did. Was this all meaningless? Did it really matter if we won or lost? That our trophy was in this case? Is it really important to be remembered? And remembered for what, hitting a leather ball with a wooden bat?*

"I heard you went yard yesterday," said a skinny freshman as he loudly slapped me five as he walked by.

I turned to Cullen. "A reporter called me last night. I don't even know how he got my number."

"It's called the phone book," he said.

"I didn't know what to say to the guy."

"Remember, the more light you shine on your teammates, the more light is reflected back on you."

"How much more publicity do you need?"

Fulbright walked up to us, holding a computer printout. He looked at me. "Five-twenty-nine." And then at Dorian. "Five-twenty-four. You two have the highest averages in school history. Even if you don't get a hit the rest of the season, you'll still bat over four hundred."

Fulbright stared at the printout and rattled off the name of every hitter in the top ten on the Shore, and I, who last month couldn't hit my way out of a wet paper bag, was on top. "Jake, you and Dorian are the two best hitters on the Shore."

Delaney stepped up and ripped the printout from Fulbright's hands. "These aren't the best hitters on the Shore."

"What are you talking about? They have the best batting averages, the most hits," Fulbright argued. "It means they're the best. Numbers don't lie."

"Of course, they do." His eyes zeroed in on the printout. "Numbers lie all the time. Let's see who on this list gets drafted. And then we'll know."

The bell reverberated down the hall, and Delaney pulled me aside.

"You're feeling pretty good about yourself, aren't you?"

I shrugged, feigning modesty.

"Remember, the time when you're playing your best, the time when you think you have it all together, is the time you're most susceptible to being tripped up."

NW

Chapter 48

The night was hazy. The clouds smudged the moon, blurring its light as we drove silently to Cullen's house through the hovering mist. We pulled off the main road, and the car was suddenly enveloped in a lush fog. "I can't see a goddamn thing," Cullen said as he violently yanked the knob to the brights.

"Don't," I knocked his hand away.

"What the hell, man?"

"Bright lights blind ya in the fog."

He leered at me and accelerated into the thick bank of gray, yanking the car back and forth, cutting a jagged path through the blinding mist. I grabbed the wheel and straightened it.

We turned onto a street outlined by enormous oak trees; their long, thick, crooked arms reaching across the road, forming a long, blind tunnel. We sped past large white houses with tall, thick pillars and wraparound balconies. "I can't believe you didn't tap that PhD ass." He shook his disappointed head.

I shrugged, silently.

"Another missed life opportunity for ya."

"I think Cox lives around here," I tapped my window. "His dad must be a player."

"Nah, middle management," Cullen scoffed. "My dad pays more in taxes than his makes all year."

We drove on silently, Cullen jerking the car back and forth, in and out of the other cars, as if his embattled mind was steering.

"You closed the deal, yet?" he asked after an extended silence.

"What deal?"

"Dawn."

"Uh... not really."

"Not really?" he snapped. "You either did, or you didn't."

"I didn't," I confessed.

"Goddamn, it ain't that hard. All you gotta do is show a little interest and she'll be on her back faster than a no-armed wrestler."

"I don't know," I said. "It's not right. I respect her too much."

"You know what your problem is. You believe your own bull-shit."

"It's not bullshit."

"I understand. You gotta talk that talk. But you don't have to live up to all that garbage you spout. All successful people are full of shit. They sell it. They just never buy it themselves."

"It's not garbage," I said feebly.

"Regardless, tonight's finally gonna be your night," he declared. "That is my mission. I promise ya. It'll be my early birthday present to you. You can't be an 18-year-old virgin."

"I hate getting older," I admitted. "I hate birthdays."

"You haven't had enough of 'em to hate 'em."

"I don't do birthday presents anyway." The car fell silent.

We pulled into his sprawling property and drove up to his house at the top of a long, undulating cobblestone path. The house was alive with pulsating lights, dancing shadows and hard pounding music. He leaned against the hood of his car. "I went to see her yesterday," he confessed.

"Who?"

"My mom. You know, surprise her, ya know, before she left for the coast."

"How is she?"

He exhaled uneasily. "Not good," his voice suddenly turning low and sad. "It was weird. She wasn't wearing a wig. She was just sittin' on her bed, bald. Her face was all gray. Her eyes were sunken in. It scared the hell out of me. She looked like a skeleton..." He looked down at his shoes. "And then she asked me how she looked."

"What'd you say?"

"I said great, you're beautiful, Mom." A lone tear slithered down his cheek. "She even knew I was lying. But she smiled anyway and kissed my cheek." He looked off into the black night. "I don't think she's gonna make it."

"Don't talk like that. She'll be all right."

"How d'you know?"

"I don't," I said. "I just..."

"Don't tell me she'll be all right when you know she won't be. Don't tell me she'll get better when you know she's gonna die." He shook his head. "That's the worst kind of lie. False hope."

We walked through the huge front door into a mass of people swaying in unison, like one big organism.

"Look, if Dawn won't do it with you," he told me, "there're a lot of other women who will give you what you need."

"Who?" I asked quickly.

He spread his arms out over the mass of people. "They're every-where. That one, and that one." He pointed at different girls. "Goddamn! Life's one giant banquet. Step up to the table, son, and help yourself. It's easier than you think."

"Maybe for you, but not for me."

"Jake, I'm gonna make a man out of you before it's all over."

"I am a man," I said as I walked to the other end of the room.

Alone on a couch in a far corner sat Laticia. Her face was fallen, eyes drooping, corners of her mouth sagging. She looked sad, which made me sad. Their hope had given me hope, but now it was gone.

I walked over to her. "Are you OK?"

She nodded, but said, "No."

I sat down next to her. "If you want to talk about something, anything, I listen pretty good."

"Talking won't fix anything," she leaned away from me. "I shouldn't have come. I thought maybe just seeing him would help."

"I'm worried about you... and Dorian," I stared into her deso-late eyes. "I care about you. This is so unfair."

She shook her head. "I'm sure there's something I did to de-serve it."

"No, there's nothing you did..."

Her body started to shake as tears flowed down her cheeks. "I love him so much. I miss him so much." She writhed in pain. "It hurts so much."

I wrapped my arms around her and pulled her into my chest. "It's OK, it's OK," I whispered as I petted her hair. "Everything will be all right." She leaned into me, her warm tears seeped into my shirt.

"I don't know what to do," she sobbed.

I held her, stroking the length of her back, not knowing what to say. When her tears finally stopped, she sat up and wiped the water from her eyes.

"I know this is hard," I told her. "But I'm here for you. Whatever you need."

"Thanks, Jake. You're a good guy." She squeezed my arm. "Thanks for coming over, but you don't have to babysit me. I'm fine."

"You're not fine."

"Seriously, go and enjoy the party." She pushed me away. "Don't worry about me. I'll be OK. It was good just to cry."

I walked back over toward Cullen. He was smiling loudly. "I see ya. Not bad for a quick pop."

"No... No..." I stammered. "It's not like that. That isn't right."

"Sure, it is."

"I couldn't hurt Dawn like that?"

"Forget Dawn," he snapped. "She went out with her friends tonight instead of being with you."

"I'm not forgetting her," I said. "And besides, I couldn't do that to Dorian."

"Jake, she's fair game. They don't see each other anymore. They can't. She's capable of making her own decisions."

"She's not capable of making any rational decision right now," I told him. "I'm worried about her. She's totally messed up emotionally."

"That's the best time to pounce," he said.

"That's so wrong," I told him. "And I'm not stabbing Dorian in the back."

"Who else in the world would he want her to be with other than his best friend?"

"I'm not his best friend," I said without thinking.

"Good, then you don't have to worry about hurting your best friend."

"She wouldn't want to hurt him either."

"It's your life. You only go around once."

◆◆◆◆

Laticia stood and walked toward the stairs. The currents of the teenage flesh bounced her around like a bottle tossed into the sea. She emerged on the other side and floated up the steps. She leaned against the white banister, looking out over the party like she was searching for someone.

Derek climbed the stairs and stood uncomfortably close to her against the rail. I stood up and watched them.

"You better act fast or Cox will beat you to it," Cullen said as the two were locked in an intense conversation. "Live for the moment, bro."

Derek placed his meaty hands on her shoulders, turned her,

and backed her up against the wall. I forced my way through the mass of dancers and sprinted up the stairs. He pressed his chest into hers, trapping her against the wall. She pushed on his chest, straining in vain, red-faced, her hair scattered in all directions.

"You know you want it," he leaned his lips towards hers, but she twisted her face away, and he caught her ear.

"Stop it!" she shrieked as his body smothered her in the corner.

I grabbed Cox's shoulder and pried him away from her. I pressed him against the wall with my forearm under his chin. "Get the hell away from her!"

I grabbed Laticia's hand and pulled her to my side.

"What are you gonna do?" Derek chided me.

I cocked my balled fist. "I'm gonna pound your face in." He recoiled.

"No!" Laticia screeched as she pulled on my cocked arm. "Stop!"

I jabbed my forearm into the base of his throat, and he gagged as I pushed myself back. "Don't touch her ever again. Nobody touches her."

"Fine, take her. She ain't worth nothing, anyhow," he said, walking toward the stairs. "She's all used up."

She grabbed my hand and led me into the nearest bedroom. Tears streamed down her face as the grandfather clock struck midnight with 12 long, ominous tones.

"Thanks for saving me," she sobbed as we sat down on the end of the bed.

"I'm sorry," I said.

"Sorry? For what?"

"The entire male race, for anyone who's ever hurt you."

"I don't care who's hurt me. I just want to feel normal again." Tears bubbled up in her eyes. "I just want to feel something again, anything. This pain is too much." She leaned into me, and I leaned back into her. We sat on the edge of the bed, our bodies holding each other erect. She turned and looked at me through bleary eyes. "Thanks," she whispered.

"For what?"

"For being a good person. For being a good man."

"I just hope you're OK."

"I don't think I'll ever be OK," she confessed. "I don't know what to do anymore."

He would want you to be with her echoed in my brain.

"I don't know what's right or wrong, good or bad anymore. I don't know what to do." She buried her face in my chest.

I wrapped my arms around her. She sighed heavily as she pressed into me and I pressed into her; her soft skin, her warmth. I stared down at her, and she peered up at me, melting in my arms. Our lips moved toward each other until they met.

I knew while it was happening it was wrong, but I couldn't stop myself. Each touch, each kiss, each discarded piece of clothing was a compromise, a compromise of myself, and of everything I stood for. I traded it all for a brief moment of pleasure. *What had I become? Why did I allow it to happen so easily, without a fight?*

When I look back on this moment, I see it as an outsider, as an innocent bystander helplessly witnessing a heinous act. My soul is tainted by its mere reflection in my mind's eye. But I know it's no stranger who I see committing that unforgivable sin. It's me, and there's nothing I can do to erase it.

I leaned over and kissed her on the mouth. She looked at me and smiled sadly. I guided her back onto the bed and spread her out on the flowered comforter. I climbed up on the bed and pressed my lips against hers. I could feel her tortured heart pounding.

The sins that I had bottled up for so many years spewed forth. It felt good, but I knew, even at the time, the pleasure was strictly temporary. And I failed to understand that I incurred a debt I could never repay.

At the end, with eyes closed and a deep breath, she sighed a single word. "Dorian." It hovered in the air like a profound mist. I rolled off of her and rose to my feet. I stepped around her scattered clothes and underwear, almost afraid to touch them.

I started to dress very deliberately. She stared at me, I looked at her, and we froze, our eyes locked in our immediate regret. We both knew it was wrong. It did not make anything better, only infinitely worse. She looked away as her eyes glistened, and a lone tear ran down her cheek and disappeared among the tiny beads of sweat on her cheeks. She looked up at me as a contorted look of revulsion grew across her face, and I stared back at her, unable to speak. I stepped to her, and she buried her face in the pillow. "Go away," she murmured through the pillow. "Just go away." And she started sobbing.

I pulled on my pants and left the room with my head down. I looked over the railing. The grandfather clock read 12:18.

"I see ya, Jake. Thirty seconds over Tokyo, huh?" Cullen beamed a proud parental smile. "I knew you had it in ya."

"I don't know man." My eyes diverted to his feet.

"Relax," he threw his arm around my shoulder, squeezing me tight to him. "This is a good thing."

"I don't know if it was right."

"She wanted it," he snapped. "She needed it."

I stepped away from him. "I think it might've been a mistake. What I did was wrong."

"Shhh." He pulled me to the corner. "There is no mistake, especially with someone like her."

"You don't get it." I walked away and trotted down the steps to get as far away from my sin as possible. I felt like I was going to throw up. The downstairs was still overflowing with teenagers, oblivious to my desecration.

What have I done? I watched Derek Cox and a thin, dark-haired girl rubbing up against each other. Why? I lost it all and for what? A sweet, metallic odor emanated from every pore of my body, so strong I feared everyone could smell it, too. I wanted to go home, jump in a cold shower and scrub it off my body, but I knew how it got there and who I became because of it could never be eradicated. There is no magic elixir to purge me of what I had just lost.

◆◆◆◆

"We shouldn't have done that." Laticia stumbled up to me as the clock struck one, a beer in each hand.

"Yeah, I just got caught up," I agreed.

"It just made everything worse." She took a generous swig of the beer. "It hurts even more. I have to make this pain go away."

"I don't think getting drunk is the answer. You'll regret it tomorrow."

"That's not the only thing I'll regret in the morning." She finished off the beer.

I nodded as we walked to the stairs.

"I don't know how I'll explain this to Dorian," she said.

"I don't... you don't have to tell him anything."

"He'll want to know."

"I don't think he will. Don't say anything to anyone. It was a mistake. Let's just forget about it. Take this to our grave."

She staggered up the stairs, missed the top step, stumbled into our bedroom, and collapsed on the bed. I shut the door and stood on the steps watching the party, trying to make sense of myself, trying to fit that last hour into my eternal vision of my life.

I then saw Dorian bobbing about in the front corridor, craning his neck above the crowd, searching. I sprinted down the steps and spread my arms from wall to railing blocking his path. His eyes looked past me up the stairs.

"I'm trying to find Laticia. Have you seen her?"

I looked away and shook my head.

"You sure? I gotta talk to her."

"I haven't seen her," I said impatiently.

He looked over his shoulder and then back at me. "Do me a favor, will ya? Check up there and I'll check down here. Her mother told me she'd be here."

I walked up the stairs and down the hall overlooking the party, watching Dorian slice through the thick crowd. I opened a door and stumbled upon a couple in bed who shrieked, "Get out!" I closed that door quickly, and opened every door in the hall, pretending to search for her.

I trotted down the front staircase and forced my way through the mass of teenagers. I looked in the dining room, living room and kitchen for Dorian. He was nowhere in sight. Jay was rummaging through Cullen's refrigerator.

"Hey, have you seen Dorian?" I asked.

"Yeah," he said, taking an aggressive bite of an oversized sandwich. "I saw him heading up the back steps about two minutes ago."

I pushed through the crowd and sprinted up the front steps. I peered into the bedroom. The lights were blazing. She was curled up on the bed in a fetal position with eyes closed softly and mouth opened slightly.

I tiptoed into the room and stood at the end of the bed, staring at her. She slept peacefully and she breathed without a sound. I pulled the blanket up, wrapped it around her body and tucked it in under her shoulders. I fixed her pillow and placed my right hand on her left cheek. The corners of her mouth rose up in an unconscious smile. I brushed her hair from her face and gently ran it behind her ear. I turned off the overhead lights and opened the bathroom door enough to allow a wedge of white light to cut into the darkness to protect her. I went to the door and turned back for one final, desperate look. She rested there in the dark room, simmering in the weak glow of the bathroom light. I shut the door gently and stood outside guarding it.

"I haven't seen her all night," I told Dorian as he walked up the stairs toward me.

"You sure?"

"Yeah, if she was," I led him back to the stairs, "I'd have seen her." I feared he could smell her smell on me, and he would know. "I heard there's another party at Carter's house, maybe she went there."

"OK, it's worth a shot. You stay here, in case she shows up." He trotted down the steps and out the front door.

I went back into her room, sat down in the corner, and watched her sleep until the party died down around two. Jay gave us both a ride home. I walked her to her front door. Her mother took her from me, and led her inside with one word, "gracias."

Jay turned to me in the front seat. "You're a good guy, doing all that."

I shook my head. "No, I'm not." Paltry gestures don't amend life altering sins.

◆◆◆◆

The next morning that sweet metallic smell was still there. I walked to the window, and it followed me. It was everywhere, marking me, repulsing me. I ripped off my clothes and stepped into the shower. I scrubbed every inch of my body; every crevice, every corner, with all my pent-up fury. I dried myself, but I could still smell it. I couldn't escape it. A constant reminder of my sin. I stood in the middle of my room shivering.

"What are you doing?" my sister stood in the doorway behind me, back home for a visit. She was tall and thin, with long hair, black like our father's.

I fastened a towel around my waist. "Nothing," I said.

"It doesn't seem like nothing," she smiled. "You're not that good looking," she said and turned to leave, adding, "You're weird."

"Wait," I stopped her.

"What?"

"I think I did something really wrong last night."

"So, I'm not the only screw up in the family?" she laughed. "The golden boy's got himself into some trouble?"

"Shut up, I'm serious."

"So am I," she shot back. "Now you know how I feel."

"I may be in real trouble," I confessed.

"Who is she?"

"Who's who?"

"Who's the girl that got you in trouble?"

"How did you know it was a girl?"

"Men are so stupid," she shook her head. "Soooo stupid. It's always a girl. They throw their life away for nothing. What did the parents say?"

"Didn't tell 'em," I admitted. "No one knows."

"Then what's the problem?"

"It was wrong. I shouldn't have done what I did."

"Did you kill someone?"

"Of course not."

"Did you ruin someone's life?"

"Uh... I don't think so."

"Can you fix it? Can you change it?"

"No."

"Don't worry about it then."

"How can't I?"

"If you worry about things you can't change, it'll ruin you." She turned and left me there alone.

I pulled on my shorts, sneakers and a t-shirt, and went downstairs. Uncle Roth was sitting at the dining room table.

"Heeeey, the next Mike Piazza? Best hitter on the Jersey Shore, huh? How about that? Your old man's been keeping me updated. I had to come and see it for myself."

I smiled and nodded at him, embarrassed.

"He's so proud of you."

I didn't know what to say to him. The hope and optimism he had in his eyes for me was too painful to behold, so contrary to reality. I couldn't take it, so I pushed open the front door, and ran down the steps. I ran along the boardwalk, with the waves crashing to my left, the cars roaring to my right, and God's burning eye following my every step. I wanted to get as far away as possible. I wanted to run away from myself, from my life. I kept running and running even after my legs ached and my lungs burned, but I couldn't outrun His scrutiny.

When I could no longer take another step, I stopped. My clothes, my shoes, were dripping with sweat, the impurities purging out of my skin. I was standing on the wooden boardwalk alone, overlooking a small cove of Long Beach. I looked up at the bright sky. The fat cumulus clouds were moving hard to the west as the gauzy cirrus clouds were spinning off to the east. It appeared as if the heavens were unraveling before my eyes.

And then, in a whisper, the ocean called to me in the echoes of the waves, in each stroke of the sea wiping the slate clean, redrawing the lines, tempting me to step into the gray, to accept the iniquities of the world, of myself, so I could love and be loved.

◆◆◆◆

I was miles from Galilee and started the long walk back. When I finally arrived home, Dawn was sitting on the top step of my front porch, her arms wrapped around both knees.

"Where were you last night?" She stood and hugged me. "I looked for you everywhere. I thought something bad might've happened." My sweat absorbed into her fresh clothes.

"Me and Quinton got hammered." I pleaded down to the lesser crime. "I'm trying to sweat it out of me."

"Everyone's entitled to one night like that, especially on your birthday." She handed me a carefully wrapped present. "I wanted to give you this." She kissed my cheek.

"What is it?"

"Open it."

"I don't want to yet."

"It's your home run ball. I had it mounted in glass for you."

I looked at her basking in the glow of her optimistic innocence, and I couldn't believe how lucky and stupid I am. "You didn't need to do this."

"I wanted to. You deserve it. You're such a good person."

"No, I'm not," I said.

"You're one of the best people I know."

I could barely look at her. I didn't deserve the love she offered me. "You better get a new group of friends." She smiled, thinking it was a joke.

NW

Chapter 49

"We're gonna get hit!" my mom screamed as the storm pounded our house. It was in the early hours the night before our last regular season game. The driving rain and cutting wind buffeted the house all night as I drifted from sleep to reality back to sleep, floating in a semiconscious fetal state filled with anxiety dreams: sprinting toward a home plate that I could never reach; facing an unending barrage of baseballs streaming at me that my flailing bat was unable to touch.

I didn't hear it. I felt it. It jolted me from my surreal dreams and almost shook me out of my bed. And then a cool wind swept over me, like an ethereal baptism, billowing my sheets half off the bed. Then the water rushed in, pelting the walls and the hardwood floors. Bare feet, slapping against the floors, ran from room to room.

"Is everyone OK?"

Sirens screamed through the beating rain, louder and louder until the red and white lights were swirling across my room. The rest of the night was a series of sirens and lights, firemen in and out of the house until it was safe to go back in and go to sleep.

◆◆◆◆

I awoke the next morning to thin beams of sun piercing my room as if nothing had happened.

"Can't believe you guys got struck by lightning last night," Jay said, as he, Quinton, and I drove to school.

"We knew we would at some point," I said.

As I saw the sun spread its light over the shore, I was hoping it would get hot enough to burn off the water on the field.

"I hope we're rained out," Quinton said.

"I don't. I want to earn the undefeated season, not back into it," I told him. "The year Ted Williams hit four hundred, he could've sat out the last game, but he played and got three hits. He earned it."

"Thanks, John Houseman," Quinton said.

"We're gonna lose, anyway," Jay predicted. "No team's ever gone undefeated. It's impossible."

"If you keep talking like that, it is," I said.

"Relax," Jay told me. "I'm just out-jinxing the jinx."

"Great, you just jinxed the out-jinx of the jinx," Quinton said.

"That doesn't matter, anyway," I said.

"Yeah, none of this baseball crap means anything," Quinton said. "In the grand scheme of things nothing nobody does means a damn thing."

"Nothing?" Jay asked.

"Nope, not one damn thing." Quinton repeated. "Not baseball, not college, not making money, nothing."

"I disagree," I argued. "What about doctors? They do important things. They save people's lives."

"Yeah, but they just save the lives of people who do nothing important," Quinton said.

"What if they saved the life of another doctor?" I asked.

"Everything's meaningless. Everyone's forgotten, Jake," Quinton said. "That's why at funerals they always say, 'He'll never be forgotten,' because we all know he will be forgotten."

◆◆◆◆

"Hell comes when the man you are meets face-to-face with the man you're meant to be." Delaney's voice resounded across the field as I spoke with Fulbright before the game.

Fulbright wiped his forehead with his forearm. "It gets hotter and hotter, earlier and earlier, every year."

"I don't know if it's hotter, or I'm just less tolerant," I said.

"The sun's moving closer and closer," he said. "The earth is in a degenerating orbit. Every year, our path around the sun grows shorter and shorter, and the years go by faster and faster."

Coach Delaney walked up to me. "Ed McPhee from the Mets called this morning," he said. "He's seen you play."

"What did he say?"

"He said you got a lot of tools, a lot of ability, but questioned how much you know the game," he flashed a disappointed smile. "Catching's more than framing a strike or calling a pitch. The defense begins and ends with you. The catcher's the leader. He instills confidence in the team, in his pitcher. You have to start asserting yourself. Lead. He's gonna be at the game today."

♦♦♦♦

As the Mercer team was taking infield practice, Cullen sat down next to me in the dugout. "They say once you pop your cherry, it adds 50 feet to your long ball."

I shrugged and shook my head in shame.

He threw his arm around my shoulder. "Cheer up, you should be proud of yourself."

"Proud of what?" I asked.

"You finally stepped up and became a man."

"What I did was wrong." I led him to the side of the dugout.

"You didn't do anything wrong." He took the ball from my glove.

"Yeah, I did. She was not in a good place," I tapped my head, "when I was with her. She wasn't thinking right. She didn't feel good about it after."

"So, you're a bad lay. What d'you expect?"

"That's not the point."

"You didn't do anything illegal. So, why worry about it? If it's not a crime, don't do the time."

"I don't care if it's legal. It was wrong." I said.

"Jake," he said, "you know what your problem is?"

"What?"

"You have too much of that Catholic guilt in you."

"The world could use a little more Catholic guilt," I replied with disdain.

"The only thing that'll get you in trouble is your goddamn conscience."

"At least I have a conscience."

"The human conscience is the most counterproductive by-product of human evolution," he said. "Think about the word conscience. Con meaning against, science meaning science, against science, contrary to rational thought. It's irrational, impractical to have a conscience."

"So, we can do whatever we want without concern for right or wrong?"

"Sure," he shrugged. "There is no right and wrong."

"It doesn't work that way."

"What doesn't?"

"Life."

"That's exactly how life works," he said, looking upward, sweat beading on his forehead. "Where's a good cloud when you need one?"

He shielded his eyes. "You know how they catch monkeys in Africa?"

I stared at him vacantly.

"Hunters place a wooden box with a hole in it in the middle of the jungle with a banana inside. Monkeys reach in the box and grab the banana, but they can't pull it out. The hole's too small, but the monkeys refuse to drop the banana. The hunters return and find these monkeys just sitting there with their hand in the box, almost waiting to be captured. They'd be free if they'd just let it go." He looked straight into my eyes. "Drop this goddamn banana."

"I don't want to treat people like that."

"People?" he scoffed. "What are people? We're all just a conglomeration of cells. Nothing more." He stood to walk to the field. "You'll only get in trouble if you keep talking about it. No matter what your conscience says, admit nothing. Take it to your grave."

◆◆◆◆

"I thought you had to kill a chicken and burn it on second base?" Quinton asked Jay as he was aligning his wristbands and readjusting his socks in the dugout.

"All that stuff doesn't do a damn thing," Cullen said to Jay.

"Of course, it does," Jay said as he re-tied his shoes. "I don't want to jinx us."

"If we win or lose because you did or did not wear the right underwear, why'd we show up? Why even play the game?" Cullen flipped his hands. "It's not a damn dressing contest. We win or lose because of what we do, whether we make the plays. I determine the course of my life. Your rituals don't. I take full responsibility for my play, for everything I do."

◆◆◆◆

"This pitcher's fastball poses no immediate problems," Fulbright explained as he walked into the dugout. "His off-speed inventory appears quite mundane.

Mercer stayed with us for seven innings, but we held a one-run lead when Quinton stepped on the mound with runners on second and third. We were three outs away from history.

The next Mercer batter tapped the middle of the plate with his bat, and his fleshy torso wriggled. I flashed my right index finger, high fastball. The pitch sailed out of Quinton's hand, and the black aluminum bat flashed across my eyes the moment my palm stung. His bat was a half second late. The next pitch was the same as the first; a high fastball and a late swing.

Then, I decided to show how smart I was. I knew he'd be gearing up for the fastball, so I squeezed my right hand into a fist signaling change-up. Quinton nodded and lifted his hands over his head. The ball tumbled out of his left hand and sailed toward my mitt in the same trajectory as the first two, but the pitch was still out in front of the plate when the streak of black flashed across my eyes.

The white ball pinged off the black and beamed to right-center. Dorian galloped toward the white streak as it faded into the alley. He dove headlong, and the dying ball nestled in his outstretched glove as he slid across the grass. He popped up and fired a strike to me, holding the runner at third.

Delaney stumbled out of the dugout, waving his arms. I met him at the mound. "How dumb are you?" he shouted, staring right at Quinton. "Huh?"

Quinton started right back, the veins in his neck popping out.

"Don't ever throw a change-up to a guy who can't hit a fastball." Delaney motioned his hand across his throat as he glared at me. "High heat, high heat! You should know better than that, Jake!"

Delaney then looked at the batter at the plate. "This kid's been on fire." He turned back to Quinton. "Walk 'im."

After the intentional walk, the bases were now loaded. Quinton stood on the mound. His eyes were two black holes staring like lasers into the emptiness as he held our destiny in his left hand. I trotted out to the mound, hoping my energy would not only give him confidence, but display my leadership.

"Don't worry about a thing, Q." I pulled off my mask. "Two outs to go. I'll catch anything you throw, anything. Don't short arm your curve or choke your heat. Forget about the guy on third. He's going nowhere. Go after the hitter. I will catch anything you throw, anything. I'm a human backstop," I stared right into his eyes, trying to inject him with my confidence. "There's no such thing as a wild pitch. Get the hitter." *If he believes in me,* I thought, *he'll believe in himself.* He stared at me blankly and shook his head.

As I settled in behind the plate, Quinton inexplicably stepped off the rubber, wound and threw the ball toward home. It left his hand high and I reached my glove up above my head as it began to rise. It rose and rose and rose, sailing over my head, over the backstop, until it banged against the hood of our team bus and rattled from car to car. The crowd erupted as the runners on second and third crossed home plate. I stood in disbelief.

"How about that one, Big Shot?" Quinton screamed. "Can you catch that one?"

The Mercer players mobbed the runner as he raced across home plate with the winning run.

I walked to the bench. Delaney stood on the lip of the dugout, his mouth agape. "I guess we're taught a lesson every day," I said as I walked past him.

"Yeah, don't bring in a fruitcake to close the record-setting game," Delaney said.

◆◆◆◆

I sat in the far back of the bus. I wanted to be alone, to reorganize my thoughts, reshuffle my goals, restack my priorities, and redefine my life.

Delaney sat down next to me. "There's always another day." His voice was ragged. "Another game."

"Is that a good thing or a bad thing?" I asked.

We drove on for a while without another word. As we reached the school, he turned to me and said, "If we took all the money and man hours the world spends on something as silly as baseball, do you think we could put an end to world hunger?"

"We probably could do it without doing away with baseball," I said.

NW

Chapter 50

"The best hitter on the Jersey Shore," Fulbright winked at me as I walked through the halls. I finished the season two points higher than Dorian, the first time I ever beat him in anything. While I reached my depths as a person, I soared as a player.

The next day, Delaney stood before the team. "The playoffs begin Saturday. Do or die. There are no second chances. Everything moves faster, is more intense, so you cannot divorce yourself from your techniques. Your fundamentals are your best friend. They are what you fall back on when everything else goes to hell. When you're staring down a 3-2 count in the bottom of the seventh, you'll hold on to them with all your being. Fundamentals bind your physical, mental and spiritual being. Believe in them."

◆◆◆◆

I went out to the field early the next day to take extra batting practice. I wasn't going to quit while I was ahead. I continued to work, hone my fundamentals. But I also believed sports were cleansing, purifying, that hard work would purge me of my inequities, the sweat seeping from my pores would draw my sins out of my body and restore the purity to my life.

Dorian sat in the dugout watching me with detached interest. I felt self-conscious. Did he know something? Should I just keep my sin hidden? Ultimately, I knew there was only one way to free myself of my sin. I couldn't sweat it out of me. I would have to own up to it. It wouldn't be pleasant. It wouldn't be easy. I could lose him as a friend.

I walked over to him. "Remember last week at Cullen's party?" I said as I studied his face for a reaction.

"Uh..," he thought for a second. "Yeah. What about it?"

"Well, I did see Laticia there," I confessed, tentatively.

His eyes rolled to mine. "You did?" He seemed more curious then suspicious.

"Yeah, she was there." I inched toward my confession, like creeping toward the edge of a cliff, tempted, yet frightened. "She was upstairs and I was up there with her before you came."

His eyes were riveted on my mouth, watching my every word

to understand each one.

"She..." I began. "We... I mean... I... I went in... the room... and... I..."

"Yeah, I know. She said she was in rough shape that night. She said you took care of her. She said you were good to her."

"No, not really," I started to say. "In fact, I..."

"No, no. I appreciate what you did. Thanks for looking after her, protecting her. I know you didn't want me to see her like that. You're a real friend." He walked away slowly.

Nothing made sense anymore. Everything was spiraling out of my control. I always had the things of the world in a neat, tidy order. Everything had its place. But now wrong was right, right was wrong, up was down. My life had been upended and I didn't know where to begin, what part of my life I should pick up first and put back in order.

◆◆◆◆

I went to see Ms. Vivaqua after practice. I thought she could help me, not just with calculus, but she may be able to give me something that would put all of this in perspective. She could point me, at least, in the right direction. I climbed the dimly lit staircase.

The name *Sylvia, Sylvia, Sylvia,* pounded in my skull. It is a beautiful name, I thought. I wasn't sure she'd be there. It was late on a Friday evening. No one else was around. The school was dark, only dim peripheral lights by the lockers and along the corridors were lit.

The main lights of the administrative wing were off, but a hazy yellow glow from the Student Guidance Offices simmered in the darkness. She was there. Her light was on. I knew it. The main door was closed but unlocked. I opened it and stepped into the foggy light.

Her door was slightly ajar, and the thinnest slice of light cut through the crack, projecting a yellow sliver across the carpet onto the far wall. I walked slowly toward her light like I was on a long dark road. I stepped to her door, and gently knocked on the black painted name **DR. SYLVIA A. VIVAQUA, PhD.** The door fell open, and a dingy yellow light swept across my vision revealing two dark shadows embracing on the couch.

I stood in the doorway, motionless, staring at the fading image of all that I'd hoped for disappear, until the slow-moving door banged the wall. They snapped their heads at me, and scrambled to their feet, fumbling to re-engage shirt buttons. "This is not what you think," her voice pierced the silence.

I groped the wooden door for the knob, backed up and pulled it definitively shut behind me. I ran toward the stairs. "Jake, Jake, Jake!" Cullen's voice bounced off the walls, as I bounded down the long staircase. "Goddamn it!" he said as I sprinted away from them like I had done something wrong.

◆◆◆◆

I came home that night and went straight to my room. I was in no mood to see or talk to anyone. I sat in my pitch-black room. The only light was the golden twinkle of the crescent moon looming over the ocean, and the only sound was the splashing of the soft waves against the sand. Staring into the darkness, everything became so clear. The world had no meaning, no goodness, no purity.

My mom knocked on the door and entered, carrying a turkey sandwich on a plate. "You hungry?" she asked.

"No," I shrugged. "Not really."

"Nervous for the big game?"

"No, it doesn't really matter."

"Of course, it does," she said. "All that time and effort you put in means something."

"Not really, maybe it's just a waste of time. Maybe I wasted the last 10 years of my life with baseball."

"It wasn't wasted."

"Isn't this all pointless?" I asked. "Isn't all of life, everything we do, meaningless?"

"Life's meaning is what you believe life means," she answered. "If you believe baseball is the most important thing in the world, then it is, and if you believe it's a waste of time, then it is. If you believe life is meaningful, worthwhile, deserving of love and commitment, then it is, but if you believe everything we do is meaningless, then life is meaningless for you."

◆◆◆◆

The following afternoon, I stood on the hill looking out over our baseball diamond glistening in the summer sun. I wondered where it all went wrong. The lines of the field were so clean, the edges were so sharp. The field made sense, everything was clearly defined, a binding simplicity. Baseball was the only thing that still made sense to me. It clarifies. It separates. It exposes. It reveals.

"About that thing, in Vivaqua's office," Cullen walked up to me as I was snapping on my gear before the game. "You gotta make hay while the sun shines, you know what I'm saying?"

"Nope, I don't," I said. "Why her?"

"Why not her?"

"Can't you just leave one thing alone, one thing pure?"

"Nothing's pure," he winked at me. "Besides, nothing happened, thanks to you." And he trotted out to the field.

◆◆◆◆

The ball popped up easily in the top half of the seventh inning. All three base runners were running on the crack of the bat. The ball floated high above the infield, and Cullen settled under it. He didn't wobble or stagger. He had it the whole way. The ball hung high in the air, and then it dropped out of the sun, hit the heel of his glove, and landed at his feet. He scrambled, picked it up, and fired it to first base two steps too late, as two runners scored extending their lead to six.

Delaney stood on the top step of the dugout as we trotted in, looking right past us in disgust.

"I lost it in the sun." Cullen tossed his glove at the bench pre-empting Delaney's attack.

Delaney grabbed him. "It's been there since the beginning of time. And it's gonna to be there till the end of time. Make the damn catch."

"If the ball's in the sun," Quinton smirked, "just catch the sun."

"We can't be losing to these fools." Curtis threw his glove against the dugout wall.

"It's embarrassing," Delaney said in disgust. "Second year in a row, knocked out in the first round."

I pulled off my equipment and tossed it into a heap in the corner of the dugout. That's the last time I will ever wear that stuff.

"We must applaud their mettle. Valor, resilience, fortitude, temerity." Fulbright heralded the virtues of second place.

I didn't know what was worse – losing or conceding defeat.

"Everybody hits." Dorian's cleats screeched on the steps of the dugout. "They still got to get three outs. They can't just run out the clock. We're the clock."

As I walked to the plate, I told myself to be the leader, be the spark plug. On a 2-2 count, the pitcher threw me an outside fastball. I waited, kept my weight back and then brought my hands. I laid the sweet spot of the barrel on the ball, and it exploded toward the right center gap. It had triple written all over it. I hit the inside of the first base bag and arched toward second. The ball bounced off the fence and rolled along the warning track. I ran and ran with my head down. I jammed my right foot on the inside corner of second base and drove hard to third. By the time I looked up, I was halfway to the base, and Fulbright was frantically waving at me to stop. I saw him too late. I couldn't return, so I lowered my head and slid hard into the third baseman's glove, knocking him down.

I rolled on my back. I could smell the freshly cut grass. It was a beautiful day. The sky was blue, the clouds were soft, the sun was bright, and I was out.

Fulbright leaned over me like a giant eclipse. "The greatest sin of all is greed." He reached down and pulled me to my feet.

Delaney met me at the top step of the dugout. "Never, ever make the first out at third," he seethed. "You learn that in Little League."

"There are 10 more ways to score from third than there are from second," I muttered as I walked by him.

"There are none from the bench."

Dorian planted his feet firmly in the middle of the box, hitched up his pants, and stared resolutely at the pitcher.

He worked the count to 1-2, and then deflected a curve off the chain link fence. He took a ball and then sliced a fastball into the stands. He stood in the box stoically, waiting for his pitch, and the balls kept coming from all directions, all angles, fastballs, curveballs, sliders, changeups, and he surgically cut them out of play, down the baselines or back into the screen. Nothing could get by him. He would not give in. He would not succumb. It was as if he was toying with the pitcher, like he and the pitcher were playing a simple game of pepper.

"This is the most unbelievable thing I've ever seen," Delaney said. "I've never witnessed anything like it, not in my 53 years of baseball. What's it been, 15?"

"Sixteen, coach," Jay said. "Sixteen foul balls."

"That's gotta be some kind of high school record."

Finally, on the 20th pitch, Dorian stroked a ball about eight feet off the ground, just beyond the reach of the shortstop's glove, that didn't stop until it clanged against the fence on one hop. He rounded first base and watched the center fielder's throw to the second baseman.

And then everyone did indeed hit that inning. Bloopers fell into holes, slow bounders found small cracks, rollers snuck through legs. We walked. We were hit by pitches. No one could make an out. It went on and on until the umpire called the game after Jay sprinted across the plate with the winning run.

◆◆◆◆

After the game, I walked away from the field with a mixture of shock and relief.

"Hey, great game! Way to go!" My uncle met me at the top of the hill.

"It was ugly," I said in a daze.

"It was a win," he corrected me. "You never need to apologize for winning."

That game showed us how good and how bad we could really be. We felt the finality of defeat and the invincibility of victory all in one game, in one inning.

NW

Chapter 51

"The Dodgers just picked you in the third round," Delaney told Dorian as we warmed up before practice. Dorian just nodded as if this type of thing happens every day. The next day, I was selected by the Mets in the 50th round.

"Congratulations!" my dad said, reaching out to shake my hand.

"For what?"

"Getting drafted," he said.

"So what?"

"The next Mike Piazza."

"I'm not wasting my life in the minors," I told him.

"It's an honor just to get drafted. There are thousands of guys who would kill to get drafted by a major league team."

"It was the 50th round, which means there are a thousand guys better than me."

"Piazza was drafted in the 62nd round."

I didn't know what to say. Either my dad actually thought I had a shot, or he was just trying to make us both feel better.

◆◆◆◆

The next two weeks, we rolled through the playoffs. No team stayed close to us for more than a couple of innings. We came together. We believed in ourselves and each other, and we reached further than we had ever dreamed.

Dawn came to every game, no matter how far. She sat next to my father and uncle, and saw every inning, every at-bat, every pitch. For the first time, someone was watching me play, not to see how good I was or to see me to do something special. She was there to see me, nothing more, and that nothing more meant everything.

◆◆◆◆

"If I get two strikes on a hitter today," Cullen told me before the State Semi-Final game. "I'll do this." He swiped his glove across his belt. "That's the signal."

"Signal for what?"

He grabbed my mitt. "You see this edge right here?" His thumb flicked a bent rivet on its heel.

"That was like that when you gave it to me."

"I know," he said. "Rub the ball against the rivet like this," he cut into a ball with a quick flick. "Don't gash it. Just give me a smooth cut or a rough edge, right below the seam," he showed me the nefarious scar beneath the red stitching.

"That's illegal."

"Don't give me that boy scout crap. It's only illegal if you get caught. So, don't get caught."

"I'd rather lose honestly," I stated proudly, "than—"

"No, you wouldn't," he shot back. "You want to win just as bad as me. There's no honor in losing. Not even Rommel or Lee were noble in defeat."

"It's wrong," I said.

"There is no right or wrong, only wins and losses."

"It's cheating."

"If you ain't cheating, you ain't trying."

I walked away. I didn't understand. He didn't need to cheat. He had already pitched 30 consecutive scoreless innings this year, two shy of the state record. It didn't make sense.

◆◆◆◆

"The wind resistance generates the action of the ball," Mr. Fulbright explained to me minutes later. "The more wind resistance against the ball, the more action, so cuts, blemishes on the ball, increase the movement. It's impossible to execute a breaking pitch with, say, a billiards ball. The ball's too pristine. It possesses no imperfections, engenders no resistance, rendering it immune to the forces of the wind. That's why big leaguers cut the ball."

"Then you couldn't throw a curve in a vacuum, either?" I asked.

"That's impossible," he pointed his finger at me. "You can't throw a ball in a vacuum. Vacuums don't exist. Nature abhors a vacuum. Nature always fills the void."

"But, imagine how fast you could throw a ball in a vacuum," I said. "With no wind resistance."

"You can't live in a vacuum, Jake. You need the wind."

◆◆◆◆

In the sixth inning, leading by five runs, Delaney brought in Cullen to mop up the game, so he could save Quinton for the Finals.

The first batter of the seventh inning took the third pitch for strike two. Cullen ran his glove across his belt. I stood up, and stealthily slid the ball against the rivet, leaving a jagged slice just below the stitching.

Cullen caught my return throw, saw the marred ball and nodded. His next pitch started down the middle and sliced hard inside. It struck the heel of my mitt, bounced between my legs and rolled to a stop at the foot of the umpire. He picked up the ball, tossed it into the dugout, and fired a new one back to Cullen. The ump crouched behind me, and placed his chin on top of my shoulder, "I don't know how it got there," he whispered firmly, "but if I find another one, you're gone."

Cullen walked the first batter and struck out the second, but the third batter laced a double in the left center alley, making it second and third with one out.

The next batter hit a high bounder that Cullen snared. He stepped to first, and the runner on third darted to home. Cullen then wheeled and fired a strike right at me. The runner skidded to a stop halfway to home and sprinted back to the base. My throw to third was high, pulling Jay off the bag. Jay pivoted and fired a strike to Quinton at first trying to nab the batter who had rounded the base too far. The runner on third sprinted back toward home, and Quinton snapped the ball to me, trapping him in a pickle.

We chased those three runners around the infield like a team of seven-year-old sand-lotters. It took 14 throws to finally make the out we should have made with one easy toss to first base.

Delaney stomped out to the mound flailing his arms. "The play was to first!"

"I thought we wanted to keep the run from scoring," Cullen said.

"You're not smart enough to think." He shook his perplexed head. "Ahead by five in the last inning. We trade runs for outs. Runs for outs!" His booming voice echoed across the field.

◆◆◆◆

Delaney sat down next to me on the bus back to Bainbridge.

"Did you see it, Jakie? Did you see it?" His voice beamed with the excitement of a Christmas Day child.

I looked at him. "See what?"

"The people. Old men, kids, women, too. They were pointing at us, whispering, 'There they are. Those are the ones. They're going to States!' Nothing like this, Jakie. Nothing in the world."

◆◆◆◆

"You're a good man, Charlie Brown," my uncle said to me that night as we watched the Yankee game. "Never forget that."

"I don't know," I shrugged.

"It's the most important thing," he told me. "When this happened," he wiggled his mangled fingers at me, "it destroyed me. I let it destroy me. I let it destroy my marriage. This took baseball, but I let it take everything. Baseball is baseball, and life is life. Don't confuse the two. Don't let anything stop you from being the good man I know you are."

"It's hard sometimes," I confessed.

"I know it is."

"I don't know what the point of all this is. I keep searching for something, some meaning, but I can never seem to find it."

He looked at me. "T.S. Eliot said, 'Never cease from exploration. And the end of all our exploring will be to arrive where we started and know the place for the first time.' It's like in baseball. The goal is to find your way back to the place where you started, home."

◆◆◆◆

The morning of the State Finals, my father drove me to the school to catch the team bus. We both just stared ahead without speaking. He was edgier than I was. His knuckles were white and the veins in his arms pulsed as he gripped the wheel, changing lanes and weaving past the other cars. His mind seemed to be racing faster than the car.

My mind was on other, more important things.

"Can I ask you a question?" I broke the tension.

"You can ask me another one, too," he said, with a smile.

"Do you think I'm a good person?" I asked.

He looked right at me. "Do you think you're a good person?"

"I don't know."

"You don't know? Well, I think we have a problem then. Why don't you think you're a good person?"

"I don't think I'm not a good person. I just... I don't think I know what a good person is, anymore."

"Of course, you do," he said quickly. "A good person is someone who does the right thing."

"I don't know what the right thing is, then."

"You don't?" He snapped his head at me. "How can't you?"

"I know what the wrong thing is," I replied," I just don't think I always know what the right thing is. I know when you do something wrong, it's a sin."

"A sin isn't only when you do something bad. Sometimes a sin is when you do something good, but that good isn't as good as you could've done."

"Some people sin all the time, and nothing bad ever happens to 'em. Other guys do the right things and they get screwed. Where's the justice in that?"

"No matter who you are, how smart you think you are, how great the world tells you you are, we all get our comeuppance, one way or another. It's unavoidable."

"I'm not that optimistic," I said.

"All you have to worry about today is hitting the ball. All that other stuff will take care of itself."

◆◆◆◆

The team was silent as we began the hour drive to the State Finals. No one said very much. We were very subdued, very businesslike. Fulbright stood in the front of the bus. "We scouted their semi-final game. They're a formidable foe, very productive offensively, tremendous explosive power. They tallied 17 runs..."

"Yeah, it looked like the Wilson ball factory blew up," Delaney added.

The bus pulled to a stop in front of a green light, as the flashing red and blue lights of motorcycle policemen halted traffic in all directions. And then, a procession of cars crawled by, an endless train of BMWs, Mercedes, and Porsches connected by solemn purple and gold flags.

"Don't breathe," someone whispered, as a square black hearse inched by. We all fell silent as our grim futures crawled before our trepid eyes. All movement, all sound stopped on the bus.

Delaney turned to Fulbright. "There goes some poor sonavabitch who doesn't give a damn if we win or lose today."

"Extensive caravan," Fulbright said. "He must've been a remarkable human being."

"Two Yugos and a moped will take me to my grave," Delaney lamented.

"It's an omen," Jay said.

"What does it mean?" I asked.

"It's a sign," he answered.

"I know, but of what?"

"I'm not sure if it's a good omen or a bad omen. It's just an omen. We'll find out after the game."

"You know someone dies every day," I said.

"Every day?" Jay responded. "Every hour."

"Every second," Dorian added.

Quinton looked up. "Someone just died. Someone just died. Someone just died. Someone just died. Someone just died. Someone just died."

"We get it Q," Delaney yelled back at us. "You better get your game faces on."

"I always have my game face on, Coach," Cullen boasted.

"If you always have your game face on," Quinton whispered to me, "it wouldn't be your game face. It would just be your face."

We pulled into the parking lot next to the championship field and Coach Delaney stood up in the front of the bus. "Men," he began with a low, sober tone, "no one has given you a damn thing this year. You are here today because you earned it. You deserve to be here, and if you deserve to be here, do not doubt for one second that you deserve to win." His words emanated from the pit of his stomach. "I have just one thing to say before I send you men out onto that field. Just one thing," he held up his right index finger and paused. "Cease the day."

"It smells like a carnival," Quinton proclaimed as we stepped off the bus into the popcorn and cotton candy filled air.

◆◆◆◆

"He delivers his pitches with a great deal of acuity," Fulbright said, pacing in the dugout before the game.

"He's a phenom," Delaney told us unequivocally. "He's got a major league curveball."

"A daunting adversary," Fulbright retorted. "I concur."

The All-State pitcher stood on the mound, flipping the ball up in the air, waiting to dismantle us, but Quinton matched the phenom pitch for pitch. He stepped up and kept the game close for six innings against the best pitcher and the best team in the state. He pitched like he didn't give a damn, like he didn't realize the magnitude of it all. He didn't rise to the occasion as much as he brought the occasion down to him. He just threw and threw, challenging every hitter with every pitch.

We trailed 3-1 going into the last inning. The whole season, everything that we dreamed of, came down to three outs. I sat on the bench shaking as I removed my gear. The more I tried to control my body, the harder I shook.

My first three at-bats, I did not place my bat on even one pitch. Nothing was working. It didn't matter what he threw: fastball, curve, change-up, I couldn't hit it. Nothing I did the last month of the season mattered now. The pitched ball didn't care that I led the Shore in hitting. I had to prove it again. The game never stops, never slows down. It's constantly challenging, confronting, exposing your validity, every day, every at-bat.

The pitcher struck out Wally and Jay with a curveball and a slider to end the sixth inning, no fastballs, so I inched myself up in the box, anticipating his junk. I sliced his slider foul, and then pulled the curve into the stands.

The pitcher wasted no time. He grabbed the catcher's return throw out of the air, and without waiting for the sign, began his wind-up. The next image I saw was four seams of the ball spinning away from me. By the time I realized that it was a fastball, the bat felt too heavy to swing, and the only thing I heard was the hard pop of the catcher's mitt and a loud "Steeeriike thrrreee" from the plate umpire.

Quinton drew a walk on five pitches, and Curtis beat out an infield single. Cullen stepped to the plate with Dorian on deck. He planted his back foot in the box, signaled timeout, and turned toward third base. Fulbright feverishly rattled off a series of signs. Cullen dropped his chin and dragged his bat up to his right shoulder. The pitcher stared in, shook his head twice before nodding and settling into his stretch position. He peeked over at Curtis, they locked eyes, both afraid to blink.

The pitcher began his motion and Cullen casually turned his shoulders, squaring toward the mound with his bat parallel to the ground. The ball rose as it approached the plate, and Cullen lurched the meat of his bat at the ball. The white sphere shot straight up in the air and hovered above the infield. Curtis, moving on contact, kicked up dirt as he planted his right foot. The ball looped in front of the plate and landed softly in the mitt of the catcher, who quickly pivoted and fired a strike to the first baseman. The umpire signaled out; it was over.

Curtis stood on the infield dirt, frozen and dumbfounded.

"Put the fucking ball on the ground?" He tossed his helmet toward the dugout.

"I hit the ball 400 feet," Cullen ranted, under his breath, "not four."

I stood on the lip of the dugout, watching a group of green uniforms dive on top of each other by first base. I had the feeling I'd never stand on that spot ever again. I sat down on the bench and lowered my head into my hands.

There was a great buzz throughout the field of both joy and regret. It was all meaningless. All of my hard work was like chasing the wind. Fulbright walked into the dugout, "For as down as we are, that's how high they are. Every pitch, every inning, every game makes one side happy and one side not happy."

We filed onto the bus too stunned to speak. I sat in the last row with Jay in front of me.

"Why did Delaney have him bunt?" I asked Jay.

"Move the runners into scoring position, let our best hitter drive him in."

"Why not let both of 'em try to drive 'em in?" I asked.

"The chance both get a hit isn't as good as one getting a hit," he explained. "Play the percentages."

Delaney climbed on the bus last and staggered up the aisle as we pulled away. He moved from row to row until he finally found a place next to me.

"Everything we did this year means nothing." My words were stained with self-pity. "You're either the champion, or you're nothing."

"Is that the only thing you took from today, from this year? That we lost?" Delaney said to me.

"No," I snapped.

"What makes baseball so great makes it impossible. Baseball's both redemptive and unforgiving at the same time. It's relentless. There's always another game, another at-bat, another pitch. There's always another day to prove yourself or expose yourself. It just keeps coming and coming and coming."

NW

Chapter 52

I went over to the beach when I got home. I didn't want to see or hear from anyone. The late afternoon sun hung over the cold beach, and the sand was littered with driftwood and seashells. Serene waves rolled in thick and fast, one after another, forming a continuous blanket of foam. The brand-new beach carried the luster, the sheen, the untainted gloss of origination.

I walked down the beach, stopping on the water's edge, staring out at the repetitive waves. The icy water ran up my ankles and stabbed my skin. A thick rainbow sprung out of the blue horizon, the offspring of a far-off storm. The bands arching across the sky on the far side of the world were so bright, so colorful, I felt I could reach out and grab them, but I knew they were eternally out of my reach.

"I think the ocean likes me." A little voice rose up from my knees.

"Is that right?" I looked down at two big blue eyes peering out of flowing white hair. "How do you know?"

"It's been playing with me all day." She reached into the white waves and pulled up a handful of foam that she threw to the sky.

"Well, you better watch out for the jellyfish," I warned.

"I didn't see any jellyfish," she said thoughtfully, "but I did see a peanut butter fish."

◆◆◆◆

I sat down on the rocks and stared at the waves, hoping the repetitive rhythms of the sea would reset or redefine my life.

"Melvin!" rang out, as the painfully familiar black and green wet suit waddled across the dunes, toward the bubbling waves. His egg-shaped body strained the seams of his rubber suit. A square plastic mask covered his eyes, and the snorkel's mouthpiece rested uncomfortably against his gums. The people shook their heads and murmured as he waddled by, and the young boys laughed and catcalled him, "Melvin! Mel-vin!"

He just smiled and waved, unaware of his own embarrassment. His flippers flapped sand and water high into the air as he walked into the oncoming waves, and then swam across the top of the water.

A row of girls stretched out on their stomachs with their bikini straps undone, browning in the waning sun as two young boys lobbed tennis balls near them hoping they would sit up, which they never did.

"When I was your age," a salty, leather-faced fisherman said as he cast out his line with a quick whir, "if people dressed like that, they'd have been arrested."

"What're they supposed to wear?" I sneered. "This is a beach, isn't it?"

"We had something called modesty, self-respect, back then."

"Just because that's the way it was in the old days doesn't make it right. Why are old people always criticizing us?"

"I ain't criticizing, just commenting."

"Leave us alone," I snapped, "we're just trying to be happy like everyone else."

"Be happy," his crooked and broken teeth grinned at me. "I lived my life. I had my happiness. See these lines?" his scarred muscular fingers prodded his face. "The wrinkles go where the smiles were."

"And the frowns," I corrected him.

"And the frowns," he repeated quietly to himself.

We sat in each other's silence for a few minutes, and then I said, "Ya know, there isn't much difference between fishin' and sitting on a rock like a fool."

"A bad day of fishin'," he inspected his empty lure, "beats the hell out of a good day of workin'." He threw out his line. "God teaches us something every day."

"What?" I asked. "What did he teach you today?"

"He taught me," he cranked his reel, "that everything I pull from the water is a gift."

"Everything? Even today?"

"Even when I pull nothing," he nodded. "It's a gift." His empty line swung in toward him.

"How's nothing a gift?"

"Today, that nothing reminded me that any something is a gift." He grabbed his empty lure. "And that's a gift, if you know what I'm saying."

Melvin, meanwhile, had long disappeared under the surface. Just as I began to worry, he burst from the depths spraying water out of his air pipe like a whale, gasping for oxygen.

"What does that boy do under the water?" he asked. "It's too dark to see anything."

"I don't know, go ask him."

"Son," he paused, "you're too young to be this bitter."

"You sure got a lot of opinions about me for someone I've known for a minute. I'm just minding my business, looking at the waves."

"What are you looking at those waves for?"

"I don't know," I shrugged. "They make me forget."

"Forget?" his voice cracked. "What are you trying to forget?"

"I don't know," I sneered. "I can't remember."

"The ocean'll do that to ya. It grabs ahold of ya and never lets go. Everything comes from the sea." He pressed his fingers against the dark, painful patches on his naked scalp. "We all come from the sea. The sea's in us. Two-thirds of the world's covered by ocean, and our bodies are two-thirds saline. Think about that one."

◆◆◆◆

Out over the horizon, another small rainbow sprouted out of the black clouds, like the fledgling progeny of the first. Both arches stretched from one side of the world to the other, as though they were wrapping the earth in one big, colorful ribbon.

The blue sky and the blue water met seamlessly at the edge of the world and I couldn't tell where the sky began and the sea ended, and it appeared that the blue water stretching out before me, turned upward and flowed overhead, and the boats sailed in the sky, and the clouds floated in the water.

In the distance, the young blonde girl and her father splashed in the waves which rolled in, layered one on top of the other, like the white curls cascading down the side of the little girl's head. She drew a picture in the sand that a rogue wave tumbled in and wiped clean. She ran after the white foam like chasing big balls of cotton candy. Another wave snapped at her feet, and she fled up the dune with a shriek. She chased the bubbles up and down the beach again and again, and fatigue slowly overcame her. The ebb and flow of the white foam lured her closer and closer to the darkness. Then the ocean receded farther, and she followed it down, deeper than she had ever been. She stopped, distracted and tired.

And then the wave reached up, snapped down and grabbed her legs, pulling her into the shoal. She slid down the slope of the beach and into the mouth of the ocean, disappearing undetected, her footprints and finger scrolls washed away, her existence erased. It swallowed her up. She was gone. I popped up off the rocks.

For a few brief seconds, her father waded in the water unaware. Then panic struck. His head whipped back and forth. His eyes shot glances over the black waves. I ran toward the father. In a moment of optimistic denial, he turned and scanned the beach. Then frantically, he sprinted and leapt into the dark water, diving under the surf grasping for his lost child, coming up time and again empty-handed.

A whistle shrilled, and the lifeguards bounded off their benches, kicked up sand and dove into the waves. They bobbed up and down like dolphins, hunting for her in vain. Women stood close, touching each other for strength, their thin hands cupped over their opened mouths as the men dove into the water haphazardly.

I stood on the water's edge looking into the black water. I couldn't see a thing. I didn't know where to begin. I dove into the waves and clawed around in the darkness, groping for anything I could find. All I came up with was sand, and shells, and stones. I couldn't see a thing. I popped up looked into the black water. I never felt so helpless, so inadequate. The girl was dead, I told myself. She died the moment that wave grabbed her. Even if they find her and managed to pump the breath of life back into her motionless body, that little girl scrawling pictures in the sand and chasing the white cotton candy with all the hope and innocence will never return. It didn't matter what happened to her now. Her fate is sealed. It didn't make any sense. How unfair it all was. What did she do wrong to deserve that fate?

Just when all seemed lost, growing out of the surf like a rolling wave, a figure adorned in complete scuba gear emerged from the depths, staggered up the beachhead, cradling the pink swim suit across his outstretched arms while her white feet and wet curls dangled limply in the air. The crowd fell in behind him as he marched up the dune, and carefully placed her on the sand as the people silently encircled the child. Two lifeguards sprang into action and worked fast and together, as a siren blared in the distance. I stood and watched. I didn't know what to do. There was nothing I could do.

He was out there. I don't know why. I don't know what he'd been looking for in that black water. But he was out there, searching. Maybe, just maybe, he finally found what he's been looking for all this time.

NW

Chapter 53

The lonely eye of the moon gazed down on us, half-open, tired, and sleepy as we drove into the vague night.

"Is Bruce really playing tonight?"

"How many times are you gonna ask?" Cullen complained.

"I don't want to go all the way to Asbury for nothing," I said.

"My dad knows his agent. He wouldn't steer us wrong."

"Why at the Stone Pony?"

"That's where he started. He plays there two, three times a year. This'll be good for you, I promise," Cullen said, as he blared his horn at a meandering car in front of us. "The sign says stop, not park!" he yelled. He crossed the double yellow lines and sped past the sputtering Chevy.

"Delaney's so smart, he's stupid," he proclaimed. "I hit home runs. I don't bunt."

"He's a book coach," I told him.

"He needs to get a new book then."

"Let the players, play," I agreed.

"But you know what, I could care less."

He slowed the car down. She was walking by herself along the sidewalk next to the sea wall, wearing khaki shorts and a light blue windbreaker. He slithered the car onto the shoulder next to her. "Where's the All-American kid?"

She continued walking with her head down. He tapped the horn softly. She didn't look up, just quickened her stride.

"Wait, wait!" The car crawled along the broken shoulder, keeping pace with her.

Laticia looked back, saw me, and stopped. "I need to talk to Jake," she said coldly, and my heart trembled for a second. "Come here." She waved me over.

"You can say it in front of me," Cullen said.

"No, I can't. It's just between him and me."

I climbed out, and we walked over to the sea wall. She turned to me with her arms hugging her chest.

"What's up?" I asked anxiously.

She looked up; her misty eyes cut right through me. "I don't know how to tell you this."

"What's wrong? Tell me," I prodded.

"I knew it was wrong," she said.

"What was?"

"I'm pregnant," she spoke those two dreaded words with a tinge of satisfaction. My heart stopped and my mind raced.

"I've already been to a doctor."

"OK," was the only word I could think of. I became very calm, my mind subconsciously shutting down all of my other emotions so it could handle the flood of this one. "What are you thinking?"

"I'm keeping it," she said.

"You can't raise a baby by yourself," I told her.

"I won't be by myself. I'll have you to help me."

Cullen blared the horn. "Come on. I don't got all night."

I staggered over to the car and opened the door. My mind was spinning. How would I explain this? How would I look at my parents, anyone, myself again?

Cullen looked right at me. "She's pregnant, isn't she?" he whispered, and I nodded as I climbed in. "That's what you get for batting without a helmet," he quipped.

"I don't know what to do."

"Relax, I got this," he said, frighteningly casual.

"What d'you mean?"

"I'll take care of it," he winked. "This isn't my first rodeo."

He pulled the car alongside her. "Hop in. I'll give you a ride."

She shook her head. "No, I'm alright."

"C'mon," Cullen urged, "you shouldn't be walking by yourself at night."

She hesitated, then reluctantly climbed in the front seat as I flopped in the back.

He raced down Ocean Avenue zigzagging around cars and passing trucks on the double yellow lines. Laticia reached for the radio, but Cullen knocked her hand away.

She recoiled. "Don't touch me again."

"Do I know the father?" Cullen smiled smugly.

She cut her eyes at me indignantly. "That was just between—"

"Or better yet, do you know the father?"

"The father..." she reached forward, spun the knob, and cranked up the volume, "is in this car." The car squealed to a stop at a red light.

"What about the All-American kid?" Cullen asked.

"I don't think this is any of your business, Cullen."

"It is my business. I don't want you pinning this on Jake, just because you don't want people to know you had a kid with your brother."

"It's not Dorian's," she said. "It's impossible."

We drove on in intense silence, and then Cullen turned to her.

"You can't take care of this baby by yourself," he argued.

"My mom raised me by herself."

"It's not fair."

"Fair? Fair to who?"

"To you, the baby, whoever the father is," he told her.

"We know who the father is," she said. "And I know he'll do the right thing." She looked back at me. "He's a good man."

I didn't say a word. There was nothing to say. I was wrong, and these are the consequences. My mind raced into the future, picturing myself, my life, in this new reality, this new existence.

She placed her hand on her stomach. "This baby'll make my life better."

"It'll ruin your life," Cullen said. "You'll end up a 60-year old waitress with a daughter who hates your guts."

"I know what I'm doing," she said.

"Listen to me," Cullen turned to Laticia. "My dad knows a doctor. He takes care of this sort of thing in 20 minutes all the time. And I'll pay for it."

"Why would you do that?" she asked suspiciously.

"Jake's my boy. And I take care of my boys." He looked back at me. I kept my mouth shut. "We take care of each other."

"But this is a one-time offer. Now or never. You have 72 hours to get it done or the money's off the table." He stopped suddenly at an intersection, staring at a green light like he was waiting for it to change. I didn't say a word. He looked over at Laticia and back up, he then saw the green light and his car shot through the intersection.

"I'm not having an abortion," she said incisively. "I'm having a baby." She placed both of her hands on her stomach lovingly.

"What about adoption?" I asked, a last gasp to retain a semblance of my life.

"I can't do that again."

"Again? What d'you mean again? This isn't the first time you've been knocked up?" Cullen asked.

She shook her head sadly. "No."

"This isn't a game. You can't play with other people's lives like this," Cullen said sharply as we accelerated past a pick-up truck. "This is real life. We can take care of this in 15 easy minutes."

I closed my eyes and silently prayed she would take his offer. I didn't want my life defined by one mistake, by my worst 18 minutes. The speed of the car and the sharpness of his turns increased, as the intensity inside heightened.

He pulled out a wad of cash. "What will it take?" he said as he peeled off five one-hundred dollar bills. He reached over and tried to stuff the bills in her hands. "Here, take this," he said. "This will take care of everything."

"No." She pushed his hand away and the bills scattered across the dashboard.

◆◆◆◆

That split second changed the course of everybody's life. The light was red. Cullen still maintains that it was yellow, and he will take that to his grave. But I saw the light was red.

When I first saw the light glaring yellow, I thought we could make it, so I said nothing as we sped to the crossroads. But then I saw the light turn red. I hesitated. We were too close to stop, but too far away to make it. We were in the perilously narrow no man's land, going too fast, or not fast enough.

Our future was set the moment the light turned yellow and I kept my mouth shut. I could have stopped us, but I didn't, so my silence continued. He wasn't paying attention. He assumed the lines and stoplights were for other people, and they would keep us all safe. Cullen snapped his head and eyes back toward the road, and in that one instant, it all come together; the speeding car, the red light, the truck. Remove any one from the equation, and we were safe. But each one was scheduled to come together at that same point and time.

I heard long, high squeals of rubber vainly trying to grab hold of the black asphalt, and then everything was a blur, the cars, the white lines, the streetlights, all became long streaks of color, except for the two big headlights looking down at me. An unsuspecting truck driver rolled through the jug handle and accelerated into the green intersection. The screeching of brakes and the squealing of tires preceded the crash.

The truck's ominous headlights still haunt me, like two enormous eyes staring down at me. I heard "Goddamnit" shouted from the front seat, the moment before impact. A light from above suddenly flashed around me and every bone in my body was jolted to its marrow. A paralyzing bang was followed by an eternity of slow silent spinning. Shattered glass floated around me. My flickering eyes captured snap shots that are imprinted in my mind like a catalogue of still photographs.

My body slammed against the door; my head bounced violently off the side window. I fell face first in the back seat. When we finally stopped spinning, the night was peaceful, everything was still and black. Even the radio was silent. A horn echoed through the darkness, and the cool ocean wind swirled through the shattered car. A soft faint voice moaned in the front seat, whimpering like a fatally wounded animal. Warm sweat rolled off my face. I was too scared to move as I lay covered in shards of glass. The car collapsed around us. I didn't feel any pain, but I was breathing hard and my heart pounded. I don't know how long we were resting there in silence. And then the sirens rose to life, faintly in the distance as mere echoes, and then grew until they were pounding on top of us.

"Take her first," a heavy voice commanded. "She's the worst of 'em."

I lifted my head to see what was happening, but a paramedic's hands pressed on me. "Stay there, don't move."

"Three back boards and neck collars!" a voice barked. I lay in my own world hidden from the clamor, waiting for them to come and take me, hoping they wouldn't.

"Careful, careful. Take it slow, take it slow." They methodically strapped Laticia and Cullen onto back boards and slid them out of the car. And then they found me, hiding in my shame. I now knew I would have to make peace with the life I've forsaken.

They carefully but firmly taped my head and strapped body to a stiff wooden board and carried me to the ambulance. I lay there, straight as an arrow, finally.

"Are they gonna be OK? Are they gonna be OK? I didn't see

them. I swear. I didn't," a frenetic voice pleaded. "They came from no-where. Tell me they'll be OK."

As they wheeled me from the ambulance into Riverside Hospital, all I saw were the shimmering stars against the black night. They X-rayed and scanned my entire body, the doctors examined me, and then released me four hours later, unharmed.

My father drove me home late that night. His eyes were red and exhausted. He looked old. We rode home without speaking, and when he was helping me out of the car, he grabbed me, and hugged me. "God blessed us tonight. He keeps his eye out for the good people."

That was the only untruth I ever heard him utter.

◆◆◆◆

The sun came up. It actually rose the next morning. Its rays peeking over my windowsill awakened me. The dust danced on the sunbeams pouring through my window, mocking me. The throbbing in my skull electrified with each movement. I didn't have the strength or the desire to lift my head. Its weight was too much for my aching neck muscles. But the feeling of emptiness hurt the most.

I staggered over to the mirror and looked at myself for who I really was. I fooled everyone. I fooled no one. I didn't even fool myself. I saw the truth and the truth was ugly to look at.

I dressed without showering and eased down the stairs. My mom was already at the table, drinking her coffee with the sun on her shoulders.

"How are you feeling?" she asked as she rose and walked toward me.

"I'm fine," I lied. "I'm fine."

"You don't know how lucky you are. The officer said you should've been killed. No one survives..."

"I know. I know."

"God must be saving you for a reason. Protecting you for a special purpose," she told me.

"I don't know. What could God possibly need me to do?" I asked.

"I think that's for you to figure out."

I turned to walk out of the room. "Oh, I almost forgot," she said.

"Mr. Clayborne called this morning. He wants to meet with you today, sounded important."

◆◆◆◆

I stepped through the tall wooden doors, into a cavernous room with mahogany walls and built in bookshelves. "Your dad must not like trees very much." I quipped.

"He likes the natural look," Cullen nodded.

I walked over to the piano in the middle of the room. "How's your mom doing?"

He stared at me with a far-off look and shrugged his broad shoulders. I sat down on a piano bench.

"Don't sit there. It's antique. Just sit over at the desk. I'll go get him. He'll straighten everything out," he said casually, as if this sort of thing happened every day, like we had just broken the neighbor's window playing ball. I looked up and saw the two of us standing shoulder-to-shoulder in their full-length gold mirror. We were, in fact, the same height.

"Nothing's gonna happen to us." He massaged his forehead. "It was an accident, a freak accident. It wasn't my fault."

Mr. Clayborne's desk was cluttered with ragged books, torn envelopes and overstuffed folders. A silver revolver with a long fat neck was lying on top of a stack of documents like a makeshift paperweight. I lifted it in my hands. I had never held a gun before. It was cold and heavy. I ran my fingers along the rivets on the butt of the handle and spun the cylinder until it clicked to a stop. I read the serial number at the bottom and wondered about the guy who owned the gun with the number 00-000,001.

The head of the gun looked inviting. It offered a solution. There was a reality to it, a finality. It held out so much promise, so much power. My finger ran along the narrow ridge of the trigger. If I possessed an ounce of courage, I would end my pain, silence the echo of my iniquities, and finally get what I deserved.

But even in the face of death, I worried about the disappointment, the utter embarrassment my final act would bring myself, my family, my image. How would they look at me? How would I be remembered? If I used the gun the way I so desperately needed at that moment,

I would expose my frailties in a way that I've tried to keep hidden for so long. I would put an exclamation point at the end of my failures. Even then, I did not possess the courage to perform the definitive act of cowardice.

"Are you a collector?" He walked toward me, interested.

"No, I have never held a gun before," I said.

"Why don't you give it to me before someone gets hurt." He stepped toward me and wrapped his palm around the top of the barrel. He walked away and placed the gun on the far mantel.

"Here, take some." He shoved a waxy brown paper bag in front of my nose, as he sat down facing me. "They're gourmet."

"No thanks," I coughed.

He placed a pretzel in his mouth, and his molars grabbed a rounded edge and broke off a piece. "It is imperative," he began between crunches, "that everyone involved is on the same page. Even the slightest discrepancy will convict the most innocent man. We cannot panic. Panic is fatal. We all must tell the same story." He over-emphasized each word.

"Which is?" I was confused about the story. And I was sickened by the garlic spices that spewed forth with each syllable and by the sound of his teeth gnashing against the hard sourdough. Pretzel after pretzel, bite after bite, as his hand rustled in the bag and pulled out several more. I felt sick. My stomach was churning. I got up and went to the bathroom.

Looking into the mirror, my skin was pasty white, and little balls of sweat poured down the sides of my cheeks.

I had wanted to live in a world of absolutes, right-wrong, good-evil. But my frailty forced me into a world of maybes.

I could no longer judge another. My sins have silenced me. I am no longer separate from the crowd, I have been thrust into the middle of the crowd, and discovered the people around me are like me, and have come to this place from similar circumstances. But there is a comfort in the gray, hidden and safe in the crowd where there is no magic, no virtue, no distinction.

This realization came much too late. I saw the truth like the light from a dead star light years away whose fire has been extinguished for a million years. And we are left to observe the brilliance of a dead past.

My head was burning. My cupped hands threw water on my face. I turned on the fan and bent over the toilet. My back curled forward, and every muscle in my body locked into place, and with each violent convulsion, my body rejected everything inside of me, expelling the deep dark sludge in the pit of my stomach into the shiny porcelain bowl.

I then sat on the cold marble floor panting for breath, dripping in sweat. A chill crawled up my back as I sat there shivering. The smell didn't even affect me, I was glad to have it all out of me. Finally, I stood, wiped my mouth on an embroidered towel, and sprayed the can of potpourri over the room, masking my foul stench.

"Two things. One," he held up his index finger, as I re-entered the room, "he was going 45 miles an hour, and two, the light," he emphasized this point most, "was amber."

I did not know what to say or how, so I said nothing. His eyes studied me as he waded in my silence. I barely nodded.

"Good, that takes care of that," he offered his hand to me as if in congratulations. "That solves that problem."

We script our futures by the way we rewrite our pasts.

NW

Chapter 54

"She lost the baby. I'm sorry," the doctor told me stone-faced in the hospital corridor later that morning. "But she's lucky."

"Lucky?" I looked at him.

"To be alive. Are you family?" he asked. "I can't tell you much else if you're not."

"I was in the accident with her. But he's her brother," I pointed to Dorian walking toward us.

"I'm Doctor Diamond," he reached his hand out toward Dorian.

"What's going on?" Dorian asked.

"Well, as you know, the front passenger side accepted the brunt of the collision," he explained. "Her lower back was at the point of impact. She ruptured her spleen, so we removed it," he looked down at her file. "She has transverse fractures in seven places on her spinal column. We were able to stabilize the spine, but she has bruising on her spinal cord. It wasn't severed, thank God." He peered at us over the frames of the glasses hanging off the tip of his nose. "But we don't know the extent of the impairment. The swelling's under control, and she has partial movement in her fingers and toes, so that's a good sign."

"So, she'll be OK?" I asked.

"No," he took a breath, and massaged his eyelids. He had muscular, disproportionately large hands. Must have been a ball player. "There's something else," his thick fingers nimbly flipped through the fragile thin papers of her file. "Something... further," he looked down at the file. "We're most concerned about her kidneys. They were both compromised and... her liver was lacerated."

"Compromised?" Dorian asked quickly. "What do you mean compromised? Just tell us what's the matter. Speak English."

He pulled off his glasses. "Her lower back was at the epicenter of the collision. Her kidneys were damaged severely. They've shut down. They're dying. She needs a transplant."

Dorian walked straight ahead in a daze and collapsed into a chair.

"I'll let you know if anything changes." The doctor turned to me. "You're lucky, too. That was a classic T-Bone collision. No one walks away from that. God must've been watching out for you." He placed his hand on my shoulder and hurried down the corridor with the ends of his coat and stethoscope flopping.

I went to Dorian, but just as quickly as he had fallen into the chair, he popped up and walked purposefully down the long hall after the doctor. I chased after him.

"I'm her brother," he was telling the doctor, when I caught up to them.

"Then you might be the best candidate," he paused, "the only candidate."

"Do they need my left or my right?"

Before I could process this new information, Dorian was following a nurse down the corridor for preliminary tests.

"What's going on?" I grabbed the doctor. "Where's he's going?"

"Your friend is a very brave young man."

"What are they going to do to him? Why him?"

"There's only one viable organ for every five transplant candidates. So, if it doesn't come from a live donor, she'll most likely die waiting."

"You don't understand how much he'd be giving up," I told him.

"She's dying," he said sharply. "Her body can no longer remove her waste naturally. She's slowly being poisoned by her own waste."

"Couldn't she just stay on the machines?"

"We can only keep her alive with machines for a short time. A live donor is the best option, her only option. We can't wait."

"Can't we find someone else to do it?"

"He's the best candidate. He's as genetically close to her as anyone. His organs offer the best chance her body will accept them."

"But…"

"You need to stop questioning everything and be supportive."

My head was spinning. "This is all just too much, too difficult."

"Actually, it's rather an easy procedure," he explained. "Three simple connections. The vein, the artery and the urine tube. A second-year resident could do it."

"So, it's not a big deal?" I said.

"Listen, son," he explained. "Whenever the human body is exposed to this type of surgery, there's always a risk of complications."

"What complications?"

"Infection, hemorrhaging, hypertension, possible death."

"Death?"

"There's a chance, but there are a lot of other factors to consider as well," the doctor said.

◆◆◆◆

I walked into his hospital room. He was already wearing a blue gown, sitting upright in a steel bed with his hands behind his head.

"You can't do this," I said. "It's too risky for you."

"It's too risky for her if I don't."

"You just don't decide to have a major organ cut out of you."

"I have two and she has none. It's simple math."

"You'll never play ball again," I said.

"I don't care."

"What about Karen? If you make it to the bigs, you can give her a better life."

"I can give Laticia life."

◆◆◆◆

I walked out of Dorian's room, and he met me in the hall and pulled me aside. He was a tall, thick man with light brown hair slicked to the side. His over-inflated bicep and chest muscles smoothed out the creases in his freshly starched blue uniform. His silver badge glimmered in the white lights of the hospital. He stared at me through the mirrored lenses of his steel frame sunglasses. "Come with me," he peeled his glasses off and smiled. His teeth were white, and his eyes were blue. He led me down the hall, swaggering in front of me, with the heels of his leather boots clicking, and his hips swaying side to side with the weight of his gun hanging off his belt.

He led me into an empty conference room and sat down in front of me. He seemed a nice enough man, likable. He appeared genuinely concerned as he inquired about how I was feeling. He smiled after each sentence and laughed at his own subtle jokes. I liked him, but I knew I couldn't give him what he was looking for. He pulled out a well-worn note pad and asked me three straightforward questions, to which I answered, "Nothing," "I don't know," and "I wasn't paying attention." I wanted to be honest with him. He was a good person, just doing his job, protecting the public, looking out for everyone's welfare. My answers were neither the truth nor lies. They were somewhere in that safe, non-descript place between fact and fiction.

He closed his notebook, clicked his pen and thanked me for my valuable time. He left the room with the same swagger he entered with, and I never heard from him again.

◆◆◆◆

"How are you hanging in there?" my uncle asked that night after my parents went to bed.

"I'm not," I replied.

"This is a lot to handle. No one should—"

"It doesn't make any sense."

"What?" he asked.

"I don't get it. Why was I protected? Why did I walk away from it and she's in ICU, can't feel her toes?"

"I don't have an answer for you Jake," he said. "You'll never have that answer."

"Why was I the lucky one?"

"You know, very few people ask that question. It's rare, most people ask, why was I so unlucky?"

"OK, why was Laticia so unlucky?"

"You know, I don't believe in luck."

"So, you believe everything happens for a reason?"

He shook his head, "No, I don't believe that either." He held up his right hand. "I can't."

"So, what do you believe?" I asked.

"I believe you were in that accident because your car and that truck came to the same place at the same moment. She got hurt and you didn't because you were in different places in the car. That is neither lucky or unlucky, meaningful or meaningless. It just is."

"It just is?"

"Yes, and there is nothing more to take from that."

◆◆◆◆

When I returned to the hospital early the next day, Laticia's nurse informed me that her condition was downgraded from serious to critical. I looked into Dorian's room. He was lying on his side away from the door, speaking with Laticia's mother. I quietly stepped back into the hall.

"You don't have to do this," I overheard her tell him in a desolate voice.

"It'll be all right," he replied.

"It's not supposed to be like this!" she wailed. "I see her with all those tubes and machines. She looks in so much pain. Maybe it'd be best if we just let her go."

"No!" he popped up. "I need her. Even if we can't be together. I need her in my life."

"She loves you very much," she stroked the hair off his eyes. "I never saw her so happy. No matter what happens, nothing could break the bond you two have."

"We're bonded by some idiot we don't even know," he said, almost as an afterthought.

"He wasn't an idiot. He wasn't evil. He was weak. I was weak. We didn't have the strength you have. Don't hate him."

"I don't hate him. I just hate the idea that half of me is him."

"Your father was a beautiful man," she said wistfully. "A weak, beautiful man."

"Maybe beauty isn't all that it's cracked up to be. Maybe it would've been better if he were ugly and stayed."

"Better for both of you," she pined.

"If it weren't for him, we could be together," he said.

"If it weren't for him, you wouldn't be alive."

"Don't give him too much credit. We were both his accidents."

"There are no accidents," she told him. "Every child is a gift from God. And God doesn't make accidents." She kissed his forehead and walked out of the room.

I entered his room tentatively, but Doctor Diamond swept in past me. "Good news," he announced. "You're a match. Five out of the six markers in the blood match."

"When will you do it?" I asked.

"First thing tomorrow morning. We'll do the kidney first, and then the liver."

"The liver? Wait," I said, "he's donating his liver? How can he give something he only has one of?"

"The human liver consists of nine sections. We can split it, and both can work extremely efficiently. The biggest question is whether your liver will take in her body. We will actually give her about 60 percent of the liver."

"Why does she get more? He's bigger! He needs a bigger liver!"

"You don't understand."

"I don't. How can he live with half a liver?"

"His liver will grow back almost to its full size," he assured me. "I know this is a very emotional decision. I'll give you time to talk about it," the doctor said, and left the room.

I looked at Dorian and saw in his face that he had already decided to go through with this. It was all my fault, and I had to watch one of the most beautiful things I've ever seen be carved up.

"What about your life, your future? Baseball?"

"I love baseball," he told me. "But there's only one choice for me here."

"But you'll never play again," I said.

"I'll play again," he predicted, as if by saying it, it automatically came true. "All I need to know is she's OK, and I'll be able to play."

"No pro team will touch you," I said. "You'll be damaged goods. They won't risk that type of money on someone whose insides were just carved up. They don't take a chance on anybody with one of anything. One eye, one ear, one arm, one nut or even one kidney, or a half a liver."

"If they don't, they don't. That's their decision and this is mine," he said, placidly.

"Your decision is their decision. And even if you do get a shot, you could die right there on the field."

"If I die, I die. We all die, Jake. Life is just one brief moment between two eternities."

"Don't give me this 'we all die' crap, like it doesn't matter if you die today or 50 years from now."

"It doesn't, if you really think about it. Fifty years is a blink of the eternal eye."

"Death doesn't scare you?"

"Death scares the hell out of me, but do you know what scares me more than dying? Living. Living knowing that I could've saved her, and I didn't. Living as the person who chooses a baseball career over her life. It's not how you die that's important, it's how you live. If you act like this is going to last forever, you're wrong. The only permanence in life is death."

"If you believe there is no difference between life and death, then why was it so important to save her life? Wouldn't you, in fact, be doing her a favor by allowing her to die, according to you?"

"You know the answer to that," he said emphatically.

"Maybe I don't know anything anymore." I turned to leave.

"Hey, Jake," he stopped me as I reached for the door. "Thanks."

"Thanks?" I stared at him curiously.

"Thanks, for trying to talk me out of this." Our eyes locked for a moment, and then I quickly turned and walked away.

◆◆◆◆

I returned to the hospital that evening just before visiting hours ended. His room was dark and empty, and for a moment, I thought he had left, had finally come to his senses.

"He's with her." The nurse's voice rolled over my shoulder as I stared into the emptiness.

I walked down the hall to Laticia's room and peered in the half-open door. Her room was dimly lit by the full moon hanging in the far window, and the flickering of the TV screen in the corner. Dorian sat by her bed watching her sleep, brushing her hair with long strokes of his open palm.

◆◆◆◆

The next morning, I sat in a plastic-covered waiting room chair, amid random people flipping through magazines, staring at the television or engaged in mundane conversations, connected by shared separate anxiety.

I thought about his opened side, and about my sins. I thought about the short sharp knife cutting into his side that morning, leaving a long clean precise incision, and I felt I was holding that scalpel.

Fulbright sat down next to me. "How you doing?"

"Why do bad things happen to good people?" I asked.

"Why is a great word. You can always ask, why? That's the eternal question. But it doesn't mean there's an answer." He grasped my bicep with his stringy fingers and led me out to the hallway.

"He doesn't deserve this," I said.

"Deserve? Deserve?" he repeated. "No one ever gets what they deserve." He looked me squarely in the eyes. "That's a good thing."

"Good? How is that good?"

"We don't want what we deserve," he explained, "because we all are given better than we deserve."

"Dorian was given baseball, and now it's gone. Where's the justice in that?"

"Do you really want justice? Is there anybody who has lived such a good life, that they are immune to the horrors of justice? I don't want what I deserve. I don't want justice. If God was really up there tallying my good deeds and subtracting my bad, I'd spend eternity in hell. The human mind cannot comprehend the horrors of infinite justice."

"So, justice is not a good thing?"

"Where justice reigns, there is no compassion, no forgiveness, no courage, no humanity," he emphasized the last word the most. "Injustice makes us human. In a perfect world, a just world, in this nirvana you're searching for, good and evil are not delineated. We all become the same. There is no greatness, no virtue, no beauty. The imperfections make our world beautiful."

He stopped as his words flooded over me like a series of waves.

"Black is white. Up is down!" I screamed. "I wish God would just tell us what the truth is!"

He grabbed my arm. "Truth is overrated. Knowing is easy. It takes no strength to know things. It takes no courage to trust facts. Belief, that's where true courage lives. Life cannot be read in a store-bought philosophy book. You can't put your $19.95 down on a counter and purchase the answers to life." He turned and walked away.

I walked back into the waiting room, sat down, and waited.

Both operations lasted over eight hours and both patients were immediately wheeled to the Intensive Care Units.

NW

Chapter 55

"Laticia is doing fine," the doctor explained. "Everything came right together. Dorian's — her — kidney pinked up immediately and started producing urine within two minutes, perfect! But with Dorian, there was some bleeding. We're keeping him in the ICU for right now as a precaution, of course."

I walked six miles from Riverside Hospital to Galilee. At the small white church with the big red door, instead of turning left to my home, I continued straight down the road I had walked years before to my Little League field. The bright yellow earth moving machines rested between the mounds of dirt.

"What was wrong with the old field?" an old man sitting in the bleachers asked as he looked out at the torn-up field, massaging his swollen knuckles.

"It was old, worn out," I said.

"Just because something loses its shine, doesn't mean it no longer deserves respect."

"I didn't mean to disrespect," I told him. "Mr..." I stretched out my hand.

"Hendricks," his large gnarled hand engulfed my fingers. "Charlie... Hendricks."

"St. Louis Browns Charlie Hendricks?" I asked.

He nodded.

"This is your field? Wow, a real live big leaguer."

"Yes," he turned his head, appearing embarrassed. "I had a cup of coffee in the bigs, a long, long time ago."

"I loved this field," I told him. "But time moves on. Time's unforgiving. The young replace the old. Vets retire so rookies have a chance. Every vet was a rookie once. It's funny; kids want to be men, and men want to be kids."

"I wouldn't want to play nowadays," he said. "We played just as many games and were paid peanuts. We had to work in the off-season, real work, steel mills, farms. We didn't need psychiatrists or damn motivational speakers. Feeding my family was the only kick in the ass I ever needed. Now five million bucks isn't enough. You know what I would've done for a million bucks? I would've swept the stadium, scrubbed the toilets. Today, five million is an insult."

"You're absolutely right," was the only thing I could think of to say.

"You know what would've happened to a batter if he admired his home run?" he continued. "The next ball he saw would've been the one the trainer pulled out of his ear. We were embarrassed when we hit a home run. We put our heads down and ran around those bases as fast as we could. We respected the pitcher, respected the game."

Anger flowed out of him, not because of what the game has become, but because of what he had become: powerless.

"We loved the game. No one loves to play anymore. At least, not like us."

"Must've been awesome. If I got just one at-bat in the majors, just one, I'd be set for life."

"They say the best thing about getting old is a lifetime of memories," he shook his head. "That's the worst. My memories are a curse. The bad ones remind me of all the pain I felt, and the good ones remind me of all that I have lost. No wonder old folks are so damn determined to forget everything. I remember all the things I used to be able to do, the plays I made, the balls I hit, and I know I'll never experience that again."

"It's better than having nothing to look back on," I said.

"It doesn't seem real. My past life seems like a dream, like I was never part of it, and I know I'll never be a part of it again. Life takes everything you have and leaves you with nothing but your life," he added. He stared at the torn apart field, then said, "Do yourself a favor, kid," his gaze shifting to his warped fingers. "Don't live long enough to see your legacy die."

◆◆◆◆

Dorian emerged from Intensive Care thin and pale. When I walked into his room, it was the first time I had ever seen him weak. His body was stretched out in the stiff hospital bed with white sheets covering him up to his neck, needles and tubes sticking out of both forearms.

The doctor walked in, read his chart and inspected his incision. "I'm checking your system for integrity."

Dorian nodded with his eyes.

"How are you doing, young man?" the doctor asked.

"The worst pain I've ever felt," he told him between heavy

breaths.

"Hang tough, D," I tried to encourage him.

"It will take some time for your body to acclimate," the doctor told him. "But, it will. Everything looks sound. Hang in there."

"How's she doing?" he asked.

The doctor took off his glasses and rubbed his eyes. "The operation went extremely well, no complications. But we cannot deem the procedure successful until we determine that her body accepts your organ."

"It will," Dorian nodded. "I know it."

"What do you mean?" I asked the doctor. "She could still die? He could've done all this for nothing."

"It would never be for nothing. He gave her the best possible chance at life, and that's everything."

◆◆◆◆

Laticia's mother staggered out of her room as I walked in. Laticia was awake, but her face was blank, and each breath was long and labored. Her eyes rolled up and locked into mine, a faint smile crossed her parched lips. "Hey, Jake," she whispered. She motioned to the pitcher of water on the table. I poured a glass and brought it to her. I carefully placed the plastic straw between her pale, dry lips, and she weakly inhaled a few sips. Clear droplets clung to her parched lips.

"How you feeling?" I finally asked.

"Horrible," she managed a laugh as pale as her face.

"What? Is it your kidney?"

"No, no. That's fine," she whispered.

"Then what is it?"

"Why did he do it?" She stared out the window. "I'm not worth it."

"You are." I fixed her covers and petted her shoulder.

"How would you feel if the one person you love, the person whose happiness you want above all else, gives up his chance at happiness, for you?"

"I don't know. No one would ever love me that much." I looked away. "You just get better and he'll be happy. I promise you that."

◆◆◆◆

My father dropped me off at the hospital early the next morning. His door was open, but I didn't go in. I stood like a ghost in the threshold. The room was uncommonly white. Every piece of furniture glowed, the steel of the medical equipment reflected a blinding white light.

His mother stood over him. Her hard features had fallen soft and a slight color had overtaken her white face. "Something happened overnight," her words were hesitant as she groped for just the right ones, trying to find the perfect words that would make what she had to tell him less profoundly permanent. "He said it just quit working, then everything else shut down. There was nothing they could do. They got to her too late." She reached to him and ran her fingers through his hair. His head was turned toward the window. "I'm sorry," she whispered, then turned and rushed by me.

Doctor Diamond walked in with uncombed hair and an unshaven face. Dorian peered up at him, pleading for an answer.

"First, the liver shut down," he said in a numbing voice. "And then the kidney, and that set off a series of multiple organ failures. I don't know yet what caused it. We gave her a renal exam last night, all of her numbers were within the range, but if one thing is compromised, it places too much stress on all the other parts of the system. Hers were fragile to begin with. I'm sorry." He pulled his glasses off and massaged his temples. "I'm terribly sorry."

I stepped into the room with light footsteps, and Dorian's head flopped toward me as I walked to his bed. We stared at each other; no words spoken. He seemed helpless, wrapped in white sheets and blankets like a newborn. Finally, the moisture in the near corner of his right eye welled up and formed a ball which grew too big for his lids to hold. The clear ball snuck past his lashes, rolled along the contour of his nose, and then fell easily into the corner of his chapped lips. That was the only tear I ever saw from him.

I left his room more quietly than I had entered, not saying a word. To myself, I kept repeating she died, she died, she died, over and over and over again as I walked down the hall, staring at the sky-blue floor. What a waste, I thought.

I was struck to still by a piercing inconsolable shriek of "No,

No, Noooo... !" that ripped into the stifling sadness. She held onto the last "no" with the heartfelt strength of a world class opera singer holding onto the last note of the final tragic aria. And for the entire time she held that aching note, you believe that it will last forever, suspending her tragedy, keeping death at bay for eternity. But the tragic desperate note grew too big to hold and she let it go softly like a faint whisper in the night, dying into silence, leaving only a fragile echo of her agony floating in the long dark corridors of our souls, as her final lasting memory.

Laticia's mother, out of breath, walked backwards and fell against the cement wall with a soft thud. Her legs buckled and she melted to the ground, landing in a desolate heap. She lay in the corner, her nylons torn, her skirt crumpled, her face fallen. Her head was buried in her tiny hands, silent tears pouring from her, her body shuddering in inconsolable grief, as two nurses struggled to pull her broken body to her feet.

Laticia's death cut my legs out from under me, too. Through all that had happened and everything Dorian was doing, I always believed that everything would somehow magically work out. But now, I could not escape the fact that ultimately, I had killed her, that I was responsible for her death. No one would slap handcuffs on my wrists and throw me in prison. No one would point an accusing finger at me and shout, "You killed her." But I set in motion the series of events which culminated in her death. That was inescapably the truth, and that truth rang in my ears over and over again. You can talk yourself into and out of many things, but the truth is always with you deep down in the dark recesses of your conscience. It never leaves you. It follows you forever, haunting you like a hideous, deformed shadow. My truth shredded all that I wanted to be into little unrecognizable pieces.

NW

Epilogue
(June 1999, age 17)

There are no innocuous sins. There are no benign acts. We are either corrupting or redeeming. There's no in-between. Everything we do, good or bad, adds to or detracts from the collective unconscious of the human experience. A sin against one is a sin against all.

Sin is God's way of reminding us of who we are, and of our humanity. Forgiveness is God touching us with his grace. Our sins beget his grace. We will all be humbled someday, not by our own badness but by another's goodness.

As I look back at my life, I can now see how I settled for the ordinary instead of fighting for the extraordinary. I see people like me, scurrying around in their little lives like rats hiding between the rocks, afraid of the sunlight, convincing themselves it is better in the darkness.

The squeaking of her sneakers against the loose wooden floorboards of my porch startled me, and I felt her tiny hand rub the top of my back as she sat down on the step below me.

"I didn't see you at the funeral," Dawn's sad, hollow voice said.

"I watched it from the jetty."

"Why?"

"It's too real," I looked away from her. "It's all too real to be that close."

"We should've been there together." She let her hand fall lightly against the length of my back. "Dorian was there."

"Yeah. I went to see him last night," I sighed. "He showed it to me."

"Showed what?"

"He showed me his scar." I peered up at her again.

A horrid look stole over her face. "He did?"

I nodded. "It started at his spine, and it went all the way around to his belly button," I traced its path along my side. "It was long, it was thin, and it was dark purple. The skin all came together evenly," I was afraid to look at her. "The doc said it would fade over time, into an invisible line."

"Really? It's hard to believe any of this would fade over time."

"Why are you here?" I asked without looking at her.

"I wanted to see if you were all right," she said in soft, caring voice as she held my left wrist. "You've been through a lot, too much. I care about you."

"Don't you know? Don't you know what I did? Who I am?" I wiggled my arm free. "Why would you care about someone like me?"

"Because…" she waited a moment. "Because, I love you."

Those three words flowed over and through my body, like a soothing warm bath, cleansing me. I never heard those words spoken to me that way, and my mind drifted to a place I had conjured many times, free from all the darkness in the world, a place of green pastures and still waters. I rested there in peace until I saw myself in that idyllic place, and the image screeched to a shuddering halt.

"How could you love a jerk like me?" I snapped.

"I would do anything for you," she said.

"I don't deserve your love. You're wasting it on me."

"Love is never given to the wrong person." She stood and leaned against the railing with her back to me. "If we all went by your criteria, no one would deserve to be loved, and if no one deserved to be loved then everyone would need to be loved." She turned to me. "Love doesn't belong to the perfect, the sinless, the blameless, the worthy. Love is precisely for the people you don't think deserve it. It's a gift and all we have to do is receive it."

"But you don't know about…"

"I know the whole story, Jake, everything. I'm not happy about what you did. But, that's not who you are. I know it."

"How can you still love me, then?"

"Love isn't easy." She shook her head as her eyes remain fixed on mine. "Love touches every part of your soul. The parts of you that you keep hidden, that you never let anyone see because they could destroy you. But the hard love is the only love, the most beautiful kind there is."

"What did I do to deserve this?"

"Nothing," she said. "Through it all, everything that has happened, I still see that little boy I danced with such a long time ago. For us to have shared that moment, that boy had to have an innocence, an idealism, a purity that's rare today. I still see that boy, that little lost boy searching for meaning, searching for goodness. It's nothing you did. It's what you are. It's what we all are. There's no deserving. Everything's a gift, the good and the bad. God is good even on the worst day of life."

I looked up at her. "I still remember him. I remember that little boy I used to be, but I blew it, I had a chance at greatness, at living a life that no one has ever lived. A perfect life, a life worthy of that love. But now it's all gone. Now, I'm like everyone else."

"You were always like everyone else," she said. "We all have that little boy, or girl, somewhere deep inside of us."

"What I did was unforgivable," I said. "I can't just erase 18 minutes of my life."

"Nothing's unforgivable," she said. "It's not up to me to forgive you. It's only up to me to love you. God forgives." She walked over and kissed my cheek.

No one deserves the love we give to each other, I thought. *All we are asked is to return the love we are given because nothing is more untenable than unrequited, unconditional love.*

I reached out and took her hand in mine. They fit together, not perfectly, but they fit. We sat, holding hands without speaking, just listening to the waves off in the distance. I then knew there was nothing I could have ever done to deserve what she had just given me.

"Let's go hit!" My father stood in front of us holding my bat and a bucket of baseballs. "There's still enough light for a bucket."

◆◆◆◆

Dawn watched as I picked up the bat and dragged it to home plate with my head down. I didn't want to look at my dad. I stepped into the batter's box, and the wind stopped, all became quiet and peaceful like I was standing in my own private nirvana. But we need the wind. The wind gives us wings. The wind makes us soar.

I looked at the vacant sky. It was clear, and the sun shone bright. From the sun, we must look like a grain of sand or a drop of water in the vast sprawling universe. But the sun was still not any bigger than a nickel, which reminded me of great distances, its burning light so far from me. Standing under its brilliance, I felt small, but that was a good thing.

At that moment, I realized maybe the sun is not the burning eye of infinite judgment, maybe it's the glowing eye of eternal compassion.

Maybe always doing the right thing is not right after all. Maybe right and wrong are at best meaningless, at worst our enemies. Maybe we are supposed to live our lives without regard for right and wrong, for good and bad. Maybe they are the tools of the devil, the building blocks of injustice. Maybe we are simply to follow our hearts, so we will be revealed honestly to the world.

Maybe we are not placed on this planet to accomplish great things, or to become a great person to prove our worthiness. Maybe we are here simply to live and to love.

Love makes the lines unnecessary; love makes them melt away. Love washes away sin, erases envy, emasculates pride, dissolves hate.

I anchored my feet in the center of the box. He picked up a ball, wound and fired. When the ball approached, I waited on it with my hands back until it was on top of the plate, and then in one quick motion, I drove my hands through the center of the ball. I slapped it on a line back at him. It felt good. It felt safe. My mind was freed from the shackles. There we were, under the waning summer sun, a father and a son playing ball, a firm toss and a quick swing. I forgot about the wind. I simply concentrated on hitting the ball back through the center.

The End

~ About the Author ~

Judd Garrett grew up on the Jersey Shore and Cleveland, Ohio. He writes from his home in Texas, where a recent non-writing job was as Director of Advanced Scouting with the Dallas Cowboys.

The Garrett name is well known in college and professional football. Judd's father, Jim, was a legendary coach in college and with several professional teams, as well as being a longtime scout with the Dallas Cowboys. Judd's brothers Jason and John also played and coached professional football.

A 1990 graduate of Princeton, Judd was an All-American football player and also played baseball for the Tigers. He was drafted by the Philadelphia Eagles of the NFL.

After six years as a professional football player, including with the 1993 Super Bowl Champion Dallas Cowboys, he began a 12-year coaching career with the Saints, Dolphins, Rams and Cowboys, and served another 12 years as a personnel executive with the Cowboys.

Judd has written two screenplays, and is a frequent contributor on the topics of sports and politics to *Real Clear Politics*. *No Wind* is his first published novel.

Judd is married and the father of six children.

Made in the USA
Middletown, DE
04 October 2020